THE CHAINED ADEPT

Karen Myers

THE CHAINED ADEPT

The Chained Adept: 1

Karen Myers

PERKUNAS PRESS • Tyrone, Pennsylvania

The Chained Adept

The Chained Adept: 1

Perkunas Press
2635 Baughman Cemetery Road
Tyrone, Pennsylvania 16686
USA

PerkunasPress.com

Author contact: KarenMyers@KarenMyersAuthor.com
KarenMyersAuthor.com

Cover and Illustrations: Jake Bullock, http://ohbullocks.com
The Kigali, Zannib, Rasesni, and Ellech languages: Damátir Ando, http://damatir-ando.tripod.com/conlangs.html

Published 2016. First Edition.

Trade Paperback
ISBN-13: 978-1-62962-029-9
ISBN-10: 1-6296202-9-7

Library of Congress Control Number: 2016932083

ALSO BY KAREN MYERS

The Hounds of Annwn

To Carry the Horn
The Ways of Winter
King of the May
Bound into the Blood

Story Collections
Tales of Annwn

Short Stories
The Call
Under the Bough
Night Hunt
Cariad
The Empty Hills

The Chained Adept

The Chained Adept
Mistress of Animals
Broken Devices
On a Crooked Track

Science Fiction Short Stories

Second Sight
Monsters, And More
The Visitor, And More

See KarenMyersAuthor.com for the latest information.

CONTENTS

CHAPTER 1

Penrys was crouched on one knee, slamming the *rysefeol's* recalcitrant wooden joint with the back of her hand by way of a delicate adjustment, when the sudden transition hit.

"Oh, *thennur holi*," she said, under her breath, but the oath that started in her well-lit workroom finished in swaying light and strong shadow. Already off balance, she tumbled on her backside. The soft surface took the sting out of it, and her hands, spread wide to break the fall, told her of carpet and, below that, uneven ground. A gust of wind blew smoke in from outside and the walls fluttered.

A tent, she realized, and a very large one.

She saw the people, then, and froze, stifling a sneeze, but they didn't seem to have noticed her. *No, that's not it. They aren't moving at all.*

Perhaps no one's moving but someone's talking. She tilted her head and pinpointed the voice—it came from something like a mirror suspended from a metal stand in front of the nearest tent wall. She was too close alongside the same wall herself to see anything but the edge of the frame.

The flickering light from the glass-enclosed lanterns on the tables and chests in the tent cast moving shadows on the faces of the people. It gave the illusion of life, distracting her for a moment, and then the words from the voice in the mirror penetrated.

"…a field test like this is always useful for a new weapon. I look forward to greeting you in person, when you arrive for a permanent visit."

She wrinkled her nose at the lazy baritone drawl. *That can't be good. What's happened to them?*

Glancing over her shoulder, she spotted a red lacquered chest along the tent wall and scooted back a couple of feet to set her back against it, taking care to stay out of the line of sight of the mirror. She crossed her legs and made herself comfortable on the rug, licking her dry lips as she tried to focus.

She steadied her breathing, then, and reached out with her mind to the people in the tent with her. She could only see a few of them from her position on the ground, but her mind told her there were seven. All the minds projected fury and fear, but one shone more clearly, aware of her, and able to respond silently when she focused on him.

*Who are you? No, never mind. Can you help us?*

That gave her pause.

What have we got here? Something from the mirror, smothering them all like a thick fog. But not me—probably doesn't know I'm here. At least, not yet.

She braced herself, and then raised a mind-shield around the one who'd asked for help. Immediately she felt the force shift and bear down upon her, but she diverted it around them both and let it flow away.

*Much better. What about the others?*

She judged the force that beat at her. _*Maybe one or two more.*_

*The Commander, then.*

Penrys couldn't drop her concentration long enough to look for him. _*Show me.*_

He gave her the flavor of the other man's personality and indicated a direction. That matched up with one particular mind, and she extended her shield to him.

The lights dimmed for her as she took on the load. She closed her eyes to remove the distraction and listened to the muttered conversation in the tent.

"What…?"

"Not now, Commander-chi. Temporary defense. Pick one more man."

Silence for a moment.

"Make it Kep, then."

*This one, please.* Her first contact pictured another personality and direction for her, and she extended the shield one more time, hoping it would hold.

She gritted her teeth and focused on the task. At least the load was steady—she could bear the pressure for a little while, if it didn't change. _Why so few? I should be able to support more of them. But it doesn't feel like that would work just now._

"I'm not sure what you hoped to accomplish, Menbyede, but I think you may have misjudged our strength. Kep-chi, see to the men and prepare for attack." She recognized the voice of the second man.

"At once, Commander-chi."

The air shifted as someone left the tent.

The voice in the mirror was quiet, but the force increased against her shield, probing and shifting. She strengthened the shield further, clenching it solid, until the sounds outside dropped away.

A finger tapped Penrys's shoulder and the familiar mental voice that marked a wizard followed. **You can stop now.**

Cautiously, she loosened the shield enough to look, and found the pressure gone. Her whole body ached as she released the shield completely, and she slumped to loosen her muscles, her dark shoulder-length hair falling into her face as she rotated her head and felt the neck joints crack.

"You didn't hear me speak to you," the man said, his deep, resonant voice low and private against the bustle behind him in the tent. He crouched next to her on the balls of his feet.

Sandalwood? She sniffed again and lifted her head. The honeyed voice belonged to a smooth-shaven Zan traveler, his hair concealed under a small maroon turban. His dusky robes of an overall small-figured fabric had been shortened for ease of movement, and his loose breeches were bloused over decorated but well-worn leather boots. He regarded her soberly, and then his dark eyes widened. He reached out and pushed back her hair on one side to confirm his glimpse, exposing her ear—her shaggy, mobile, fox-like ear.

She jerked her head back and staggered upright. Glaring down at him, she shook her hair loose again to cover her ears.

He rose more gracefully and made her a sketchy half-bow. "Your pardon, *bikrajti.* I was just… surprised."

Penrys looked beyond him and realized the tent was large and multi-part, four square bays surrounding a central square, the ties at the corner seams marking its origin as five separate structures. It was dark in the corners but full of activity. *Uniforms. So, I was right—this is a military camp. But where?* Her companion seemed to be the only Zan—none of the rest, bare-headed or not, showed the loose curly hair she would have expected. To a man they had short, straight, black hair, and several cultivated wispy beards. A glance out of one doorway confirmed that it was still nighttime.

A courier had arrived and was reporting to Commander Chang, easily identified by both his voice and his location—anchoring a wide camp chair, fronted by a large, portable table, little of which was bare of papers, and commanding a view of the tent entrance, where an armed man stood ready on either side. A quick glance confirmed that the mirror was gone from the stand by the tent wall.

The dark Zannib wizard followed her gaze. "Locked away it is, where it can do no more harm." He paused. "We *think* it can do no more harm."

"I'm called Zandaril," he said. "We must talk, soon as he's free." He cocked his head over at Chang.

He drew her over to the Commander's table and they waited for the courier to complete his report. The smoky cressets outside the tent flap still held the night at bay, but the clamor of a roused camp belied the darkness. Voices called back and forth, and hoofbeats pounded by. As Chang leaned forward in his chair for emphasis, it creaked and his black leather jerkin reflected the candle light dully.

Once Chang had dismissed the courier, he turned his full attention to Penrys. His lined face was impassive, the eyes narrow.

"Who are you? What just happened? And how, exactly, did you happen to turn up, in such a… *timely* way?"

It was clear from his face and the tone of his voice that he didn't believe in coincidence.

"It's complicated, sir." She cleared her throat. "There was an accident…"

At the sound of her northern Ellech accent, Chang's eyes met Zandaril's. The Commander and the rest of the men in the tent, with the exception of Zandaril, had the look of the eastern Kigali folk, their eyes tightened against the ancestral wind and their beards sparse.

She forged ahead. "M'name's Penrys, and I was in Tavnastok a little while ago. But not now, I think."

"No." Zandaril blinked. "Indeed not. It's far from the Collegium you are, way up in the valley of the Mother of Rivers." At her blank look, he added, "Near the western border of Kigali."

Penrys closed her eyes briefly and shook her head. *Thousands of miles if it's a step, as much south as west. What have I done? How will I get back, with nothing but the clothes I stand in? How can I tell them at the Collegium where I am?*

She studied the two faces before her, one stern, one curious. *Well, that may not be my most urgent problem. They think I had something to do with this attack.*

She straightened up. *First order of business—stay alive and out of prison.*

CHAPTER 2

Penrys waited in Zandaril's company while the Commander made certain that the threatened attack was not about to materialize, based on the reports of his returning scouts as they continued to come in.

She glanced at her oh-so-polite custodian. *It's not like I can go anywhere, from the middle of an armed camp. That they know of, anyway. Guess they don't see it that way.* In spite of herself, she yawned and belatedly covered her mouth.

At Zandaril's raised eyebrow, she protested, "I've come west a great distance, so my night just got a lot longer."

She left it at that, not wanting to admit that the shielding had also had its cost. *And just why did I have to stop at holding three under my mind-shield? Where did that limit come from?*

"Who was in the mirror?" she asked him, quietly.

"Menbyede of the Rasesni."

"I've read about them—they're your neighbors to the west, aren't they? Who's this Menbyede fellow?"

He narrowed his eyes at her suspiciously, without comment

"No, I don't know," she said, answering the unasked question. "Hey, I can name several colleagues from the Collegium who will vouch for me and where I was last night. Um, this night."

"And what should we do with you while we wait for messages to go and return, all the long way?" Zandaril said. "Or perhaps you have a better means of communication?"

His eyes slid to the spot where the mirror had been.

She swallowed and decided to resume her silence. As if to contradict her resolve, the smell of the hot, bitter *bunnas* sitting untouched on Chang's crowded camp table made her stomach growl, audibly. She was always hungry after a prolonged effort, but it was food she wanted, not that foul stuff.

That's not actually a bad idea, though—using a mirror to cross distances. How did they attach sound to the vision? How do they focus it? How far can it go? And how do they send an attack through it, like the one I shielded?

She settled down to ponder ways and means, her fingers itching for something to write on.

With the camp on high alert until daybreak, but no enemy detected, Chang finally returned his attention to her. Two of his officers stood behind him and waited. She could feel the suspicion radiating off of them.

"I would like an explanation," he said. It was little short of a command.

May as well tell them part of the truth, anyway. Not that they're likely to believe it.

"I was at my workshop, at the Collegium. Working on my…" She paused. "You see, I made this *bendu*, a device, kind of a detector, a *ryskymmer*, like a bound-circle, only the reverse…"

They looked at her blankly. *These are Kigaliwen, and they don't have the terms.*

She started over. "Look, if you take a defined space, like a big box, you can cancel out the magic inside the space." She framed the concept out with her hands.

She glanced at Zandaril. He was nodding as if he'd heard of the theory.

"Most people stop there," she said, "but I thought if you could set it up right, you could use it to find active magic somewhere else."

Zandaril stopped nodding, but she pushed on anyway. "And if it's big enough…" She spread her arms wide to illustrate. "You could maybe go where that magic is." *If you were fool enough to stand on the inside of it.*

There was silence for a moment, broken only by the spitting of the cressets outside.

"What, seven thousand miles?" Zandaril raised both eyebrows this time.

"Well, I had it set up to look for the biggest activity it could detect. I didn't think it would go further than the Collegium. After all, there's plenty there for it to find. And besides, I wasn't trying to use it—the full-scale version wasn't working yet."

Didn't think about what I was doing. Idiot.

Zandaril said, "So the Rasesni tried out their new weapon, and…"

"It sucked me in. I was on the inside, tinkering with the framework's joints, but then I, um, hit it and, wham, here I was."

She could feel her cheeks heating. "Guess it worked."

Zandaril and Chang exchanged opaque looks.

Chang began again. "You sound like a Northener, but you don't have the look."

"No. No, I don't." She cleared her throat. "About three years ago, they tell me, there was a disturbance out in the forests of Sky Fang in the Asuthgrata region, enough to bring Vylkar, the local wizard, out to track it down."

"You?" Zandaril suggested.

"Well, I'm what they found." She raised a hand and fingered the heavy chain resting high around her neck like a collar.

Waking up at the base of a rough-barked tree, surrounded by torches and strange, armed men. Waiting for them to speak and then tapping them for the language.

"And where had you come from? How did you get there?"

"Wish I knew. That's all there is, nothing further back."

"But you knew the language?" Zandaril asked.

She compressed her lips. "I know all the languages. I get them from the speakers."

She looked at them pointedly. "Yours, too, you may have noticed."

Chang glanced over at Zandaril for confirmation, and Zandaril shrugged.

"I've never heard of that," the Zan remarked.

"Yes, that's what Vylkar said. It's true, nonetheless."

He let it pass, though his skepticism was plain on his face.

"So, you ended up at the Collegium."

"They figured it was the best place to… examine me. They gave me a name and a bunch of tests." She half-smiled. "Then they argued a lot."

"You're what, then? An apprentice? A *nal-jarghal*?" Zandaril asked.

She snorted. "No, they couldn't really make me fit properly anywhere in their system. Old Aergon declared they should revive the ancient title of *hakkengenni*, um, 'Adept.' All I wanted was a place to work, and to persuade them there was no harm turning me loose in the library. Help 'em with the catalogue."

"And they did? They just took you in and exposed everything to you? The Collegium, with its reputation for stringent qualifications?" Zandaril snorted.

"And what's the first thing you did, eh?" Penrys said, and cocked her head at the corner where she'd arrived. "Tried to find out what I was and what I could do, didn't you? You're no different then the rest of your wizardly colleagues."

She heard her voice rise. "Made m'self available for experiments, I did. That was the exchange. Made some devices, too, not that they're any too eager to use 'em. Why? You want to come up with some tests yourself?"

"Enough," Chang said, and she subsided.

"Sorry." *Don't be a fool. Don't alienate them—they may be your only means of getting back.* She took a deep breath, and sneezed from the smoke of the cressets drifting inside.

"Whatever the Rasesni had in mind seems to have been called off. I'm going to stand down the camp." Chang waved over one of the guards at the entrance.

"Take our… guest over to Jip-chi and have her assigned quarters for what's left of the night." He glanced at her. "Under guard, if you please."

Zandaril stroked his beardless cheek as he settled back in the folding camp chair and watched Chang's face. The quiet discussions elsewhere in the tent gave them a bit of privacy. "What did you think of her story?"

"She has to be a Rasesni plant," Chang said. "Nothing else makes any sense. Accent or not, she's certainly no Northener, not with that dark hair. Not skinny enough, either. Or tall."

"She is what, then? Who are her people? Not the bandy-legged Rasesni." Zandaril let that hang there for a moment.

Chang nodded, reluctantly. "No. Not a pure-blood anyway. Probably some sort of border family, mixed-blood. Or something else."

"I know what I saw." Zandaril shook his head. "I don't know any border families with pricked animal ears, Commander-chi. Do you? Not even in the old granny tales."

Chang glared at him. "You have a point?"

"You should believe her story for now, as long as it doesn't disturb your mission."

"And what's to keep her from vanishing the same way she materialized?"

Zandaril had been facing that corner of the tent when he was locked in place by the Rasesni attack. He'd seen her arrival, tumbling on her rear with her arms flailing. *That was the clumsiest entrance I've ever seen. Hard to associate that with a secret enemy.*

He poured himself a mug of the still-hot *bunnas*, lifted it to his nose, and inhaled before taking a sip. "If she needs a large device to travel, as she claims, we can prevent it. If she lied about it, and needs nothing, how could we stop her?"

"Chains," Chang said, with a frown.

Ah, yes, I want a closer look at that necklace she keeps fingering. I didn't recognize the style.

He put the mug down on the ground beside his chair.

"I'll take charge of her," he said.

"What, in Hing Ganau's wagon? And won't *that* start rumors."

"Oh, come now, a young girl she is not, Commander-chi."

"As if that mattered." Chang narrowed his eyes. "She's young enough, and I didn't hear mention of a husband. Still, the idea has some merit—who better than you to defend us if she's not what she says?"

He thought for a moment. "All right. If she can ride, we'll mount her, else she can bounce along in your traveling warehouse with the rest of the odds and ends. Think you can catch her if she makes a run for it?"

Zandaril raised one robed arm and let the sleeve flutter gracefully while his hand waggled in the air. "Outride me she will not."

"Then she'll be in your charge tomorrow. You've just made yourself responsible for her."

Well, I asked for it, did I not?

CHAPTER 3

"Stow your gear in the *puichok*. Hing Ganau will show you where." Zandaril turned from the horse who was hitched to the side of the wagon and waved vaguely in the direction of a soldier in the process of loading up.

He returned to his task of checking the tack of his black mare. She was fit and energetic, though somewhat round and sturdy. Penrys did not recognize the pattern of the simple saddle. Except for the short stirrups there seemed to be nothing to it but shaped leather pads, decorated with punchings like his boots, and colorful wool fabric beneath, over a sheepskin.

Dropping her shoulder, Penrys shrugged off the worn pack Jip had issued her last night and set it down with a metallic thump. 'A soldier's gear,' he'd called it. It seemed half empty, and the clanking of the eating kit had been an annoyance the whole way as she'd followed her guard to Zandaril's place in the breaking camp. There hadn't been time to go through it yet, though she'd been grateful for the blanket fastened to it, in the middle of the night. She was even more grateful for breakfast, salted dough on a stick with smoky bacon wrapped around it, shared by her escort at the cook-fire of a group of troopers.

She'd still been licking her fingers when she'd spotted Zandaril, supervising the loading of his wagon at the rear of the camp. Four mules had already been harnessed up to its shaft, the nearest one an elderly gray that was almost white, and the rest ordinary bays. The wagon looked like all the others she'd seen so far—tall iron-tired twelve-spoked wheels in back, with smaller ones in front, and a body about five feet wide and ten feet long. The wooden walls rose about four feet, surmounted by a high arching framework covered in canvas that was partially folded aside—only the long pole affixed to the side of the wagon-seat that flew a colorful pennant distinguished it from the rest of the nearby vehicles. She thought the device on it might be some sort of many-spoked wheel, when she tried to make it out as it flapped in the gusty wind.

The smell of tar wrinkled her nose—it looked as though the seams of the wagon's boards had been tarred and caulked.

Her guard had handed her possessions over to the wizard and released her, and she tipped her head to him in farewell. *Well-mannered he was, and he provided breakfast. Could have been worse.*

She glanced at the older, uniformed man who was busy with the last of the gear, spry despite the splint and wrappings around his right leg. She surveyed the narrow wagon seat and asked Zandaril, "Will we all three be sharing that?"

"That depends. Can you ride?"

She smiled broadly. "Indeed. That would be much better." She paused and looked down at her feet, shod for indoor activities. "Although boots would make it more comfortable." *At least I'm wearing my work clothing, not something more unwieldy.*

"Maybe I can fix that," Zandaril replied. "You'll need some sort of coat or cloak, too. Any clothes in there?" He pointed at the pack on the ground.

"Not that I could see."

He nodded, and called out to the man who was tying down the bundles in the wagon bed. "Hing-chi, errands I'll have for you to the Quartermaster at our next stop. Meanwhile, please have someone fetch something suitable for our guest to ride before the Horsemaster gets too busy."

Hing Ganau started a bow but converted it into a clumsy wave and limped off to corral an errand boy.

Penrys raised an eyebrow at the performance and Zandaril coughed politely. "I have here no official rank, but it seems to be hard for him to break the habit." He paused. "Only three weeks ago I was assigned to him, when I joined the expedition at the Meeting of Waters. Posted he was to drive a wagon until he could ride again. Doesn't like it much, and who can blame him? A *kwajigomju* is used to getting things done with his men, and frustrated at being alone."

He looked down at the little bundle the guard had handed him—the pouch and knife that had hung at her belt. "Here, *bikrajti*. You'll want these."

That's gracious of him. Also says something about how much he fears me, which is not at all. Is that a good thing?

"Thanks," she said, and left it at that.

She attached both items to her belt and felt complete again, if somewhat under-dressed for the weather. As she recalled from the maps, Kigali was about as far south of the equator as Tavnastok was north, and autumn was starting in the south. She smelled a faint crisp chill in the air, under the blue cloudless sky, but there was nothing she could see along the horizon in any direction over the low, rolling grasslands, to account for it. If this was truly a valley, it was wider than she could see, and the actual Junkawa, the Mother of Rivers as they'd called it, could be anywhere out of her view.

We'll be delayed waiting for the horse. Let's see what I've got.

She knelt on the ground, on the damp grasses which had been trampled by the camp traffic and were still giving up their pungent juices. "Spoon, fork, metal cup and plate, well-scoured and well-used." She ticked off the inventory and glanced up at Zandaril. "Might as well have been a set of bells for all the noise it makes."

"I think the practice is to wrap each of those in articles of clothing. Muffles the noise, keeps it from shifting," Zandaril contributed, gravely.

"Sounds right. Well, a nice big packet of salt, a bag of…" She opened it and sniffed. "Ugh. *Bunnas*," she said, wrinkling her nose.

"Glad I would be to remove that burden for you," Zandaril remarked.

'That's right—*bunnas* comes from your folk, doesn't it? What'll you trade for it?"

"Not very good quality that is, that they buy for the troopers."

"No point bad-mouthing it to me," she said. "I can just ask your Hing Ganau."

A faint smile crossed his lips. "You can trust me for an honest price. When you find something you want, we'll talk again about it."

She dug through the rest of the pack. "Looks like wrappings for bandages, soap, and that's about it. No clothes, like I thought. Not even a comb. Nothing to read." She began to put everything back in.

Zandaril cleared his throat. "I may have a *sushnib* or two. Books."

"Yes, a wizard would, wouldn't he?" She tied the straps at the top of the pack and stood up.

"I'll show you a bit tonight, when we camp up again," he said. "In *wirqiqa*-Zannib they are written, so it may be they are of no use to you, *bikrajti*."

She said to him, in his own language, "If I can speak it, then easily enough I can read it, with a little instruction in the script."

He stared at her in silence.

"Didn't believe me, did you?" she said, with a quirk of her lips, as she returned to the western Kigali-*yat* dialect she'd been speaking since her arrival. "There were a few *wirqiqa*-Zannib scrolls at the Collegium, but no native speakers, so I appreciate this opportunity to truly learn the language."

Looking at her with interest, he said, "Do you retain the knowledge after your source departs, *bikrajti*?"

"Only if I've taken the effort to master it m'self, and make it my own."

This was more than she'd intended to share, and the clop of hooves provided a welcome interruption as a young trooper led a saddled horse and hitched him to the cleats on the side of the wagon walls, next to Zandaril's mare. The mules already in their traces turned their heads to watch.

She laughed out loud when she saw him—a piebald gelding, quiet and deliberate. She couldn't picture him bestirring himself to a canter.

I bet that mare can run rings around him.

"Not taking any chances, eh?" she commented to Zandaril.

He bowed in her direction with a smile of his own, and she sketched him a comic salutation to honor his precautions.

CHAPTER 4

Penrys restrained herself from burying Zandaril with questions until he had worked the kinks out of his lively mare. The two of them trotted up one of the rolling slopes some distance northwest and then turned more directly west to parallel the men riding below them. Her horse maintained a steady pace, and eventually Zandaril's mount settled in beside hers and they both slowed down to match the main body of the expedition.

Scouts rode in pairs barely within her sight well in front, vanishing forward as she watched, and she could just make out other outriders on the far side of the line of march. The primary force rode in columns of two at a walk, with the supply wagons behind them, two dozen large ones with six-mule hitches, and not quite as many smaller ones pulled by two mules. More outriders brought up the rear behind the herds of horses and mules not in use and the cattle herd. At this distance, the constant noise faded into the background, and only the occasional shout made itself heard.

Looks like about five hundred men, and maybe another five or six dozen in support. There must be close to fifty spare horses. And dinner on the hoof. Probably a good idea in this empty landscape.

She'd seen cooks and a doctor on her way through the camp in the morning. A blacksmith, too. There were a few women doing laundry or managing supplies or horses, but it was clear that soldiering was a role for men in Kigali, on the whole.

Time to find out what I've fallen into.

She looked to Zandaril, riding to her right, on the outside. *What, in case I make a break for it on Lead-foot here?*

"So, where are we, exactly? What's this all about?" She gestured at the moving squadron below them.

Zandaril turned his horse's head uphill. "Follow me."

They rode a hundred yards at a slant to the top of the low, grass-covered ridge and reined in their horses. The chill wind from earlier in the morning freshened the air and she inhaled deeply.

From where she was, on horseback, Penrys estimated she could see about thirty miles. The air was exhilarating, but the view was not—in all directions, grasslands on rolling ground stretched out, interrupted by occasional wooded streams, with no sign of habitations anywhere.

Zandaril smiled at her expression. "Not what you expected, eh?"

"I thought there was this big river, and mountains all the way around."

"That's right. Let me explain." He used his hands to illustrate. "We are in the center of the world here." His deep voice made the pronouncement sound irrefutable.

She laughed at the hyperbole.

He glanced at her, deadpan. "I'm only repeating what the Kigaliwen say. We Zannib say the same thing about our own land—so does everyone.

"Have you seen the steppe hounds, the ones with the long, thin bodies and elegant necks?"

"I've seen drawings," Penrys said.

"So. Think of one, facing right, to the east, lying down on its belly, its head erect like the noble beast it is, with a leg stretched out in front, and an extra-long tail with a puff at the end." He cupped his hands in the air to represent the puff.

She smiled at the image, and he nodded in encouragement.

"That is the world. Now," he held up a finger, "Your Ellech is the hinge of the open mouth between the long snout and the heavy mountains and frozen ears of the upper face. Yes?"

"I can see that."

"Good. We will not waste time on the over-lengthy neck, with its hot and uncivilized peoples, but come with me down to the body of the hound. Here there are bands along the side, like the coloring of the actual beast." He swept his hands back and forth.

"On the spine and the shoulder are two nations—Fastar to the west, and Ndant in the east."

His hands sketched out rough forms in the air. His low voice lent gravity to his description.

"Below them is a line, the Kunlau Mountains. That is the northern border of Kigali. But Kigali is also the chest where it meets the sea, and the beginning of the foreleg, and part of the front belly. You see? Yenit Ping, the Endless City with its great harbor, is on this belly piece."

"The capital?" she said.

He nodded. "From there, Kigali merchants sail all over the world. From Kwattu, too, on the chest. That's how they send goods to your Collegium, without going all the tedious way around the front leg first."

He leaned closer, conspiratorially, though no one was within hundreds of yards of them to overhear, and dropped his voice even lower. "Kigali wants Shirtan-pur, too, the harbor on the spine at the base of the tail, but it doesn't belong to them."

He pointed northwest of their current position.

"It's that way. You go up the Neshikame river to the end, then overland a bit through Lomat, then down the Kabanchir. If they had that, they'd have a harbor on all three sides of the hound's body. Merchants, they want that. Very good for business. But it means war. No decisions yet."

"Is this something recent?" Penrys asked.

"No, no—many generations. Sometime merchants push, sometimes not. But never final. Always problem. Sometimes Rasesdad, sometimes Fastar. Sometimes both."

He waved his hand as if to dismiss the unresolved territorial ambitions of Kigali.

"Now we come to the middle band of the hound's body, below the mountains. This is the valley of the Junkawa, the Mother of Rivers."

"The largest river in the world."

He smiled at the remark.

"Yes, exactly. Two big rivers, running east. They join at Jonggep, the Meeting of Waters, and reach the sea at Yenit Ping. Many little rivers and not so little rivers go to them. Most of Kigaliwen are on a river somewhere."

He looked at her. "We are now between the north branch, the Neshikame, and the main south branch, Seguchi, four hundred miles west of Jonggep."

"The hound's liver?" she suggested.

That surprised a grin and a nod from Zandaril. "The nearest mountains in any direction are the Lang Nor, the Red Wall, about three hundred miles west of here. This whole valley, if you can call it that, is roughly six hundred miles wide, north to south. A giant valley for a giant river."

She pulled her reins to keep her horse from cropping grass with his bit in place. He raised his head and shook it, and the bit clattered. She patted him absently in apology, then leaned forward to scratch his poll.

"What about the Zannib?" she asked.

"Ah, we are more modest, as befits the rest of the belly and the back leg. Between us and Kigali are the Ardib Yakush, what they call the Minchang Mountains. We have not so many rivers, but much grass and fine horses, all the way to the cold sea at the bottom of the world."

"So I see." Penrys cocked her head at his mount, the small, shaggy horse she associated with steppe nomads.

"Yes, I brought my *lubr mar-az*, my string, with me when I came to join. Everything had to come on horseback over the passes, no wagon. Chang let me use a wagon. And Hing Ganau."

"This horse, too?" She gestured at her sturdy mount.

"He is from the troop herd. But is he not fine, in his own way?" he intoned.

"Very fine. He can probably keep a walk going all day long. I've named him Vekkenfet, Lead-Foot."

He grinned again. "Ah, but wait—I am not finished. I forgot the rump of our hound, and part of the tail. That belongs to Rasesdad, who borders both our lands, Kigali and *sarq*-Zannib.

"Not all neighbors can be friends," he said, glancing at her slyly. "The Rasesni, maybe they have friends up the tail, but they have few here on the body."

"But they're mountain folk, aren't they, not a great nation?" Penrys tried to recall the geography books she had glanced at in the Collegium.

"For people who are not a great nation, they are big pains in the rear of this hound." He smiled at the image.

"So. Word came downstream from the western border of raids and people evacuating. Neshilik has always these problems. The Rasesni would take back more of the headwaters if they could, and so they test Kigali readiness to defend them. Every generation or two, they do this. If they can ever reclaim and hold the land up to the gorge at Seguchi Norwan, the gates of the Seguchi, it might be difficult even for the Kigaliwen to shove them out again."

"The gorge?" she asked.

"You'll see. In about two weeks."

Penrys sat her horse and digested the information. *That's another three hundred miles, at the usual pace. So what's this Zan fellow doing here, in the middle of Kigali?*

"What brought you into this expedition?" she asked.

"The Kigaliwen are great merchants and not bad farmers. They build well, too. Make things."

He gave her a sidelong look. "But they are not famed for their wizards. Not like the Zannib."

She stifled a smile, apparently unsuccessfully, for he frowned at her.

"With the first word out of Neshilik came stories that spoke of wizards. The Rasesni are like the Kigaliwen—no wizards—so where does this come from? Where? Or is it a lie?"

He straightened in his saddle. "Commander Chang was appointed to lead this expedition, I suppose because he was already at Jonggep, the Meeting of Waters. Or because he is experienced."

"Or both," she said.

"Or both. Chang asked for assistance from *sarq*-Zannib, and we listened. Neshilik is on our border, too, and so is Rasesdad, to the west. I agreed to come, and joined him just after they started west."

"Why did you volunteer?" His deep voice was misleading—every time she studied him she was surprised how much younger he looked than he sounded. *Looking for adventure, were you?*

He spent a few moments fussing over his mare's mane before answering, with his face turned away.

"I have been to Kigali before, several times. I have visited their cities. It… interests me, how they do things, how they *organize* things."

He glanced over at her to see if she understood what he meant.

"This expedition, it is like a building project in some ways—it is an *organized* response to a problem. I have not traveled with soldiers before, so all of this is new experience for me."

She nodded.

"We do not *organize* like this, in *sarq*-Zannib. The Zannib-*hubr* have independent routes for our *taridiqa*, our annual migration, and even the Zannib-*taghr* work independently, farm independently. Our merchants do things in small groups, not large ones—not the caravans, not our western fishermen. Even our clans and tribes are small, compared to Kigali."

He gestured at his turban, and Penrys wondered if that identified his clan, if she but knew how to decode it.

"Wizards work alone. If something happens, we talk about it. A lot. And do little."

He looked over at the soldiers riding steadily along.

"Long time we have been friends with Kigali. Trading partners. Kigali stands between us and all others. They fight for both of us."

He turned to face her directly. "This is not proper, for adult peoples. It is not safe. How will we fight, if we have to?

"I am a wizard, so I am interested in how to *organize* wizards. This is my journeyman project, how I become a master. I would like to go to your Collegium and find out, but it is too far away and, besides, maybe I don't meet their standards. So, I go with troopers instead during my *tulqiqa*, my journey time, so I can at least learn this."

He set his mare on a downward diagonal off the low ridge and cantered slowly back to the level they'd started at, expecting her to follow, but refusing to turn his head to see if she did.

I'd be more impressed with that if I thought the sound of Vekkenfet's hooves trotting behind him weren't audible.

He would never have fit in at the Collegium, I think. They don't organize either, not really—they'd rather work alone, too, even if they speak about sharing knowledge.

She pursed her lips. *So what happened last night? What are they marching into?*

Penrys caught up with Zandaril once he'd fallen back into a walk to keep abreast of the troopers.

He seemed to have thrown off his embarrassment at revealing so much of his personal feelings, and smiled at her when she trotted up at her horse's stately speed. "See, he can go fast enough to run down Badaz when you want."

Falcon, it meant. She ignored the tease. "What about last night? Where did that mirror come from?"

He sobered. "What about you? Where did you come from? Geography lesson free. Time for trading now."

All right. Why not? I don't have to tell him everything. "Agreed," she said. "You first."

Their horses walked companionably side by side, Zandaril again on the outside.

"Mirror was a stupid trick. Stupid for us, I mean. Old mirror, used by Chang whenever he travels."

"Part of his furnishings, you mean? For his own tent?" she asked.

"Right. Last night, first time, it spoke to us, showed us Menbyede of Rasesdad." He wrinkled a lip. "So it said."

"In the command tent. With the senior officers."

"Bad idea. I examined it while Rasesni talked. Don't know how it worked. Picked up a cloth to throw over it, then... nothing."

"You were frozen in place."

He nodded. "I saw you. Pop! Then... thump, as you fell down."

Penrys felt herself flush. "I was in my workroom. I'd tried my little model of a *ryskymmer* and it seemed fine. So I got inside the framework of the full-sized detector to make the same adjustment. There was this one lower joint I thought was the problem. When I stepped back out and tried it again, it didn't work. I did this three more times. It was exasperating. Finally, I just gave the thing a good whack, not remembering I was in the wrong place."

"And that time it worked," he said.

"Yeah, I was stupid, too. I never thought it would go far if it did work, anyway, so I wasn't worried. The more fool me."

She glanced at him. "I still don't know what happened, exactly."

She rode in silence for a moment, the ache in her unaccustomed muscles from the morning's ride grounding her in the reality that she had come a quarter of the world from her refuge in the time it took her to fall to the ground. *Try again with a new device, built in a wagon from scraps, or walk home? Great choice. And what do I do for power-stones?*

"What are you thinking?"

The low voice interrupted her thoughts.

"I was thinking about the difficulty of getting home. Getting back, anyway," she said.

"Everyone wants to go home sometimes."

She muttered, "Doesn't feel like home. Just someplace I... work."

"Work is good. But it is not the same."

She grimaced. "Your turn now. What did the Rasesni say and what did you do with the mirror?"

He grinned broadly. "This Menbyede, he said we should not bother coming, that he had already taken back Neshilik and fortified the Seguchi Norwan gorge with fine new weapons. He was prepared to talk treaty terms, instead, and warned that we were surrounded. Here! In the heart of Kigali!"

He slapped his thigh. "Our blood was hot, and then we were… stopped. Very angry, and nothing we could do. Maybe he lied about attack, but maybe not."

He snorted.

"Then, when you released Chang, he bluffed right back. Excellent plan. Now Rasesni don't know what happened. Don't know about you. Don't know why it didn't work the way they wanted. And we are still coming to Neshilik."

He straightened up as if he were about to charge that instant.

Penrys hooked a thumb down at the expedition. "But isn't that an awfully small force against an invasion?"

"Who says Kigali is invaded? Kigali is very, very big. Very many people. Rasesni live in mountains—not so many people. They attack Neshilik, yes, and they have some new weapon, yes, but more likely this is all a trick to make Kigali give up. We go to see what is really happening. Then we fix it, or we send for real army. Army has a long way to travel, but they are not easy to stop."

He looked at her. "I think maybe we fix it. We have new weapon, too."

Her ears drew back on her scalp. "Me, you mean."

"Of course, you." He stared at her with friendly interest. "What can you do?"

CHAPTER 5

Despite herself, Penrys could feel her face freeze. *What can I do, is it? Well, that's a change from Aergon and his colleagues. They just wanted to know what I was—the rest didn't matter. Here at least maybe I can be useful.*

"Um, you know about the languages." She paused. "I didn't think—would you rather we spoke *wirqiqa*-Zannib together?"

He shook his head. "I need practice with Kigali-*yat*." He stopped with his mouth half open and crinkled his brow. "But you do not get Kigali-*yat* from me? You speak it better than I do."

"No, I'm using them." She pointed down at the troopers.

"Ah! So, how far can you go for language?"

Farther than I'm willing to admit. For now. "Pretty far."

His expression told her the evasion had not gone unnoticed, but he let it pass.

And this? You can hear this?

She answered him just as silently. **As you know from last night.**

"Not all wizards can do this," he commented, "to speak in this way."

You have no idea. Almost none in the Collegium. And the few who did didn't understand how to take it further. "Is it common among the Zannib wizards?"

He pursed his lips while he considered.

"Almost all—it's usually how we first know we are maybe going to be *nal-jarghal*, apprentices. It is a great blow when a young wizard fails at this, for it is harder for him to find teachers."

All! They'd be wasted at the Collegium.

The cry of a hawk hunting overhead drew both their gazes and gave her time to recompose her expression. "Do you study all in one place, then, like they do in Ellech?"

"No, very different. Some *taghulaj*, teachers, they specialize in the young ones, giving them basic instruction and keeping them from trouble—those usually live a settled life in the winter villages. As younglings, those who want to pursue the craft seek out a mentor willing to take them on, if a parent can't do it, and they stay together until both are satisfied or the student is dismissed." More quietly, he added, "Or the student dismisses his *taghulaj*."

Penrys filed that away for later. "So, is there a place, a repository, where all, um, craft knowledge is kept?"

"*Sushnib*, books, you mean. Wizards have their own books and pass them along to other wizards, their friends or students. Like I said, it is not *organized*, the way the Collegium is."

She could see the envy in his eyes. *It's not fair to let him cherish that illusion.*

"It's not what you think, the Collegium." She touched the chain at her throat. "The books are there, like you'd expect, and the wizards and students can use them, but they don't talk to each other, not about important things, and new books, serious ones, don't get written. The senior staff, they're mostly off working on their own narrow specialty, focused on past glories. The young ones, well, if they don't make themselves fit in, they don't last long."

He narrowed his eyes. "I do not think you fit in, with your new detector."

Devices, experiments, disruptions—no, I do not fit in.

"What do your wizards *do*? How are they useful?" Zandaril put the question politely but Penrys thought he was on the verge of outrage.

She spoke frankly. "I am not involved in Ellech politics, sheltered at the Collegium, but it seemed to me they do not do much of anything of worth, except produce more wizards like themselves—qualified, unimaginative, and timid. The knowledge is there, but not the will to try new things, to fail until something works. The merchants come with requests, sometimes, but not much happens."

He laughed. "Almost you make me glad I have not gone there. If it weren't for the books…"

"Yes, if it weren't for the books."

They walked on together for a few moments, upright but swaying slightly to accommodate the movements of their horses. Breakfast was beginning to seem like a distant memory to Penrys and she unhooked the canteen that was affixed to the saddle, hoping that a couple of swallows of tepid water would mollify her stomach for now.

Zandaril waited until she was done.

"You are hungry? We will all stop when the sun is high, but we can find something for you now if we ride down."

"No, I can wait. Thanks." She tried to remember whose turn it was, but Zandaril beat her to it.

"You knew the mind-glows last night, the ones who couldn't bespeak. I showed you Chang and Kep, and you shielded them from the Rasesni."

She nodded.

"What about them, below?" He cocked his head at the moving men and baggage train.

She opened her mind briefly. "Too many to count, but in range."

"Men? Women?"

"Yes."

He paused. "Horses?"

She smiled. He was clever. "Yes, animals, too. Have to be choosy about that—do you have any idea how many critters live in the grasslands around us?"

He grinned wolfishly at her. "Dangerous mice, must be careful or they'll attack." He glanced up. "Hawk would like that."

"Can you…?" she asked.

"Not the same for me. Just the mind-glows nearby, and only people."

He cocked his head and looked at her. "Maybe you can teach me, *bikrajti*."

"I can try. Um, sometimes that gets a bit… personal. More than mind-speech gets through."

At his expectant look, she added, "I don't recommend that lesson on horseback."

"Tonight, then, after dinner." He nodded briskly as if it were all set. "Language, too?"

What have I started? "I don't know if that can be taught."

"Maybe we can practice on your language."

Her muscles tensed. "And what would that be?" she muttered, bitterly. At his look of puzzlement, she continued, "Do you know Ellechen-*guma*? We can try that."

Zandaril closed the *sushnibtudin* and retied the heavy cords over the leather wrapping that enfolded the trunk. Putting aside the volume he'd extracted, he shifted it back into its place in the corner of the wagon and evaluated the cleared area he'd left free for lessons, in front of the sacks of beans that still made up most of its load. The square carpet that filled it, with its border pattern of intertwining vines in a riot of colors brought a fond smile to his face. *It was good that the jimiz, the scholar's rug, could serve its proper purpose, even if this would be a meeting between bikrajab, not a lesson from taghulaj to irghulaj, teacher to student. This is my first offer of nibar, hospitality, as one bikraj to another. Not what I expected.*

He could have used their tent, but he'd wanted more privacy for this. He'd sent Hing Ganau off and now all he was waiting for was his guest. Or prisoner. Or even, if Chang's worse fears had any basis, a spy.

He didn't think the latter was true, any longer, not after a day in the saddle together, exchanging stories, asking careful questions. He wanted to know much more, but better to go at it slowly, in these long days covering the vast distances, feeling his way, rather than damage, by clumsy interrogation, what he thought could become an alliance of colleagues. For all her peculiarities, he thought Penrys might have much to teach him.

He did, however, take his responsibilities seriously, and Chang had put her in his charge. He kept a mind-touch on her while she took care of "private matters" after dinner, just to confirm her location. She'd offered as much when she brought it up. "Better a mind-touch than a tether," she'd said.

He felt her approach now and moved forward to greet her as she came to the back of the wagon and walked up the steps that Hing had placed there.

"Come in," he said. "I've made us a place. You can lean against that." He pointed at a partly filled bean sack over which he had draped his red *uthah*, the printed mythical animal figures seeming to move in the lantern's light.

"This is for you, for now." He presented the *sushnib* to her with both hands, pleased with her obvious delight. She ran a hand over the cover and held it up to her face to sniff at it, then she opened it to look at its contents while walking blindly to her place, and stumbled a bit over the sack as she settled herself cross-legged on the rug, still intent on the pages.

Zandaril smiled to himself. *Anyone that clumsy should walk first and read later.*

She looked up as he seated himself and leaned against another sack draped in his sky-tree *uthah*, all blues and greens.

"This is a basic primer on magic, for a young student, isn't it?" she said. "What are you doing with something like that? Did you learn from it, yourself?"

"Yes, it's the one I used. Good to be prepared when you meet a new student."

"It's cut down from a scroll, isn't it? Don't see many like this at the Collegium."

"It's sturdier, as pages between boards. Hard to get rid of the curl, though—it's an art, flattening the parchment of an older work to bind it like this."

She grunted, and lifted a page to note the absence of text on what would have been the back of a scroll.

He baited his trap. "But I thought you would need help with the letters."

"Not when you're so close," she said, absently, buried again in the first few paragraphs. Then she started, and shifted her glance to him in alarm.

"Ah. So it is more than language, is it?" he asked, mildly, and watched her cheeks redden. Through his soft mind-touch he could feel her chagrin. The flickering light from the lantern hanging low overhead from the central bow supporting the canvas cast deceptive shadows over her face, but her mind was not so easily disguised.

"So," he said. "Can you show me?" More softly, "*Will* you show me?"

She exhaled and lifted a finger as if to ask him to wait a moment. "When you said it was hard for a student to find a mentor if he couldn't mind-speak, what did you mean? How do you use it with your teacher?"

"The teacher shows the student what to do, how it looks, from the…"

"From the inside?" she suggested.

Zandaril nodded.

"What about private thoughts?" she said. "Unintentional sharing?"

"That is not done," he said, drawing himself up.

"Isn't done, or can't be done?" she persisted.

On the point of sputtering a reply, Zandaril caught himself. *She deserves an honest answer.*

"It is not proper to try, but I cannot say that it is impossible. There are rumors of wedded couples, close friends…"

She smiled faintly.

"But there are also rumors of powerful men, misuse…"

She nodded as if he had confirmed something for her.

"When Aergon and the others began to examine me, three years ago, they asked me to show them what I could do. I should have asked them to go first, but I didn't know any better. I… scared them."

She looked away from him and cleared her throat. "After that, I couldn't find anyone willing to learn from me or to teach me, not in that way."

She stuck two fingers inside the front of her collar chain as though it were too tight and she wanted to loosen it, and then glanced back his way. "I wouldn't want to scare you, too."

Zandaril's skin chilled. *Do I trust her in this? How badly do I want to know? What secrets do I have that really matter? I don't know what she can do—maybe she can kill me and escape. Do I think that likely?*

He tasted her mind again and felt a stubborn loneliness and the bitterness of old failure, but not deception.

"We will try this thing, *bikrajti*," he said. "Please, can you describe it?"

"I can't tell you what it will be like for you, only for me," she said.

"Of course."

"For me, it's as though there were different layers. At the top, I can touch a mind, over a distance, and know something of the person by its flavor. If I've met him already, I can identify him."

This was familiar, and he nodded. "I showed you Chang last night that way, and you picked him out of the others."

"That's right. That's simple. Then, if they are capable, I can mind-speak with them, as I have done with you. Most can't, and it's like talking to a deaf man—the inability to hear is obvious."

Zandaril squeezed the corner of his bean sack in a clenched fist, on the side she couldn't see. "Not the same for me. I cannot know a person is mind-deaf—only he himself knows when the mind-speech fails to come to him."

"So, someone could lie about it, claim to be mind-deaf and then eavesdrop on a conversation?"

That was a disturbing thought. "Maybe he could pretend, but you can't overhear mind-speech the way you can spoken words."

"Are you sure about that?" she asked.

"Yes, of course. I mind-speak *to* someone, not to the air."

"Hmm," she said, noncommittally. "Perhaps."

"You do not agree?"

"I haven't tested it, but I wonder if a mind-cry for help to whomever could hear it wouldn't work."

That jolted him. *Ah, like in the old tales.* "There are stories, for children…"

She nodded. "I wanted to experiment with that in the Collegium, but…"

"They wouldn't allow it." He could picture prim and affronted elderly *bikrajab* reacting to such a request.

"It would've been like shouting in the library. I just couldn't do it."

They shared a smile.

"And, then," she continued, "there aren't very many there who can mind-speak at all."

"No?" he asked, startled.

"Hardly any. In fact, you'll find if you terrify half a dozen, you've pretty much run out of experimental subjects." A sardonic grin flickered across her face.

Oh. This paints an unflattering portrait of the great school of wizardly knowledge. Mind-deaf like the Kigaliwen.

"Truly?"

"Truly," she confirmed. "Anyway, what I've described is the top layer, as I think of it. Below that…"

She looked at him directly as if to judge his reaction. "I cannot see a man's thoughts, only his emotions, because he doesn't know enough to suppress them successfully. Like a deaf man babbling, he doesn't realize he's giving himself away. But the things he's learned by rote, the things he's an expert in—those things are deeply part of him. And I can share in that, to some extent."

No man I know can read another's thoughts, but how would I know if she is different?

"Language," he said.

"Yes, the earliest thing he learns that way. Reading, too. But only m'mind knows it, not the body. I can read your *wirqiqa*-Zannib script, because you can, but writing it would be difficult, my fingers clumsy and the letters ill-made. I speak with an accent, because my mouth is not accustomed to forming the sounds the same way that you do."

He nodded. "Compared to your native tongue."

"I have no native tongue," she spat. "I have nothing more than three years old. I've had to work all this out experimentally."

She pulled at her collar chain again.

"Why not take that off if it bothers you?" he suggested.

"Ha! How?" She leaned toward him and held her hair up off her neck. "I would be grateful if you could remove it, believe me."

Zandaril bent forward at the waist and ran his fingers along the outside of the chain, careful to avoid touching anything else. He could feel no clasp, no break in the perfect links. It was between gold and bronze in color, but did not have quite the feel of either metal. It left no mark on her bare skin, as brass might. The thick links hugged her neck without apparently impeding her ability to breath.

"Jewelers cannot cut it?" he asked, as he sat back again.

"No, nor blacksmiths. Nor any devices we could come up with. It came with me."

"What about your clothes? Any clues there?"

"It was me, a collar, and a great deal of cold, wet snow. Quite the spectacle."

She grimaced and gathered her hair again, finger-combing it off her face and holding it back with both hands. "And before you can think of a polite way to ask, the ears came with me, too."

She sat stoically while he leaned forward again for his first good look. They were furred all over, the outside dark brown and dense as her hair and the inside paler and sparser. They stood upright and pricked, but attached to her skull where normal ears would be, not high on her head like a hound, and not too large to be hidden by her thick hair. As he watched, one swiveled to focus on a footstep passing by outside.

He eyed the tension in her posture and sought a way to return the mood to the joking conversation of earlier in the day.

"Why, this is better than any story," he said, and applauded lightly. "Tell me, quickly now, is there more? A tail, maybe? I've always wanted a tail."

It startled a smothered laugh from her, as he'd hoped it would, but a shadow crossed her face. *There is something else, isn't there. What?*

She let her hair drop again. "Where were we? Ah, yes, expertise. Do you play a musical instrument?"

Her eyes narrowed a moment and, before he could answer, she said, "I see that you do. I can tell what stops on the strings produce which notes, and what the positions are for certain chords, but my fingers would be like sausages, trying to play. There's no shortcut for the body to learn things deeply, in the muscles."

As she continued her lecture, her voice cooled. "There are other kinds of expertise. If I'm in reach of a doctor," she tapped her forehead, "I know more about medical symptoms. A sword-smith's mind can inform me about the folding and welding of a blade. I may not be able to do what they do, but I can know a lot about it. The longer I borrow their expertise, the more it becomes my own, at least the mental part."

"And a military commander?" Zandaril suggested.

She assented soberly. "Yes, him, too. From someone like Chang, I can learn what to look for in junior officers, or how to read a landscape for defensive positions. But not actual troop movements, or what his orders are. Or what he had for breakfast, either."

He smiled. "And how do we know that?" he asked.

"Yes, that's the problem. Why should you believe me?"

She sighed, and they stared at each other a moment. "I *can* show you, I think, if you are willing."

"I said I would try this," Zandaril said, and bowed briefly from the waist.

"Then let's begin with language." She scooted herself around the rug until they were sitting more side by side than facing each other. He let her set the conditions as she wished.

An evening breeze rattled the canvas around them, and he tasted the remains of his dinner, the *wishkaz* he had added to give more flavor to the sauce. *How did she scare the wizards of the Collegium?*

She placed her right hand on his left knee, palm up. "It's usually easier if we touch."

He swallowed and laid his left hand down on top of hers, loosely. She made no attempt to clutch it.

See. The surface of my mind touches the surface of yours. Nothing more.

It was a strange sensation, as if their heads were joined, but there was no sense of invasion. *Would I be able to tell? Did she hear me thinking that?*

Let's look together at someone in the camp.

Penrys sent her attention outward from the wagon, letting it unfocus to cover a wide area and bringing him along somehow with her. The mind-glows of the humans were scattered across the near landscape, in a way familiar to him, but this was more crowded. He recognized the herd of horses by its direction. *So that's what animals feel like. And horses, so different from mules, and both from cattle.*

With that clue, he found the camp dogs, and even some of the smaller life, in the thatch of the grasses.

So. Let's pick someone.

She settled on a person nearby. **He's not moving. In his tent, maybe. What is he?**

Quietly she inventoried him. **Kigalino. Feel the language flow?**

It was the difference between describing a wine and drinking it, the difference between his painfully studied knowledge of the language and this unimpeded stream.

I understand, he told her. **But I don't think I can do this myself, bikrajti.**

Maybe all you need is to be shown. What else do we know about him?

He felt her somehow weigh the man's skills. **Whittling. He carves things, toys. And he has the common joy of singing, how to harmonize. I can feel him juggling, which might as well be magic to me. And, of course, he knows how to ride and set up a camp, how to fight, how to care for horses.**

He believed her, but he couldn't feel it, not the way he did the language. She'd gone beyond his ability to follow. **Did your wizards of the Collegium do any better keeping up**

They all fled in panic before getting this far. You're doing well.

His internal snort of disagreement was ignored.

Let's see if we can find another language speaker, one whose language you don't know already.

That will be difficult. They will surely all be Kigaliwen in this camp.

But not you or me. Maybe there are other strays.

He could feel the humor underlying the thought. He tagged along as she cast widely again, quickly filtering out all the minds whose flavor was, to her, "Kigali-*yat* speaker."

Ah. Here, near the horses. One of the herdsmen, perhaps. What language is this?

He perceived it, as she did, but it wasn't until he tasted the elaborate consonant clusters that began the words and felt the distortion in his mouth as he tried to pronounce them that he recognized it.

He snatched his hand up in surprise and broke their link. "That's Rasesni," he said, scrambling to his feet. "Can you find him, on the ground?"

She blinked at him, and he stretched out a hand to help haul her up.

"Leave the book," he said, as she bent to pick it up. "Hurry. We can't let him vanish on us."

CHAPTER 6

"Where is he? What direction?"

At Zandaril's urgent whisper, Penrys pointed again, like a hound aligning her body along a scent trail. They were striding through the evening camp, back toward the horse herd, as quickly as they could without attracting attention.

"How can you be sure he isn't just from some border family?" she asked.

"The horses… This expedition would be useless if something happened to the horses. Bad place for him to be, if he is really Rasesni."

He spared her a glance as he all but dragged her along. "I have to see what he's doing."

"Don't you think you could use a little help?" She gestured at the bodies by the campfires all around them.

His mouth quirked, just visible in the reflected firelight. "Well, and I may be wrong."

He pulled at her sleeve. "You find him again."

"I could show you how to do it."

"No time." His stride lengthened as the campfires became more sparse, and she had to stretch her legs to keep pace. They left the conversations and laughter around the supply wagons behind, and the tents, glowing from inside, were fewer. She had to watch her step now, the pools of darkness on the ground hiding ankle-turning hummocks. She concentrated on the mind she'd picked out from Zandaril's wagon.

If I could stop a moment and catch my breath, I might be able to find out more about him.

"Slow down. Give me a chance to think," she said, and dug in her heels.

Reluctantly, Zandaril stopped, peering off into the darkness as if he could see their target.

She bent over at the waist and breathed deeply. When she

straightened up, she concentrated on the Rasesni-speaking mind. Horses, he understands horses. What else? The turns of his knowledge seem familiar—what is it?

Then she realized—he reminded her of Vylkar, the wizard who had found her. It was wizardry this mind knew.

"Hurry up," she said, and trotted past a surprised Zandaril.

They crouched together outside the picket of riders walking their quiet circuits around the grazing herd. Zandaril peered through the darkness.

"That's him," Penrys whispered. "On the gray."

The horse glimmered faintly in the starlight. There was nothing suspicious about the scene, but what was a wizard, of any sort, doing riding night watch?

"Now what?" she said.

"Don't know. Didn't think that far," Zandaril whispered back. "He'll have to change horses, to give the one he's on a rest. We can stop him then."

"Just the two of us? What do you plan to use for weapons?"

He made no reply.

She persisted. "Why not tell Chang and have him do it right, with a mounted squad?"

He gave her a frustrated look.

Oh. Of course. If he fetches Chang, that leaves me on my own. Or, worse, able to contact a possible enemy. If he sends me, maybe I'll just escape. If we both go, this horseman may vanish. If we both stay, how does he know I won't side with the enemy?

She chuckled. "You have yourself quite a problem," she said, and he glared at her.

We will wait until he goes to swap horses and confront him ourselves.

The horse shied, as if its rider had jerked on the reins, and his head went up. The guard turned to face them, then took off, away from the herd, at a gallop.

They stood up and watched him vanish, the hoofbeats drumming on the soft turf until lost in the distance.

"Can you follow him? Track him?" Zandaril asked, frustration and chagrin in his voice.

"Not forever. He'll be out of range soon enough, if he doesn't stop."

They lingered there for several minutes. The scents of the quiet night and the peaceful shifting of the dozing horses filled in the gap where the horseman had been.

Finally, Penrys sighed. "He's gone."

"There aren't any others? You're sure?"

Chang was not pleased with them. Penrys spared a bit of sympathy for Zandaril, who was withstanding the worst of the Commander's wrath, currently in full spate. He'd admitted his fault, that he'd been more eager than prudent, and he was now standing, head bowed, waiting for the flood to pass.

"I couldn't find another native Rasesni-speaker in the camp," she said, diverting some of Chang's ire.

He eyed her as if considering an appropriate punishment, but passed on to the Horsemaster, whom Zandaril had had the foresight to fetch along with them before reporting the disaster.

"What was a Rasesni doing with the herdsmen?" Chang thundered.

The short, stocky gray-haired man said, "And how was I to know? He had no accent, and he was willing to stand night watch. He called himself Mu Wenjit—good Kigalino name. There's no way to screen all the civilians. And a hard time we have getting them, too, sometimes. Not everyone wants to hire away for months."

It's tough to tell if Chang's actually grinding his teeth, with that bit of a beard in the way.

She fought to keep the smile off her face.

"It's clear he was up to no good, by the way he fled after he heard us," she said.

"Not 'us.' Me," Zandaril muttered. "My mind-speech, he heard."

"We don't know that."

Zandaril looked at her and rolled his eyes. "We do now."

He turned to the Horsemaster. "What did he look like?"

"I don't know—ordinary. Um, I remember one eye drooped a little lower than the other."

"Menbyede, from the mirror," Chang said. "Maybe you're right, Zandaril-chi. Maybe this is a big bluff."

Penrys watched him drop into intense consideration, all the frustrated anger forgotten. No one moved, hoping to avoid notice.

She tried to yawn surreptitiously, her mind on the bedroll Hing Ganau had fetched for her, back in Zandaril's tent near his wagon. *I'm not used to riding all day like this.*

Chang turned back to her. "You think he was a wizard. Like Zandaril."

"No, not like Zandaril. Like one of the Collegium," she said.

"What's the difference?"

"I haven't met other Zannib but the books said, and Zandaril's like that, too, that the Zannib wizards are famous specialists in *beolrys*, the mind-skills. The Ellech are more interested in *raunarys*, the thing-skills, controlling physical objects."

Chang stared at her blankly.

"Moving things, binding things, destroying things." In exasperation, she continued. "That's why there are devices, to amplify or control that. It's what much of the Collegium is for, the study and development of that craft. Anyway, it leaves a different flavor in the mind, as a baker and a brewer do, though both are concerned with the transformation of grain using yeast."

In the silence that followed, she seized her opportunity. "I want to examine that mirror. Maybe it can tell me something."

CHAPTER 7

"Are you saying this Rasesni was trained at the Collegium?" Zandaril asked Penrys as he led the way to an armory wagon, one of several that housed the squadron's inventory of weapons. The mirror was stored there, to take advantage of the guards already in place.

"No, I don't know that," she said. "There may be many places where similar work is done."

"Skill, blood, and power," Zandaril muttered. At Penrys's look, he explained. "Magic comes in different forms and is born in blood. In bloodlines it lives and sometimes skips generations, like hooded eyes or notable noses."

She nodded.

"Skill can be learned," he said. "Anyone with magic can better their skills. But power, well, that is partly inborn."

"And partly not," Penrys said. "There are ways to get more power."

"And you are a maker of devices. You know something of how that can be done," he said.

"Yes, I do." She eyed him, sideways. "And you do not?"

How could he explain to her?

"It's not right, to do this. Not… proper." He could see she didn't understand. "Good people don't…"

He cleared his throat and tried again. "The little gods, the *lud*, would not…"

"Approve," she suggested.

He detected an odd note in her voice. They walked on carefully through the darkened camp, where most of the fires burned low and the lights in the tents were extinguished. An occasional touch of smoke drifted their way.

"You know," she said, at last, "the Collegium would almost agree with you. Except that they would consider the line to be drawn immediately after the inventions of the prior generation. It's only advancement from that point that they consider… unsanctioned."

This time the bitterness in her voice was clear.

"Yes, I make devices, I spent much of my time there learning how to do that. I'm sorry if it offends you."

I'm not the one offended. "It's not my affair," he told her.

She made no reply.

"Truly, it is not. We of the Zannib do not do this, but other people have other gods."

He glanced at her. *Who are her gods, if she can remember nothing? Do they remember her?*

He pointed to the guard walking a path around a group of wagons, drawn together side-by-side. "There, that's the wagon where they put the mirror. Can you feel it?"

Penrys glanced at the wagon, its high wooden walls topped by a white covering looming out of the darkness in the distance. If not for the watch-fires nearby, she wouldn't have been able to make it out. She noticed that the fires burned inside the guard's circuit, so that his eyesight looking outward was not affected. The watchman silhouetted against the fire-light hesitated and then came to a stop to wait for them as he saw them headed his way. She couldn't make out his back-lit features.

She checked to see if the mirror was detectable, slowing down as she concentrated, and Zandaril matched her pace. She scanned the wagon for a device's power-stone, trying to see it clearly through all the iron and other metals stored there. Yes, there it was—a faint throb with an odd signature. *What is that? What does that remind me of?*

Cocking her head as she took another step, she poked further into it, and it vanished. Her instant of puzzlement was overwhelmed by the punch of air that knocked her down and tumbled her backwards. In the confusion, she glimpsed Zandaril rolling until he fetched up hard against the wheel of the wagon they had just passed. *What happened? Why can't I hear anything?*

Time seemed to slow. She stopped moving, having ended up on her right side facing what was left of the armory wagons. The one she'd been examining was gone, utterly. A rain of objects flew through the air towards her. She tried to lift her arms to cover her head, but it took far too long. All around her she saw them hit the ground, some bouncing, and some sticking—fragments of swords, unidentifiable crushed metal, in silence, like a dream. Something heavy thumped her on the left shoulder and her arm went numb.

In the deathly stillness, she saw people running through the fire-lit darkness, flickering in and out of the dusty air. Their mouths were open, as if they were shouting. *Where's the guard?* With her good arm she groped the ground, trying to brace herself to stand up, but she was clumsy and couldn't seem to organize herself.

She gave up and looked for Zandaril again. He wasn't moving. Leaning on her right arm, she hitched her way on her side in his direction, pulling herself through the trampled grass. She felt the juices sticking to her bare arm. *Why is my arm bare?* People ran past and ignored her. It was strange to see so much activity all around, and not hear a thing, not even her own heartbeat. Her left arm didn't hurt, but it flopped around loosely in a way that worried her, distantly. She avoided looking at it.

One thing at a time. Let's find out if he's alive. She blinked and felt tears trying to wash the dust out of her eyes. *Come on, it's not that far. Is he breathing?*

She started to bespeak him, to check on him, but stopped. *I shouldn't do that.* That puzzled her. *Why not?* Something inside told her, *it went wrong last time.* She didn't understand why she hesitated, but didn't let it stop her from dragging herself closer to the wheel where Zandaril lay, crumpled sideways on the ground.

She reached one out-flung foot, stocking-clad. *Why was he out here without his boots?* The other leg was still shod, and she couldn't make sense of that. She glanced at her own feet. *Still have my own shoes. That's good.*

She pulled herself up alongside him and leaned on the wheel next to his body. *Skin to skin should be safe.* She held her right hand up in front of her face, surprised at how filthy it was, clods of dirt and bits of grass smeared everywhere. Reaching over her left side, averting her eyes from whatever was wrong there, she laid it along his throat.

It pulsed, and she could feel the shallow breaths. *Good.* She lay back against the wheel to rest. *I think I'll just sit here a while and see if things get any better.*

From a great distance away, she could hear a dull wash of undifferentiated noise. She half-closed her eyes and let her vision blur to match it—the shadows and movements were restful, undemanding.

CHAPTER 8

"There they are."

Penrys flinched as her body was jostled. Her left shoulder throbbed,

"What about him? Is he alive?" A woman's voice, this time.

They were talking about Zandaril. She opened her eyes and threw her right arm over him protectively. Someone gently pried it away and told her, "He'll be fine. We'll take care of him."

She clutched her injured shoulder instead and tried to make out who it was, but the face was unfamiliar.

"Let me see," the woman said, and pulled her hand away again. The man accompanying her raised his torch closer for light, and she was fascinated for a moment by the warmth and the busy movement of the flame. She inhaled sharply as the fingers probed, and then exhaled in relief when they stopped.

"Dislocated," the woman commented to the torch-bearer. She grabbed Penrys's wrist and twisted the whole arm until, with a dull snap, it settled into place, almost before Penrys could exhale from her sharp and surprised gasp.

"Let's get it in a sling for now." She pulled a cloth from the satchel slung over her shoulder and folded it into a large triangle. Then she bent Penrys's left arm at the elbow and cradled it in the cloth, slipping the ends around her neck and knotting them just below her right collarbone.

"What about the Zan?" her companion asked.

"I can't find anything 'sides a knot on the head. He's lucky he wore a turban. We'll have to let him sleep it off, and set a watch in case it gets worse."

Penrys cleared her throat. "What happened?" Her words sounded slurred to her.

"Well, we don't really know, yet. Something destroyed one of the armory wagons."

"I remember." She thought about it a moment. There was a

question she wanted to ask, from before. "What happened to the guard?"

The woman's lips thinned. "Not much of him left, I'm afraid."

Penrys swallowed.

The doctor continued. "We're still finding people like you and fixing them up. Maybe a dozen dead, so far."

The mirror. I was looking for the device. That's what set it off.

Dead, a dozen dead. I caused that.

Her stomach clenched, and she leaned over to her right and retched onto the ground. The woman held her forehead until she was done.

"Get me up," she said, flailing with her right arm. "I have to speak with Chang."

"I don't have time to waste on this." The doctor stood up and closed her satchel.

"It's important," Penrys insisted, and the doctor threw up her hands.

"Stay here. I'll send word," she said.

The man with the torch had waved a couple of men and a stretcher over for Zandaril, and they helped haul her up and steady her as she limped over to a camp seat one of them found. She watched them carry the Zan away and hoped for the best.

She sat on her flimsy support and endured the dizziness, trying not to tumble off of it. Waves of nausea wracked her, and she wished for a canteen, anything to take the taste away. She bent her head and concentrated on staying awake and controlling her stomach, staring at the grass in front of her.

Eventually, a pair of black boots intruded into her view. They were no longer highly polished.

She blinked and lifted her head.

Commander Chang loomed above her, his face smeared with soot. Several men with grim expressions trailed behind him.

"How's the Zan?" he asked.

"They took him away somewhere, with a bump on his head," she said.

He glanced at her sling without comment, and she shivered.

"Well?"

"I think I know what happened," she said, her voice low.

Chang waited.

"I checked on the mirror while we were approaching. From outside the wagon. It was a device. They didn't just *project* through it last night—the mirror itself did some of the work."

She cleared her throat. "Devices use power. When my mind touched it, the power released, all at once, like an overloaded spring."

She looked down again. "That's not supposed to happen."

"It was a trap," Chang suggested. "For our wizard."

"That's what I think." She picked at her guilt again. "How many dead?"

"Too many," he said, and she winced. He paused for a moment. "But it was *my* mirror. Could you tell when it was tampered with?"

"I never got a good look at it. Could have been a long time ago."

"Or it could have been by our Rasesni spy, now gone. Yes?"

She nodded. "Why not? If he was undisturbed, if he had tools and knowledge, sure, he could've done it recently. It's not a device I know, but they all have similarities."

She shivered again.

He raised his head and turned to one of his staff. "*Tatgomju*, have someone get her to bed in the Zan's tent. There's still work to be done here."

Penrys didn't get a good look at the trooper who helped her hobble back towards Zandaril's wagon and tent. Her surroundings seemed to fade in and out as they made the slow journey, and she gave all her attention to not falling down. When he stopped moving she lifted her head, surprised to find their tent in front of her, its flap open and a cresset burning in front of it.

"Is this the place?" he asked her.

"Yes," she croaked.

"No one's here. D'ya need help?" He peered at her more closely. "You don't look so good."

All she wanted was to collapse. "You should get back to them. I'll be fine, thanks."

He looked at her dubiously, then nodded to her and turned away to jog back toward the disaster. She watched blearily as he vanished.

She swiveled her heavy head back to the beckoning darkness of the tent's interior and shuffled carefully inside, aiming for the nearest bedroll on the ground. She hadn't slept there the night before, and she wasn't sure if any of the bedrolls were hers, or even if there were enough of them. *Doesn't matter—Zandaril's somewhere else.*

Mindful of her injured shoulder, she lowered herself carefully onto the closest bedding and rolled over on her back, shoes and all. The sudden change of posture dizzied her and she closed her eyes to recoup, just for a moment.

Someone passed a cool, wet cloth over Penrys's face, and she blinked.

Hing Ganau sat beside her, his splinted leg stretched out to the side. He'd placed a bowl on the ground next to him, and kept up a low, running monologue as he worked.

"They fetch me to keep watch on him, and I do that, and then he wants to know where the other one is, and nobody knows, and he's out again. And the healers won't talk to me, too busy, they say, go away, they say, ask someone else, they say. And nobody knows what's happened."

He caught her looking at him, but carried on as if nothing had changed.

"And I come back here to get clothing for him—and what became of his boot, I'd like to know—and look who's lying on his bed like a cuckoo in a nest where she don't belong, in her dirt and her rags."

She opened her mouth to protest, and he gave it an extra-heavy swipe that shut it again.

"And how did she get here, all the long way, I wonder? She never walked it, like that."

She nodded her head carefully, and watched his face. He was older than she'd realized, his face wizened and his hair going gray.

"I had help," she whispered.

"'Help,' she says. Didn't do much for her, did they, just tied a scrap around her neck and called it done."

"Not high priority," she croaked, and he snorted in response.

He reached behind him and brought out a flask. He helped her lift her head and monitored the two careful sips she took. Whatever it was, it burned all the way down.

It tasted of peaches, somewhere underneath the fire, and the aftertaste in her mouth was an improvement.

"How is he?" she asked, choking on her dry throat.

"Talking, is she, and won't wait for some good, fresh water."

He clambered up and fetched a stoneware pitcher and a cup. He sat himself down again next to her and poured out the water. She could smell the moisture of it and tried to rouse herself enough to reach for it, but he gently batted her hand down and once again helped her lift her head.

"Slowly, now, I don't want to be seeing it again, coming back up."

She'd thought she could drain the cup easily, but after making it halfway she lost the energy, and he let her slip down again.

"All right, then, she's been a good girl. How is he, she wants to know? The Zan's got a bump like an egg on the back of his head, is how he is, so he don't stay awake for long, but I've seen the like before. He'll have a headache like a signal drum for a couple of days, no worse. Bad enough, he'll think it."

Hing rinsed out his cloth.

"How many killed?" she asked, trying to keep her voice steady.

"Not saying yet, are they, and some of the survivors ain't likely to. Survive. A mess, it is. Don't know if we'll march tomorrow or not. Decision in the morning, they say."

All this time, he'd been continuing the work with the wet cloth. He'd ripped off the rags of her shirt, wiping her down impersonally afterward, like a horse. For all his muttering, he'd refastened the sling on her left arm after giving the bruises a thorough look.

It felt wonderful to have her face and hands clean. She couldn't bring herself to care about the impropriety of her clothing or, rather, the lack of it. She groped up to her neck and felt the chain. *Still there.*

"Weren't you going to have clothes for me?" she wondered, sleepily.

"And a good thing you weren't wearing them yet, or I'd have to fetch new ones, wouldn't I. Never you mind, you won't need them tonight at any rate."

She realized her shoes were off, and she felt the blankets pulled up over her, the sheet beneath them smooth against her bare skin.

"Don't you stir, now," he said to her, looking down sternly.

She smiled faintly. *Small chance of that.*

CHAPTER 9

"Sixteen dead—two of them afterward—and another eight wounded badly enough to be incapacitated," Penrys said.

"I'd rather be up than lying here like a lump." Zandaril glowered at her from his cot at the far end of the healers' tent, set up in a cross of five squares, like the command tent. He transparently envied her relative mobility. Without his turban, his black hair hung in loose curls to the line of his jaw.

Penrys ran her hand over the smooth green tunic and brown leather over-jerkin provided by Hing Ganau. The choice in civilian clothing was limited. The clothes fit her well enough, but she wasn't used to them, particularly the boots, and she hoped they'd be more comfortable after a bit of wearing. Everything ached at the moment.

She leaned forward on her camp chair, careful not to knock her arm in its sling.

"Listen—you've already faded out a couple of times since I've been here. Nothing wrong with you that time won't cure, but no use pretending you're fine."

He glared at her.

"Or would you rather hop on a horse right now and go scouting for that Rasesni, eh?"

She was amused to see him turn pale at the thought of a swaying horse.

"Thought not," she said.

He subsided for a moment, then changed the subject.

"Have you seen the place in daylight?"

"I took a walk around it earlier this morning. After Hing let me get up."

He grinned at her. "Don't let him bully you. He will, if you let him."

"He was with *you* most of the night, you know. I told him to go get some sleep himself." She chuckled. "He might even be doing that."

"What does the damage look like?"

She sobered. "That wagon is just… gone. Everything inside came flying out and embedded itself in the nearest target. Luckily almost all the people were already settled for the evening, but some tents were too close…" She nodded her head at some of the other occupied beds.

"We were lucky, we were just far enough away to miss the worst of it. Two more of the armory wagons were badly damaged, and they're repairing what they can."

"It was the mirror, wasn't it? When you… touched it."

She swallowed. "It was prepared to dump its power if someone mind-probed. Think if we'd been inside the wagon with it."

He closed his eyes. "Two more dead, then."

She nodded.

"That Rasesni, he didn't have time to set the trap when we surprised him," Zandaril said.

"No, it must've already been arranged."

"Maybe it would have gone all the way back to Yenit Ping before a wizard touched it. Or ended up in Chang's *samke*, his family's compound, and killed even more there."

"A nasty bit of work," she agreed. "Indiscriminate. Aimed for you, I would think."

"And it almost got me."

"Oh, that reminds me. I have good news." She reached behind her. "I found your boot."

He smiled incautiously. "Still don't understand how that could've come off."

She presented him with a tattered bundle of leather. "Better for you that it did, considering what happened to it."

He held it up and looked at the holes pierced through it. His face fell, and he leaned back again.

"I'll just see if Hing wants this for a souvenir," she said, plucking it out of his hands. She stood up to go, but a commotion at the tent's entrance flap stopped her.

"Look who's here," she murmured to Zandaril.

Commander Chang and several other men were making their way through the tent, stopping at each cot to speak briefly with its occupant before moving on.

"Headed our way," Zandaril said.

Penrys agreed. She put the boot down. Some of the faces seemed familiar from the night before.

She waited beside Zandaril until all had come to a stop. Staff followed them in to deposit camp seats for each of them, then left again. All remained standing until Chang spoke, directing himself to Zandaril.

"Since the doctor wouldn't let you come to us," he cocked his head at the woman trailing behind him, the one who'd treated Penrys the night before, "we decided we would come to you. We want a wizard's opinion in our counsel."

"It's good we have you both." This time his glance included Penrys.

He sat down, and his staff followed his lead. Penrys took her own seat, next to Zandaril's cot.

"Tell us again what you saw last night," Chang told her.

She recounted the events one more time, and added her interpretation. A hard-faced man with a square jaw scoffed at her account.

"I'm sorry, Commander-chi, but she shows up one day ago, the next night a so-called spy is found, and then the evidence disappears and we lose sixteen people. What sort of idiots do the Rasesni take us for?"

Zandaril raised himself on his elbows to protest. "I was there for all of it, Sau-chi. I'm the one who scared off the spy. I suggested she look for the mirror from a distance, and watched her do it."

The staff officer did not look convinced, but a lifted hand from Chang quelled the discussion.

"I want to address any other immediate threat," he said. "Is the Rasesni still gone, or has he returned in the confusion."

Penrys stared at him. "I hadn't considered that. I'll look."

She knew the spy's individual mind now, and that helped her sort through the camp quickly. She then swung out to the edge of her reach, but couldn't locate him.

"Nowhere I can find him."

Sau muttered loudly, 'So she says."

"And how far is that?" Chang said, ignoring him.

"I'd need a known person at a known location to serve as a measure of distance, but I think it's at least a couple of miles." *This relatively level terrain would make a good place for some tests, once Zandaril is recovered. If I'm still at liberty by then.*

The officer's blunt antagonism was the first overt enmity she'd encountered, but a quick glance at the emotions of the men around her confirmed that he was not alone. Chang's mind was controlled over a roiling simmer of rage at the moment, but not actively hostile.

"No other Rasesni in the camp?" Chang asked.

"I don't know." Before Sau's outrage could provoke him to speak, she continued. "I found this one by looking for someone whose native tongue was not Kigali-*yat.* I was showing Zandaril some things, as a colleague."

Zandaril nodded to confirm.

"I didn't find any other native Rasesni-speaker, but that's not to say there aren't others who mean you harm, whether or not they learned the language later."

Zandaril spoke up. "She thinks that mirror was set to release its power catastrophically at the touch of a wizard, any wizard. It might have done so at any time."

He cleared his throat. "I've been thinking—nothing else to do here. What if it's not the only device planted in the camp? Why would there be only one? Seems like a waste of a good spy."

Penrys could feel her ears move back on her scalp, and the council was thrown into consternation.

"Can't you look for them, the way you did the spy?" Chang asked her.

"And what if that makes them explode the same way? In someone's pack, or in a tent somewhere? I can't know it's there until I touch it with m'mind, and then the damage is done."

She thought about the uses of traps. "I'll bet he didn't modify the mirror itself. He probably just attached something to it. Might've been small. Something that small could fit anywhere. People wouldn't know it was around. What if there're lots of them?"

Zandaril added, "The Horsemaster said he'd been with us since Jonggep. That's weeks he had, to tuck his treats away, before she even joined us."

"If there are any at all," Sau said.

"Yes," Penrys said. "If."

"Maybe he expected to trigger them all himself, when he could do the most damage," Zandaril suggested. "If he gets close enough, maybe he can still do that."

"Good that we're beyond his reach, then," Chang said, but Penrys shook her head as he spoke.

"He's out of my range, but we may not be out of his. Every wizard's different."

She could feel panic beginning to tinge the thoughts of two of the council.

Chang addressed them. "We'll handle this now. Assemble the men on the south side of the camp, and everyone else—all the *yekungno*, the civilians—on the north side. Everyone to strip down to their clothing and empty their pockets, then walk away from their packs and other possessions…"

He paused and looked at Penrys.

"About a hundred yards," she suggested, with a shrug.

"Yes. We'll send you down behind them to look at the gear. Once that passes the test, everyone to pick up their gear and bring it that extra hundred yards out of camp. Then the supplies and other group equipment, with no one closer than a hundred yards."

One of the officers spoke up. "Do the saddles and horse gear the same way, first. That way we can leave the troopers armed and mounted while we continue."

Chang nodded. "Then the wagons should be separated first, before examination. Set them in two columns, drive the first two a hundred yards down and separate them, then unhitch the horses. Test those wagons, then hitch up the horses again, move them a safe distance, and go get the next pair."

"It'll take all afternoon," someone objected.

"And much of the night, too, I don't doubt, but we're not moving until I'm sure nothing else has been left behind by the enemy, and I plan to move on in the morning, so the sooner we begin, the more sleep we'll get. Have the cook wagons and gear go first so they can start preparing supper for the camp. There'll be enough grumbling about re-erecting up their tents, no reason to make them wait for their food."

The Commander eyed Zandaril, stretched out on his cot, then turned to Penrys. "Looks like you'll have to look at everything the same way you did the mirror. Everything. Can you do it?"

She swallowed. "Don't know if I can stay on m'feet that long, but I'll try."

Chang turned to one of his men. "Get her a horse or, better yet, a cart and driver. After she goes up the lines of people and loose gear, she can remain in place for the columns of wagons."

She looked at Zandaril. "You could join me in the wagon, and watch over my shoulder."

Chang chopped his hand through the air. "I don't want the two of you in the same place until this is done."

CHAPTER 10

With much hollering and confusion the unusual instructions were carried out. In the end, they decided to leave the tents in place but to move as much gear out onto the grass as possible before walking what Penrys hoped was a safe distance away.

She'd examined her driver and the small two-wheeled cart before they hitched up its horse. As with the rest of the loose horse tack, she'd found nothing.

They walked the horse from the back of the encampment to the left and just on the inside of the long lines of sullen troopers, stretched to the west on the south side of the camp. She looked again for native Rasesni-speakers and sampled their mood as she passed. They were suspicious and uncooperative. Yard by yard she surveyed the packs and tents, looking for the power signature of any magical device. Her muscles were tense, making her sore left shoulder ache, as she expected at any moment to trigger an event like yesterday's, and she had to keep reminding herself to relax or she'd never last the day.

About halfway down the column she glanced casually with her mind at one small pile, too far away for her to make out individual contents, and bolted upright. *Was that it?*

Before she could confirm it, there was a white flash and small objects shot out harmlessly in all directions. A cry went out from the men, and one trooper shouted, "Stop! Stop! Don't do any more."

He reached a shaking hand into his pocket and withdrew a small object. He laid it gingerly on the ground and backed away, pulling at the arm of his companion who was still staring in shock at the explosion far out in the grass.

"That was his," he said, cocking his head at his buddy. "We both have these. Is that what did that?" He pointed out into the field. "I didn't take mine off—he said we shouldn't ever take them off if we wanted them to work."

A burly man thundered down upon him. "'Everything out of your pockets and off your backs,' I said. You heard me." He eyed the guilty men. "Anyone else not inclined to obey orders?"

The unit looked properly cowed.

"All right, back off," he roared. "Over there, by the trees. Move!"

Penrys climbed down awkwardly from the cart and bent over to look at the object. It was a wooden charm of some kind, painted in bright colors. She straightened up to look at the driver. "Better go join them," she said.

Movement caught her eye—Chang was approaching to see what had happened. She turned to the man in charge of the troopers. "Better yet, *Kwajigomju-chi*, can you mark this with something? Then let's all get out of here and meet him, in case something goes wrong."

He bellowed to his retreating men to bring him a staff, and one of them returned on the run with an eight-foot whippy pole. The *kwajigomju* untied his neckerchief and fastened it around the top like a flag before sticking it in the ground, none too close to the cheerful charm. He climbed into the back of the cart, and all of them drove at a good trot over to intercept Chang and stop him from coming any closer.

"You found one," the Commander said. He pursed his lips and nodded. "There will be more."

"We may have found two of them." She cocked her head at the *kwajigomju* to finish the story.

"Two of my men—friends they are—one of them emptied his pockets like he should, and that's what went off. Turns out the other one didn't."

Penrys explained. "He put this thing… I don't know what it is, a charm, maybe? Anyway, it's out there where the pennant is. I'm not sure how to look at it without setting it off, but I could try ordinary tools."

"Are you sure it's another device?" Chang asked.

"Well, no. To do that I'd have to trigger it. If it is, I want to see how it's made."

"Dangerous work," he commented.

She cleared her throat. "I'd rather save it until last, if I could. I want to find the rest of them first."

Chang nodded. "*Kwajigomju*, set up a guard around that item, a hundred yard circle. Don't let anyone approach."

"I'll use the unit that caused the problem, sir. We'll keep everyone away from it." He hopped down from the cart and humped off toward his men.

"And find out where they got those things," Chang called after him. "I want to talk to them."

He waved his hand in acknowledgment without turning around.

Word spread down the line, and soon there was a small amount of traffic crossing hurriedly back and forth ahead of them as the contents of incompletely emptied pockets were suddenly added to the piles of items waiting to be examined.

Behind Penrys and her driver, the soldiers whose possessions had already been tested walked back to retrieve them and return them to pockets, packs, and tents.

One tent went up with a hollow noise when she probed it.

"Whose was that?" she asked the shocked men, and four of them reluctantly raised their hands.

"I'll need a list of absolutely everything that was in there, no matter how small or trivial."

She glanced outward and saw Chang's party riding on a parallel track outside of the column of soldiers. He dispatched someone to collect the four men for interrogation, and she drove on.

The rest of the troopers' column was clean, but it wasn't the same for the civilians. Her driver turned the cart at the head of the column where there were dozens of men working on lining up the column of wagons for the third pass, and she began making her way back down the north side.

Almost at once, she felt something briefly from a laundry crew's supplies. There was just enough to confirm the same signature before the distant air was full of dried soap flakes. The men and women of that crew were collected by Chang's men.

Penrys glanced over at her driver. "Chang has a system going here, doesn't he?"

"Always was one for organized effort," he said. "This ain't no different."

A food dump went off next, within seconds, and she slowed down to make sure she probed absolutely everything. Altogether, she triggered four devices on that side of the camp.

By now the afternoon was beginning to approach dusk, and they broke for a few minutes before starting on the wagons. The healers' tent had been cleared at the start by the simple expedient of carrying off the injured men on their cots far enough to let it be probed safely. Penrys dismissed the driver when they got there to go and care for the horse and return in an hour or so.

The wagons are going to be a problem. That's where the mirror was. They're the easiest to sabotage.

She wasn't looking forward to it, and could already feel herself dragging. She yawned, and walked into the tent to see how Zandaril was doing.

He was sitting up, eating his dinner, and Hing Ganau was supervising the procedure.

Zandaril swallowed his current mouthful when he saw her. "You've been busy, busy, busy. Stories everywhere."

"It's not even half done," she said. "The wagons'll be worse."

"Maybe not," he said. "I hear they changed their minds. These troopers had nothing to do today, and Chang doesn't want to lose more wagons. So, they took each wagon, unloaded it, and ran it out to the side. Maybe if something goes whoosh, less will be damaged."

"That's a lot of work," she said.

"Chang's in a hurry, he is. Doesn't want to stay in one place. He thinks, better men be tired and safe, then rested and in danger." He grinned at her. "The men agree. Glad you're getting rid of threats."

She glanced around the healers' tent. *After I killed sixteen of them and hurt all of these.* She looked at Zandaril. *And you.*

"Are they going to reload the wagons in the dark?" she asked.

Hing shook his head. "Everyone's praying it won't rain, aren't they?"

CHAPTER 11

Rather than go up one side of the unloaded wagon column and back again, Penrys decided to drive straight to the head of the line and start a hundred yards in front. From there she could go back along one side of the spine, probing the goods on the ground in their two parallel lines.

It was tricky—she had to do the supplies a hundred yards before she got to them, and the wagons on either side as she passed, and it was hard to remember which of the piles of supplies she had already examined.

The first explosion, however, woke her right up, her heart pumping in recollection of the night before.

Her expectation had been that the goods were most at risk, like the mirror, but it was a wagon which blew apart initially. She stopped to let Chang's outriders identify whose it had been and retreat from the dangerous neighborhood before she went forward. And she was glad she'd waited, because the wagon beside it, already riddled with wood fragments from the first one, went up next.

The driver focused on reassuring their horse that these loud noises were nothing to be alarmed about, and Penrys straightened up and concentrated.

They managed a few more yards before the first supply load boomed into the air, well ahead of them.

Their progress down the line was slow and tedious, and the damage in their wake was substantial—four wagons, and five loads. It was too dark to tell just what could be salvaged from the sabotage. *Well, at least it was balanced. Would have been smarter to target more wagons, force them to leave supplies behind. Guess they didn't think the wagons and supplies would be separated.*

What if that Rasesni spy had triggered all of this instead of just fleeing? Why didn't he? The only reason not to would be to trigger them later, when the surprise had more value.

Maybe last night was lucky, despite the cost. If they'd had to face all of this, unwarned…

She thought of the deaths that might have resulted, as they reached the end of the wagon column, and was more reconciled to the disaster of the previous night.

One of Chang's outriders rode up to her as she clambered down to the ground. "He wants to see you."

She stifled a yawn unsuccessfully. "Doesn't he ever sleep?"

A fleeting grin flashed over his face. "Not tonight. We'll be off tomorrow, mid-morning, after we re-load all the supplies. Those pack mules will earn their keep, for the leftovers."

Penrys limped into the command tent, silently cursing new boots and long days. Her stomach rumbled at the smell of roasted beef, and her head turned involuntarily to a table along the tent wall, covered haphazardly with wooden platters and used metal dishes.

Chang, behind his table, noted her entrance and waved her over to the food. She seized one used dish, emptied its scraps onto another one, and carved fresh bits of beef onto it, with some slices off the loaf to eat them with. She dumped the contents of one stoneware mug into another, and looked for pitchers. The empty ones smelled of stale beer as she passed them by, but the water pitchers were hardly touched, so she filled the mug, drained it on the spot, and filled it again.

She found an vacant seat, placed the mug carefully on the ground beneath it, and balanced the plate awkwardly on her lap, the arm in its sling not much use in keeping it steady.

Chang left her alone for several minutes to let her wolf down the food. Her shoulder still ached from her tumble the night before, but her appetite had returned. As she slowed down, she glanced up tardily to find his eyes on her.

She used the last bit of bread to wipe the grease off her lips, and swallowed.

"Sorry there was so much damage, Commander-chi," she said. "I still have to deal with that one thing, that charm. Could it wait until daylight?"

He held up a hand to stop her and turned to the man who had been sharing the thin end of his table, a discarded plate shoved away from the sheets of paper in front of him. She'd seen his face repeatedly since last night—dark and broad, middle-aged, and sparsely bearded.

"This is Tun Jeju, my *Notju*, Intelligence Master," Chang told her. "He's been running the interrogations—everyone whose property was compromised."

She tipped her head to him. "You must have been busy today."

He smiled slightly. "We've discovered some very interesting things while you've been turning the camp upside down."

She rolled her eyes and tried not to belch while he continued.

"About half of the losses are not accounted for by the owners of the property or the drivers of the wagons. That is… not unexpected, if these are small devices, easy to hide."

He paused. "But there's a common thread running through several of the others. The first one you triggered, the soldier with the *juk*, the charm?"

She nodded.

"Well, two of the men in the destroyed tent also had similar charms they left there. And the list of items for two of the others, the laundry supplies and one of the food dumps, included charms, stashed there by the workers."

"That's awfully suggestive," Penrys said.

He lifted a finger. "There's more. We spoke at length to the rest of the herdsmen, as well as the *lakju*, the Horsemaster. When your man fled last night, all he had was what was on him. When we went through the possessions he left behind, we found more of those charms."

"But I examined everything he abandoned first, before I did the main camp! Did I miss those?"

Chang interjected. "When we're done here tonight, I want you to go look again. We've pulled them all out together and taken them a safe distance away."

"But…" She stopped and stared off into space as something occurred to her. "Maybe I didn't miss them. Maybe they aren't… prepared yet."

She focused on Tun Jeju. "I need to see everything he had, every scrap. He may have had tools and other things."

"That will be your job in the morning, after you confirm they're not dangerous," Chang said. "We had your trooper who carried the charm in his pocket walk it back to the same place, separate from the others, so everything suspicious is in one general location. It's under guard for the night.

"It'll take most of the morning to set things back in order and prepare to move forward. I want you to take that time to tell me what you can find out."

"All right," she said, slowly. "What did that trooper tell you? Was the Rasesni giving those charms to others?"

Tun Jeju said, "Selling them when he could, giving them away when he couldn't. We don't know how many." He looked at her. "The owners said he told them they had to wear it on their person for the charm to work, day and night."

Penrys felt the blood drain from her face. "So he sold them death."

She turned to Chang. "I believe we were wrong to think of this as a trap for Zandaril—that was accidental. This was a long, slow, thorough seeding of destruction throughout the expedition, waiting for an outside trigger, by the saboteur himself, I should think."

"Yes, we've come to that conclusion ourselves," Chang said. "The cost has been high—three percent of my men, the loss of some of our supplies and transport—but much less than it might have been, and not when the enemy planned it."

"Why didn't he trigger it all when he fled?" she asked.

"I'm sure he thought he could return and do it later. There was no reason to think we'd find any of his work, and now it's too late for him."

"If we'd known what it was, exactly, we could have saved some of the destruction today," she said.

"Better to be sure, and no more men lost," Chang replied. "And morale is back where it should be, now that the men have seen the threat removed for themselves."

She could feel his confidence. *A military leader's answer—men first, logistics second. Merchants figured costs and benefits differently. And wizards? They interchanged knowledge and power so frequently they forgot which was which. Men hardly counted at all.*

CHAPTER 12

"We're moving out."

Hing Ganau's head popped into the back of Zandaril's wagon and vanished before a startled Penrys could look up.

"I'm not ready yet," she muttered, and Zandaril, lying flat on a pallet surrounded by boxes and sacks grinned at her.

"Maybe you better tell Chang to wait for you," he said.

She glared at him and did a quick look around to see if everything was tied in place, nothing in danger of tumbling down onto Zandaril.

"Wish I could have taken that one specimen with me," she told him, "but it was just too dangerous." She'd probed the device inside the charm as slowly and carefully as she could to identify its structure, but it had exploded almost immediately, like all the others.

The rest of the Rasesni's possessions were stored in four large packs, stashed at the back entrance of the wagon where they would be accessible as they traveled. The charm blanks were harmless, and contained no power sources.

"Weren't they surprised when a herdsman turned up with three extra horses and their packs?" Zandaril wondered.

"Apparently some of them do that work year-long and bring all their possessions. It wasn't that unusual," Penrys said. "We're lucky we caught him on duty and he had to leave it all behind."

"What happened to the horses?"

She was amused by the greed in his eyes. The Zannib, the horse-hungry.

"Mine," she said, "by right of, um, conquest."

She laughed at his disappointment. "I might be persuaded to share them with you. The three he left are running with yours for now. Alas, he took his saddle with him."

A knock from the front bench through the opening was a warning they were about to set off.

Zandaril called out, "We're ready."

His words were followed by an unanticipated lurch that jerked the standing Penrys off balance. She swore when her left shoulder hit a box, and groped with her good hand for one of the more stable bean sacks. Carefully she lowered herself to sit cross-legged on the wagon bed between the foot of Zandaril's pallet and the back of the wagon.

"Today we're going to learn about devices," she told Zandaril, in her most pedantic tones. "We're going to go through all his stuff, however long it takes us, and see what we can discover."

Zandaril thought the bouncing of the wagon had to be worse than riding a horse, but he was under strict orders to stay flat all day. He'd suborned Penrys into helping him get propped up with a sack as a backrest, on the pretext that he couldn't watch what she was doing otherwise.

She lost no time in claiming the space where his feet had been. The first pack had yielded clothing in the Kigali style and personal gear. Neither of them could find anything notable in that, but buried in one of the shirts were three small books. One was in Ellechen-*guma*, and she recognized it.

"I've read this already. *The Principles of the Physical.* It's good, well beyond the basics." She handed it back to him. "D'ya know it?"

"I've heard of it," he said, dryly. *And quite a denunciation went with the hearing, too.*

She glanced at him as if she'd heard the thought. "Read Ellechen-*guma*, do you?"

"Well enough. Most of the great books have not been translated, so if you want to study them…"

"It's the standard edition," she said. "Could have come right off the shelves at the Collegium."

She hefted the next tome—paper bound between carved wood, like the first one, but when she held it up to her nose, the smell was different. The ink, maybe. "D'ya know the language of this one?"

"That's Rasesni. Can't you read it?"

"Not any more—my source is gone. That's a weakness of borrowed knowledge. Make it your own or lose it." She shook her head. "How about you? Can you read it?"

He shook his head. "I can speak it a bit, but there's little need for us to learn the writing, beyond the letters. Don't see many books, don't know if anyone has."

"This one, too?" she said, holding up the third book.

"Same."

"Well, we can puzzle through them together as best we can. There are lots of illustrations."

She sat back on her heels, balancing as the wagon swayed. "Somehow I think we'll have some Rasesni in range again before we're done, and then we'll see what we can find out."

She flipped to the front. "Looks like there's a name written inside the cover, on the first page."

She showed Zandaril, and he puzzled out the letters. "Veneshjug, I think. That's a Rasesni name," Zandaril said. "Do you suppose it's his?"

He looked at the titles again. "Seems that 'Venesh' word is in both of them."

Penrys laid the two books aside.

"Let's see what else we've got." She waved her hand at the other three packs. "I just skimmed through them in a hurry before breakfast, to get a quick idea of what there was."

She reached into the second pack and pulled out a soft leather drawstring pouch, the size of a human head. "Ah, here it is. There's another one around somewhere." She loosened the drawstring and spilled some of the contents onto the unoccupied foot of Zandaril's pallet. Several handfuls of pea-sized faceted stones gleamed dully in the daylight filtering through the white canvas top of the wagon.

He leaned forward to look. The colors were various and muted, and they looked nothing like valuable gems. If he'd seen them on a beach at Shimiz, he would have ignored them. But the hand of man was evident in the care with which they had been cut.

When he sat back and looked up at Penrys, he found her watching him quizzically.

"D'ya know what these are?" she asked.

He shook his head.

"Power-stones."

He could feel his nose wrinkle at the name. *So these were hadab makhtab. Such small things.*

There was no way to avoid unhallowed knowledge. Not if the enemy was using it. He made himself ask. "How do they work?"

"What do you know about *raunarys*, thing-skills?"

"Not much. We don't test for it, and if a wizard has it, he doesn't speak of it." *And I don't want to know if I have it.* The very idea made him feel dirty.

"Hmm." She thought for a moment, eying him and his obvious discomfort.

"Here's what we'll do. You don't have to try anything—you can watch through me instead. You already know I'm… hopelessly contaminated, but there's no need for you to end up that way." She offered him a half-smile.

"I can do that," he said. He braced himself for the experience.

She slipped into the mode of teacher to student, familiar to him since his apprentice years. "The commonest form of *raunarys* is simple movement." Off the floor of the wagon she picked a small clod of dirt, the size of a thumbnail, and laid it down near the stones, less than a yard from where she knelt.

"Watch, now." He peered through her mind, as he'd done when she'd showed him how she found languages. She reached out to the little clod and wrapped her focus around it. Then, with significant effort, she picked it up, without touching it with her hands, and moved it a few inches to the right, setting it down gently again. He could feel that it was a strain, and he could perceive some of the work it took for her to do it smoothly.

"You see? It's not easy. The heavier the object, or the further away, the more difficult it is to do, and the sooner you get tired."

"But what's it good for?" he asked, surprised to see so much forbidden effort devoted to such paltry results.

"With the unaided mind, not much. Perhaps you could turn a key in a lock." She watched his face. "Or stop a heart."

He felt his skin chill.

She looked away and cleared her throat.

"The power-stones are amplifiers. There are two parts to an amplifier. One is to channel power to the will of the wizard. The other is the power-source itself, usually another stone."

She plucked a stone from the pile. "An unpowered stone provides more control, but requires just as much power as using no stone at all. Like this."

He watched through her again as she picked up the clod and moved it. It seemed to take the same effort, but the smoothness came more easily.

"Not much good by itself. But if you add a powered stone…"

She took a second stone in her hand and concentrated on it for a moment. She didn't invite him to watch from the inside, and he left her in privacy to do it.

"Now." She held the two stones together and he saw the clod lift easily, sail once around his head, and return to its starting point.

His eyes widened. "How did you do that?"

She repeated the maneuver with him monitoring. The second stone glowed in her mind, nothing like its visible appearance, and she drew upon it for movement. The glow visibly diminished as he watched. When she opened her hand, he could see no difference in the stones with his eyes, nor could he tell which was powered, and which not.

He held out his hand, and she dropped one of the stones into it. "Which one is it?" she asked.

He closed his fist against the little prickle of the pointed facets. He couldn't tell how to detect it.

He shook his head and offered it to her again on his palm. "It's not in me, I think." He could hear the relief in his own voice.

"Why is it forbidden to a Zan, if you can say?"

"Unclean, unnatural." He looked at her apologetically. "Not you, of course, *bikrajti*."

"Of course," she agreed, dryly. "Dirty, perverted, action at a distance…"

He lowered his eyes.

"What is a thrown spear but action at a distance?" she said. "I can see the emotion in a man's mind without seeing his face, but any man can see emotion in the face of another. Are these truly different in kind? We call one of them magic, but not the other."

"I can hear a man's language in his mind, but any man can hear it in his voice. These things are all similar." She waved her hand in an arc. "Wizards are at one place on the map, but everyone is on the map somewhere."

She lowered her voice. "Physical magic is just another tool, like a knife, or a loom, or the ability to read, or the skill to lead men."

He heard her words, but the strictures of his youth were resistant, and he knew how his colleagues would react. He wanted to reach an understanding with her—she had so much to teach him.

"Let us agree to not agree," he said. "I think well of you. I've never met a *jarghal* with your strength—maybe they are all like you in Ellech, how would I know? But that's not what matters."

He spoke as sincerely as he could. "I've tasted your mind, and it is *not* unclean or unnatural. I can't explain how that is, but I know what I've seen in you. I will try to learn whatever you care to teach me, *bikrajti*."

He bowed at the end of his little speech, from his backrest, and when he lifted his face he was shocked to discover her bent away from him, her face hidden. A delicate probe revealed a roil of emotions, more than he could name.

"What's wrong?" he asked, gently. For a moment he thought she wouldn't answer.

"Perhaps I *am* unnatural," she said. "Not because of physical magic," she waved her hand dismissively, "but because of what I am."

"Yes?" he said, encouragingly.

"I am *not* like the wizards at the Collegium. They don't learn the languages and knowledge of the people they are near. They can't power a stone as easily as I just did. They grope at the principles of powered devices which seem clear as glass to me. To some ways of thinking, I'm only three years old! That's all I remember. How is this possible? What am I? What happened to me?"

Her voice shook.

"They certainly don't have furry ears. Or…" she trailed off.

He wondered what she'd stopped herself from saying.

"I'm *not* in any of the books, none of this is—I've looked. They named me an Adept because they couldn't think what else to call me. Made it easier to deal with me without thinking about it."

She swayed, and he remembered that she'd been assaulted by the blast just as he had, and how little sleep she'd gotten, how little time to recover. Her control was unraveling.

"You know what I think, sometimes?" she said.

"What?" he murmured.

"I think someone made me, maybe, constructed me, to be a sponge and suck up knowledge. And when I have enough, he'll take me back and wring me out, and start my memory over again. The world's a big place—maybe he's done it before. I think that's where the chain comes from."

She paused a moment. "You know who wears chains? Slaves do."

"That's not possible," he said.

"Who knows? I'm not possible, either. And I demonstrated just a couple of nights ago how a body can be transported a long distance."

She leaned against the pile of the Rasesni's packs, and set her face to the back of the wagon, away from him. "I'm sorry," she said, over her shoulder. "Let's pick the lesson up later."

CHAPTER 13

Why did I reveal myself like that?

Penrys was dismayed at her breakdown before Zandaril. She took a few deep breaths to steady herself, disturbed at the quaver in her throat, as if she were near to tears. None of this was his fault, and he was doing his best to keep an open mind about *raunarys.*

I must be more tired than I realized, and I wasn't prepared for his offer of friendship, of respect. No one back home at the Collegium had been half so welcoming, and she'd been there three years, not just three days.

Back home, was it? Nothing home-like about it. Do I really want to go back? What for, besides the books I haven't read yet? That's not much of an excuse for a life.

What do I really want? To find out what I am and where I came from, I guess. They had no answers, so where will I find them? From other wizard communities? Like the Zannib?

She leaned on the packs and rested her head on her folded right arm, staring out over the tailgate at the receding plains and the wagons that were further back in the column. She'd gotten comfortable, and the view presented to her eyes was restful. She half-closed them to keep out the dust.

A jolt from the wagon woke Penrys and she clutched at the packs to stay upright. She ran her hand over her face and swung around to see how Zandaril was doing. He was reading, a book propped up on his knees, and he stuck a finger in it to hold his place.

"Must've fallen asleep," she said. "Sorry."

"You needed it," he said. "Too bad it wasn't longer."

He looked down at the pallet of blankets. "I was thinking… There's enough space here, I could scoot over and give you room to stretch out."

She flushed. "No, no, that's all right."

He looked at her earnestly. "I wish you would. Better for you."

She spoke past her embarrassment over her loss of composure earlier. "I still need to go through the remainder of these packs. Chang's expecting a report."

"Chang can wait," Zandaril said, hotly, and she raised her eyebrows.

"*Bikrajab* aren't made of steel, any more than the rest of his men. And if we make mistakes, it costs too much."

She paled at her recollection of the triggered mirror, and he exclaimed, "No, I didn't mean that—no one could have suspected that. But what if you'd been too tired to find all those traps yesterday?"

He drew himself upright from the backrest and intoned, "*Bikrajab* have a duty to keep themselves fit, and you've been violating that."

She smiled. He had a point.

He seized the advantage. "It's almost lunchtime. Afternoon naps for both of us, then back to teaching. Yes?"

"All right," she said, and began gathering up the power-stones from the foot of the pallet. "What are you reading?"

"*The Principles*," he said, showing her the book he'd avoided when she'd pulled it from the Rasesni's pack.

"Will your friends still speak to you, after?" she teased.

"I don't plan to tell them," Zandaril replied.

Penrys spent the early part of the afternoon dozing on the side of the pallet, her back to Zandaril. For a while, trying to balance without touching him in the narrow space kept her restless, but eventually the swaying of the wagon did the job, and she slept solidly for a couple of hours.

The world seemed brighter when she woke up and she looked over her shoulder cautiously to see if Zandaril was still reading. He'd dropped off himself, the book fallen from his hands, and he himself still sitting half-upright.

Didn't want to wake me by sliding down. She shook her head and pried herself up carefully, trying not to disturb him. She slid over to the Rasesni's packs at the back of the wagon.

As quietly as she could, she finished laying out the contents of the second pack. She looked up when she was done and found Zandaril awake and yawning.

"You were right," she told him. "Things seem better now."

"I am always right," he said, thumping his chest outrageously.

"Hmm." She waved at the pile beyond the foot of the pallet. "Shall we continue?"

He stretched in place and nodded. "Tomorrow we ride. Nicer outside. No more lying down."

"Better do demonstrations today, then—hard to do on horseback."

Penrys ran a hand over her mouth and returned to lecture mode. "So, when we stopped, I showed you how a powered stone makes physical magic stronger. But how do you put power into a stone?"

She lifted a finger. "It's like lifting a weight with a rope and pulley. Instead of lifting it a little way and then dropping it, over and over, you lift it all the way up, and drop it all at once. Same effort, but concentrated release. You understand?"

Zandaril nodded.

"Power-stones are rare. Wizards who have them carry them around and spend spare moments acting on them without really acting. They don't move the stones, but they fill them with the effort of movement, if you see what I mean."

Zandaril stirred. "But when you did that, it only took you a moment to power the stone."

"That's right. Good for you for noticing."

He smiled at the praise.

"That's because I cheated," she said, soberly, and his smile vanished.

"I tapped this." She rested a finger on the chain around her neck. "You can't tell a powered stone from an unpowered one, but some other wizards can. What they can't see is that this chain is powered. I can't see it myself—mirrors don't work for this—so I don't know if it might be visible to someone else like me."

If there were anyone else like me.

Zandaril said, "I saw the powered stone get dimmer for you as you used it. Didn't look like it would last very long."

"That's right. There's a limit to how much power you can stuff into a power stone. Some of them are better than others. I didn't spend long filling that one, and over time it would gradually leak out."

She cleared her throat. "I could have filled it to destruction, from this." She tapped the chain. "And quickly."

He hesitated. "And how do you refill the chain?"

"I don't. It has never seemed diminished."

Silence fell for a moment while Zandaril considered that.

"Then can you pick up this wagon with your mind and spin it around?" he ventured.

Her mouth quirked. "Mules and all? I suppose the chain might have enough power, but there's a connection issue. For physical magic, wizards can use their natural power, which is weak, or amplify it with a power-stone, and I have the same limitations. What the chain helps me do is overcome the inherent disadvantages of power-stones, with near-instantaneous replenishment.

"So, to answer your question, I would have to find and fill a very large power-stone to transfer that much power. And keep it filled, or drop the wagon."

He said, slowly, "Or maybe a bunch of small stones?" He pointed at the sack next to her knee.

"Yes, maybe. I used an array of them to power my detector device, borrowed from the Collegium resources." She ran her hand over the smooth leather of the bag. "This many in one place is quite a treasure. He must have used one or two on every device. A good one was probably worth the value of the wagon it was used to destroy."

She hoisted the sack in her hand. "He has two full bags of these stones. Expensive sabotage," she said. "Wasn't there any cheaper way?"

She shook her head in disbelief. "And that's not the only puzzle. The traps that were set are still a mystery. You can fill a stone to failure. There's a sort of… resistance that tells you when that's close, but when it happens, the stone just breaks. Might cause a little fire, maybe. You can prepare a stone in a device to make a thing happen when it detects some other thing, so you could make a trigger that would react to a probe. Those traps probably had something like that. But I don't know any way to make them give up their power all at once to cause the… explosions. A sudden drain wouldn't do that, and the energy in them wouldn't be enough, I think."

"Maybe the Rasesni books…?" Zandaril suggested.

"I hope so, because I'm not looking forward to random experimentation. Too dangerous, for one thing."

She looked down at the contents of the second pack lying at her feet. "The rest of this is tools and raw materials."

She opened a small rectangular box and revealed a set of nested lenses and a stand. "That's for fine work, making the devices."

"The charms, you mean."

"Actually, no. Those are just shells. He brought hundreds with him—he must have just gotten started planting them because one of those packs contains nothing but the painted exteriors. I have to unpack them completely to be sure there's nothing else, but that's all I saw."

She waved at the fourth pack. "That's where the devices are, small pre-built frameworks, more than enough for all those charms, and a good bit more."

She stood up and unlashed the top of the pack. Then she groped inside and brought out a flat wooden rectangle, about the size of two little fingers side by side. Holes were sunk along the surface.

"There must be hundreds of these in here. They don't weigh much. See the holes? Those are for power-stones, but I don't recognize the configuration. The assembled device would fit nicely inside a charm, or maybe on its own, tucked away somewhere unexpected, and then triggered."

She tossed it back into the pack and refastened the top.

"There are more tools here—for faceting, for cutting wood, for drilling holes. He had the setup for a regular manufacturing operation."

"Where did he do the work?" Zandaril asked.

"I don't know. Look how much of it seems to have been pre-assembled and brought with him. Maybe all they expected him to do was to put things together and then plant them where they could do the most harm."

"The cost of the stones, the scope of the attack—this comes from a government. It's official." He pursed his lips. "Only one attacker? Not likely."

"I didn't find any other native Rasesni-speakers or other devices."

He waved that aside. "They could be ahead of us, waiting for us to get there. They could be allies of the Rasesni, speaking other languages. Who can say?" He snorted. "But I don't believe he was by himself, this Veneshjug."

"You're only three weeks out of, what's it called, the Meeting of Waters. Maybe he was just the first and he hadn't met up with the rest of them yet."

"And now he's out there, giving them a big warning," Zandaril remarked, glumly.

"Worse," she said. "Didn't you say the Rasesni weren't known for wizards? That they were like the Kigaliwen that way? So where is all this expertise coming from?"

CHAPTER 14

Tak Tuzap groped with his bare foot for the next slick rock, careful to keep hold of the cliff wall with both hands. The guards at the top of the gorge were distracted by the boats trying to run the Seguchi Norwan, the great Gates of the Seguchi River. He'd counted on that, sure that they wouldn't be watching halfway down the southern cliff for movement in the dark.

The shouts that trailed up faintly from the roar of water below him betrayed at least one overturned and destroyed boat. *They're dead. Told them it wouldn't work.*

He didn't look down. *Slide one foot, and then the next. Don't let the pack pull you away from the rock face. Keep the wet braid from getting in your face.*

I guess they couldn't have gone this route with the little kids. Should've stayed and waited. Yenit Ping would be sending an army. There'd be fighting. Getting out then might've been easier.

He snorted as he inched his way along. *So why didn't I stay, if I believe that?*

The truthful answer came, unbidden. *Because Uncle Tak's dead, and I couldn't hide anymore. Because whoever's coming is going to need another way in.*

He stopped for a moment at a slightly wider spot in the ledge to rest his muscles. *Look at me, big hero. Six inches at a step. This is no way in for an army.*

He thought about the hill passes far to the south, the ones he'd heard about but never seen. The border folk had Zannib blood, they said. And there was the pack road over the Red Wall ridges, the one they used to travel before they channeled the river in the gorge a hundred years ago and sheltered the trade road alongside it. Sometimes a peddler came over the old road, instead of going the whole long way up to the Gates of Seguchi.

Gotta keep going. Can't afford to stiffen up.

It was still dark when the boy reached the last ledge above the river, nearly forty feet up. The wreckage of the boats had long since passed, and he knew the guards would be patrolling the roadway on the other shore, not this side, where the river ran right along the cliff face.

From here the going was easier, but it was almost half a mile before the pass widened enough to leave bare ground on his side. He was confident his dark clothing would hide him if he didn't do anything to attract attention, but he still moved cautiously, testing his footing with each step until he reached river level and solid, if muddy, soil. He stepped carefully to obscure his footprints.

The invaders ran patrols outside the gorge, too. He'd still have to creep along once he reached the bank, but he wanted to make as much distance as he could before dawn. Then he could hole up and sleep during the day.

He passed bits of broken planks on the left, turning in the little backwaters spun off by the main current, and he didn't stop to look at them—what would be the point. One time he saw what he knew was a body, floating face down, drifting back and forth as though the river were debating what to do with it.

Fish'll take care of that one.

The sky in front of him was beginning to lighten, and he searched for a good place to move away from the river into the scattered groves, raised slightly above the flood plain. When he turned and looked behind him, he couldn't see any guards, and the distant far side of the river, which had broadened now that it had passed its constraint, was still in darkness, shaded by the sheer wall of the north-eastern cliff.

Just as Tak Tuzap was about to turn away from the water, he heard a desolate cry, like the dawn song of a waterbird. He didn't recognize it but thought of breakfast and moved stealthily left to the river shore to see what it was.

After the second repetition he paused in mid-step. It was a person, a kid, voice hoarse and babbling.

No one could've survived the gorge.

For a moment he was tempted to turn around, but then he blushed for shame and crept forward until he could see.

This boat was still floating, despite its damage, and was loosely wedged against the mud of the bank. The only movement he saw was the head of a seated child who was babbling desperately at something in the bottom of the boat, and hitting it with both small fists.

He swallowed, and came out into the open. When the child saw him, she screamed incoherently at him and pointed down. Her bright red face was streaked with tears under her short black hair.

"Shush, now," he said, as calmly as he could. "Let me see."

He walked over and looked into the little boat. It was half-filled with water, and he saw the woman he had expected to find, not moving. Her forehead had a deep gash that didn't bleed.

I can't take her. She's too young to toddle all that way. What is she, three, maybe? Four?

Yeah, but I can't leave her, either.

He ran both his hands through his hair. Then he bent down and picked the little girl up, and hauled her up the bank a ways until he could sit down with her—she was too heavy for him to carry for long.

He held her on his lap and wrapped his arms around her while she hiccuped and clung to him.

He stared at the boat while his mind worked furiously looking for a solution. The stern of the little boat floated up and down, pivoting against the wedged prow.

Do you suppose it still floats, really? If I could hide it somehow during the day, I could launch it tonight and be out of their reach.

She could come with me that way.

The warm, damp weight in his arms drew his look. She was sleeping in exhaustion.

He made his decision. He laid her down gently and shrugged off his pack and put it next to her.

There was no way to bury the mother and, if he could have, the next flood would just have taken her away. So he searched her pockets and took her rings for her daughter, then tilted the half-submerged boat enough to let her body float free downstream.

Once she was gone, he was sickened to discover a baby underneath. His eyes watered and he blinked, then he gritted his teeth and made himself pick the boy up and tuck his blanket tightly around him. Him, too, he consigned to the impersonal mercy of the river.

The oars were gone, but there was one pack still aboard, shoved into the narrow space at the prow and soaked. It contained a man's clothing and heavy cookware. *Her husband.*

He glanced over at the sole survivor, asleep like the dead up on the bank. *May they all meet together again, and wait for her.*

The boat itself seemed to have no serious holes in it, though part of the upper strake on one side had broken off. He could see across the river, now, as the true sunrise approached.

If I can see them, they can see this boat. But if I submerge it in the shallows and weigh it down with mud, I can dig it out tonight and empty it, and we can float away.

I'll need to cut a long pole to steer it.

He looked up to the grove beyond the crest of the flood line, making plans. *The man's pack up the bank to the kid, first, then sink the boat and scoop mud into it. Then one pack to the trees, kid to the trees, and then the other pack.*

Better get moving.

CHAPTER 15

The two wizards reined in their horses on the crest of a small rise. The terrain had become more rolling in the last three days, and there was a blur on the western horizon that Zandaril claimed was their first glimpse of the Lang Nor mountains, the Red Wall.

Penrys was trying out the small chestnut gelding in her new string. She leaned far forward over her horse's neck and scratched the sweaty spot on his forehead that always seemed to itch.

"Isn't there supposed to be some little, insignificant river around here someplace? Where's it hiding?"

"About twenty more miles that way, then we'll turn northwest and follow it another six days or so to Seguchi Norwan." Zandaril pointed due west. "Chang took us straight across the prairie from Jonggep to cut off a big curve—that's why we had to bring our own cattle instead of stopping at the river towns to requisition supplies. We'll catch up to it soon. Then you'll see."

"So you keep saying."

The air had turned cool, under the cloudy sky. As far as her eye could roam, the grasses were sprinkled with the last of the autumn flowers, their colors muted in the dull light.

"Where is everybody?" she asked. "Where are all the farmers and towns?"

"East," he said. "East, where the great cities are, and the granaries near them. Out west the settlements are all along the river and its tributaries. All this, out here in the grasslands, there's no one—the winters are very bad, snow very strong. No trees for a reason. The towns cling to the river valleys, and send their produce downstream, and wait for spring.

"Soon the herds of wild cattle will come down from the hills for their winter pasture—surprised I am they're not here already. I expected to see them by now."

He used his hands to sketch two long horns reaching out from his head. "We make too much noise." He pointed down at the expedition, marching in a shallow depression to their right.

He's right. Penrys could hear the creak of the axles and jangle of metal clearly, and she didn't doubt that every creature within earshot had headed elsewhere.

She followed that thought with an actual probe, scanning as far as she could reach in all directions, even back along their trail. No other horses or mules besides those with the expedition, no other herds of cattle—nothing but the small animals on and below the ground, and the hawks in the air.

No people, besides their own.

Zandaril watched her, his mind touching hers lightly and monitoring the probe.

"Where are they hiding?" he asked.

"Maybe he was the only one, this Veneshjug."

He cocked his head at her. "Do you believe that?"

"No."

"Is he shielded from you, somehow?"

Penrys shrugged.

Chang sent scouts out daily along the line of his march, screening the surroundings for several miles, but it wouldn't be hard for a small number of people to lurk undetected. Still, it was the more serious threat that concerned them as they approached the river towns—word was beginning to come in again about the disturbance on the border, in Neshilik.

No traffic had come down the river or by land from the west in over a month. Riders skirting the Red Wall were discouraged from getting near the Gates by patrols much larger than their own parties, and better armed. The opinion from the river towns was that these were their old enemies the Rasesni, but they'd never behaved like this before, seizing and holding their old territory instead of raiding, and they hadn't appeared east of the Seguchi Norwan in generations. The townsmen hadn't tried to talk to them. It was the army's job, they said, to take them on.

Members of a few of the clans who had family in Wechinnat, in northern Neshilik, had ventured off toward the old Red Wall crossings, but none had returned. Speculation was everywhere, but nothing confirmed.

The camp had felt on edge to Penrys, these last couple of days, with the soldiers sharpening their weapons and a buzz of energy in the air. She and Zandaril spent their evenings experimenting with the Rasesni's gear, trying to puzzle out just what sort of weapon he had deployed. Chang was impatient with their lack of progress, and so was she.

"All you have to work with are moving and binding," she blurted out, speaking her thought and startling Zandaril.

"Ah, that again," he said.

"Yes, again, until we figure it out."

"You said 'destroying' once, too." Zandaril pointed out.

"Well, yes, technically. All that really means is you can kill a power-stone." She started over. "Moving is 'push,' binding is 'pull,' and destruction is 'fizzle.'"

Zandaril laughed.

"No, it really is. Not much happens except your expensive power-stone doesn't work anymore and everyone looks at you as if you're an idiot."

"What happens if you try to push and pull at the same time?" he asked.

She held her arms out in front of her, with reins loosely looped around one of them and gripped her two hands while trying to pull them apart sideways. "Like that. Lot's of tension, no result."

"So what happens when you let go?"

"There's a rebound, of course…" Her voice trailed off. "Could you make something of that? Put a strong move and bind together, then suddenly release them?"

"Like two horses yoked to the same thing but pulling it in opposite directions, and then it breaks," Zandaril suggested.

"Don't know. Not sure how you would set that up, but I wonder if that might work."

She glanced up at the angle of the sun. "Wish we could read those books. We'll have to go look at those illustrations again."

"Tonight's not the night for it," Zandaril said. "Rain coming. Lots of it."

Penrys put aside the remains of her beef stew next to her bedroll with distaste. Despite the early afternoon halt before the soaking rains hit, it had been impossible to keep dry. The tent's ground cloth sported muddy puddles, her clothing was sopping wet from tending to the horses and the dash out to the cook fires to fetch dinner, and both Hing Ganau and Zandaril had vanished, Hing to an evening with his men. Penrys could imagine the scene of drink and gambling he was anticipating in someone's crowded tent.

She didn't know what had happened to Zandaril. After their mad dash to strip the horses and stash the horse gear under shelter, the rain had hit as they watered them at the creek which paralleled their line of march. At least it had made the evening currying moot. Between them there were seven horses to care for—Zandaril's four and the three she'd acquired from Veneshjug. The morning routine of watering and grooming lasted about an hour, but mostly they were allowed to graze morning and night when not on the move. Any supplemental grain was added in the evening, but not on a night like this when it would be soaked, even if served in a nosebag.

She'd ridden a number of times in Ellech—hard to avoid it while Vylkar was her sponsor—but the care had been left to the grooms. It was a pleasure to her now, to feel the relief of the horse she'd been riding all day, as she brushed and combed all the itches away. She had just the one road horse, while Zandaril had two, but at the pace they were traveling they held up fine under the daily work. The pack horses were getting fat and lazy by comparison.

Zandaril was somewhere around Hing's wagon, she could tell. Every couple of days another sack vanished into the camp kitchen as the supplies were slowly consumed by the expedition, freeing up a little more space for their evening studies. The squadron was headed for garrison at Shengen Ferry, the biggest town on the river near their destination, Hing said. Keelboats had been ascending the Seguchi for their resupply, ever since they left Jonggep.

We should get an early start on our lessons, I suppose. Too much trouble tonight. It's a night for feeling wet and miserable, like a drowned rat.

She snorted at the self-indulgent whine in her thoughts, and shook her head. A rustle at the tent flap drew her attention, and Zandaril stepped in, careful to contain the dripping of his cape as close to the entrance as possible.

He gave her a little formal bow, which raised her eyebrows. "I've come with an invitation," he said. "Tonight is a holiday, in *sarq*-Zannib—the *kuliqa*, the turning home, when we turn on our outward migration and face the winter villages again. When the day and the night are of equal length."

He glanced up through the tent's ceiling at the hidden sky. "You may have to trust me for that."

Penrys grinned. *This sounded interesting.* "What happens on this holiday?"

"Come and see," he said, and waved his hand to beckon her outside.

CHAPTER 16

Zandaril scrambled after Penrys up the steps and into Hing Ganau's wagon, hauling the tailgate up behind him and pulling the cover tight to keep the persistent rain from penetrating the waterproofed canvas.

The two of them dripped at the very end of the wagon, and he held up his hand to keep her from moving. "Wait."

He pointed at the clean woolen robe he had been saving as an overrobe for winter use, draped now over one of the bean sacks. "I will turn my head, see? And you will drop your wet clothes here where we can hang them. Once you're dressed, and I am dressed, then we will celebrate the holiday, dry and comfortable."

He handed her a cloth to towel her hair and turned away, listening for the squelch as her clothing hit the wagon bed. When she cleared her throat uncertainly, he turned back. As he'd expected, his robe was long on her, not quite to the ground, and large enough that the sash he'd provided held it well-wrapped against her body. The dull blue was a good color, he decided. Her hair was wet and shaggy, but no longer dripping.

She picked up her sopping clothes and wrung them out one by one over the edge of the tailgate, then hung them over the rope he'd stretched where they could drip without soaking anything else. Out of long habit, Hing had found a slight upslope to park on, so any liquid that accumulated ran out the back.

"Now you must turn your back, please," he said.

He wore his only other robe and it was soaked, but he'd laid out his formal robes. *Good to get some use of them, and suitable for the kuliqa, the turning home.* Since this included breeches and undergarments, he was much better clothed than his guest once he was done, but it couldn't be helped. He left his hair bare like Penrys, to dry—too wet for the turban.

Once he'd hung his own discarded clothing, he offered Penrys her choice of his clean socks or his too-big tent shoes of soft leather, and she chose the long woolen socks.

"Well arranged," she commented. "And I like your robes. For ceremonial occasions, I presume?"

"I debated whether to bring them, but then, maybe I would be the only Zan where I was, and wanted to represent my nation with dignity."

"And very fine you look," she added, in *wirqiqa*-Zannib.

Zandaril broke into a broad smile. "Yes! Let us spend this evening in the language of my home, if you will. In honor of the day." It was a relief to shed the constant struggle with Kigali-*yat*, like removing a blanket from his thoughts.

"Come, take the guest-seat." He gestured toward the bean sack, covered in the red cloth of life. "I will be host, under the sky." He waited for her to sit cross-legged on the edge of *jimiz*, the scholar's rug, before he lowered himself across from her to lean on the sack with the sky cloth.

Penrys glanced curiously all around. "You brought all of this with you?"

"You must pardon me—this is but a meager setting," he said. "We should be under the great *kazr* with its central sky hole or, better, under the open sky if it were clear. All the clan assembled, at least those of the *taridaj*, with the noise of the *yathbantudin*, the children newly old enough, and the smells of the cooking fires."

He pointed at the tiny brazier placed behind him, with its curl of resinous piney smoke, and her nostrils flared to catch the scent. "This is all I could bring, for my private celebration."

"How many people would there be?"

"As few as eighty, perhaps, or as many as two hundred." He smiled, picturing his relatives settling into place in clusters of families and friends, the gossip quieting down as the evening began. They would all be doing this tonight, the *taridaj*, those on the migration, all across his nation.

"The *zarawinnaj*, the leader of the migration, the *taridiqa*, would stand, and everyone then would hush, until all you could hear would be the fires crackling, and the bells of the herd leaders. He would announce the day, as if that were needed, and recite the *tahaziqa*, the traditional verses."

He leaned forward. "The young matrons, when they can, try to time their births for the winter camps, so many would be pregnant, and oh, so proudly so, with their husbands behind them trying not to swagger."

"There would always be some new *yathbantudin* that year, so the *zarawinnaj* would call each of them to the central fire and recite both lineage and accomplishments on this, their first *taridiqa*."

He remembered his first time, his fear that he might bring dishonor on his family, and his relief that he had been judged worthy. Now, of course, he realized he had almost never heard of a failure. There was always something good to say about *yathbantudin*, some way they could fit in and serve the needs of the clan.

"Is this the first time you've missed it?" Penrys asked.

"The fourth. I was ill-prepared the first time, and it was very sad for me, not joyous like it should be." He gestured around the little space within the wagon. "But this time I am ready. Would you like to see? Few outsiders have ever attended."

He felt both curiosity and sincerity in the light mind-touch they maintained. "Please, show me. I would be honored."

"Well, as I said, it begins with smells, so many of them, but perhaps you can imagine with just this." He opened the pouch near the brazier and added a pinch of *yawd-suragh* to the *yawd-rub* already burning. He could feel the muscles of his face relax in the familiar, dusty scent, but a sneeze from Penrys recalled him to his duties.

"And then the sound of the herd bells. I brought a little one." He pointed to a brass ram's bell, dangling on a string from the side of one of the bows supporting the roof canvas. He leaned sideways and shook the string to let it jangle freely, then picked up a short stick bent at one end with a leather-covered striking surface to tap it lightly like a rough gong, without activating the clapper.

He pointed at an improvised stand that displayed a portion of a scroll, his own preparation, the ink painted on with a brush of his own goat's hair, the same one that had provided the skin. "The recitation of the verse." He cleared his throat—he had never done this with someone else listening. "If you will allow me… Close your eyes and listen."

When she had obeyed, he intoned,

> *"Under the sky is the fruit of the land and its beauties.*
> *The little gods watch us to keep us in touch with the right.*
> *Our faces are turned to the end of the year and our duties,*
> *To strengthen the clan and bring it again to the light."*

As he recited, he tapped the bell with the stick in the rhythm of the verse, and marked the end with a louder strike that he let die away.

The throb faded under the noise of the rain on the canvas and Zandaril felt his whole body melt into it, his spine anchored between earth and sky, even while sitting in a wagon instead of on the good ground.

His guest held her position in silence, and he could only hope some of it reached her, too, but he left her mind in privacy to feel what it might, outsider that she was.

After a moment, she murmured, "Who are the 'little gods' in the verse?"

Zandaril felt a spurt of approval. She questioned, as a child should question.

"The *lud*, the manifestations of the *dunaq wandim*, the world-that-surrounds."

At her puzzled look, he sighed. "It is hard to explain to outsiders. The Zannib do not have the dozens of gods, large and small, that the Kigaliwen and Rasesni do. We do not see our world in that way. A… benevolence created our world, and we honor it. It is not much concerned with us as individuals, but we have a duty to that same benevolence, to righteous behavior. Sometimes we meet little manifestations of that spirit in the world."

He rose and led her back to his portable shrine. In honor of the day, he had unrolled it onto the top of a stack of food stores to display his two stones and the thunderbolt, a bit of iron ore fused by lightning in the ground. He picked up the first stone and placed it in her hand.

"See the movement in its form, feel its personality, judge its balance. I found this one day, when I was a child in the *zudiqazd*, the winter village, too young to go on *taridiqa*. I had lost two ewes from the flock I was in charge of, and was ready to give up and go home, since I had never been so far away before and I was afraid. And when I stared down at the ground in despair, this… winked back at me and captured my soul. It was beautiful. It spoke to me."

He glanced at her attentive expression. "Not in words, mind you, but a sort of resonance. As if it had endured trouble, and would continue to endure, and the experience had shaped it." He had bowed to it and stopped for several minutes considering, before he decided to take it with him. "If I had taken it, and not persisted until I had found the sheep, that would have been… unthinkable. A slap in the face of the world."

"And you would have been a coward not to take it, is that it?"

"Exactly!"

She sniffed the stone, then returned it to him, and he gave her the second one.

She weighed it in her hand. "It's sad, isn't it? Yearning."

She glanced at him for the story, but he just took it back and replaced it on the soft sheepskin of the shrine. Not for strangers was his determination go wifeless yet, his conviction that his *nayith*, his masterwork, must go on, whatever the cost.

"This one is different. I saw it born." He picked up the thunderbolt which still reeked of iron to his nose. "Lightning hit an oak tree not far from the camp of my *taghulaj*, my teacher. The tree was riven, but what was truly strange was that another oak nearby was also killed, though it hadn't been struck. My teacher could not say why, but I wanted to know. I looked carefully along the ground between them and discovered traces of a line where the grass was damaged. I dug there, and this is what I found."

He handed it to her, and she smelled it as he had. "You can smell the iron—this was in the low hills where we sometimes dig for the ores that produce iron. The lightning made it all by itself. I don't know why."

Something about power, he thought, but it didn't make sense to him. Not yet.

He shook off his thoughts. He had a guest to consider.

"Please, sit. Now we drink."

She raised an eyebrow, but returned to her seat obediently. He picked up his *binwit*, his mead kit, and brought it back to lay between them, on the *jimiz*.

"This is lovely," Penrys said, stroking the fine leatherwork of the rolled kit.

"It was a gift from my *tigha*, my first brother," he said, "the day I became a *tushkzurdtudin*, a man of the tribe instead of a boy."

He started to untie the straps that held it together. "It is a customary gift, from a parent or a brother, or a close friend. Every Zan you meet will have one of their own, and sometimes more, waiting for the right recipient."

He unwrapped the three stoneware *jukwit* bottles, each the size of two fists, with an indentation around the middle for hanging from a cord, and the two rough stoneware cups, the *abin*, that fit his hand perfectly and sang out their presence. His brother had chosen well. He pulled the stopper from one bottle and offered it for Penrys to sniff.

"Sweet! Honey?"

"Yes. *Khimar* is almost a 'little one' for us, like the trees and rocks we get it from. The liquor from grain or grape is just drink. But mead, *baijuk*, is for special times, like this one. Even the bottles and cups are passed down in the family, when possible, or traded for."

He filled a cup for each of them, and restoppered the bottle. "It is not for drinking alone. You do me great honor by sharing with me."

They sipped in silence for a moment, and he felt the heat permeate his limbs and warm his chest. The rain sounded cozy now, defining their shelter by contrast. With the verse said, a brazier for a central fire, and a guest to share with, however strange this *bikrajti* might be, it began to feel like a real *kuliqa*, even far away in alien Kigali.

"Tell me of your family," Penrys said, and her voice had an odd, constrained sound.

He took another sip of the mead. "I am Zandaril, son of Ilsahr of clan Zamjilah, of the Shubzah tribe, and my mother Kazrsulj is daughter of Khashjibrim of the same clan.

"I am second-son, my brother Butraz being a scant year older, and celebrating the *kuliqa* on the *taridiqa* this night, as we are. His wife Yukjilah and our first-sister Ghuruma are both in the *zudiqazd* of my clan, awaiting births and tending their little ones."

He smiled fondly. "Ghuruma swore she would let our mother raise her infants so she could return to the *taridiqa*, but the babies changed her mind for her. Once they're grown enough, she'll return."

Penrys asked, "You don't take children on the migration?"

"Only those nine years or more, the *yathbantudin* who have proved their readiness, though sometimes an exception is made. Better for the younger ones to stay in the *zudiqazd*, under their mother's care or a close relative.

"Next are my two sisters, Rubti, almost sixteen, a *tushkzurtudin*, and Washi, and the youngest boy, Nirkazdhal, on his first *taridiqa* this year. I am sorry to miss it."

"Six children!"

"Yes, I believe my mother is done, though she has not said so. She returned to the *taridiqa* six years ago, when my brother married and provided a caretaker for her youngest. It's what our women do—travel with the herds when they can, unless they are too old, or have some specialty that keeps them in one place."

Zandaril noticed his cup was empty, and Penrys's, too, so he refilled them both. It felt good to speak of home.

"Is yours considered a large family?" Penrys asked.

"Not at all. My father has seven siblings that lived, and my mother eight."

He felt her surprise and hastened to reassure her. "Not all in the same clan, of course. A few of the women married out-clan, and one of my mother's sisters surprised us by joining the Kurighdunaq clan of the Undullah tribe, many miles away. I've never met her family."

"You must have dozens of cousins!"

He cast her a puzzled look. "Well, yes. Everyone does. It's very handy, good for introductions or trade."

He reached for the bottle to top up their cups, and was surprised to find it empty. When he glanced at his guest while he worked on the stopper of the next bottle, he thought she was looking more relaxed. *She's smaller than I am, she'll never be able to keep up. I should be careful about that.*

"Can you name them all?" she asked.

He straightened up. An easy challenge—all his brothers and sisters had learned the list, adding new members to it as needed.

"In birth order or by branch? My father's line first, then my mother's, and then those of their parents."

He started out, hearing an echo of his brother's voice reciting with him as he went along. "My nephews and nieces…" As he continued he found his tongue betraying him and a growing smile on Penrys's face, so he switched to mind-speech to remove the impediment. *…*and Ilbirs, Nibarzan, and Surbushaz, the sons of my father's second brother, and their children…**

Penrys kept count for him, but he began fumbling badly in his grandparent's generation and had to stumble to a stop. **If I had the family scroll, I could continue for quite a while, but I will admit the baijuk is a handicap. And the younger ones do keep having children.**

Reminded of the cup in his hand, he took another sip. His touch on Penrys's mind turned up peculiar emotions, with envy and loneliness chief among them. And not nearly as much drink confusion as he expected. He prodded her with a silent inquisitive. *Hmm?*

Seventy-three first cousins in your own generation, and more coming still. I can't imagine it. And you've met them all?

Most of them, except the very youngest. A few are close friends, the ones in my own clan. Like brothers and sisters, after a fashion.

No one is without family, then? Even orphans or foundlings?

Zandaril sputtered out loud. "There's always room for one more, somewhere. Of course there is."

He could feel her becoming more sober by the minute. He held up his cup and looked at her. "I don't understand—why aren't you drinking anymore?"

She smiled sadly. "It doesn't last very long, so after a while it's pointless. Doesn't mean you should stop, though."

"I've had enough," he managed, with dignity. "I brought the blankets from my bedroll, in case we did not feel like returning to the wet tent. People curl up around the fire to finish sleeping out the night—it's customary."

"Would you care to stay? No harm will come to you," he said solemnly, blinking in the lantern light swaying overhead.

His last clear memory was of someone tucking him into a blanket and the soft feel of the *jimiz* against his face.

CHAPTER 17

Despite her best intentions, Penrys knew her manner was still uncomfortable when she thanked Zandaril for his party the night before. When she tried to divert him by teasing him about his throbbing head, she could feel his concern and puzzlement, and pushed it away, returning to their professional discussion of the day before about how Veneshjug had been using the power-stones.

He went along with her and they were still arguing about it inconclusively when they crested yet another low ridge.

Penrys stopped in mid-rebuttal, stunned. Below them, a quarter of a mile away, rolled a brown river, wide and unstoppable. The bluffs were cut cleanly through for its passage, as if with a gigantic knife. Small wooded side streams snaked into it on both sides. There was no settlement here.

"Well?" Zandaril said, looking with satisfaction at her stupefied expression.

"You were right," she said. "It's big."

He beamed proudly as if he'd created it himself. "And this is just the south branch, and well upstream. You should see it at Yenit Ping where it enters the sea. The Endless City is perched well above, and still someday they will have to move it when the Junkawa eats away at the land and makes Pingmen Bay even bigger."

"No town here?"

"There are big streams below here, two of them, and that's the last of the biggest towns. Only smaller towns upstream. This is low water—the spring floods fill the channel."

Penrys blinked and re-evaluated the landscape. The ridge she stood on bounded one side of a large, level plain, and a companion ridge ran along the south. The river flowed down the middle between them in a broad braid of meandering channels, but it wasn't difficult to envision it spreading out smoothly all the way from one side to the other. *That's how that flat ground was created, in the middle of these low rolling hills. No wonder no one built here.*

"Is the ground solid, d'ya think?" she asked.

"This time of year, I think you can go right to the bank in most places, if you're careful. It's all dirt, this land, all the way down. No rock until the mountains, almost anywhere."

Penrys wanted to get a closer look, but they were expected to stay close to the column. "Is Chang going to cross it?"

"If we were just a merchant train, no—he wouldn't have to. The road through the gorge takes the left bank, as it flows—that's this side. But if we have to fight our way in…"

Penrys had marveled over the efficiency of the one river crossing she'd seen, the wagons driven through a ford and helping to break the flow for the herds swimming downstream. The troopers swam, too, clinging to their horses' manes, and everyone else either did the same, or found a place in one of the wagons.

In retrospect, that now seemed an insignificant stream, shallow and fordable. *How would you cross this with a supply train?*

"Is there a bridge?"

"Only ferries, until well within Wechinnat, on the other side of the Gates."

She walked her horse back up a few yards so she could see down the other side of the slope. The column was clearly aiming for a point further upstream.

"Can't we go take a look at it?" she said.

"Tired of walking, are you?" Zandaril replied, with a gleam in his eye. "Let's see what that new horse of yours can do."

He pointed his black mare at a diagonal down the slope and took off. Penrys was left behind, and then she pulled herself together and followed. When they reached the flat they stretched into a smooth canter, keeping a sharp eye out for burrows and holes that could trip up their horses.

She laughed with the exhilaration of speed. They kept the easy pace for a while, until she judged they had come as far on the flat as the head of the column on the other side of the ridge. When she cast her mind out to check where they were, relative to them, she picked up two people on her own side of the ridge, near the river, and spun her horse in a quarter circle to find them.

Zandaril followed. **What?**

People. Kids.

She found them where a small stream wandered in from the north. A small copse of water-rooted trees hid them, but she trotted straight at them. She already knew they weren't the Rasesni she was looking for, and one was very young.

She felt the older one's fear and pulled up several yards away. Zandaril trotted up behind her and stopped.

A dirty Kigali boy, not yet full-grown, stood up from his hiding spot below the stream bank. He had a toddler by one hand, and the other hovered close to his belt knife.

This wasn't the Kigali army Tak Tuzap had hoped to find. The man was clearly a Zan, both by his turban and his robes, and the way he sat his horse as if born to it was unmistakable. He didn't know what the woman was, and when she called to him, her accent was strange. But he'd heard merchant trains before, and the noise in the distance sounded like it might be an army. Now that he'd met them, would anyone listen to him?

Gailen held his hand and half-hid behind his leg, and stared at the woman from there, fascinated. He was embarrassed by her clothes, a mix of what he'd found her in, cleaned, and a cut-down shirt from her father's pack.

The woman dismounted and tossed her reins to the Zan. She glanced at Tak briefly but focused on Gailen.

"Hey, little one, what's happened to you?" She kept her voice low and her approach calm. "What's her name?" she asked him.

"I don't know, she won't talk to me. I've been calling her Gailen, 'Sunshine.'"

"I'm Penrys, and that's Zandaril," she said, keeping her eyes on the girl. "We're with the column just over there." She pointed north.

"I am Tak Tuzap, *minochi*. We've come out of Wechinnat."

"Through the gorge?" the man said, with a tone of amazement.

Tak nodded. "Three days ago."

He stood there in his muddy rags with a little girl waif and drew himself up to his fullest height, an inch or two shorter than the woman.

"I want to see the man in charge. I have things to tell him he needs to know."

Zandaril bit the inside of his cheeks to avoid any suggestion of humor and nodded soberly in reply to the boy's demand. "I think our Commander Chang will want to speak with you," he assured him. "Can you ride? It's not far—we can go double."

Tak Tuzap hesitated. "We have two packs."

"Show me," Zandaril said, and he dismounted. He looked over at Penrys and caught her kneeling in front of the child and murmuring something softly.

"If you'll hold the horses, I'll get the boy's packs tied on," he called to her.

"Let's go see the horses," she said to the little girl, and she picked her up and tucked her on her hip. The child clung to her as if she'd always been carried that way.

When Penrys came up to take the reins for both horses, she told him, "She's scared, hiding. Something bad happened."

"The boy's not her family, so you can guess…" Zandaril said.

She nodded. "I'll carry her."

"The packs, too," he said, as he saw the boy struggling with two backpacks, one larger than the other. "I'll take the boy."

He opened the two packs and rebalanced the contents, moving some of the metal cookware to the smaller one so that they weighed roughly the same. Then he tied them top-to-top together so he could drape them over the rump of Penrys's horse and fasten them to the saddle tie-downs as a single unit.

Penrys handed the child to Zandaril so she could mount and, before the little girl had time to protest, took her back again and curled one arm around her, holding both the reins in the other hand.

Zandaril mounted his own horse and reached one hand down to swing the boy up behind him. "Wrap your arms around my waist and hold on," he told him.

He looked over at the child fused to Penrys's hip, a leg on each side, and smiled fondly.

"What?" she said.

You look like you've done that a thousand times. You must have children.

He felt her anguish, as sharp as if he'd slapped her.

And are they wondering where I am, three years gone?

She shut him out and turned her horse away.

CHAPTER 18

"What's this?" Commander Chang said. "We don't have time for every stray along the river."

He turned aside to finish a discussion with Tun Jeju.

Penrys waited patiently with Zandaril and the children in the command tent. Zandaril gripped Tak Tuzap's shoulder in a strong hint to stand still, and the little girl was subdued and quiet.

The expedition was setting up for camp in mid-afternoon. There would be a review of the incoming information from the settlements and then a planning session that was anticipated to go on for hours.

Penrys's thoughts still roiled from Zandaril's casual remark down by the river, and she avoided meeting his troubled gaze. She hadn't dropped her shield to mind-speak him since.

Children. The thought haunted her. *Women my apparent age do have children, mostly. Zandaril's sisters and cousins do.* Even the other female wizards at the Collegium had families, if they were old enough, and no one thought it strange.

There were no stretch marks on her body, but then she had no marks at all. Nothing left a permanent mark. Even liquor rolled off her after a while. *My makers built me well, if makers there were.*

She was tired of these bitter thoughts, but had no defense when they returned periodically to batter at her.

She leaned down to sniff the head of the girl wrapped around her hip. Under the dirt, she inhaled the child-scent, and she felt a pinch at the bridge of her nose. *You can't have her. What if you vanish again in a few years? Better she not get attached to you.*

She told herself she was only carrying her because the boy was too small to do it, that the girl was comforted by the feel of a woman's body—any woman would do.

Tak looked up at her face with a questioning expression, and she tried to smile reassuringly.

Chang returned his attention to them, and Zandaril said, "Tak Tuzap here says he made it through the gorge three days go. He came to find you."

Chang's eyes narrowed, and he turned to the boy. "You knew we were coming?"

Zandaril dropped his hand and the boy stood on his own, ramrod straight. "I knew someone would come, Commander-chi. Yenit Ping, the Endless City—they were never going to let the Rasesni just take Neshilik away from them. That's what my uncle said."

"And who is this uncle?"

"Tak Paknau, of clan Cham. He was the leader of the *tengom*, the trader's guild, at the head of Gonglik Jong, the Steps, where all the caravans resume. Those who want to continue west by water take their goods past the rapids to where the river runs smooth again."

Penrys heard the quaver in his voice.

"We were going to come together, but… he got caught."

He looked down for a moment, but then raised his head again. "I know I'm young, sir, but we rehearsed what we would say together, and now there's just me."

Chang glanced at the girl on Penrys's hip and lifted an eyebrow.

Tak said, "I found her along the way."

Penrys and Zandaril had already heard much of that tale, on the ride to the camp.

"You can't go in through Seguchi Norwan, sir."

"Start at the beginning, boy, and tell me what happened."

Chang gestured an invitation to sit. Penrys pulled two camp chairs together and settled the girl in one of them, hoping she might sleep. "I already sent for some food for the kids," she told Chang.

The boy cleared his throat and began his story.

"It was the beginning of summer, sir. The fields were all planted and growing, and those with the better ground had taken their first cut of hay. We'd had the spring traders, come and gone, and most of the summer ones had arrived and were busy with the *gepten*, the trade fairs."

He stopped to explain. "The towns run the *gepten* in a sequence so the merchants can get to each town, one after the other. They'd worked their way down to Song Em in the south for the small villages and were coming back along the western border when we first heard about the fighting."

He watched Chang to see if he was following along. "You know, most of the herds are in Song Em—it's sheltered, see, in the winter, with the mountains on three sides. Most of the towns are in the north, in Wechinnat, near the river."

"Did the attack come down out of Nagthari?" Chang asked.

"No, that's what was so strange. We expect those raids—there are forts and men on watch, and a series of alarm beacons, y'understand? That's where they always come from. They plunder what they can, and then they leave."

With a quirk of his mouth, he added, "My grandma used to say, they come to see what we've done with the place since they left."

Chang nodded.

"This time they came down through the mountains on the border of Song Em and drove people north. They kept the herds."

He swallowed. "The traders who got out, they came and talked to my uncle. They said the Rasesni brought women and children along, too."

Tak stopped for a moment, remembering. "It was bad. They all thought it meant the Rasesni were going to settle in Song Em, and they started to make plans about taking it back. Things were quiet for a couple of weeks, and the towns in Wechinnat busied themselves making room for the new folk from the south."

He rushed on. "But then, all in one night, they came at us down the river from Nagthari, and out of the south, too. We were caught between them, and lots of people tried to get out through the Gates, but then we found out that some of them had crept along the Craggies in the north to Koryan. They came down at the Gates and blocked the road, and so we were bottled in."

His voice had risen and Chang gave him a moment. "When was this?"

"About, um, ten weeks ago. Not yet mid-summer."

He clenched his fists. "There weren't nothing much we could do about it, y'understand. The bigger towns put a delegation together and sent it to find the head guy, but they never came back. That scared everyone, and things started to fall apart.

"Y'see, the mountains around Neshilik aren't really that bad. There are passes, and old roads—some are well known and some are kind of kept in the family. But none of them are good for more than a few folk at a time, and the townsfolk couldn't get out that way. And some of them didn't want to, leave everything behind, lose it all. And no one trusted anyone else."

"But you got out," Chang said.

"One group wanted to run the gorge in boats. That never works—the river's too strong at the Gates—but my uncle couldn't stop them. He told me, 'Let them do it if they must, and we'll leave the same night.'"

He bit his lip. "Someone must've betrayed him. A couple of Rasesni *salengno* showed up at our camp with swords, and clubs…" His voice caught. "I grabbed my pack and got out while they were busy."

He wiped his hands along his breeches and took a deep breath.

He cocked his head at the girl, sleeping quietly. "She's the only survivor from the gorge, far as I know."

Tun Jeju picked up a brush and readied some ink and a piece of papyrus. "Names, son—I need as much as you can tell me about the raiders and whoever is leading them."

Penrys heard a disturbance at the entrance to the tent. She could smell the arrival of roast fowls without turning her head.

Tak ignored it. He bowed to Tun and leaned forward in his chair. "Everything I can, Notju-chi. But most important, I need to tell you about the passes. My uncle took me with him, all the time. I know where lots of them are."

CHAPTER 19

Penrys admired the bustle and long lines as she gave up her spot in the bathing tents. All the water-based businesses had been quick to take advantage of the unusually early stop and the nearby river to get as many things clean as possible, clothing as well as people.

She found Tak Tuzap and Gailen where she'd left them, seated on the ground at the feet of the formidable Rai Limfa. The woman was in charge of three cloth and laundry wagons, with her tailor husband, three laundresses, and assorted helpers and drivers. Her almost-grown son traveled with her, as well as her youngest child, a girl about Tak's age.

Penrys had noticed they each wore their hair in a single braid, like the boy from Neshilik. Perhaps the troopers kept their hair short for helmets.

Rai had offered to house and feed the two strays for a while, and Penrys could see that progress had already been made. Gailen was washed and tidy, and sat quietly on a small blanket on the ground, looking around her with interest. The boy wore fresh clothes, wrinkled from his pack but clean, and his wet hair, slicked back and tidily rebraided, framed an expression more carefree than when she'd first seen him.

Must have been a relief to deliver the news the way his uncle wanted him to. And he no longer has to worry about taking care of a little girl. He's done well.

"All cleaned up?" Rai asked her.

"Hing Ganau's been keeping up with the clothing, but it's good to get the smell of horse off the rest of me."

She looked down at Tak. "You going to be all right here, for a while?"

He nodded. "Rai-chi is just fine with Len-len, too."

"I miss my littlest one when she was this age," the woman said, reaching down to stroke the child's soft hair.

"She's looking much better," Penrys said. "Has she said anything yet? Her name, maybe?"

"No, but they can get like that after a good fright, and she's lost everyone, hasn't she, poor little thing. It'll wear off, likely, and she'll be chattering away again."

The boy tilted his head up at Penrys. "What'll happen to us?"

"I don't know yet. You'll come with us for a while, at least."

Rai asked him, "D'ya have any family, boy?"

"Not out here, beyond the Gates," he said, with a frown. "I want to go home. I want to take it all back and push 'em out again."

Rai glanced up at Penrys.

"Is Commander Chang going to do that?" Tak asked, looking at each of their faces.

"That why he came, isn't it, to find out what's what," Rai answered him. "Now you let the woman go along and get ready for that big meeting they're talking about."

Penrys headed for Zandaril's wagon. She had pen and paper there and the makings of ink, courtesy of her travel companion, and she wanted to add to the notes she was writing about Veneshjug's devices.

She found Zandaril standing outside, expectantly, as if he'd been waiting for her, and her step slowed.

He opened his hands wide and walked toward her. "I'm sorry," he said. "I didn't mean to upset you this morning, when I mentioned children."

She flushed, guiltily. "I know you didn't. It's just a sore spot for me. Not your fault."

She realized she was still bottled up tight inside her mind-shield, and relaxed it. **No reason you should have to guard what you say or think around me. It just surprised me.**

I'll try to be less thoughtless.

He tilted his head and said aloud, "You worried me. I hadn't considered what it must be like, not to know. I know I have no wife, no child. If I vanish, then…" He shrugged. "The weave of my family's life will continue."

"And I don't know," she said. "Maybe there's no one, that's probably it." *And I might as well behave as if I believe that, since I'm never likely to find out.*

She walked with him back to the wagon and swung herself up into it over the open tailgate. Hing Ganau had already erected the tent where they would sleep, so the new custom was to set up the interior of the wagon like a small traveling study once the wagon was done moving for the day.

Zandaril leaned on his elbows on the lowered tailgate while she poked around. "You must always look forward," he said, seriously. "Never back. Nothing to gain, looking back—only sorrow, regret. Life is always in front of you, never behind."

She stopped fidgeting around and looked at him. "I'm tethered to my empty past, by this…" She slapped the chain with her hand. "… and by the very emptiness. How can you build anything on bottomless sand?"

"Bah! If you think like that, always you will be afraid to build. No one has any certainty—all building is on sand. But if you don't build, you can't live."

He straightened up and tapped his forehead. "You're not stupid. You should know this." And he stalked away as if ashamed of her.

She blushed, unwilling to scan and confirm how he thought of her. *He's right—I'm afraid to try. What sort of special cowardice is that?*

"From what the boy says, Neshilik's been overrun and there's no effective defense left." Chang held up a finger. He was trying to cut through the fruitless session once again by summarizing what little they knew.

The tent was hot and crowded, despite the cool air outside. Penrys watched from the corner with Zandaril and tried to be inconspicuous. Chang had told them to attend, but they were the only ones in the gathering not part of his actual command—Zandaril as an ally volunteer, and herself as… what? A guest? A suspicious visitor? As Zandaril's colleague, she decided—they apparently valued another wizard, and her action with Veneshjug's traps seemed to have earned provisional acceptance from most of them, though Sau Tsuo was still something of a stubborn antagonist.

Chang ticked off another finger. "Our primary mission is reconnaissance and we're only one *laigom*, just the one squadron. We don't know how many Rasesni entered in the first wave, or how many have poured in since."

One more finger. "It looks like they intend to stay. They brought families, and they didn't destroy the herds or take them back into Nagthari."

Last finger. "They've fortified the Gates."

"And they have outriders roaming well outside of that, as a screen," Tun Jeju added. "What do they intend, besides this initial invasion?"

"And how many are there, and why haven't there been any attempts to negotiate?" Chang continued. "The boy says the townsfolk didn't succeed, and the Rasesni certainly know we're here."

Sau said, "They have hostages, don't they? Thousands of Kigaliwen. They going to keep them alive?"

"Depends on what they plan to do with the land," Chang said.

"They'll do what they did before." Sau snorted. "They never forgave our taking it finally, once and for all."

Tun commented, sardonically. "Well, they seem to have taken it back, so maybe that wasn't so permanent."

Zandaril filled Penrys in silently on the history. **Neshilik was Rasesdad land, guarded by the Gates. Wechinnat's their name for the north cove. They don't have much good land for food, near their capital, and they clung to it hard. It was a raiding base for hundreds of years. Then, three generations ago, the Kigaliwen fought their way in with a great army and forced the border upstream to Nagthari, where it has remained. Linit Kungzet, the fort there, must have been captured.**

Penrys asked, **What happened to the former inhabitants when the Kigaliwen won?**

The Kigaliwen say they pushed them back into Nagthari, those who would go. I suspect the Rasesni have a different tale—some of them were pushed all the way over Jus Sidr, the High Pass, into sarq-Zannib. The Kigaliwen didn't waste any time worrying about it. Lots of settlers wanted the land—more fertile than the open plains and better sheltered. They channeled the Seguchi away from one side of the gorge, made the trade road through the Gates, and built prosperous towns.

Built the road? Built towns? Civilized the place? The mind-speech allowed the sardonic flavor to get through clearly.

Zandaril confirmed. **Just so.**

Penrys thought his own commentary had the flavor of a circumspect junior partner, part of a people allied to the Kigali people, but not their equal in power.

The tone at the front of the tent changed.

Chang said, "We don't have enough men or resources to repulse an invasion, no matter how favorably we estimate their forces. So what *can* we do? We can keep them penned in Neshilik, hold them at the Gates. We can establish communications with them and find out their intentions. We can attempt to secure the safety of our people held captive.

"Behind us, Yenit Ping is assembling an army of thousands, and they've been getting our couriers, as we have theirs. But we must know more about what's going on. I have no stomach for a blind assault on the Gates into the unknown."

Tun Jeju said, "So we must send in scouts. Over the Red Wall passes the boy described?"

"Yes, some. And some around the outside of the Gates to the passes of the Craggies in the north."

Chang raised his head and looked over to Zandaril. "I wish we had enough time to approach from the south, through *sarq*-Zannib, but the distance is just too far. The Rasesni have the inner lines of communication."

"All of this we can do. But there is one more issue," Tun said. "A new one. For the first time, the Rasesni seem to have wizards, and they've found a way to make them a military problem. Luckily, we have two who can find out more for us, if they're willing."

Zandaril stood. "I'm proud to help our Kigali allies. It was for this that I came."

He glanced down at Penrys and lifted an eyebrow. She blew her breath out and considered. "We haven't solved the mystery of the Rasesni weapon," she said. "If we are both away, and their wizards return, what will you do?"

Tun said, "A wizard in war is like an excellent bowman. He may be invincible against a single target, by one means or another, but he can't truly influence a fighting force in any significant way."

At Penrys's skeptical expression, he said, "And just how would you attack a large force over unprepared ground?"

She mentally reviewed devices she had worked on or read about, and nodded, reluctantly. They just weren't suitable for mass assault. "But what about prepared ground? That's what that herdsman was doing, wasn't it—preparing the ground, in our camp."

Chang shrugged. "We've sprung that trap. Can they do it again? Not so easily, I think."

"But your scouts, they'll be able to blend in, hide among the Kigali people." She cocked a thumb at the standing Zandaril. "Not him. And not me either."

Zandaril grinned down at her. "They don't catch us, it doesn't matter." He made stand-up motions with his hand. "Think what we might be able to do."

"Building on sand, eh?" she muttered, but she couldn't help grinning back, and stood up. "I'll go," she told Chang.

"Together," Zandaril said. "We must go together. Wizards are better in pairs."

CHAPTER 20

Penrys and Zandaril left two mornings later. The first pair of scouts had been cast off the morning after the meeting, headed southwest to a little-used pass into Song Em.

Tak Tuzap had spent that day advising all the potential scouts about clothing, pack horses or mules, and especially directions for recognizing the blazes that marked the passes. He couldn't help the men who would try to enter from the north over the low ridges of the Craggies, except to give them the names of the passes they should look for.

"I've never been there myself," he'd told them, "but we do get traders that way, so the people on the north side should know where they are. All the famous ones will have roads leading to them, but some will be barely visible, starting at the back of someone's farm and little used 'cause they're less convenient."

Zandaril had spent some time choosing saddle horses and pack mules from the squadron's herd, and Rai Limfa had busied herself making clothing suitable for unremarkable Neshilik folk, at Tak's direction. The animals would stand out as military issue with their brands, and so would their gear. Each scout would have to try and remain unobserved, at least while mounted.

When Penrys dropped by Rai's wagons to pick up their clothing after that day's march, Tak blocked her path.

"I'm going with you two," he'd said. "I've done everything I can, like my uncle would have wanted. Now it's time to go back, and I reckon you're the ones who can maybe do the most damage, if I can get you close to the workings at the Gates."

It had gone against the grain for her, to bring a kid into danger, one that was no more than three quarters grown.

"How old are you?" she'd asked him, but Rai intervened.

"He's old enough. Old enough to fight for his home."

The two women had stared into each other's faces for a moment, then Penrys yielded. "Be at our wagon at daylight," she'd told him.

He'd grinned and then wiped it off his face and assumed a dignified expression.

Now, under Hing Ganau's disapproving scowl, Penrys checked the girth of her saddle horse one last time, while both Tak Tuzap and Zandaril inspected the loads on the two pack mules to make sure they were well-balanced and secure.

"Mules. Not how we do things at home," Zandaril muttered. He hadn't wanted to put his own pack horses at risk and was now forced to learn in a hurry from Tak.

"Ready?" Zandaril asked. He looked strange to her, no longer in his robes, with his head bare.

Penrys mounted and Tak handed her the lead rein of the first mule. Zandaril led the other.

The boy looked small on his rangy buckskin. Penrys had suggested a smaller horse for him, but Zandaril pointed out that any of them might have to ride any of the horses.

"See you in a few days," Zandaril called to Hing. "Take care of everything for us."

"I'll send Chang-chi in after you, if you don't show up."

Penrys snorted at the unlikeliness of that. "Stay out of trouble yourself," she told him.

They turned west, toward the river.

By the time they reached the bank, they could hear the creak and jingle of the camp behind them as it broke down and prepared to get underway.

A small break in the land here had provided a broad stretch of shallows for the river to cross and, at this time of year, in low water, it was only as deep as the horses' hocks. This close to the mountains, the dirt had been washed away from exposed, worn rock, and the horses picked their way carefully over it.

The early morning had brightened by the time they reached the other side. When Penrys looked back, she caught the tail end of the expedition's cattle herd, following the column. The water flowing incessantly over the riffles drowned out any sound, and then they passed out of sight.

"We should cross the old trade road soon, coming down from the north," Tak Tuzap said.

They were three days west of the river, and finally the mountains were close enough that they could make out individual details. Penrys had extended her mind as far as she could, looking for people, but there seemed to be no one else on the land for miles.

"There's nobody around. Why would there be a trade road?" she asked.

The boy pointed north. "Up that way is Shaneng Ferry, both sides of the river. Big ferry there. Used to send traders this way, south to the pass, but the road at the Gates stole all that traffic, and the traders didn't have to cross the river to use it."

"And the road is still there?" Zandaril asked.

Tak shrugged. "Not much rain, this side of the Red Wall. Takes a long time for old roads to go away."

"The mountains don't look that high," Penrys said. "I'd expect there'd be lots of places to cross."

Tak was shaking his head before she finished speaking. "Not high, not like Mratsarnag, but very, very crumpled." He squeezed his hands together to demonstrate. "Landslides, pocket canyons, dead ends."

He tilted his head back and scanned the mountain range that filled the western horizon, running south all the way to the *sarq*-Zannib border, and north to the Gates.

"All the *gwatenno*, the traders, have stories about people getting lost, about finding old bones." He looked earnestly at Zandaril. "If you find old bones, people bones, it's a very bad sign. It means they didn't get out, from where they were, and now you're in that same place."

Up ahead, the dry grass was interrupted by intermittent patches of bare soil. When Penrys stopped her horse there, she could see a faint trace running away from her in both directions, parallel to the ridges in front of her.

"The road from Shaneng Ferry?" she asked Tak.

He smiled. "See, I'm a good guide."

He swung left along it, and Penrys and Zandaril followed.

Two days later, Penrys was thoroughly sick of the twisty pack road, scarcely wider than a well-laden mule. They'd climbed, and climbed, one dusty yard after another, and nowhere a view to break the monotony.

The boy was in the lead, with Penrys immediately behind. He was right—it was a maze of short trails. If the blazes on the old trees had been erased or the rock cairns scattered, it would have been almost impossible to make their way without an endless series of dead ends.

This was the high point of the pass, Tak Tuzap had said, and Penrys wanted a view. She looked up through the narrow sides of yet another canyon, and her shoulders ached with longing. If she'd been alone, she knew what she would have done to see the view from the nearest peak. As it was… *well, maybe at dusk, if I can get away for a moment.*

They turned the corner around the knee of the ridge, and the trail widened out into a sparse upland meadow surrounding a small seasonal pond.

"This is the mid-point," the boy said. "It's always got water unless there wasn't much snow the winter before. Everyone stops to camp here."

The view extended to some of the ridges on the western side of the range, but not all the way out to the protected valley below. The sinking sun shone warmly on their faces, but Penrys knew the chill of the heights would be upon them when it was gone.

They fell smoothly into their camp routine. Zandaril tended to the horses and mules while Penrys fetched water, and Tak laid out the cooking gear.

Penrys looked up at the gathering twilight. "I'll start getting wood," she offered, anxious to get off by herself for a few minutes. She strode off to the wooded margins of the meadow and used the remaining light to pull dead branches out of the thickets into the grasses, where it would be easier for her to pick them up on her way back. Zandaril had surprised her the first night, in his refusal to use anything but fallen wood. "The trees would not like it," was all he would say on the subject.

Done with her task, she walked upslope looking for a standpoint higher than the trees with room enough to launch.

You should tell them about this.

She'd had this argument with herself before. They already looked at her as if she had two heads. *Be honest. You don't care what the kid thinks, or the Kigali people back in camp. They don't know what wizards can do, not in detail.* Though she wondered if maybe Tun Jeju was more knowledgeable than most.

No, it's Zandaril. He knows what's impossible. He likes to think I'm just some sort of minor mystery.

It would be the end of their comfortable friendship, letting him see this. Can't explain this away so easily. It was worse than the ears.

The light was fading quickly. If she was going to do it, it had to be now. She looked up and took a running step… which she stumbled over as Zandaril appeared at the upslope edge of the trees, calling her name.

Her aborted movement must have caught his eye.

His deep voice carried over the distance. "What are you doing up there? Get lost?"

She coughed. "Just looking for a view. Stay put, I'll come back down."

He waited on her, a puzzled expression on his face.

"Not safe to wander off by yourself," he said. "I came to help you with the wood. Saw you found some on the way up."

"Sure, we'll just grab it as we go back." She set off in front of him to keep her face hidden. *That was close. I should have checked where everyone was first.*

He looked at her oddly as she went by. "I wanted to talk to you," he said. "I thought of something."

"Hmm?"

"Did you learn to ride in Ellech?"

She bent over to pick up the first pile of branches. "Um, no. No, I could already ride."

"Didn't you think that odd?"

She straightened up with her armful of wood and looked back at him, in the dusk.

"Well, where did you learn to ride? Everyone remembers that," he said.

"I don't know," she said. "I told you that."

"But your body knows. Your body remembers."

Her stomach clenched.

"What else does your body remember?"

He picked up the loose branches she hadn't been able to carry and passed her on the way down to the next pile, leaving her staring off after him.

She followed, slowly, lost in thought.

What skills did her body have, that first year at the Collegium? She could ride and swim, read and write, but her writing was ill-done at first, and still clumsy. *Maybe that's not the language or script I learned on.* The language proved nothing—she pulled that from the people around her, and what language her first thoughts were in when they found her was gone. She couldn't draw, but she could sing—she'd discovered she had a trained voice, but no repertoire. There was no weapon that called to her, but she knew how to wield a knife for slicing food, had a hand for kneading bread. Cloth and fiber didn't speak to her fingers, but leather did.

All of these things she had discovered gradually, living with other people and sampling what they did. For wizardry, it was more difficult—the models she could test herself against didn't exist. She knew how to mind-speak, how to sense the minds around her, but she'd had to find out for herself that other wizards had smaller ranges, that animals weren't visible to them. They couldn't even shield themselves well, as she discovered when she was first surrounded by them and her own shield popped into place. *Is that true for all of them, or just the ones in Ellech? Could they have learned, if they'd been willing to?*

The books had helped, then, describing things that were similar to what she could do. It was that resemblance, before she learned to be more closemouthed about the differences, that led them to call her an Adept, like one of those mythical creatures no one really thought had ever existed.

And she didn't either, since the books never mentioned animal ears, or unbreakable chains of power.

Or flight, which she'd only discovered by accident. What else was still hidden?

CHAPTER 21

Zandaril puzzled over Penrys's behavior well into their simple meal of grain cakes and smoked fish. *What was she doing way up the slope, as though she were about to run off somewhere or meet someone?*

He cast around and found no other people, no refugees from the cove below, and no Rasesni prowling this high up.

All through dinner Penrys had seemed lost in thought. When he raised an eyebrow at her, as she wiped her plate clean, she flushed and commented, "A cook who could ride and sing, with a strange fondness for leather. Can't see that that's much help."

He snorted, but Tak Tuzap was completely stumped, and stared at her.

She glanced at him. "Never mind—something Zandaril said to me earlier. Now, whose turn is it?"

They'd started to tell stories of an evening, to spend the time before going to sleep. They'd heard about Tak's uncle, and the death of his parents years before. Zandaril had talked about crossing the pass at Jus Shamr, the Low Pass, to join Chang's expedition.

So far, Penrys had ducked her turn. Now Tak swallowed his last bite, and then told her, "You know it's yours. I want a story about…"

He broke off.

"About wizards," she said, and the boy nodded.

"What's the fun in traveling with wizards if they don't tell stories about it?" he said.

Zandaril commented, "He has a point."

He expected her to refuse again, but she surprised him. "I'll tell you a story." Her eyes slid sideways to meet Zandaril's. "A story about a meeting of wizards."

She sat upright and crossed her legs. She drew her open hand across her face as if she were wiping it clean, and her expression changed. She focused on Tak as she spoke.

"Now, I was there for much of this tale, but some of it I heard from others. This is how they tell it, in far-away Ellech, at Drosenrolkentham, the Collegium of Wizards in Tavnastok, a quarter of the way around the world."

The boy's eyes widened.

"On a cold, snowy, winter's night, not many years ago, in the forests around Sky Fang, the wizard Vylkar was quietly reading in his study when he felt the tug of power, like a burst of a wind funnel, somewhere nearby. His old mother, a wizard before him, called down to him from her chamber, having been woken from her sleep."

Penrys leaned forward and waved her hands before her to illustrate her words. "They agreed that they both felt the disturbance in the same place, and that it was nothing they had encountered before. So Vylkar summoned his huntsmen and some of his grooms for, you see, it was a fine hunting estate he was at, the treasure of his family. The horses were surprised to be turned out of their warm stalls into the chill of the night."

She wrapped her arms around herself and mock-shivered.

"It was still and overcast, and the men lit torches to find their way, holding them well away from their horses, accustomed though some of them were to the task. Vylkar could feel something where the surge of power had been, and he used that as a guide."

Zandaril watched the fire's embers between the three travelers flare up as if they envied the torches.

"The paths led sometimes toward it, and sometimes away, but always they got closer, winding around the side of Sky Fang, and it was awkward riding with their torches through the trees."

Zandaril was as rapt as the boy. *She should add 'storyteller' to her list.*

"At last, Vylkar drew his horse to a stop. 'Here,' he said, 'Somewhere around here you should find something.' He and his men dismounted, and began to search through the trees on either side of the path.

"One voice cried out, 'Over here!' and the others joined him. There, at the base of an old oak tree, in the snow, was the naked body of a woman."

Tak asked, "Wasn't she cold? What was she doing there?

"She was asleep until they startled her awake with their noise and their torches. Then, yes, she was very cold, and wet, too, from the snow.

"'Who are you?' they cried, and 'What's your name?' but she just shivered and didn't speak, so they wrapped her in two cloaks and lifted her onto a horse to ride double with one of the grooms."

"Were her feet bare? No clothes at all?" the boy asked.

"Nothing but a cold chain around her neck."

The trance was broken, as Tak Tuzap realized this was her own story and stared at the chain that hugged her throat.

She went on as if she didn't notice.

"It was faster coming back than going out, for they knew their way, and soon they had her in the hunting lodge, wrapped in warm blankets, and Vylkar's old mother pouring hot soup down her."

Her voice trailed off for a moment, and then she continued.

"They were kind, these men, and waited until she had stopped shivering before they asked her again who she was. She answered them this time, in their own language, that she had no name, she had nothing at all. The earliest thing she could remember was the torchlight reflected from the snow.

"Then, when the wizard Vylkar went to probe her mind to see if that would tell him more about her, she shut him out, and he couldn't get in. That's when he knew she was another wizard, though what all of that meant was unknown to her."

She stopped, and swept her hand through the air. "*Sennevi.* It is done."

Silence fell, until the collapse of some of the coals broke it. Penrys laid her hands back into her lap.

"That's enough for one night," she said. She rose up clumsily from her cross-legged seat and walked away, out of the firelight.

Tak looked over at Zandaril, across the fire. "That wasn't the sort of story I expected," he said.

"Nor I," Zandaril said, thoughtfully.

At last. People.

Penrys turned her horse off the trail and pulled the pack mule along behind her. She stopped there to concentrate. The trees and grasses were greener, on this side, and the air had been getting moister for some time now.

Behind her, she heard Zandaril call out softly to Tak Tuzap to keep him from riding ahead of them.

They were still well up in the pass on the western side, about halfway down from the crest, but for the first time in days she could feel the mind-glows of other people in the not yet visible valley below them.

"There are small clusters of men, women, even kids—well scattered. Families and villages, I would guess."

Tak had turned around and come back up to watch. He nodded. "That's what there should be, down there."

"Are they Kigaliwen, or the Rasesni invaders?" Zandaril asked.

"Can't tell from here—too far away for language. Just ordinary folk, no wizards," Penrys said.

At Tak's puzzled look, she added, "If they're Rasesni settlers, they might be a lot like the people they displaced."

She looked at Zandaril. "It would be useful if they were Rasesni, and a bit closer. Think of those two books." The spy's books, power-stones, and a few of his pre-built device forms took up part of her pack.

Tak ignored her aside. "That's our land. What about the people who lost everything?"

"It was Rasesdad land before that," Zandaril commented. "And I'm sure Chang is intent on making it Kigali land again."

"Point is," Penrys said, "these aren't likely the primary folk doing the fighting and planning. It's not them we're looking for, but the leaders and especially the wizards, if they have any."

Zandaril coughed. "We'll be just as dead if it's the herders and farmers who catch us."

"True." She twisted in her saddle and grinned at him. "Got to survive long enough to get further into Wechinnat and find out about the situation there. Glad you came?"

She laughed outright at the glare he directed at her, and turned to the boy.

"What's the best method of working our way north without being seen? Can we stay in the foothills? As far as the Gates?"

"The hills are no good—the trails go over them, not the other way, north and south. The trade road on this side runs along the valley edge for a few miles before it joins up with the main road. That might be empty, I suppose, if you go at night."

He pursed his lips. "Can't you just make yourselves invisible or something?"

"Wonderful that would be, if we could." Zandaril nodded slowly. "Horses, too?"

Tak's face fell.

"And then there's all those footsteps, and creaking leather, and jingling harness."

Penrys chimed in. "Not to mention the smell when one of the horses decides to…"

The boy's face flamed red. "How do I know what you two can do?"

"Sorry, Takka," she said, "but it's just not that easy. We can sneak around a bit, but not with all this gear. What we have to do is meet up with your uncle's colleagues at Gonglik, if they're still around, and get some information."

"And then we have to not get caught, any of us," Zandaril said. "And get a message back to Chang."

She looked at him. "And how were you planning to do that, by the way? Smoke signals?"

He looked at her, deadpan. "I thought we could seal up some clay bottles with messages inside and float them down the river. What do you think?"

She laughed, unable to contain herself. "No, really, how will we get messages out?"

"We'll carry them out ourselves." He looked at her seriously. "This is something I intend to survive."

CHAPTER 22

I don't like this. The boy's overdue.

Penrys and Zandaril communicated silently. They were mounted and held all five animals quiet in the patch of woods on the edge of the little farm village that Tak Tuzap had named Lupmikya while they waited for the boy to return from his reconnaissance.

He hasn't moved much for half an hour.

She'd had her mind on him as he worked his way into the center of town, but it was like following one fish in a multitude, with all the people going about their business in the early evening. She couldn't detect any wizards, so she thought she could safely bespeak Zandaril, but she couldn't shake her uneasiness, recalling how Zandaril had accidentally spooked the Rasesni spy that way. *We don't really know what they can do.*

You'd know if he was hurt, yes?

She nodded in response to Zandaril's question, confident he could make her out well enough in the dusk.

There are Rasesni here—can you feel them?

Penrys had wanted to stop and look at the books she'd brought with her from the spy, now that it would be possible to read them. Her fingers itched to dig into her pack and pull one out, if she could only strike a light.

I don't get that much detail.

She could feel Zandaril's hesitation, before he continued. **How do wizards fight each other?**

Wish I knew.

Biting her lip, she looked away from him in the dim light. **There were books in the index, in the Collegium, but they didn't let me in everywhere.**

In sarq-Zannib, they have contests, one on one. The winner is the more powerful.

She saw him tap his forehead.

And if he is a man of… bad character?

He swept his hand sideways in front of him. **Several can overpower one.**

Ah. So, no wizard-tyrants, then.

His head dipped in the dark. **We call them qahulajab. But mostly it's just feuds and boasts. Unorganized, like everything else. What the Rasesni are doing, that's different.**

Organized, as you would say. She smiled to herself. **It's a function of the devices for physical magic. You can accumulate tools, and that provides leverage. I imagine it's like producing weapons on a large scale—now you can have an army. But, just like an army, it needs social and political organization, too. And people willing to be subordinate to the whole. They don't have that in Ellech—too much independence.**

Kigali has the organization, but not the wizards. Tun Jeju was ready to think that way. But what about Rasesni? What's happening with them?

She let Zandaril's question hang unanswered, and concentrated on following Tak's progress.

He's moving now. Two more coming with him.

It didn't feel right to her to let a kid take on this danger, but they were relying on his contacts and had to trust he could look after himself.

Seemed like Zandaril could pick the boy's mind out, now that he was closer. **He's left the other two back at the fence.**

Penrys waited for him to get there. **He's upset about something. Bad news, maybe. His uncle?**

A low whistle penetrated the dark, and Zandaril whistled back.

Tak slipped back into the little hollow where they waited. "Found them," he said.

"What about the two who came with you?" Penrys asked.

She felt his surprise. "Wizards, remember?" She smiled when she said it, and after a brief hesitation she saw his own answering grin gleaming in the night.

"I wanted to come back first, by myself. I know one of them, Zau Tselu, he was a friend of Uncle Tak. He vouches for the other one."

She heard the echo of grief in his voice. "You heard something about your uncle, didn't you?"

He choked. "I… I knew he was dead. Had to be."

Zandaril murmured, "Not the same as hearing about it for sure."

The boy nodded.

"They want to take you somewhere for a meeting, One of the farms. They've got a stable where we can put the horses and stuff for a while."

What do you think?

Penrys snorted. **Well, I can monitor them well enough to tell when one's about to betray us. Just before he pulls his knife out.**

To the boy, she said, "Well done, Tak. Go ahead. Take us to them."

Tak Tuzap mounted his own horse and led them out along the margin of the field to join the two men waiting on foot at the fence nearest the lane.

Penrys detected suspicion but no malice in them. The first one, stout and middle-aged, held up a hand to stop Tak from introducing them and brought them in silence down the lane. She made no demurral. *Introductions can wait.* The second man, tall and elderly, followed in the rear, the gray in his braid visible in the faint light.

She kept her mind lightly on the half-dozen Rasesni-speakers in the area, but she was sure none of them were wizards. That didn't mean that no one else in the village would betray them—there was no way to tell what hostages had been taken and how each person's situation would shape their actions.

They walked quietly for twenty minutes along the grassy roads on the outer edge of the main settlement, and then at last turned away from the distant lights and back towards the woods. When they reached it, the *samke*, the farm compound, was a dark mass cut out of the sky, and Penrys sensed no one inside, or anywhere nearby, besides themselves. There was enough starlight to make out the side path that led around back to a stable, barn, and other outbuildings, all as deserted as the main compound—no livestock in the fields or the paddocks, and no recent smell of them, either.

She shivered. Had they been victims of the invasion here, or did they leave for somewhere else?

Their guide drew back the bar that closed the stable door. They dismounted and he led them over the threshold with all their animals. He raised his hand when Zandaril was about to speak, and the question died unuttered. Both of the villagers walked the length of the stable, seven empty stalls and one still filled with straw for bedding, and closed every wooden shutter. The stout one even laboriously climbed the ladder into the loft, and Penrys heard shutters drawn together there, too. She listened to him grope with his foot for the top rung, and then make his way back down in the pitch blackness.

Finally, the old man struck a light and touched the wick of the lantern he'd carried all the way. The sudden light dazzled Penrys's eyes for a moment before they adjusted.

Zandaril sneezed from the dust that had been stirred up, and Tak let loose a startled laugh.

The boy caught the eye of the stout man. Something he saw there reassured him, and he bowed to him. "Zau-chi, these are the wizards, Zandaril and Penrys, sent by Commander Chang."

To his own travel companions, he said, "My uncle's friend, Zau Tselu, and Nek Kazu. They said they'll listen to you."

Zau said, at once, "We make no promises, mind. Rasesni are bad enough." He scowled at the boy. "You said nothing about a Zan and…" He waved his hand dubiously at Penrys.

Zandaril bowed. "We want only to find out the truth of what has happened in Neshilik, *binochiwen*, not to cause you any further trouble."

Penrys nodded. It was clear the villagers distrusted foreigners, and wizards, but that was no surprise.

The two men looked at each other. The old one said, "If you're found, we shall deny we ever saw you, you understand? It's too risky. They've taken some of our youngsters in to serve them."

Penrys looked him in the eyes. "We won't betray your help, and the boy's already proved his own courage."

Zau said, grudgingly, "Aye, his uncle would've been proud of him, that's a fact. Down the gorge and back over the Red Wall, is it?"

He considered them. "Well, no light outside at all, none of you. This family won't be coming back, but there's neighbors might wonder if they saw a light or any of your beasts. We'll be back come morning with some food and maybe the *yankatmi*, the headwoman. You all stay put, hear? No wandering around."

Zandaril bowed again. "We'll do whatever you ask, and thank you for your hospitality."

Zau thinned his lips, but made no reply. They left the lantern behind on the floor of an empty stall so that its light would be masked when they opened the stable door to leave.

It creaked on its hinges, and Penrys listened for the sound of the bar being thrown to shut them in, but it didn't come.

Zandaril chuckled. "Thought they'd lock us in, after all that."

"I thought they'd be pleased to see you." Tak Tuzap's disappointment was clear in his voice.

"Never mind," Zandaril told him. "There's Rasesni blood in the old families here, from before, and they're remembering their great-grandparents and wondering if they can just all get along again. Might not want the army showing up and forcing them to choose. 'Sides, having their kids or grandkids held hostage is a powerful incentive to leave things be."

Penrys picked up the lantern and inspected the stalls and the leftover tools. "There's not much here, but we've got our own canvas buckets if we can find some water. Must be a well somewhere in the yard. The hay still looks fresh enough, and we've got grain in the packs."

She hung the lantern on a high hook over the main aisle. "Let's get the animals settled and catch what sleep we can. We'll see things more clearly in the morning."

CHAPTER 23

The sound of rain on the wooden shingles of the hay loft woke Penrys before Zandaril came to get her at the end of his watch. They had split the night, watching for anyone approaching from the village. The precaution might have been unnecessary, but Penrys couldn't maintain any sort of shield while she slept, nor was she even sure that the shield was a good idea—the wizard who ran the mirror seemed to have been attracted by it—so this was the best they could do. She checked the surroundings now. She felt Tak Tuzap, still sunk in the sound sleep of youth, and Zandaril preparing to catch another couple of hours before the sun was properly up, but no one else nearby.

She yawned, grateful for a roof this wet morning, even if only a hay loft, half-full of bales. *Daylight soon—I can start with the Rasesni books!*

She pulled on her boots and stepped carefully down the ladder. The horses and mules were dozing, standing hip-slung and quiet. She picked up two of the buckets that had been left behind and went out the human door on the side, calculating the driest route to the privy, and then to the well to bring back water for the animals and themselves.

When she returned, dripping, she set the buckets down inside the doorway and looked over at her pack, the one that held the bags of Veneshjug's power stones. She closed her eyes. *Yes, I can feel them, but only just, unpowered as they are. Couldn't do that from the yard.*

There was no telling what Veneshjug's colleagues could manage. She kept her own shield up lightly, now that she was awake. Just because there didn't seem to be a wizard within range didn't mean none was there. *We don't know what they can do. I'm not back at the Collegium, where my range is longer than anyone else's. It'd be stupid to think that's true everywhere.*

She'd tried to teach Zandaril to shield himself last night, but it was slow work—apparently wizards didn't hide that way in *sarq*-Zannib. Their best defense was going to have to be not to draw any attention to themselves, and to find out as much as they could without alerting any Rasesni wizards.

She snorted quietly. *That'll be a neat trick.*

"Listen to this." Penrys's voice drifted up from the far side of the stable.

Zandaril sighed. Penrys had buried her nose in the first Rasesni book from the moment there was enough light to make out the letters on the page. She'd commandeered an empty stall, opened the shutter on its window, and dragged a bench into it as a makeshift work table so she could follow along with experiments as she read.

While he and Tak Tuzap had watered and fed the animals, and set up a watch for their promised visitors, she'd been calling out the highlights of device techniques that were apparently new to her.

He'd popped in once to look over her shoulder, but he still couldn't read it. She tried to show him something with the wooden forms and loose stones she'd brought with her, but he just shook his head and backed out again.

"Aren't you worried about having all that… stuff out in the open with other people around?" he asked.

"I'll put it away before they get here. The book, especially—wouldn't do to have a Rasesni book around, under the circumstances, I suppose."

Zandaril rolled his eyes. "Come have some breakfast."

"Later… Who knows when I'll be able to read it again…" Her voice trailed off as she flipped a page.

"Everywhere in Neshilik there will be Rasesni," Zandaril muttered under his breath as he joined Tak on a bench against the wall, as far as he could get from her experiments. The boy grinned at him.

There was a sizzle and a spark from the stall, and dust rose over the partition.

"*That's* how that works. What a clever idea!"

"Is she always like this?" Tak asked Zandaril.

"I hope not." He had visions of this unbridled enthusiasm at work in the hallowed halls of the Collegium library.

"Try not to blow us all up if you figure it out," he called.

"They're coming," Penrys said. She stuck her head out of the stall doorway to make sure she'd been heard. There was dirt on her forehead and down along one cheek.

Zandaril grunted. Apparently she hadn't been so entirely absorbed in her research as not to maintain a watch. Her range was greater than his, but soon he could feel the approach of four people, the two from last night, and two others.

Penrys disappeared again, and he heard her sweeping her things into a pack. She emerged from the stall with it over her shoulder and hoisted it up the ladder to bury it in the loft.

"No sense leaving it around underfoot," she said, as she passed.

"Wash your face," Zandaril called up after her. "Experimental smuts."

"The badge of a hard-working technician" drifted back down.

Tak Tuzap paced nervously, and Zandaril stopped him with a hand on his shoulder. "No fault to you if they're difficult," he said. "You've done what you could."

He timed their approach and went to open the human door for them as they entered the farmyard. Zau Tselu paused to look around the yard first, as if seeking traces of their presence, then led the way into the stable. He was followed by a middle-aged woman and a young man, and Nek Kazu brought up the rear. Between them they carried two leather sacks and a couple of covered baskets.

Zandaril bowed to them and Penrys and Tak came up to help with their wet cloaks and hats. Penrys found pegs for everything, and soon the scent of wet wool joined warm horse and loose hay.

The woman cocked her head at Zandaril, and he felt the full force of her inspection. When she got a better look at Penrys's face, an eyebrow rose.

"Introduce us," she told Zau.

"This is Wan Tawa, the *yankatmi* of Lupmikya," he said. "Her nephew, Wan Nozu."

He looked over at Tak. "I've told her what you told us."

With Tak's help, Penrys pulled the benches into a rough open triangle. "Thank you for coming, *yankatmi-chi*. Please, won't you take a seat?"

Wan Tawa and her nephew took the middle bench, Zau and Nek the second, and only then did Zandaril join Penrys on the third bench, patting the seat beside him to encourage Tak to roost there instead of pacing behind them nervously.

Nek offered the baskets to Zandaril. "A meal, for after. More food…" He waved a hand at the two wet leather sacks.

Penrys took the baskets and put them down at their feet. "Thank you, Nek-chi. We're in your debt."

"I shall explain, yes?" Zandaril asked Wan Tawa, and she waved her hand for him to proceed.

He shifted on the bench to face her squarely and sketched out his story with his hands as he spoke.

"In Yenit Ping they heard the story of Rasesdad invading your fair Neshilik. Early reports traveled downriver quickly, and the garrison at Jonggep didn't wait for orders to prepare a first probe, to find out just what had happened."

He glanced at Wan Tawa's face, firm and expressionless. "It is a very long way, and though a force left Jonggep not long after, they are only just now approaching the Gates."

"There was even enough time, apparently, to send to *sarq*-Zannib for a wizard," Wan Tawa commented, dryly.

"It was so, *yankatmi-chi*. When the ships along the coast brought the news to Ussha that there were rumors of wizards with the Rasesni, they sent couriers to my tribe's camp in the north, and word reached me. 'Could we send a wizard,' they asked, 'to the gathering in Jonggep.' I volunteered, and crossed the Low Pass with my horses. I caught them not long after they left."

"And you?" Wan Tawa's attention turned to Penrys.

"I'm an addition to the expedition, a couple of weeks after Zandaril joined. From the far North, from Ellech."

It was a simple answer, but Zandaril hoped this local headwoman had no clear concept of the tall, fair-haired Northeners, since Penrys wouldn't match that expectation.

"The soldiers reached the river south of Shaneng Ferry, a few days ago," he said, "and the Commander gathers information."

He gestured at his companions. "We're part of that. It was thought useful for wizards to explore the presence of Rasesni wizards, if any, and report back."

He laid his hand on Tak's shoulder. "We picked up Tak Tuzap here on the river at the same time, and he told us his story." He looked over at Zau. "The death of his uncle, and how he got out through the Gates."

Wan Tawa pursed her lips as if digesting the story. "There must be others scouting this side of the Red Wall, not just you two."

Zandaril shrugged. "I know little about that, *yankatmi-chi*."

"And will tell us less," she said. "But that's the way it should be." She glanced at her nephew. "So, what do you want with us? You can't stay here, people will notice."

"We won't stay, to make it dangerous for you. We want to know, first, what is the truth? What happened?"

Wan Tawa raised her head and looked away from him. "Rasesni have been here before. When we pushed them out last time, some stayed. Many of us have Rasesni lines not far back, if we're willing to admit it. They came back, is all we know, and brought the hill-tribes with them."

"Was there fighting?" Penrys said.

"Of course, but not… not like an army. More like pushy neighbors, bullies. They wanted us out of the Song Em, especially, but they're not as bloody as last time, if the old tales are to be believed."

Nek spoke up. "That's not what they say who escaped up here. Lost everything, they did."

"But not their lives, mostly," Wan Tawa said. "Poorer, but alive."

She looked at Zandaril. "We're taking in as many as we can. It helps that some of our own fled north themselves, or out through the Gates, like these folks." She waved her hand around the stable. "If they're not back soon, we'll be settling some of the southerners here."

She smoothed her skirt over her thighs. "I think they'll be staying, again. They're rededicating the temples, like last time. The priests are already here, sneaking about."

"What about north of here, where most of the people are? Like his uncle?" Penrys said, cocking her head at Tak Tuzap.

Zau said, "We keep in touch, as we can. It's just another twelve miles or so to Gonglik, and it's very quiet right now. Some folk made trouble, and some got killed, like Tak Paknau, so most everyone else is keeping out of the way and waiting to see what's next."

"What happened to Linit Kungzet, the border fort, under the Horn?" Zandaril asked.

The four villagers looked at each other. "No one knows," Wan

Tawa said. "We've seen no soldiers at all, and heard no rumors about it."

Wan Nozu said, "There are Rasesni soldiers quartered in Gonglik, and all the towns around there, but not here yet. Just some officers…" He trailed off.

Wan Tawa said briskly, "The officers take over the best properties in the outlying towns and displace the families. Rewards for them, if they stay, and control over us. That's how it works."

Zau glowered. "And they keep the young folk there to serve them."

"Hostages?" Penrys asked.

Wan Tawa shrugged. "It was expected, it's their way. So far, they haven't abused them, and we keep the peace. But that's why you must move on. They might see you. Even some of our own, fearing for their children, might decide to turn you in. We won't risk reprisals, not until there's no other choice."

Nek added, "They're better armed, and we have more to lose."

"And they already hold the south," Zandaril said. "Well, it's not our job to plan strategy, that's for more military minds."

"What about wizards?" Penrys said. "Have you seen or heard of anything like that?"

Zau looked at Wan Tawa and hesitated.

"Tell them," she said.

"The towns east and north of here, to the Gates… They talk of wizards. Especially in Gonglik, with all their temples. We don't know the truth of it."

Penrys looked at Zandaril. "Then that's where we must go." His stomach clenched, but he nodded.

"Can you help?" he asked the villagers.

"You'll never pass in daylight," Wan Nozu said. "But if you travel at night and remain indoors during the day…"

"I can guide them," Tak Tuzap said, popping up from the bench.

"No, lad, you're back home now. Time for you to stay put." Zandaril tried to push him back down, but the boy eluded him.

"That's not why I came back. You need me. I know those towns."

Wan Nozu looked at his aunt. "I could go with them, make them look less conspicuous. With their hoods up…"

Before Wan Tawa could draw breath to rebuke him, he added,

"If I don't get out of here, I'll end up a hostage, too. Better to be out there doing something."

She hesitated. "This wizard business… The Rasesni never had that before, and we don't understand it. It's worrisome, it is." She examined Zandaril and his companions and came to a decision.

"You may go, nephew, to guide them." She turned to Tak. "Can you find the big mill on the left, at the end of Lupmikya, along Gonglik road?"

When he nodded, she said, "Take everyone there, an hour after full dark. My nephew will meet you. You'll have to leave your beasts behind—the Rasesni will take them otherwise. The mill needs horses and mules to deliver its grindings—you can leave them there. Might still be there if you come back. He'll bring cloaks with hoods for you two." She gestured at the wizards. "Use them."

She looked around at the packs placed against the walls. "If you can't carry it on your backs, you'll have to leave it behind. The miller can help with that. I'll talk to him today."

She rose abruptly. "Anyone about?"

Before Zau could get to the door, Zandaril checked the vicinity, and he suspected Penrys did as well. "No one's out there in the rain, *yankatmi-chi*."

She stared at him, grimacing in distaste at the wizardly assurance.

"So. I wish you good fortune, and entrust you with my nephew's safety."

She glanced at Tak. "Can I not make you stay behind, boy?"

"No, *yankatmi-chi*." Tak sidled closer to Wan Nozu and glanced up at his face, and Zandaril thought the two of them would partner up soon enough on the road.

Penrys fetched cloaks and hats while Zau, ignoring Zandaril's words, peered carefully out through the rain, looking for witnesses.

They swept out of the stable into the muddy yard and Zandaril shut the door behind them.

"Well," Penrys said. "If anyone can survive this invasion, she can. Let's hope it gets no worse for them."

"Or for us," Zandaril said, contemplating trudging through the mud with a heavy pack.

CHAPTER 24

"Zandaril, I know how he did it," Penrys said.

It was mid-morning, and she needed to take a break. If she explained it all to Zandaril, it would solidify her own understanding before she went on. She had what hours of daylight remained to learn as much as she could from the two stolen books.

Zandaril leaned over the stall door. "Show me."

"Well, I can't quite do that without making things go boom, but I can explain it all and I understand the steps."

Tak Tuzap slipped into the stall and stood in a corner.

He's bored. Let him stay—it's not like it'll make much sense to him.

"Remember how the power-stones are used, for control or for power?"

Zandaril nodded.

"They found a way to combine all that."

She held up two small power-stones, the smallest she could find. She didn't know how to separate them again after the demonstration, and she hated to waste any of the larger ones.

"If I put these face-to-face, along the widest part of the cut stone, see, like this… and then bind them directly to each other, the way I showed you, with raw physical magic… I can attach them together along the surface in a way I don't know how to break again. Maybe there's some method for it." She waved her hand at the open book on the bench beside her.

"Now the goal is—you were right, by the way—to make them pull in opposite directions. But not at once, or it blows up in your face! What you do is…" She lifted one of the simple wooden blocks with its pre-drilled holes.

"You put them there and for each one, separately, you tell it to pull on the wooden edge." She laid the joined stones down on their side, with the outer points directed at the raised border of the slab. "You don't give them any power, yet, you understand? So they can't do much."

"Under tension, like a crossbow," Zandaril said.

"Yes, something like that. So you make a trigger, like for a crossbow. This one's a simple *detect* sensor. If it feels a touch…" She tapped her forehead. "And what that does is let a powered stone pour into the bound ones. Maybe more than one—I'm not sure how many it takes. It was the powered stones I could sense."

Zandaril said, "But what does that do? It's not strong enough, is it? Rotating the wagon, remember?"

"That's not where the energy comes from. All the power does is make it possible for the joined stones to pull themselves apart to opposite sides of the framework. Once it's been set up, then if you focus enough power on the edge of the bond, it rips apart the rest of the bond and destroys the stones, like one rock starting an avalanche. The bond bursting, according to the book, is what creates the explosion. Apparently there's nothing left afterward."

"Easy to join," Zandaril said, "Hard to break, destruction when it breaks. The crossbow string shatters."

"That's it. I don't know why that works, maybe it'll be explained further on, but that's the principle."

"Can you disarm them, once they're set, like uncocking a crossbow?"

"Not by magic. You'd have to physically remove the trigger or the bound stones."

"This is very good," Zandaril said. "You make progress."

Penrys held up her hand. "I still don't know how the mirror communication worked. That's something completely different. And if one of those devices was attached to the mirror, how did Veneshjug or whoever it was keep from triggering it at the same time? And why didn't he just blow it up right then, and kill the officers, decapitate the command of the expedition?"

"Maybe the device was on the storage box for the mirror, not the mirror itself, where it might have been noticed," Zandaril said.

Penrys turned that thought over in her mind. "You could be right—that would fit."

She looked down at the book. "But I still have a lot to do. I have to read through both of these books before we go tonight and memorize as much as I can. I don't dare take them with us, and I can't leave them behind—they're priceless, whole new approaches to physical magic. What they would give for these in the Collegium! But if we're caught with them…"

Tak Tuzap spoke up from his corner. "If they catch you, you're in trouble anyway. You don't look right. They'll know you don't belong."

Zandaril said, "He's right. If we don't get out, it doesn't matter. If we do, you'll want them with you. Keep them in your pack, with the stones. Maybe you'll get to use them."

I don't want to leave them behind, that's for sure.

"One thing, though," she said. "You told me there weren't Rasesni wizards, but it's not true. These books aren't beginners' work, they're sophisticated and clever. There's nothing like them in the Collegium."

"What does the front matter of the book say?"

She turned to the beginning. "The language is Rasesni, or I couldn't read it, drawing on the locals here. It's an older version of the language that they speak. There's a date." She pulled the knowledge of the current year in the Rasesni dating system from the occupiers in the village. "Seems to be about twenty-five years old. Name but no description of the author, no information about his sources." She sniffed at the leather binding. "Doesn't smell all that new."

She looked up at Zandaril. "This one's all about experimental techniques. The other one's theory."

Penrys pulled the second book out of the pack. "I haven't tackled this one yet, but I've got to. Different author, three years more recent, no context."

"Doesn't make any sense. We'd have heard of wizards there before now. I think that's why Yenit Ping is so alarmed."

"Look at the titles," she said. "Venesha Zhablig, Venesh's Secret Way" and "Venesha Chos, The Glories of Venesh." What are the Rasesni religions like?"

"Gods jealous of each other, with dedicated worshipers. Priests everywhere, and the Hand of the Mountains—that's the name of a group of hill-tribes—enforcing their will. Assassins, secret cults."

Zandaril's hand stroked his shaven cheeks. "We've heard rumors about this, in *sarq*-Zannib. Every now and then a small caravan returns through the High Pass in Song Em with news of a wizard born in Neshilik. Twice that I know of the child has been found and sent to us for fostering, but usually they live their lives untrained or, worse, they are discovered and killed. And there is much Rasesni blood in Neshilik."

He slapped the books on the table. "No one can visit Rasesdad—foreigners are not allowed, outside the ports. The summons from Kigali seemed like an opportunity to learn more about this. And now we *know* they have wizards."

"And esoteric knowledge, apparently. Maybe no one's supposed to know about their wizards. I guess that's part of what we have to find out," she said, as she rotated her head on her neck until the joints cracked.

Sitting back down on the bench, she picked up the first book again and opened it where she'd slipped a bit of straw to marked the page. "Back to work."

Zandaril spent much of the afternoon dozing in preparation for their travel in the evening. Part of the time he lay awake in the loft, casually monitoring Penrys's activity below. It was quiet—she'd laid aside actual experiments and was trying to read as much as she could before they had to pack up and go. The rain gradually subsided, giving way to an autumn chill.

She'd invited him to watch over her shoulder, as it were, but little of what she skimmed made much sense to him, not without her knowledge of physical magic.

And the puzzle she presented to him…

When she forgot herself in her work, it made him smile, much as he tried to hide it from her. Her enthusiasm was infectious—there was an actual gleam in her eye. It woke an echo in him, a memory of being a young *irghulaj*, a student. But she wasn't that young, not really. She seemed to him about his own age, or perhaps a little less.

It's the lack of memory, the shallowness of her remembered life. Things are still fresh to her.

His smile faded. *The truth is, she scares me, too.*

It made him uncomfortable with her. Her casual experimentation with physical magic spoke to his own childhood, when it was made clear to him that a proper Zan had nothing to do with physical magic, that it was both shameful and destructive.

Well, they were right about destruction. He was beginning to doubt them about the rest, however. He suspected he could learn, if she'd teach him, and he thought he wanted to. *Why not be as strong as possible, in all the ways I can?*

This was his *tulqiqa*, his wandering time, when he'd finished with his teachers and sought to create a *nayith*, a masterwork of his own. He wanted to see if one could work together in an organized way with other wizards. His own countrymen weren't interested in the question, and so he'd looked for foreigners with different ways, to learn from them. He'd postponed settling with his clan, finding a wife, taking students.

And fate had given him something very strange—a wizard who might be able to work with him, but was nothing like his countrymen. She was stronger than he was, in magic, and more broadly educated. *In just three years. Why can't we build something like the Collegium and learn as quickly? Or maybe it was her special gifts.*

She was his student, as much as he was hers, and he understood that relationship.

But was she even human? *You forget, when you look at her, but those ears, those animal ears…* His fingers twitched involuntarily and his mouth quirked. *I wonder what they feel like. Are they moving around all the time under that hair, swiveling to catch the sounds?*

And there was something else, he was sure of it, even if it wasn't the tail he'd joked about. Eventually she'd tell him, he thought, when she was less self-conscious about her differences. *You wanted foreign, you did, and that's surely what you got.*

Crippled, she is, with that chain around her neck, as long as she thinks it so. He remembered her bitter words that day in the wagon, when she was exhausted. *Is that all she wants, to know her own story?*

He felt her fascination with something she was reading. *No, not so—the love of learning surely drives her.*

As it does me.

CHAPTER 25

Penrys clucked her tongue to get Tak Tuzap's attention. He pulled his horse to a stop and turned his head back to look at her, and Zandaril stopped behind them both.

"Three men around the corner, not moving. One of them's Wan Nozu," she told them.

"That's the mill," Tak said.

She surveyed the village again, most of the people behind them now. The Rasesni minds seemed unaware of their presence. Beyond the mill in front of them, there were few villagers.

"The sooner we're off the road, the better," Zandaril commented from the rear. The tension pull his deep voice higher.

Tak took the remark as an order and led their little troop forward. Their horses' hooves were muffled by the dirt, but the harness clinked and the leather creaked. When they rounded the corner, a gust of wind blew wet leaves down upon their heads, and Penrys smelled the warning of winter in their scent.

There were lights showing, in the three-story mill building, and Penrys thought she heard the rumble of the wheel that must be there, on the far side where the stream flowed.

Wan Nozu waited by the turnoff, his pack resting on a boulder to keep it out of the muck. "This way," he said. "They're waiting for you."

He shouldered his pack and led them along the side of the structure, down the slope, until he reached a stable door, built into the underside at the lowest part of the building.

There were many stalls but few animals. A wagon shed with external doors was visible at the end of the main aisle, through an open doorway.

The other two men awaited them there. One was clearly the miller himself, as his brawny arms and air of proprietorship attested. The other bore a strong resemblance to him. *His son, I expect. I hope they don't suffer from helping us.*

"No names, I think," the miller said.

Zandaril dismounted. "Yes, that's a good idea. Can't tell what we don't know, can we?" He unfastened and lifted the double load down from his mule's pack-frame and separated it into the pack he would carry, and the one he would leave behind.

"A gift to you," he said, waving at all their mounts. "Whatever's left in the loads, too."

Penrys dismounted and handed her reins to the younger man. He stared at her features for a moment before taking the horse.

She'd arranged her own pack and lifted it to her shoulders. *Take the books and power-stones or leave them here to moulder away? Too late to change my mind now.*

The books were wrapped in her spare clothing, but she still felt the awkwardness of their unyielding shape and the weight of the two small bags of stones.

Wan Nozu pointed at two cloaks, draped over the wall of an unoccupied stall. "We guessed at the length for you two. See if we got it right."

Penrys picked up the shorter one. It was a dull brown, of a worn, densely woven wool that still smelled faintly of lanolin, despite its age. When she flung it over her shoulders, pack and all, and fastened it at her throat, it hung to mid calf.

The miller thrust an old front-brimmed leather hat at her. She was puzzled for a moment, and he shoved it on her head and drew up the hood over it. *Ah. The brim keeps the edge of the hood from dripping on my face.*

She nodded her thanks, and took the hat off to see about stuffing something inside to make it fit better.

"One more thing," the miller said. "I don't like to see you walk off all unarmed like that."

"Pa, they're wizards," the son objected.

"Says who?" his father retorted. "They never said anything, did they?"

He glared at his son, and then turned back to them.

"These are for you." He pointed at the thick walking sticks, leaning up against the wall. They were just well-hewn lengths of common hickory, but Tak Tuzap walked over and picked up a shorter one, clearly intended for him, with apparent delight. He stood next to Wan Nozu, and unconsciously mimicked his stance as he waited for the two wizards to finish.

Penrys commented unobtrusively to Zandaril. **Look at the two of them.**

He glanced over. **Best thing for him. We may have to leave in a hurry, and this way the two of them can get each other back here.**

"Y'know," the miller said, "I can't say the beasts will still be here when you return."

Zandaril shrugged. "We understand—do what you need to."

He added, quietly. "If any of our goods remain when you see these two again, see that they get the benefit, will you?"

The miller looked at the headwoman's nephew and the boy, and nodded. "We'll see the lad has a home if he makes it back here."

"That's all we can ask," Penrys said. "Stay out of trouble, and we were never here."

"You looked like you were sorry to see those mules go," Penrys said, as they scuffed through the wet leaves afoot, headed north. "I thought you didn't like them. Change your mind?"

"Did you see how well they held up on the crossing, with nothing but the grazing? They looked like they could go on forever." Zandaril hesitated. "Never worked with them before, hardly ever see them in *sarq*-Zannib. I wonder what sort of mules our own horses would make. Winter-hardy ones, maybe."

Tak Tuzap broke in, "You oughta like 'em—that's our own bloodline, you know, the donkeys in 'em."

He swaggered a bit. "All the traders working in Neshilik used to buy our mules. The army won't—they want to breed their own, so we sell the donkeys. Only the jacks, of course, so they have to keep coming back. They like the ones in Neshilik best."

Zandaril grunted thoughtfully and Penrys shared a glance with Tak.

"Last time you looked like that," she told Zandaril, "you were making plans to get those horses of Veneshjug's away from me. What's the matter—not happy without something to look after?"

"I do miss my herds, it's true. Not just the horses back with the squadron, but the ones my *nurti*, my second sister, has charge of, while I'm gone."

Wan Nozu spoke up. "Do you have many animals, Wizard-chi? I understand the Zannib take them up and back to their winter pastures."

"Well, much of our wealth is in herds, but I'm a bachelor still, so my mother's family holds them for me instead of my wife. My second sister is in charge of the family herds on the *taridiqa*. After all, some of them will be hers when she marries, so she takes responsibility for their well-being."

Zandaril smiled to himself, then told Wan Nozu. "She's very good about it, very serious. The best in our family in this generation. I'm always a bit afraid I'll come home sometime and find her married, outside the clan maybe, and someone else looking after the herds."

He waggled a finger at Tak. "I'd hate to to have to face any new brother-in-law tough enough that she couldn't scare him away."

Penrys laughed. "That bad, is she?"

"No, that determined."

"Then you'd be better off being the one to bring any husband strong enough for her into the family, right? Get him on your side first."

They all laughed softly, as the night air chilled around them.

From the secluded rock overhang that Wan Nozu had led them to, off the road, Penrys could feel the people of Gonglik over the rise. Even well past midnight, the glow of lights in some of the buildings reflected off the overcast sky, visible to their cold, fireless camp.

A thousand or more people were there in town, and many were Rasesni.

"There could be a dozen wizards there for all I can tell,"she told Zandaril in frustration. "I can't go through that many of them, carefully, and there's a risk I might alert any wizard, like you did with the false herdsman."

"Can't they find us easy, out here? No one around?" Zandaril asked.

"Yeah, but they have to be looking for us. Why should they think to?"

Zandaril's lips thinned. "No security in that."

"Got a better idea?"

Wan Nozu and Tak Tuzap were scouting on their own in town, trying to discover what restrictions the invaders had placed on the locals. Tak, in particular, was hoping to check the homes of his uncle's associates, to see if there was anyone safe they could approach for news.

Penrys's imagination had no difficulty painting a picture of what might happen to them if they were caught, and it did nothing for the shortness of her temper that she was forced to wait while they took the risk.

"Look,"she said, "Realistically, what's the most we can accomplish for Chang? We've heard the same wizard rumors here that he did outside. If we find a wizard, however distant, we can confirm their presence, and then get out, back over the Old Ferry trail, the way we came. Preferably before our horses disappear."

Zandaril was shaking his head well before she finished. "Never works the way you plan it. And not very useful for Chang, either. Best is we find out who the leader is, overall, what he wants, and the leader and number of wizards, and what they can do."

He paused, struck by a thought. "No, best is we kill leader and wizards."

She rolled her eyes.

"Why not plan big?" he said, with a suspicion of a smile. "Besides, worst is not so good. Worst is we are discovered and never get back."

"No," Penrys said, "Worst is we get captured, and *then* we discover who leads the wizards and he peels our minds of everything we know."

That stopped the conversation for a while.

Penrys made an effort to lighten her mood. "At least, if we don't come back, Chang will assume we found wizards."

She slid her eyes to catch the expression on Zandaril's face. "See? There's more than one way to send a message."

"Help me stay awake," Zandaril said, as he nudged Penrys whose head had started to droop as she leaned against a rock.

Her head bobbed up again and she rubbed her eyes. "What do you suggest?"

"Tell me about the Collegium, maybe." It seemed like a good moment to try and get her talking, he thought. Harder for her to dodge the questions when they were stuck together like this, just the two of them.

"What do you want to know?" He could hear the reserve in her voice, though it was too dark to make out her face.

"Well, what did you do there? Can you tell me?"

She paused. "I wanted to teach, the things I could do that they didn't know. I thought they could learn, like you are learning, but they wouldn't have it. Not even with Vylkar as my sponsor, and he was part of the governing body.

"So he arranged a different job for me, cataloguing the new works, rescuing the old ones that weren't indexed yet. It was supposed to be a dull job, a thankless job, but it left me on my own to read everything I could."

She leaned back on her elbows, on the ground. "The books that had hardly ever been opened… you wouldn't believe it. Languages I didn't know, languages no one knew. I made friends of two of the elderly librarians—they weren't too sure who I was, exactly, or what I was doing there, but they were happy to have someone else to talk to. They helped me find a workroom to call my own, showed me where to get supplies. And so I began to experiment."

Zandaril looked down on her where she lay, dim in the grass. "What sorts of experiments?"

"Things the books suggested. Old research projects that fizzled out. Requests from merchants—the Collegium turned down most of those, but I rescued a couple and worked on them. You see, the merchants expected to try things, and to fail, but to keep trying until something worked. That's what they were used to, in business. Some of them, anyway.

"They didn't understand that attitude, at the Collegium. You were supposed to focus on things that already worked, and make them just a little bit better, rather than set off after an unproven hunch."

Her voice quieted. "I had personal notebooks documenting all the things I tried, and new projects to work on."

"Where are they?"

"Back in my room, I imagine," she said, "if they haven't been thrown away by now."

"But they'll have missed you. Won't they be searching? Your friends?"

"Vylkar must wonder, of course. His mother, too. I joined them for holidays, sometimes. They would feel… responsible."

She stopped, and Zandaril wondered if she would continue.

"Friends, well… I'd scared some of them and the word spread. It's funny—they like foreigners in Ellech, not like most places I've heard about. They find them interesting, and not that many make it upstream to Tavnastok, to the Collegium. But conversations still stopped when I walked into a room, and they'd make jokes about how good my hearing must be, with those ears of mine."

She said, levelly. "I made them uncomfortable."

"And so they did the same to you," Zandaril commented. "And no surprise, an unexpected marvel in their midst."

"More like an unexpected monster," she muttered.

CHAPTER 26

"They're back."

Penrys twitched awake at Zandaril's nudge. She could smell dawn in the air and the birds had started their aubade, but there was still very little light. She rolled out from under her one blanket and her cloak and pulled on her boots.

Wan Nozu and Tak Tuzap crept out of the woods and joined them, under the shelter of the rock ledge. They were tired, but she could see from their grins that they'd been successful.

"We did it!" Tak's boast was whispered but intent, and Wan Nozu looked down upon him indulgently. Penrys could feel just as much excitement from the young man as the boy, and she bit the inside of her cheek to keep from smiling at them and offending their pride.

Zandaril pulled cold meat and bread from his pack, courtesy of their hosts in Lupmikya, and thrust it at them, patting the ground in an invitation to sit. "Eat. Talk. Take turns."

Tak deferred to his elder and cut bread and meat for them both, while Wan Nozu began his report.

"It was really late, but the taverns were still open," he said. "Not like the last time I was there—this time most of the houses were dark and quiet. No music… I remember there was music all the time, whenever I came. Not like home."

He yawned and shook his head. "Sorry. Anyway, I went and listened to the talk in three different places, and Tak Tuzap went looking for his uncle's friends. I'll let him tell that part.

"They've got their army camped right on Harlin, where the river overflows in the spring. Except it's not really a proper army, any more. They say that lots of the fighters stayed in Song Em, with their tribes, and only the real core came up through Wechinnat."

Penrys said, "Which is maybe why there aren't very many on the ground in the small villages like Lupmikya."

Wan Nozu nodded. "The top man, the Commander, is a fellow called Tlobsung. He's out there with the army. They've got the Gates blocked, like Tak said."

"So who are all the Rasesni in town, then?" Zandaril said.

"All sorts of folk. They've taken over the temple buildings, even the old ones, and changed the names back to the Rasesni names. They're full of priests, everyone says. Not sure what's happened to the priests that used to be there."

He looked uncertainly at Tak. "Probably nothing good. They control the warehouses and run supplies out to Harlin. Many of the big *samke* have people quartered on them—officers mostly. Even the smaller compounds have someone."

Tak swallowed another mouthful, and burst in. "They brought craftsmen and all kinds of people. Families, too. It's like a whole 'nother town."

"That's right," Wan Nozu said. "It's real crowded, even counting the locals who got away. And they left the old people in charge in the *zopgep*, the town council, only they report to Tlobsung, now."

"They're acting more like armed refugees than an invading army," Penrys commented to Zandaril.

"What's the mood of the townsfolk like?" she asked Wan Nozu.

"There've been killings, uncontrolled ones like Tak Tuzap's uncle, and some ugly stuff, but the people are saying it's not so bad, not what they expected, not like last time, maybe there's a way to keep doing business if they keep their heads down."

"Hmm." Penrys waved a hand at them to tell them to focus on their breakfast for a minute while she thought about it.

"D'ya think something's driving them, pushing them out?" she asked Zandaril.

"They don't have much farming land. Mratsanag, it's very large, but you can't grow a lot of people on mountains. They've got flat coast land further west, on either side of the mountains, but they've got neighbors there, too. I wonder if something's happened."

He turned to Wan Nozu. "Are these hill people, or just the folk from Nagthari?"

Wan Nozu swallowed his bite. "Mostly hill people, the old tribes, down in the Song Em. The ones in town are more…

civilized. At least, the tavern folk said they were like the ones they drove back to Nagthari, before."

Tak Tuzap piped up. "We know what they want. I found the kitchen folk awake at Kor Pochang's place. He used to trade with Uncle Tak and he's on the *zopgep*, the council. I scratched at the door and they let me in. He's got an officer there, but they got him a message without the officer seeing, and we had a long talk in the scullery, with the cook standing guard at the door.

"He said what the *zopgep* hears is that they've come to stay, that they had to come. That's why they brought families and hill-tribes. They mean to live here, and keep peace with us, if they can, or fight if they must. The council's afraid of being caught between the full might of Kigali and whatever's behind the Rasesni—they're fortifying the Gates as best they can, and there're supposed to be patrols running all over the Craggies in the north."

"Why only the north?" Penrys asked Zandaril.

"You can't get an army over the Red Wall, and below Song Em is more mountains and the empty *sarq*-Zannib, but the Craggies aren't very high or rugged. North of there is still Kigali, for a while, but the disputed Lomat is just beyond, and the west end of the Craggies joins Garshnag at the Horn."

At Penrys's puzzled look, he elaborated. "Mratsanag, the Ram's Horn—the mountain spine west of here—ends in a pincer of mountains. The south range is Damsnag, the Right Horn, and Garshnag, the Left, is to the north. Between them, they shelter Nagthari, "Between the Horns." The last eastern peak in Garshnag is called Nakshadzam, the Horn's Tip—you can see it from a long distance. That's where Linit Kungzet is, under the Horn, where the upper Seguchi crosses into Nagthari."

"So, what are you thinking? Some threat coming over the northern part of the mountains and spilling into the Craggies?"

"Maybe. Something like that." Zandaril said. "Must be big and scary if the hill-tribes have been displaced. Raiders out of Nagthari are one thing. Outsiders haven't seen the hill-tribes for generations.

"Or it could just be the Kigali army they're afraid of. If they can hold them at the Gates, what's to stop them coming in behind them, from the north?"

He paused for a moment.

"If they're really smart, maybe they want to sit tight in Neshilik and have whatever's behind them meet the Kigali army, north of the Craggies. That would be very, very clever of this Tlobsung, to bait a trap for his enemy and then duck out of the way of the big fight."

"And if Kigali wins, and they haven't been too bloody here, maybe they can work something out," Penrys said. "But it's not to their benefit to tell the Kigaliwen what's coming, is it, or they might not be willing to do the work for them.

"Of course, this is all guesswork. Still, they've done what they could to reduce Kigali's response. At least, to delay it. They tried to stop Chang's advance, but it didn't work. That's maybe as far east as they could send someone in the time they had. How did they know what to try and how Kigali would first react?"

She glanced over at Wan Nozu, and he stopped himself from his next bite.

"Which leads me to my next question, what about wizards?"

Wan Nozu looked uneasy. "You have to know, *minochi*, the townsfolk, none of us—we've never *seen* a wizard before. Don't know what they can do. Don't even know what one would look like. I mean, you two look like foreigners, sure, but not like *wizards*, if you understand." He eyed her nervously.

"It's all right, we won't be offended," Penrys told him.

He looked doubtful, but continued. "Well, there was a lot of talk about them. Very quiet talk, looking around the room, as though their neighbors might have turned into wizards overnight. It was unsettling, that."

Zandaril said, "More likely they wondered about their neighbors informing on them."

"I suppose. Still, they acted like there were wizards all over, that any one of the Rasesni in town could be one. There was talk that they'd taken back the old temple school in Kunchik, north, over the bridge, and filled it with sinister folk."

"I've got a name," Tak said. "Kor said that the council had met someone Tlobsung valued. Some thought he was a political adviser, but there were others who whispered 'wizard.' Zongchas, they said."

Penrys looked at Zandaril with a raised eyebrow.

"It's a good Rasesni name," he said. At her level look, he spread his hands and added, "Yes, I know I said there were no Rasesni wizards. I must be wrong, I admit it."

"Looks to me like they're getting their wizards *organized*, just the way you admire," she said, deadpan, and he glared at her.

"Did you two hear about any other foreigners?" Zandaril asked.

Wan Nozu and Tak Tuzap exchanged looks, and Wan Nozu shook his head. "Just Rasesni, and they don't look much different from us, especially here in Neshilik."

"Except they don't wear braids," Tak said. He laughed. "They all look like soldiers that way."

"Did they describe what it was the wizards did?" Penrys asked Wan Nozu.

"No. I thought that was funny. I expected to hear about things. It's like you two, I haven't seen you *do* anything, um, wizardly."

Tak stared at him as if amazed at his daring, and Penrys chuckled.

"It's not all that impressive, most of the time. Why, would you like to see something?"

Zandaril gave her a hard look and she shrugged.

Wan Nozu faltered. "If you'd like, *minochi*. It'd be something to tell my children about, after."

"I'll see what I can arrange," she said, dryly.

"You know what we need to do?" Penrys asked Zandaril. She spoke softly, to keep from waking Wan Nozu and Tak Tuzap who were catching up on their lost sleep in the middle of the day.

"What?" Zandaril said.

"Well, we can't sneak into Tlobsung's tent and read his orders, especially if he's the man on top. Right?"

Zandaril nodded.

She waved her hands as she spoke. "Chang's other scouts will have a lot more to tell him about military preparedness than we can. No, what we can do that they can't is look for whatever might be driving the Rasesni to invade, find out if that's what's happening and what it's like. That's the part he really needs to know."

"What, go west?" he said, "Up into the hills?"

"We can dodge their scouts easily enough." She tapped her forehead meaningfully. "And we should be able to detect whatever it is from a distance. Then, if we go north, through the Craggies, we'll come back out to the land between the rivers again, right?"

"And get back to Chang that way," Zandaril confirmed. "It would take weeks, maybe, living rough."

"Depends how close the pursuit is. If we go straight north, the shortest way, then we only have to go west far enough to confirm it. Then we get out as fast as we can."

She watched his face, unwilling to invade his privacy further to touch his mind and see what he really felt about the proposal.

He cocked his head at their sleeping companions and rumbled, "Can't take them with us."

"And that's a good thing. They won't like it, though."

"Wan Nozu will understand, I think," Zandaril said.

Penrys broke the news in the afternoon, when they sat and ate a late lunch together.

"It's the right thing for us to do," she told Tak Tuzap, firmly. "And you can be of no help to us while we do it. Better you go back to Lupmikya with Wan Nozu."

The boy looked away from her. She could read the resentment and rejection in the set of his shoulders, but he surprised her—he didn't protest.

"I'll go back to Kor Pochang's house," he said, squaring his back. "I can be more useful there. Maybe he can help me with my uncle's property."

Wan Nozu looked over at him in admiration. "Won't that be dangerous?"

"No more than waiting in Lupmikya to be a hostage."

Zandaril made a seated bow to both of them. "We are greatly in your debt for the risks you've taken and the help you've given us."

Penrys rose and brushed off the crumbs from her breeches. She'd already confirmed that no one else was close enough to hear them.

"I owe you something 'fore you go," she said.

She surreptitiously fingered the power-stones she'd slipped into her pocket, and whisked the leather cap off of Wan Nozu's head, spinning it up and out of his reach.

"So you wanted to see some magic, did you?"

She kept it dancing between Wan Nozu and Tak Tuzap for several minutes, smiling at the boyish shouts of laughter, then dropped it to hover before Zandaril's face, evading his efforts to grab it, before finally settling it delicately back onto Wan Nozu's head, letting it flutter one last time as it landed.

"There. That's something a wizard can do."

CHAPTER 27

Three days later, Penrys and Zandaril were following the rough trails in the Craggies, headed northwest. As Tak Tuzap had advised them to, they'd stolen a boat to cross the Seguchi above the series of stepped waterfalls and rapids that gave Gonglik both its name, The Steps, and its industry as a mover of goods.

Tak had warned them there would be no trading trails that far to the west on the north side of the river and Penrys had grown weary of the rough and trackless terrain. It wasn't truly steep, and you could walk over most of it without aid—though she was grateful for the walking staff given her by the anonymous miller—but it would present a serious barrier to any army with wagons to move.

They traveled by day, using their mind-sense to look for anyone within range, but Zandaril distrusted relying on that entirely. "People can be seen from further away than we can sense, if the conditions are right," he'd said, and she was forced to agree with him. They tried to keep to the interior of the hills, but water was easier to find on the outer, and lower slopes, and it was harder to walk invisibly in daylight there.

The sky was overcast, threatening more autumn rains. They trudged and stumbled along, trying to avoid ankle-turning rocks.

"How far to the Horn is it, d'ya think?" she asked Zandaril, just to hear the sound of another voice in this lonely place.

"Not sure. They say you can see it from all over the northwest corner of Wechinnat. Start looking tomorrow, I think. That way."

He lifted his arm and pointed west and a little south.

Penrys stared off in that direction, but it was just a featureless blue haze. She knew the second highest range of mountains in the world were not too far beyond the horizon, but you couldn't tell that from here.

They'd lost part of the morning taking shelter when they'd felt two Rasesni scouts somewhere on the ridges northeast of them. Penrys had taken the opportunity while waiting to pull out the second book in their language and read further, taking advantage of the connection with them that made it possible. It was frustrating, to have to steal moments like this. Fully half the book remained unread, and any Rasesni-literate contact she had might be her last. Still, at least it wasn't raining today, the way it did two days ago, when she'd had to forgo another chance at it.

There was more of a chill in the air, even in these lower hills, than down by the river. The cloak was welcome now more for its warmth, than as a disguise.

Zandaril interrupted her thoughts. "We have food for maybe two weeks, if we're careful. We're almost that far from Chang, I think. If we don't turn around soon…"

"I know, I know." A hawk screamed overhead, and she looked up at it, almost tripping with her next step. "Just two more days, and I'll call this theory unproven and head back."

She smiled over at Zandaril. "At least the packs get lighter, the more we eat."

A rain shower passed through on the next day, in the early afternoon, and washed the air of its accustomed haze. When Penrys shouldered her pack again and took her first steps, watching her feet to avoid stumbling, she almost ran into Zandaril who had stopped, suddenly.

"There," he said. "There's Nakshadzam, the Horn's Tip." And he moved aside, so she could see.

Back-lit by the sun, a dark ridge lay athwart their distant path. The higher end was to the south, jutting up above the plain of the upper Seguchi. South of that gap, she could just barely make out the tip of the Damsnag range framing the other side.

She'd thought the Horn would be a single peak, but it ran north and south for a few miles along a smooth ridgeline, only slightly lower at its northern end, high above the hills of the Craggies that piled up at its feet.

"Nagthari's through the gap, there," Zandaril said.

She looked for the fort, Linit Kungzet, somewhere near the river and the gap, but the base of the Horn was blocked from her view by the shoulders of the lower slope she stood on.

Penrys cast her mind out as far as she could, in all directions. The clarity in the air was deceptive, and the distances were more than they seemed. It seemed unnatural that no people stirred in this landscape, as far as her mind reached.

Zandaril had shared her cast and felt her disappointment.

"Eyes see further than the mind, sometimes, whatever books may tell us," he said.

This would be the last day of the search, and Zandaril was relieved by the thought. Tomorrow morning they would set their faces east again, back to Chang and his soldiers.

The ridge of the Horn was close enough now in the late morning light to make out its ragged edges. It wasn't the sheer barrier it had seemed from a distance, but something eroded, with rough trails. Whatever stone composed it was completely different from the ancient weathered Craggies, like an intrusion placed by giant hands.

He looked back at Penrys, and surprised a smile on her face which wakened one of his own. "One more day," he said.

"Let's go north and get out of the Craggies," she said, "before turning east. We'll make better time, and we're less likely to hit Tlobsung's scouts beyond the hills."

"Why don't we swing north now? We could start angling that way."

She nodded, and he turned right, climbing upward on the broken scree, keeping the Horn on his left. It seemed immediately less oppressive to remove that wall from his path, and his heart lightened. The air was chilly but pleasant, drawing off the heat of his exertion.

He reached the top of his local ridge and stopped to let his breath recover. When Penrys joined him, she paused for her usual scan of the area.

"Hsst!"

Startled, he did his own scan and felt two people moving, north of them and not far away. His eyes flicked around their surroundings, seeking a place to hide, and found a rocky depression, a hole at the base of two trees, partially masked by bushes. There wasn't room for both of them inside the hole, but they hugged the ground in and around it and covered themselves with their cloaks.

The two men passed east, out of range, and Zandaril began to pick himself off the ground when Penrys grabbed his arm. "More of them," she whispered.

He sensed two more pairs of men, both north of them. *We mustn't mind-speak.* He tapped his forehead and shook his head, and she nodded in understanding. She moved her mouth to his ear and whispered, "Rasesni. Not the same as the ones in town."

They hadn't thought it through well enough, he realized. They forgot they'd be putting themselves in the path of whatever followed the invaders.

He flattened himself, partially covering Penrys with his drab cloak, a better match for the ground than her brown. She muttered into his ear, "Think like a tree."

It was impossible to still his mind. He tried to make himself part of the ground, but Penrys's shoulder was warm beneath his chest, and lumpy, and his nose was smashed against the back of her head. He found it difficult to ignore the scent of her hair. *Not now, this isn't the time to think of that.*

He closed his eyes, but that just made him focus on his body, so he opened them again and stared at the ground, a couple of inches away, and began counting, slowly.

Nothing happened, and he started to doze off.

What have we here?

A strange mind-voice rattled him awake, and he felt Penrys twitch beneath him. He cast his mind out and felt three pairs of men converging on them, and then he couldn't feel anything with his mind. When he tried to get up, he found he couldn't move.

CHAPTER 28

Penrys's arms wouldn't obey her, and she felt Zandaril's panic at her back. She couldn't speak, and she suspected whoever this was could hear her mind-speech if she tried to reach Zandaril privately.

He knows where we are, and if he has mind-speech he knows what we are, too. Might as well try to protect ourselves. I've got to play the part of an apprentice from sarq-Zannib. Trapped by the invasion, just trying to get out in an unwatched direction.

After a few minutes, she heard the rustle of bushes and two pairs of feet crossed her line of sight. The pressure holding her immobile released, and she felt Zandaril being hauled up off of her. She scrambled up on her own without waiting for their hands, and raised her mind shield, for all the good she suspected it would be.

"Sorry, *jarghal*," she said to Zandaril, with an apologetic whine, staring at him meaningfully. "Looks like this wasn't the right way to go after all, to get away from them." She spoke in Kigali-*yat*, hoping that would be a common language shared by whoever these people were. She didn't dare use their native language, since Zandaril wouldn't be able to.

His eyes narrowed briefly in puzzlement, and then he protested fussily to the man who had hold of his arm. "There's no need for that. My *nal-jarghal* and I were just trying to leave Wechinnat and get out of the way. None of our business, this is. *Sarq-Zannib* has no standing in Kigali affairs."

The two men grinned at them. They were bearded, with shaggy hair, and dressed in dusty brown leathers. Each had a longbow on his shoulder and small throwing axes fastened to his belt, and one had a short sword. Their jackets were trimmed with dirty fur.

"That's for our Voice to decide, ain't it," the larger and grubbier one said, answering Zandaril in badly accented Kigali-*yat*. "He told us to fetch you two." The other one pulled a stout cord from the bag tied to his waist, and proceeded to tie Zandaril's crossed wrists, in front of him. He left Zandaril's pack in place.

He cut the cord, and used the remainder on Penrys. She tried to take up as much space with her wrists as she could while he tied the knots, but he yanked the cord tight as if he'd done it a hundred times before. *Maybe there's a reason we didn't find anyone out here, except the scouts on both sides. What were we thinking?*

The two remaining pairs she'd sensed appeared at about the same time. Her captor called out, in his own language, "Hey, got a bit of rope on ya?" and one of them volunteered the coil on his belt.

"Don't ya be cuttin' that now," he said, and their captor adeptly solved the problem by tying one end to Penrys's bonds, hitching in Zandaril's with a gap of about six feet between them, and tossing the remainder of the coil back.

"Ya want the rope? Then you can lead 'em."

The donor curled his lip sourly, but took hold of the rope and yanked Zandaril forward. He stumbled and almost fell, but Penrys grabbed his arm, and was pulled after him. Five of the men spread out on either side of the one with the rope, disappearing into the woods on either side while he stuck to whatever path he could find.

It didn't take long for Penrys to exhaust herself, trying to maintain her balance without her hands free, and forced at something close to a jog trot up the rough trails. Her throat was dry and she couldn't keep from coughing, hoping to clear it of the dust. Zandaril was clearly having a similar struggle.

The chill in the air helped. She tried to ignore her discomforts and concentrated on keeping her shield up. She couldn't feel anyone testing it.

This Voice her captors mentioned must be the one who had mind-spoken to her, and presumably to Zandaril, too. A wizard. These men spoke a different dialect of Rasesni than the people she'd already tapped. They looked rougher than she'd imagined.

Once, when Zandaril turned his head, she'd cocked her head at the man with the rope and raised an eyebrow, and Zandaril had mouthed the words "hill-tribes." Was the wizard who'd found them the same, or something else?

She dreaded being a captive like this, but at least they were headed to the place with the answers.

They paused after a couple of hours, and she collapsed to the ground, her chest heaving. Three of the five men came back to join them. One of them offered water from a clay bottle on his waist, getting a good feel of her while he did it. She ignored him and drank as much as she could get, silently.

Zandaril smiled at her encouragingly afterward, and she nodded back to him.

They had to survive, that was all she had to think about for now. A tug on the rope alerted her, and she struggled up again for another run.

The closer they got to the ridge of the Horn, the more people they encountered. At the base they found an encampment, strangely reminiscent of the expedition's camp out in the plains. Some of the men paused in their work to grin at the running captives, and several threw sticks, hoping to trip them up.

Penrys narrowed her attention to just staying upright, not wanting to fall and be dragged. She thought a broken leg would result in casual death.

All the men she saw had a certain tribal resemblance, and most of them carried bows or had them nearby, whatever else they might arm themselves with. She didn't see any women at all, and she set her mouth grimly as she considered what that might mean for her.

The pace slowed as they pushed through the camp to the base of the ridge. There was a trail up at this point, steep but accessible, following an old fault in the escarpment.

They waited for a man to finish his descent, and Penrys bent forward at the waist, trying to catch her breath. Her legs trembled with exertion.

One step at a time. Don't look up and, whatever you do, don't look down either.

They moved Zandaril up the length of rope so that there was about twelve feet between them, and refastened it.

The owner of the rope protested. "I ain't gonna be tied to 'em going up the Horn. I'll lead, and you all can follow." He hung the gathered coils of the rope around Zandaril's neck, in a gesture of contempt.

Penrys knew Zandaril couldn't understand what he'd said, but the gestures were obvious. With one captor in front and the other five behind, Zandaril started up the rough path, and Penrys followed.

CHAPTER 29

When Penrys found there were no more steps, she stopped and swayed, puzzled. Rude hands behind her pushed her forward and out of the way, and she concentrated on staying upright and letting her vision recover from its reddish, tunnel-focus on her feet.

Over the pounding of her heart she could hear the noise and bustle of many people. When she blinked and raised her head, she discovered the top of the Horn was a wide plateau, sloping down to the west in front of her as if there were no drop-off on that side.

An entire population seemed to be up here, dwarfing the encampment they'd passed through at the base of the ridge to the east. There were so many that they stirred up enough dust from the rocky surface to create a local haze in the air.

Their captors escorted them north along the eastern edge, where a wide space had been left open, not bothering to retrieve the rope from around Zandaril's neck. *Where, after all, could we go?*

There were women up here, she saw, part of the throng that waited, milling about. She saw no tents, and few cooking fires. *Where do they get their water? How long have they been there?*

Quiet. They were very quiet. Unlike their passage through the men down below, Penrys and Zandaril attracted little attention up here—just the occasional raised head and dull stare.

She spared a glance at Zandaril's back, but he seemed well enough, limping a bit. Like her, he was studying the situation. A recently dug channel on their left dodged downslope from the spot they encountered it and terminated in a pool where a line of people waited to fill their water vessels.

Where does the water come from? Somewhere ahead of us. She could smell moisture in the air.

There was a separation in the crowd on the other side of the channel, a gap of a good fifty yards. The people on the far side were different. She spotted few women. All of them, men or women, wore leg shackles, and their clothes were ragged. She could hear the occasional clink of chain. Thirty or more of them stood around a shallow pit, the source of the water channel.

Penrys didn't dare lower her mind-shield to check, but she knew what she was looking at. These were wizards, captive wizards. They were pulling water from the air into the pit.

She felt the hair rise on her forearms. *Were they all Rasesni?* They were too filthy for her to be sure, but she thought so. The quiet crowd she'd seen first seemed to be dressed the same way.

She tugged twice on the rope, surreptitiously, to bring them to Zandaril's attention. He nodded slightly without looking back at her.

Where are they taking us? To add us to the working slaves?

Up ahead, she spotted a cluster of tents.

Their captors walked them to the start of a guarded avenue leading through the tents, leaving them twenty feet from the eastern edge. They parked a man to the north and south, and two more on the open west. The remaining two, the ones they'd first met, trotted up the avenue past the guards and out of sight.

Penrys looked over at Zandaril. His face was set and grim, and he glanced at her and shook his head.

How long have those wizards been captive? How long do they survive?

There was movement, coming back down the tent avenue. A tall young man led the way, dark haired and clean-shaven, his unbraided hair hanging to his shoulders. *Not the same as the scouts at the base of the horn or the people camped up here.*

Behind him strutted their missing captors, with a few others, but Penrys only had eyes for him. The chain around her neck started to throb fiercely.

He casually reached with his mind for Zandaril and tore the protection of her shield from him. "Zan, this time. That's a rare flavor. Maybe we should go south, next."

Then he turned his attention to her, and his eyes widened. "At last!"

He leaned forward, and his shirt gaped open to reveal a thick chain around his neck.

Zandaril felt his borrowed shield ripped apart and his mind riffled for anything of interest. When the tall man withdrew again, his relief was cut short by the sight of the chain around his neck.

Another chained wizard! I will not be owned.

Penrys spun around. "Trust me," she cried. "Run!"

She dashed for the unguarded cliff edge, and he followed before the twelve feet of rope between them could even tighten.

She's right. Death is indeed preferable.

He was not quite even with her before they reached the edge, and she took the first leap into the void, with him following immediately behind.

The air rushed past his face and he lost sight of her, but then his arms were yanked up with all his weight on them, and he looked up to see her above him, with wings outstretched, longer than her body, struggling to support them both and failing.

The best she could achieve was a controlled fall.

As he looked at her wings in amazement, one of them sprouted an arrow and blood, and her face contorted.

Pain exploded in his left calf, and he felt a jerk above him. When he looked up again, there was an arrow sticking through her side.

Her face expressionless now, she stopped flapping and locked her wings into a glide, angled north and east. The ground still approached, but much more slowly.

Too many trees. We need open ground.

She must have had the same thought, for she slid sideways through the air, his own body trailing hers like an anchor, swinging out at the curve on twelve feet of rope.

I hope the knots hold. Wish I could drop the weight of my pack and make it easier.

There was a tail, too, he saw, flaring as it tried to keep the too-heavy mass on course.

How far can we get?

They had started from several thousand feet up but lost quite a bit of height in the first few moments. They were stable now, descending shallowly, but she had to be weakening and there was no way to defeat the pull of the ground. Distance was what they needed, and a safe landing.

Neither of them could reach a knife, with their roped wrists holding them together, so there was nothing he could do to improve her chances alone, but he was strangely relieved to think she could get away on her own, if he was captured again.

He could no longer feel his hands, as the bonds tightened even further.

How far could that chained wizard track them?

He didn't dare mind-speak to her. They were leaving no trail for the scouts, but that would be futile if that wizard could sense them from ten miles away.

The ground of the Craggies fell away below them—not as quickly as they were sinking, but it helped prolong their time in the air. Penrys slid sideways again, this time to the east, choosing to stay in the northern foothills with their pockets of shelter instead of the open plains just north of them.

Zandaril gave a passing thought to the danger of running into Tlobsung's scouts working the Rasesni back trail, then dismissed it. *Rather be captured by them than that slave camp up there.*

Their glide developed a jolt and he looked up. She was just about done, her legs dangling loosely instead of held out to lower her air resistance.

"Hang on," he shouted up to her. "Just find a place to get us down."

His eye caught the glint of water. "This would be good, if it opens up."

She revived a bit and looked more alert. "Bend your legs. It's going to be rough," she called.

The stream he'd spotted dropped over a small waterfall and widened into a pool. The low-water shingle around it made a dry, open gap between the trees, and she circled around it, coming in low over the water until his feet hit the gravel and he tumbled to the ground. His landing forced her down in an uncontrollable sprawl as the rope yanked on her arms, and she crashed with a thud and didn't move. Her wings vanished.

CHAPTER 30

The landing broke off the spent arrow that had been embedded in Zandaril's left calf and it was several moments before he could focus on checking for other damage.

Nothing seemed to be broken, so he fumbled with his bound hands until he could pull his belt knife loose. He held the blade reversed and sawed through the rope, then stripped the bonds from his wrist, dumped off his pack, and hobbled over to Penrys.

She lay in an oddly crumpled position, and he feared for a broken neck, but she was still breathing. He didn't dare try to mind-speak, not knowing the range of the chained wizard who'd captured them. He quickly cut her bonds off and pulled her pack away but left her lying on her side, the undamaged one. The arrow in her right side above her waist was still intact, the point having penetrated all the way through.

He ran his hands over her arms and legs looking for breaks, but found nothing. When he felt under her head, his hand came back bloody.

Where are the wings, and the tail? How do they attach? There were no gaps in the clothing to accommodate them.

He remembered the arrow in one wing. How could he treat that?

Calm down. She's breathing—let's keep it that way. One thing at a time. Side and head. We'll think about what to do for the wing after that.

Hot water. Nothing's spurting blood, so start with that.

He quickly gathered loose branches and built a fire under the overhang of a bushy maple on the margin of the shingle, and shoved his pan into the middle of it to heat water. The leaves of the tree would dissipate the smoke, he hoped, and make it harder to find them.

After checking her pack for a spare shirt, he tore strips off the one she was wearing and made a pad for her head. Then he sat on the gravel by her head with his bad leg thrust out stiff before him, and tilted it up so he could see, pulling her hair aside to assess the damage. He felt a bump on the back of her head, but the blood was superficial.

Don't know how bad it is inside, but nothing I can do about that.

He rigged the pad in place with a strip of rag to hold it, and laid her head back down, trying to position it so as not to apply pressure against the damage while keeping her on her side.

The water was boiling now. He dropped several rags into it, and sat down in front of her to work on the arrow. First he notched the shaft and then broke away the back with the fletching. He whittled the broken end carefully, shaving off every splinter he could find. Then, with a hot water-soaked pad ready, he grabbed the arrow just behind the point and drew it steadily out the front of the wound. A small amount of blood followed it, and leaked out the back, too, but much less than he expected.

He pulled what was left of the shirt up out of the way and probed with his fingers. He thought the arrow might have missed any vital organs, but still, there should be more bleeding. When he pressed down, a little more blood seeped out, then it stopped.

Zandaril had never seen a deep wound that behaved this way before, and it puzzled him. He'd hoped to flush out any scraps of clothing the arrow had driven into the wound, but none appeared. The shirt looked like it had been cleanly slit, but he thought it unlikely that no material had been carried in with the point, and he feared the festering that would result.

He strapped a boiled pad on it, front and back, and considered his next steps. Maybe a poultice would help draw any infection to the surface.

The throbbing of his own wound reminded him that they were both dependent on him, now.

Making himself comfortable near the fire, with the rest of Penrys's stripped shirt, he thought through what he would have to do. His boot had kept the arrow from penetrating very far, but now boot, breeches, and stocking were all involved.

He wanted to save the boot—they might have to walk a long way from here. He picked apart the seam stitches at the back until he had freed up enough to fold the pierced side's flap down and away from the broken stub of the shaft. He had to take the boot off to free the clothing beneath it, but he cursed the necessity as the pressure the boot had applied to the wound site suddenly released and the pain doubled.

He closed his eyes as sweat broke out on his forehead. He swayed and bent his head until the sensation eased and he could see again.

He pulled the leg of his breeches up, and the stocking down—both looked like clean cuts. The arrowhead was embedded in the meat of his calf with about an inch of the shaft behind it, and he was going to have to back it out the way it came, or open his leg up further with his knife, a prospect he wanted to avoid.

The sooner, the better. The boot had kept the flesh from swelling, but it was making up for that now, and any delay would make it harder.

Zandaril grabbed the broken-off end of the shaft with both hands and pulled steadily. Whenever he met resistance, he wobbled it a little to see if it had rotated from the original path.

He could feel the cold sweat dripping off his forehead and the sound of his panting breath seemed deafening, but he didn't stop. When the widest part of the metal broadhead emerged from the wound, he yanked out the rest, dropped the bloody object on the ground, and concentrated on his breathing for a moment.

When he opened his eyes, he reached for his leg and kneaded it to drive as much blood out to clean the wound as he could stand. It bled much more freely than Penrys's arrow wound, but a boiled pad and a rag tied around it finished the work for now.

He pulled the intact lower part of the boot back on his bare foot, in preference to walking without it on the shingle, and thought about the arrow through Penrys's wing.

A glance up at the sun warned him that evening was near, and soon the light would fade. He needed to treat that wound now.

He hobbled back and sat down in front of her, stretching his bad leg out straight. There was no apparent change. Would she listen to him, unconscious, if he couldn't mind-speak her?

"Hey, Penrys, you did well. We got away."

No reaction.

He leaned forward and stroked her cheek with the side of one finger. "I need your help. I need to see your wings again."

She breathed, and he kept stroking her cheek.

"Please, it's important. Wings, you've got to show me your wings. It's me, you can trust me."

She stirred for a moment, and his hopes rose.

"You can do it. It's safe." On impulse, he brought the back of his hand up to her nose to let her smell him, and she sighed.

"Show me your wings, *bikrajti*. I want to see them."

With a sudden displacement of air, the great wings appeared, and the tail.

The feathers were all shades of brown and black and dark amber and smoky gray, colored in bands like an immense eagle. The wings lay half open, draped along the ground and, when he looked closely at how they joined her body, he discovered there was a gap between the ends of the wings and her flesh, as though they were something she put on instead of part of her. The tail was the same, not actually contacting her skin. The clothing she had left moved smoothly between the gaps.

Fix first, investigate later.

He lifted the right wing that the arrow had pierced and spread it out to look for the wound. He found the blood on the feathers but, when he lifted them carefully to locate the wound itself, it eluded him. He searched the whole area but the bloody feathers were the only sign of injury.

He cleaned the feathers and let the wing retract to its original position.

"Mystery upon mystery," he muttered to himself. "And what's your relationship to our chained wizard up there, I wonder?"

It was a cold camp, and a cold meal, after the fire had been extinguished to guard them from discovery.

Before the light faded completely, Zandaril checked all of Penrys's wounds one last time. He'd been forced to wrap some of the soaked rags around his own wrists where the abrasion from the ropes had rubbed his skin raw. When he looked for similar injuries on her arms, he found no marks. He remembered seeing welts earlier when he'd cut her bonds—what had happened to them?

Lifting the edges of the bandages on her side, he was not entirely surprised to see the wounds had visibly narrowed, with no seepage at all.

"No marks," she'd said, back in the wagon, weeks ago, when she'd mentioned not having the signs of childbirth on her. "No marks at all."

He believed her, now. Still, he wasn't so sure that he wanted to move her, not until she woke from that head wound. He leaned over her, and shook her shoulder lightly. "Hey, there. You can put your wings away."

She muttered something, and he did it again. "Go ahead, put the wings away."

Wherever it was they went.

She twitched, and the wings and tail vanished.

A lump in the pocket of her breeches made him curious, and when he investigated he found she was carrying a small stone, like the ones in his shrine. It puzzled him—it was incomplete, the heavy base rounded and unstable. When he supported it in his hand he saw the movement in its form, but the lack of foundation was a defect. Well, a first *had-kighat* wasn't always well-identified. Still, she'd been listening to him. How unexpected, for an outsider.

He pulled the blankets from each pack and laid one on the ground as a pad, rolling her from one side to the other to ease her over it. The other blanket and their cloaks went over them both, as he curled up behind her to share his body heat in the chill autumn air.

CHAPTER 31

Penrys woke to the twittering of birds and the soothing sound of running water. Her face was grateful for the freshness of the cool air, but her body was warm. If she didn't move, nothing hurt.

That must be Zandaril's arm, draped around her, and she could hear a low, rumbling snore at her back.

We're alive. How far did we get? Far enough he hasn't found us yet.

She'd settle for that.

Her head throbbed, but not too badly.

Oh. The wings.

What did Zandaril think of that? *Must not be too bad, or he wouldn't still be here.*

She realized she had no shirt on, under the blanket, and his arm was around her bare waist. She took a deeper breath and it… moved. He was still asleep, but his hand had a mind of its own. It brushed one breast, still in its breast-band wrapping and she felt her belly tighten.

She cleared her throat loudly and the snoring stopped, followed by the frantic withdrawal of the hand. She lamented the draft of cold air down her back as he rolled away and stood up, clothed only in his long shirt, facing away from her.

"Sorry, um… How are you?" he said, over his shoulder, embarrassment thick in his voice.

"Don't worry about it. Something else m'body knows," she commented, dryly.

"Your body? Just your body? What, you mean in three years…" His voice trailed off.

"Nobody asked. Too scary, remember?"

He muttered something she couldn't hear.

"What?" she asked.

"'Cowards,' I said."

She thought about that for a minute and let a slow smile spread across her face. Then she held the covers to her chest and tried sitting up. Her head was sore, very sore, but the wound in her side was only a bit tender.

At the sight of his bandaged leg, she said, "The landing? I seem to remember it was pretty rough."

He looked down as if he'd forgotten it. "No, an arrow."

He shook himself as if starting over and started putting on the rest of his clothes. "I found your stone," he ventured.

She looked down. "It's not quite right, I know, but I liked the feel of it."

He stopped as if uncertain what to say, and then he tried again. "So, it *was* a tail you had, after all, wasn't it?"

She grimaced. "I'm afraid so. Sorry it was a surprise, but it just seemed like one thing too many."

One more thing to make a monster out of me.

"So, um, how does it work, the wings?"

"Don't know." At his skeptical look, she added, "Stumbled off a high balcony one day, and that's what saved me. Luckily no one was there to see."

Into the growing silence, she said, flatly, "Yes, I can call up wings. No, I don't know how they work. Do you know how your arm works?"

Zandaril patted the air. "All right, all right—I was just curious."

"Sorry," she said, looking down. "And before you ask, there's nothing else." She shrugged. "That I know about."

"Except for how fast you heal," he said. He held out his arm and unwound the wrapping, comparing it to her own wrist.

"I never did find the injury in your wing. Do you want me to look again?"

Now it was her turn to look puzzled. "How did you…"

"I asked you to show me your wings, and you did. Then you put them away when I asked."

She sat there, covers pulled up to her neck, stunned. "I don't remember."

"You trusted me," he said. "Like I trusted you, when we ran off the cliff."

She swallowed. "Yeah, well, thank you for that."

There was a moment of uncomfortable silence between them.

"Do you know him?" he asked.

She had no trouble understanding whom he meant. "No."

"But he recognized what you were."

"Apparently."

"He had a chain…"

"Just like I do. Yes, I saw." She rubbed a hand over her face. "Guess there's more than one of us."

She could see the unasked questions in his face vying with his wish to be polite, and her temper broke.

"Does he have wings? I have no idea. Can I do what he was doing, keep wizards as slaves? Don't know and don't want to find out."

She took a ragged breath. "Can't you understand? I don't know *anything* about him!"

"Except that he's stronger than you are," Zandaril said.

"Yeah, except that." *Is it innate? Learned? Special aids or devices?*

"Well, he wasn't happy to see you, I could tell that much. Maybe he knows something about you, worries him."

Penrys snorted. "Wish I knew what it was, m'self."

Penrys insisted they keep moving, east through the foothills. She didn't know how far they'd come from the ridge of the Horn—thirty miles or more, maybe—but it didn't feel like enough. Even traveling slowly, to favor Zandaril's leg, she wanted to get another ten or twenty miles away, each day.

Speed mattered, now. Their mission was over, but they still had to get back to Chang, and avoid the Rasesni between them.

No one was within her range, but now that range felt pitifully small to her, as though she stood in a shallow circle of light in a darkened room, with a ravening monster taunting her just out of her sight.

The stream they'd found meandered east as it worked its way down to the northern plain, ultimately seeking the Neshikame, the north branch of the Mother of Rivers. They followed it for three days, until it reached the open lands where they couldn't follow and still be well-sheltered.

They encountered Rasesni scouts only once, at a distance, and let them pass well to the south. She pitied them if they met the Voice and his scouts as they probed west.

The Craggies to their right grew steeper, and the open land to the north began to sprout small farms.

As they pushed past through one patch of woods, they emerged onto a clear trail, running up from the plains, and stopped to rest.

"Must be one of the northern trade roads Tak Tuzap was talking about," Penrys said. "Any idea how close we are to the end?"

Zandaril leaned down, untied the cloth wrap that held the loose flap of his boot up, and massaged around the edges of his wound. "He said there were three of them, maybe thirty miles between the first and last, and the first was just west of Koryan, above the Gates. The mountains get steeper and broader there."

"So, what, two days to reach the outside of the Gates, more or less?"

Zandaril shook his head. "Might not be good enough. Remember, the Rasesni were sending raiders out through the Gates. Who knows where Chang is now? By then, we'll have been gone more than three weeks."

He looked downslope to the north. "We'll need horses. Maybe on those farms…"

Penrys looked down at the ground. "You're not thinking… I can scout for Chang, once we get that far."

Zandaril raised an eyebrow.

"From the air," she said. "At night. There'll be fires."

Two evenings later, from the final bits of rough ground that were all that remained of the Craggies, Penrys and Zandaril surveyed the grasslands that led up to the outer entrance of Seguchi Norwan. The river itself was barely in sight as it flowed out of the far side of the Gates, already in shadow from the setting sun.

Penrys's scan turned up a few Rasesni, but most of the ones within range were inside the gorge. Harlin, where Tlobsung's army was reputed to be encamped, was too distant for her to reach.

They made their cold camp tucked behind a few rocks, and waited for full dark.

"Down the Seguchi first," Penrys said, reviewing their plan. "Then inland a couple of miles and come back. If that fails, try a loop outward from here for a few miles, and then a loop to the north."

Zandaril grumbled, "If they've moved elsewhere, we have a problem."

"Maybe not. We know they're not here. The closest we're sure they've been is around Shaneng Ferry, so if this fails, let's go there and see if anyone has word. Hing Ganau said they would garrison up there."

She dropped her pack next to his, and made sure her few necessities were well-tucked in her pockets or attached to her belt—a knife, a canteen, the makings of fire.

It wasn't quite dark enough yet, with twilight still lingering to the west, so she settled in to wait.

Zandaril cleared his throat. "Can I see them?"

"Hmm? You mean now?"

"If it doesn't make any difference…"

She was so used to hiding them, it took a moment to adjust to the request. Then she stood up straight and swept her wings into existence, stretching them to their fullest. They weren't attached to her body directly, and yet her back and shoulders always felt their presence. Her legs were a nuisance in flight, a poor adjunct to the feathered tail, but she supposed it was an acceptable compromise.

They had the air of a design, a made thing, rather than something organic, and so she thought about them that way and theorized how she might improve them.

"Can you wrap them around yourself, like a cloak?" Zandaril said, with a tone of wistfulness.

Penrys cocked her head at him.

He said, sheepishly, "I always wanted a cloak I could hide in, when I was a boy, and wings would have been even better."

"Let's see," she said, with a grin.

She found she could cross them in front, but not truly wrap them around herself, as though they were arms. They didn't bend that way, so close to the front of her body.

"Sorry," she said, and watched him stifle his disappointment.

A thought occurred to her. "Stand still," she said. She walked right up to him and stood chest to chest, and tried again. The wings did manage to close over the double thickness of torso, as she'd suspected. From above his head, almost to the ground, they were enwrapped in a tunnel of smooth, sliding feathers.

"Ah," he growled, in a low, soft voice. "That's good." His arms slipped around her to hold them together and help keep their balance.

She froze for a moment at the unexpected contact, then made herself relax and return the embrace.

They stood without moving for several moments, her cheek against his shoulder, while she inhaled his scent and the smell of her own feathers. His chest rose and fell against hers.

"I have to go," she murmured.

"I know."

He released her, and she opened her wings and stepped back.

The sky was quite dark, now, and the stars were out.

"Come back safe, Pen-sha," he told her. "We have much to discuss, and nowhere to go until daylight."

She half-smiled at him, then she turned and took several running steps, ending with a leap and a heavy downstroke that pulled her into the air.

Zandaril's senses were full of her, after she passed from his view into the dark. Those wrapped wings had been intoxicating, and he could still feel his pulse racing. He'd wanted to delay her mission, to spend the night with her instead of waiting for her return.

Maybe if she came back early… He smiled at the thought. No one could expect them to travel at night.

CHAPTER 32

Penrys flew steadily, aiming for stamina rather than speed. She knew she would be silhouetted against the stars if anyone should happen to look up, but no one would know what to make of the shadow as it passed.

She detoured around the few Rasesni she found and followed the river down, its silver channels easily visible in starlight. By counting to herself, she was able to estimate how many miles she was covering on each portion of the three planned loops. She wanted to be sure not to go so far on any one of them that she would have trouble completing the whole search tonight.

Below the Gates, there were Kigali-*yat* speakers scattered around the Seguchi, in small homesteads and occasional towns. She couldn't reach as far as Shaneng Ferry this evening, and didn't know the names of the places she passed, but nowhere did she sense the large gathering that would be Chang's army.

After about eight miles, she swung east away from the river and began another search back toward the gates. The air was still, with none of the thermals that were sometimes available on a warm day—she couldn't glide as much as she'd hoped.

Again, only a few people were in her range. She kept up her count, and thought about how she'd left Zandaril. Two weeks traveling together, on their own, near quarters before that. This development was no surprise but…

Three years in Tavnastok, and no one close to her. She was an oddity, a thing to be studied, a scholar to be tolerated. This… this was so much better. He *liked* her wings. He wasn't afraid of her.

She smiled. He'd called them "cowards." Why, and so they were.

Like she'd told him, this was something her body knew. She couldn't remember her experiences, but clearly her body did. She'd given up expecting something like this, shut it down entirely. Maybe that could change.

His voice and his scent did things to her. She wanted more. She wanted the man himself, with his odd accent and his sense of humor and his deep, rumbling voice. She knew it wouldn't be the first time for her, but it seemed like it, with nothing to compare it to.

The time flashed by, and soon she was back at the level of the Gates, turning to the east to start her next pass outward in the second loop.

Maybe I can finish early. Maybe I'll find them on this loop, and skip the northern one.

She hugged the thought to herself as she counted out the new lap.

There! There they were.

Penrys was about ten miles east of the Gates, just after her turn west again at the extreme end of her loop. She felt the horses first, then the cattle, as she came up on the camp from behind, and then the people. The glint of water marked a stream headed for the Seguchi, a few miles to their southwest.

She thought of landing now and taking two horses with her back to Zandaril, but they weren't much more than half a day from the Gates—the two of them could be here by mid-afternoon tomorrow, and that was good enough. The camp wasn't boiling with activity, as though they were about to go into action, and it would be better for the two of them to report together.

She overflew it, undetected in the night, and broke off to fly directly back to their hiding place north of the Gates by the shortest route, starting her count afresh to help guide them in the morning. She made careful note of any people along their proposed path as she passed, but none seemed to be Rasesni.

She would be back early, after all.

Zandaril woke before the birds, in the dim light of false dawn. His left arm was cramped under Penrys's head, but he did nothing to disturb her sleep, curled up and snuggled into his chest, wingless.

He brushed her hair back from her face and tucked it behind an ear, smoothing the black fur of it as he did so. Feathers, fur, and skin—so strange. And so wonderful.

She murmured as he touched her ear, and he smiled.

He didn't know her well, nor she him. He had stories to tell her, and she had none. No family.

He'd thought he was afraid of her, but he realized she was afraid of herself, not knowing what she might find, what strange feature might materialize, what the chain around her neck meant. That's what he feared, as well, not Penrys the woman. That person he found intriguing. They could survive the rest of it as it came, together.

Did she have some other family, as she suspected? He decided it didn't matter to him. If she did, they were dead to her. If she remembered them suddenly… *Ah, there was something to fear after all.*

Well, he would have to give her new memories, then, wouldn't he, something to compete with.

He leaned down to kiss her ear and breathed on it warmly. *Let's start now.*

CHAPTER 33

Penrys felt two of Chang's screen of scouts while they were still a couple of miles away from the encampment.

"Shall we let them find us?" she asked Zandaril

"Seems kinder than shaming them by slipping past."

They walked into the open, and Zandaril put his fingers to his mouth and gave a piercing whistle. Penrys could sense their sudden change of direction.

"They heard you," she said.

She shrugged her pack off to give her back a rest, and rotated her shoulders to loosen some of the stiffness. Surprised by a huge yawn, she caught Zandaril grinning at her.

"What?"

"Didn't get much sleep last night?" he asked, trying to look innocent, and failing.

She examined him—hair finger-combed, beard coming in, clothes dirty and torn, a rag holding up the top of one boot, and a smug leer on his face.

"You're no better off," she retorted, and smiled. His pride in pleasing her was obvious, and very touching.

She'd known the basics of what to expect last night, of course. What she hadn't expected was the tenderness of it, the way they'd kept exchanging casual affectionate pats as they packed up the cold camp in the morning. *Would it be even better, if we let our minds be intimate in the same way? If his people hadn't told him that was wrong?* She wanted to know what her touch felt like to him.

Getting back to the expedition would change everything. No more privacy, just the two of them. She hated to see that end.

The sound of hooves alerted her.

"Show your face," Zandaril said, and he made sure the hood of his own cloak was well back.

One scout circled behind so that they came in together from different directions, with their lances at the ready.

The nearest one reined in abruptly when he got a good look at them, as they waited with their packs at their feet. "You're back!"

He waved the other one off. "You go return to patrol. I'll escort them in."

"D'ye need any help?" the scout asked them, as he looked them over.

"We're fine," Zandaril said. "What are we, a mile out?"

"That's about right," the scout said.

"Are the others back?" Penrys called up to him.

The scout turned his horse as if he hadn't heard her, and started off at a slow and lazy walk toward the army.

She looked at Zandaril and saw the same puzzlement in his eyes.

Doesn't trust us?

He shrugged. **Maybe wants someone else to tell us. Maybe he doesn't know. We can wait—won't be long.**

In just a few minutes, Penrys heard the familiar noise of the daytime camp, talking, shouting, the clang of the farrier.

The first troopers they met called to the scout with friendly jibes, until they saw the two wizards, one of them limping, and then they stood their ground in silence. That core of silence spread, and people assembled on the edge of the avenue between the tents and watched them walk in.

Penrys's ears shifted back on her scalp. *What's wrong? Didn't they expect us? Are we that late?*

She saw runners ahead of them apparently carrying the news of their arrival back into the camp, and she exchanged a look of uneasiness with Zandaril.

He nodded to people he knew, and a few of them made jerky acknowledgments, but the mood of the camp was tentative and uncertain.

At last, they reached the command tent, where Chang himself stood outside the entry, waiting for them.

He glanced up at the scout who'd escorted them in. "Thank you. Back to your duties now."

The scout turned his horse and walked off, and the men that had gathered behind them parted to give him room. It was so quiet, Penrys could hear when he got past the edge of the crowd and set his horse to a canter.

Zandaril cleared his throat. "Are we the last ones back?" he asked Chang.

Chang's eyes flicked to Penrys's neck, and then looked at them both for a long moment. "You're the only ones back."

Penrys sat alone on a camp chair, next to Hing Ganau's wagon. Two guards stood watch. Even Hing was kept away, though Penrys had asked the guards to let him go through the wagon and find her some clean clothes, and get soap and a bucket of water for her so she could wash.

They wouldn't let her inside the wagon, so she'd held her cloak wide around her and washed as best she could with a rag under it, changing into fresh clothes a piece at a time. The cold water suited her rage, kept it alive.

Chang was still questioning Zandaril when she'd finished, so she'd begged a comb from the wagon and another bucket, and she knelt down and washed her hair, in front of the guards and the curious bystanders that they were unable to effectively disperse, angry enough that she ignored any glimpses they might have of her alien ears.

I don't care what they suspect. I'm going to look my best when they accuse me.

The guards looked embarrassed at this semi-public bathing, and she was icily glad. *Three weeks we spend, almost end up slaves, and this is what we get? No one's even asked about Tak Tuzap. Let the monstrous Voice eat them all.*

Her stomach growled, but no one had offered food. She glanced up to the empty sky. *I could fly away now, and who could stop me?*

Both their packs were in Chang's tent and they wouldn't let Hing bring her a book from the wagon, so there was nothing to do but brood. She stretched her legs out in front of her and slid down in the chair, leaning her head back and letting her wet hair drape over the canvas to dry in the chill air.

She closed her eyes, but she was too angry to drowse. She didn't want to interrupt Zandaril by mind-speaking him. He knew how to reach her when he was ready.

What was wrong with everyone? She felt the mood of the crowd—they were apprehensive and afraid, but of what? Of her?

Of Zandaril? Of the two sets of enemies in front of them, that Zandaril was telling them about?

She scanned the camp—no Rasesni natives, no other wizards besides Zandaril. What had happened while they were gone?

Zandaril held a tight rein on his temper. No one had given him a seat, and he stood, rigid, before Chang's table. Only Tun Jeju and the guards shared the command tent with him.

The first blow had come when Chang ordered Penrys off, under guard, without explanation and over his protest. He'd had both of them stripped of their packs, first, and their pockets emptied, and Tun had laid out all of their possessions on the table along the tent wall, where he was now poking through them. No one said what they were looking for.

One guard had even tried to remove Penrys's chain, and been baffled. Zandaril had winced internally at her cold and stony expression as he'd fumbled with it.

When Tun picked up the two arrow heads with their bloody shafts, he looked over at Zandaril and raised an eyebrow.

"We were in a fight over on the Horn," Zandaril said. He spoke as little as possible, but Chang's eyes slid down to the boot flap tied around his leg.

Tun pulled the Rasesni books and the two bags of power-stones from Penrys's pack and favored him with another quizzical look.

Zandaril told him. "You saw those yourself, the night we went through the Rasesni spy's belongings."

Bits of the cord and rope had been saved and were stretched out on the table, and those had bloodstains, too. The remnants of their food were examined—fragments of cheese and sausage, hard bread and dried fruit.

Spare socks, dirty clothing, a wrapped piece of soap, an iron pan. Two wooden bowls. Spoons. Knives and firestarters. Canteens. The leftover rags from Penrys's shirt.

Tun looked at Chang and shook his head.

"Where is it?" Chang asked, coldly. His Kigali features struck Zandaril as stern and alien.

"Where is what?" Zandaril replied. *What are they doing to Penrys while this is going on?*

"The *juk*. The device."

"What are you talking about?" He was too angry to be polite about it.

"The one that's used to enslave."

He closed his eyes as red washed over his memory of running, as he'd thought, to his death, over the cliff. To escape enslavement.

He opened them again and glared at Chang, all deference gone. "You can grill us all day if you like, or you can explain yourself to me. Better, you let us tell you our story, bring back Penrys. We've done nothing wrong, nothing!"

He turned his head and spat on the carpet under his feet, and heard with satisfaction the indrawn breaths at the insult. *This is how you treat disrespect, with a waste of precious water. I am shirqaj, warrior, as well as bikraj, and you Kigaliwen would do well to remember it.*

"I am ally, not one of your men. You can get truth from us, or whatever lies you already have," he said. "Your choice."

He looked for a camp chair and took it, and sat down uninvited, crossing his arms. "I was you, I'd listen to us. Big problems over there." He cocked his head to the west. "Very big."

CHAPTER 34

The bustle at the entrance of the command tent attracted Zandaril's attention. It resolved itself into Penrys, escorted in with two guards in front and behind. They dropped the flap shut behind her.

She washed up. Smart.

Her expression was masked, but he could feel the anger radiating off of her, stiffening her shoulders.

She slid her eyes sideways as she passed the table with all their belongings, and paused, taking a moment to rhetorically pull her empty jerkin and breeches pockets inside out before the gaze of everyone there, and leave the pocket linings dangling in contempt.

When she raised an inquiring eyebrow at Zandaril, he snorted. Then he stood up and got her another chair, inviting her to sit.

Chang stayed silent throughout this pantomime, his fingers steepled in front of him as he watched.

She sat and folded her hands, waiting for Chang to speak.

"While you two were gone," Chang said, "we received a letter."

Penrys said, "How, exactly?"

Chang tucked his chin in, as if surprised at being interrupted. "Tied to a lance, stuck in the ground in the path of the patrols. Written in Kigali-*yat* on paper, with a brush."

She nodded.

"It said, in short, that our wizards were spies returning to their master to report. That this master would send them back with his weapons for the next step, to turn us into slaves to fight against our countrymen."

He waited for their response.

Penrys asked, "Signed by…?"

"No signature."

"I see," she said.

There was a pause.

Tun Jeju said, "It referred to the master as 'chained.'"

"Ah," she said, icily. "And that got your attention."

She glanced at Zandaril, then addressed Chang. "His men refer to him as the 'Voice.' He has enslaved dozens of Rasesni wizards, the ones we didn't know existed. We left them at the Horn a week and a half ago and they're headed this way—it's why the Rasesni have fled their lands."

"And now, perhaps," Zandaril said, "you'll let us tell you the whole story, before they overrun you. Or slaughter everyone in Neshilik. Or both."

Penrys stayed in the command tent during a break in the debriefing, while Zandaril took the opportunity to get cleaned up. Tempers had eased somewhat in the long afternoon of reporting and questioning, but she had not forgiven Chang the treatment they had received nor, she suspected, had Zandaril. The smoking braziers at the entrance of the tent did little to melt the icy atmosphere between them.

Real damage had been done to the relationship between Chang and his wizards and, even though she knew this was one of the goals of the letter, she found it hard to set aside the effects.

The letter had played into the Kigaliwen suspicion of what they didn't understand, and it risked dividing them from their Zannib allies if Zandaril couldn't get past this.

She was personally affronted by the indisputable fact that this "Voice" was somehow related to her, as evidenced by the chain, and that the letter exploited that. *Better to save my outrage for the sender.* She snorted. *If only I could master my emotions at will.*

While she waited impatiently for some food to carry them into the next session—anything to distract her—Tun Jeju surprised her by breaking off from his quiet conversation with Chang and taking Zandaril's seat next to her.

He cocked his head at her, as if evaluating her mood. "No point being angry at what happened," he said. "See if you can convince Zandaril-chi of that."

"Maybe you better convince me first," she said. "Why shouldn't I just walk away? Declare this not my fight?"

"I don't know," Tun said, and that compelled her attention. "Why did you help find the Rasesni traps? Why did you go into Neshilik with Zandaril, and then come back and give us a warning?"

She opened her mouth, but nothing came out.

Tun looked at her with both sympathy and calculation. "Because that's what you are. Zandaril, too—that's why he joined us. That's why I find that anonymous warning... uncompelling."

The chair creaked as he leaned forward to keep their conversation private. "Chang needs you both. I don't know what that chain you wear means, and you say you don't either, but it means something. I think you want to find out what that is."

He sat back again. "Don't let resentment rob you of what you want to do anyway."

She closed her eyes and took a deep breath. "I would rather have remained friendly."

Tun half-smiled at her. "That's a luxury for civilians, not soldiers. Chang's responsible for too many lives to let that stand in his way, nor should he."

Penrys grimaced, but she recognized truth when she heard it, however unwillingly. Tun Jeju stood and walked away, and left her brooding on his advice.

When Zandaril returned, it was in his formal Zannib robes, with the more elaborate turban she recognized from the *kuliqa* celebration that seemed so long ago. Gone was her companion of the last three weeks, Penrys thought. *I understand why he's done it, distancing himself from these Kigaliwen who have so offended him. But Tun Jeju's right—if we want to accomplish anything, we have to get past it.*

He surveyed the room and its little pockets of conversation coolly, but when his gaze fell upon Penrys, it softened and he made his way through the tent to take the seat next to her that Tun Jeju had just vacated.

"Hing Ganau did quick work, I see," she said, admiring the cleaned and restitched boots.

"There's still a hole in back," Zandaril said, "not enough time to fix that right now."

"Listen, Zandaril..." She switched to mind-speech.

We've got to put our anger aside. Chang has a job to do, and we're just tools. It's not personal.

His reply was tinged with residual scorn. **This is not how a warrior leads his people.**

She took a breath. **Remember how you wanted to organize wizards? This is what it means—people filling slots professionally, being led* *professionally. Not people deciding to follow a man. Their loyalty goes to an institution, not a man.**

He made no overt response, but his nose wrinkled in disgust.

Look at you. You're clothed in your people's robes. You're filling the slot of "ally," not your individual role. You know this is how places like Kigali work, and you're using that knowledge whether you like it or not.

That goaded him into a reply. **It is not honorable. We were not treated honorably.** He glanced over at Chang, assembling a plate of camp bread and broken meats and speaking with Tun. Tun had his eye on them.

No, it isn't. Not the way you mean. But professionals have honor, too, a pride in what they do. Soldiers fight so as not to let their temporary brothers down, not because they are actual blood-brothers.

She could feel his mood begin to shift to a black humor.

Our tribes will never make this change. Maybe some of the Zannib-tahgr, the slow ones, the ones who have settled down… Of course, that is why we are such little allies for the great Kigaliwen, isn't it?

He swallowed, and then looked at her with a real smile, and said, "So, how does a professional wizard behave? Can you guide me, o Collegium expert?"

"I'm angry, too—there were better ways to handle it. But there, you see, that's a *professional* complaint."

Chang brought his plate back and took his seat behind his work table. He paused to give them both a half-nod before he called everyone back for the next session.

CHAPTER 35

Penrys listened to Tun Jeju summarize the crux of the problem in front of the senior officers. The darkness outside the tent's entrance reinforced the sense that they were focused together on a crucial decision.

"It comes down to whether you're willing to cede Neshilik to Rasesdad in exchange for their help against this 'Voice' and his horde."

Chang waved a hand dismissively. "If this Tlobsung had wanted that, he would not have tried to weaken us or to set us up for ambush from their enemy. He would have approached us for help."

"Not the Kigaliwen," Zandaril said, with a sardonic tone. "The Kigaliwen who do not trust wizards won't trust Tlobsung's wizards. The Kigaliwen who've never seen a *qahulaj*, a wizard-tyrant, won't believe us when we tell them what's coming. The Kigaliwen who conquered Neshilik permanently will not give it up again for a buffer state. The Kigaliwen will never ally with us, their traditional enemy."

Chang glared at him, but he went on. "The Kigaliwen who are bringing an army of unknown size for arrival at an unknown time are better diverted north of our seized territory, and maybe our two enemies can weaken each other, or at least give us time to settle in and improve our defenses, for when the survivor comes after us. Maybe they'll give us time to flee into *sarq*-Zannib if we can't stand against them."

"And if they ally with the horde, instead?" Chang said.

Penrys shook her head. "Never voluntarily. No one would. The only willing members are there for plunder."

She leaned forward for emphasis. "I don't know what this 'Voice' wants, but he's bringing tools with him, human weapons, not builders and settlers. And he's collecting and using wizards, which ought to scare you. It scares me."

"Says the foreigner of unknown allegiance." She stiffened at Sau Tsuo's disbelieving voice.

Zandaril remarked. "How will Kigali, the nation without wizards, defend itself?"

Chang declared, "Kigali is too large, too many people. How could a conquerer, however powerful, rule it?"

"And if he absorbs more wizards?" Penrys said. "Takes all the ones left to the unconquered Rasesni, maybe detours through *sarq*-Zannib? How much of Kigali are you willing to give up? It looked like he was struggling to get through the barren mountains, but what about when he hits the farms of western Kigali?

"It's true that he may find it hard to hold what he's taking, but I think he'll have no trouble defeating mundane armies, so who will protect the granaries? And when he gets far enough, what will they eat in the east, in the great cities?"

Tun Jeju said, "And just how will they defeat armies?"

"I remember our discussion before we left," Penrys said. "But this threat's very different. He has range, he has power. I've seen him immobilize people from miles away. There must be limits, but I don't know what they are.

"The Rasesni are device builders and he's using physical magic. Could he flood the terrain an army stood on, by pulling the water from the air? He used a lesser version of that to water the horde. Could he immobilize or kill the leaders from a distance? Pull their thoughts from their heads? He did that to us with some success, and we're wizards ourselves. With that sort of power he should be able to send objects great distances—how about a rain of devices like the ones that Rasesni spy prepared, falling onto an army from the sky and exploding?"

It was so still inside the tent that the voices of men passing by outside were audible.

Chang took a deep breath and looked at Tun. "The plan being proposed is unworkable. I have no authority to enter into diplomacy with Rasesdad to discuss territory—my mandate is to take it back, if I can, or prepare for the main army to do so. They're still a month behind, or more, and it takes days to send messages."

He turned to Zandaril. "This story… they'll never believe what you are describing as the danger. I know what their answers will be."

Zandaril nodded. "Yes, we understand. This we cannot help you with. But if your superiors truly believed there was a serious enemy, stronger and more dangerous than the Rasesni, what would they have you do?"

Tun said, "Make the right tactical decision for the situation you find, Commander, and worry about forgiveness if we live through the result."

"Or stand our ground and obey orders, Notju-chi," Chang rebutted. "You of all people know what happens to those who exceed their mandate."

Chang considered a moment and shifted focus. "If we did this thing, when would you do it?"

Zandaril said, "At once. No time to waste."

"A provisional truce," Penrys said, "in exchange for an army and especially a wizardly alliance for a joint defense. If they have ideas for attack, we want to share them. We need their wizards, we need their scouts, we need whatever they know about the horde, where it came from, what this Voice is."

"We have two wizards," Chang said, "and they have many. Why do they need us?"

Zandaril said, "We have scouts and a small force, maybe theirs is about the same size. It apparently fits in the Harlin meadow—how big is that? We have population in Neshilik who could maybe fight, if they understood the stakes. And one of our wizards bears a chain. This will mean something to them."

"But that's a bluff," Penrys protested. "I can't do what he does."

"It's a symbol, a good symbol," Zandaril replied. "Symbols are very useful."

"It still sounds like a bad idea," Chang said. "Why wouldn't they just attack us and move on out through the Gates to take their chances in the plains, if they're that afraid? I don't see how we can make this happen—they won't trust us, and we have no reason to trust them."

Tun said, "And what if it's a deception? What if they ally with the Voice and the horde, and overrun us all. Who planted that lance—a scout from the Voice, or from Tlobsung? Our army might be able to hunt them out of the plains or dig them out of Neshilik again once it gets here, but that won't do us here much good, after we're dead."

He glanced at Zandaril. "Or our wizards either, hostages with theirs."

Sau Tsuo scoffed, "You're just sending the spies on back to their master, and good riddance. They'll come to no harm, you'll see."

Penrys and Zandaril left before midnight. A draft copy of the proposed document had been given to a scribe tasked with producing multiple fair copies by morning.

When they reached Hing Ganau's wagon and the nearby tent, Penrys turned to seek her bedroll, but Zandaril stopped her, with a hand on her arm.

"I told Hing we were both moving into the wagon at night."

She examined his face, where presumption warred with hope, and smiled. *So, the Zannib robes have not changed him.*

In an oddly courtly gesture, he offered her his hand and drew her the short distance to the back of his wagon, dangling his lantern from the other hand.

A small step stool, placed on the ground, made the scramble easier, and she waited for him there, standing on the bare deck. Their blankets were spread in the hollow space between the diminished stacks of supplies, private on three sides.

When Zandaril joined her, he pulled up the tail gate and untied the canvas, letting it dangle and block the view, like a bed curtain.

"Cozy," she said. "Much better than the bare ground."

"I'm glad you think so," he said, his voice thick. "Not much room for wings, I'm afraid."

"Oh, we'll manage somehow."

She cupped his cheek in one hand, and he leaned his head into it, like a cat. "I'd like to share with you, if you'll let me," she said. "For example…" **This is what it's like for me when I lay my head to your chest and hear your voice rumble.**

She unfastened his formal robe and rough-folded it, then raised it to her nose to inhale the exotic spicy Zannib scent it carried before laying it onto a burlap sack. With his help she lifted off the shirt beneath and embraced him, her ear against his chest. **Say something.**

"I don't know if I can do that
with you," he said.

She shared with him how that sound coursed through her physically, the tingle as it passed, and the heightened senses it left behind.

She felt his knees buckle, and he caught himself. "Ah." There was a pause.

"What happens if I do this?" he murmured, as his hand reached out to play with her ear. **Or this?**

CHAPTER 36

The three emissaries met in front of Chang's command tent well after the sun had risen, mounted and ready.

Penrys smoothed the fabric of her new breeches along her thighs and concentrated on holding her horse still. She wondered if she might meet the horse's former owner in the enemy camp, if they got that far. She hoped not—too many people had died, too much damage.

While she'd been gone in Neshilik, Hing Ganau had had her original clothes duplicated from the rags that remained after the device with the mirror exploded, but in finer materials. With her cleaned and polished boots, she supposed she represented the Ellech portion of this embassy, however unofficially.

Her saddle had been fitted with a saber mount, and the hilt of the sword was tied to the scabbard with very visible red ribbons that rustled whenever the breeze picked up, an ear-twitching distraction for her horse. Hing had explained to her that the weapons demonstrated they came as free emissaries, not captives, and the ribbons showed their intentions were peaceful.

Fine as a symbol. But I've never even held a saber—would have been nice to give it a swing before tying it down.

Zandaril appeared in his formal Zannib robes, of course. But Tun Jeju, the third ambassador, was a surprise. He wore a dark blue overrobe, in brocaded silk, with flared trousers that hearkened back to Kigali's more remote past. The ceremonial black and red hat with the stiffened wings that was tied under his chin transformed his face from urbane to exotic. Penrys had seen illustrations that looked just like this, back in the Collegium, complete with the weapon hilts and their streaming ribbons.

Their herald trotted up, neatly uniformed, his long staff sporting the *leipum*, the traditional leafy branch indicating a parley. When Penrys looked closely, she saw the branch was artificial.

Sensible. Can't find a leafy branch in winter when you want one.

Chang passed two scrolls to one of his men who put them in the dispatch pouch attached to Tun's saddle, and then the Commander walked up to Tun and handed him a third scroll directly.

Tun tucked it into his robe, then tipped his head to Chang and abruptly turned his horse, joining the herald to walk side-by-side down the avenue of the camp. Penrys and Zandaril made a second pair behind them.

The mood of the camp was different from their entry, just a day ago—more settled, less apprehensive. The focus was more on Kigali pride, in the person of Tun Jeju, than on the two foreign wizards.

At the edge of the camp, they were joined by their escort, half a dozen horsemen in clean uniforms on well-brushed mounts that smelled faintly of saddle soap. The guard took position several paces to their rear, and Tun led them all off in a slow trot, west, toward the Gates of Seguchi.

Penrys scanned their surroundings every few minutes. Their horses stood in a group on the open ground plainly visible from the fortifications at the top of Koryan, on the right—the herald first, the three emissaries with Tun Jeju in the lead, and then the escort. The rest of the grassland around them was deserted, but she sensed dozens of people out of sight within the Gates and up on Koryan, as she'd reported to Tun when they arrived an hour ago. Behind the nearest people, she could feel the bulk of the Rasesni encampment on the floodplain of Harlin, well back from the Gates, but only a couple of miles distant.

The sound of rushing water from the gorge on their left carried clearly through the still air, and Penrys admired the apparently sheer walls that rose above it in the distance. The moisture in the air raised by the turbulence made itself felt whenever the unsettled breeze swung in their direction.

"Tak Tuzap crossed that rock face," she said to Zandaril. "At night. I wouldn't like to try it."

"Nor I," he replied.

Tun Jeju turned his head to the left to see what they were talking about, then resumed his relaxed posture. "It shouldn't take them this long to make up their minds. We'll give them another half hour or so, then we'll dismount to relieve the horses."

Almost as he spoke, Penrys felt a change in their observers. A group was beginning to move forward from within the sheltered Gates. "They're coming," she said. "Ten of them."

"Good," Tun said. "Matching our numbers."

He turned to look at the wizards. "Follow my lead, and don't lose your dignity, whatever the provocation."

"I still don't think it's a good idea to let them see my chain," Penrys said. "That's a mark of their feared enemy."

"And won't that puzzle them," Zandaril said, with a grin. "Make them wonder if we've got some secret weapon they could use."

"But we don't," she said.

"Quiet." Tun was monitoring the approach of the others, who came most of the way at a slow canter, then fell to a walk to cover the final fifty yards or so.

Penrys glanced at their herald, who carried a matching staff with a leafy branch. This one was real, she saw, the autumn-colored leaves barely clinging. She disregarded their escort, six riders similar to their own who hung back in a group.

The three emissaries were interesting. All three were native Rasesni speakers—they looked to her like Kigaliwen with broader faces and shaggier, unbraided hair. One was dressed in uniform, nothing as showy as Tun's diplomatic display, and the second was clothed as a warrior, leather-clad and well-armed, but not in uniform. The third was in civilian tunic and breeches and carried no visible weapons. The weapons of those who carried them were tied down with a motley collection of cords of various kinds.

They don't have truce-ribbons ready to hand. Saw ours. Had to improvise.

When she let her mind-scan sink a little deeper for the civilian, she caught his attention. A wizard. She felt the change in his emotions the moment he noticed the chain around her neck—surprise and fear and loathing, followed by speculation.

She withdrew, and nodded her head to him, then made sure her mind-shield was tucked firmly around Zandaril and herself.

After the initial introductions had been made, in Kigali-*yat*, Tun Jeju and Tlobsung pulled their horses aside from the others for a few minutes of private conversation. Penrys waited awkwardly with Zandaril, while their counterparts stared at them.

Tun turned his horse back to them. "They're prepared to talk. There will be a delay while they prepare the formal meeting."

Tlobsung had one of his escort wave a signal flag to the gates, and in a few minutes they were joined by four servants and two carts that carried small tables and camp chairs, along with refreshment for the party.

Everyone dismounted while the meeting place was assembled on the grass. The escorts took charge of the horses on both sides, and Penrys stood out of the way with Zandaril while they waited.

"I was surprised by Tun Jeju's attire," Penrys said. "Shouldn't he be in military dress clothing?"

"He's the Emperor's representative, and that takes precedence over any military rank, even Intelligence Master. It doesn't look quite proper without the braid, though."

"The braid?"

Zandaril glanced at her. "I suppose you haven't seen that many civilians yet. Didn't you notice the herdsmen and the teamsters, with their long braids? And the people you met in Lupmikya? Tak Tuzap, too?"

Penrys lifted a shoulder. "I just thought the troopers had short hair to accommodate their helmets."

"Well, yes, but it's more than that. Everyone wears the braid, everyone except the military. It marks them, in gatherings. They stand out, and it bonds them together, against the 'long braids,' as they call them. Makes it harder for them to masquerade as something else, too."

Penrys fingered her shoulder length hair and then glanced at Zandaril's turban. "We don't fit in either way, do we?"

"In Kigali, in the cities, we would never meet someone like Chang, much less Tun Jeju. Wizards not important enough. We're like camp doctors—little rank, no standing. Worse, Kigali has little use for foreigners. We don't even merit Kigali names, and that's pretty low."

Penrys blinked at that.

"I've met people like Sau Tsuo before. Zannib confuse Kigaliwen. His gods don't know what to do with me. We have no temples, but we have people in the *Ghuzl mar-Tawirqaj* at Ussha the way they have priests. So what are they?"

He chuckled. "Chang has a problem. The tribal assembly knows I am here, that they sent for someone, and Kigali may need its allies. And now he thinks he may need foreign wizards, too, if he believes what we reported."

He looked down at Penrys. "It is awkward for him. He doesn't know how to treat us, as you saw. And I am warrior, and trader, not just wizard. And you are mystery. What will he do if there is trouble?"

Shaking his head, he said, "I would not expect him to work all that hard to get us out, if something happens."

He stared at her directly. "It's not too late to turn back."

Penrys frowned. "Tun Jeju is different. I think he values us higher."

"Doesn't mean we're any safer with him in charge. You know what they say about him—he lives with his wife's family." He grinned.

Penrys lifted an eyebrow in puzzlement, and he explained. "In Kigali, the wife does not go to the husband's family, like the Zannib. They live with the more powerful family, whichever it is. Imagine people even sneakier than Tun!"

As if by cue, Tun chose that moment to beckon them over to join him. He seemed especially pleased with the hastily erected canopy, a simple piece of fluttering cloth over ten raised staffs that provided a nominal shelter for their talks. "Means they're serious," he said. "Part of their traditions."

The camp chairs were arranged on the grass three on a side, with the little tables separating them. Once they sat down, they completed the formal introductions, with Kigali-*yat* as their common language. Tlobsung, the man they had heard of from Tak Tuzap, was in charge of their military, and Pyalshrog was some sort of leader of the hill-tribes. Penrys wasn't clear on his exact role.

The wizard, Zongchas, studied his two counterparts, and questioned them. Penrys had been expecting this moment since they'd met.

"It was a surprise to us to see a Kigalino envoy with two foreign wizards," he said, politely, in excellent if accented Kigali-*yat*. "Have you been with them long?"

"I joined them to find out what had happened here," Zandaril said. "*Sarq-Zannib* has an interest in whatever happens to our good allies, the Kigaliwen."

"I see," Zongchas said, and turned to Penrys, his eyes flicking to the chain and reluctant to look away. "And you?"

Here it comes. "I was visiting from Ellech, from the Collegium..." She saw the narrowing of his eyes as he made note of the name. "When I heard the news myself."

There. Let him make what he wants of that.

"And your role with this military expedition?"

"Advisors," Zandaril said. "We help them with matters that are... beyond their military experience."

"And what sort of matters would those be?"

Penrys paused a moment and looked at him. "We met the Voice, up on the Horn. He grabbed us but we got away."

Into the dead silence, she added, "Those sort of matters."

CHAPTER 37

One day later, Penrys and Zandaril rode borrowed horses over the trampled grassy spot where the canopy had been placed. Negotiations had just begun, and their ending was uncertain, but a temporary truce was in effect and the two wizards, specifically, had been released to meet with their counterparts.

Zongchas had urged it from his side, and Zandaril and Penrys had agreed. Chang had declared them foreigners not under his direct control, and that was the end of it. For now. Penrys thought that absolved him of all responsibility for them, and wondered how they would defend themselves if it came to that.

There would be no commingling of the two armies. Too many Kigali soldiers had died from the Rasesni sabotage, and the blood spilled in Neshilik was too sore a topic. Chang had no plans to move his encampment for the moment, keeping it out of garrison in Shaneng Ferry and ready for action.

Penrys looked back just once as they joined the trade road and passed under Koryan headed for Harlin. "Aren't you worried about your horses?" she asked Zandaril.

"Better they stay with the Horsemaster in the herd, and yours, too, rather than weaken in a stable in some town, here," he said.

"I suppose." *Or he expects to lose them here, like the last ones we brought into Neshilik. And us, too, maybe. What would happen then? Would Chang try to send them back to someone in sarq-Zannib? How does that work?*

The Seguchi ran close to the road as the gorge narrowed, and the roar of the water grew louder. Penrys's nose flared to the moisture in the air that had been river moments ago. The clouds overhead threatened rain as if in competition.

At the point where the shelf carrying the road on its embankment was at its narrowest, a barricade had been erected. Their promised escort awaited them on the far side, a young dark-haired wizard with a prominent scar across his left cheek, still livid, and they passed through with no difficulty.

The escort trotted up to them on his gray horse. "I'm Ichorrog. *Brudigdo* Zongchas has assigned me to be your guide."

"We're pleased to meet you, Ichorrog," Zandaril said. "This is Penrys, and I am Zandaril."

Ichorrog nodded briefly, then moved to the front and led the way.

"Doesn't have much to say," Penrys muttered.

"Better than shooting at us," Zandaril replied. Penrys had noticed how many of the soldiers had bows, though this wizard bore no obvious weapons.

"At least he spoke Kigali-*yat*," Zandaril added.

"We've got to do something about the language issue," she said to him. "I'll bet most of them don't. You and I are going to work on it again."

He looked at her in dismay. "It'll never succeed."

"Oh, I don't know," she said. "I noticed last night you're getting much better at reading deeper into minds. Just a matter of practice."

She watched with interest as his cheeks reddened.

They walked their horses on through the gorge which gradually widened out. The road's elevated surface hugged the right edge, and between the river and the road stretched the floodplain of Harlin, level as a table top. It was filled with tents and other temporary shelters, marked here and there with patches of bright color. Well-defined avenues between them allowed for unimpeded movement. A herd of horses was confined to the grass meadows along the river, but there weren't enough for a cavalry unit—this was clearly infantry.

At this time of year, the ground was firm and covered in low vegetation, wherever it was not worn away by the foot traffic, and the Seguchi was restrained by its banks, but it was clear to Penrys that come spring it would likely all be underwater.

"Where will they move to, for permanent quarters?" she asked Zandaril.

He just shook his head.

She had expected their guide to lead them off the embankment and down into the meadow, but he kept to the road and passed the army encampment behind.

Over the next few hours, the embankment gradually subsided and the road returned to the surface of the natural land, which was starting to rise. Penrys felt the spray in the air before she heard the increased sound of water and, as they turned past a wooded hill, the river narrowed and hissed down an endless series of shallow rapids.

A good-sized village was sited there, at the base of the riffles on the north side, with an outsized set of sturdy landings for river-borne traffic, and a ferry crossing to a smaller settlement on the far bank. Tak Tuzap had described how no boats could ascend the Seguchi at this point, but the locals made a living moving goods via the trade road to the head of the series of falls, some two miles west, where local boats and barges could navigate the river again. Every outlying building they could see from the road seemed to have stables and a wagon or two.

"That's Gonglik Jong, the Steps," Ichorrog told Zandaril, pointing at the rapids. "There's a big town at the upper end, biggest one in Neshilik, on both sides of the river. It's called Gonglik, too. We're based there."

Zandaril nodded silently and Penrys kept her thoughts to herself. *That's where Tak came from, and I imagine he's there now.*

She was surprised at the solitude of their journey, as the road climbed with the land. There were no compounds here, along the ascending rapids. Only the noise of the occasional passing rider disturbed them.

"Is it the invasion, d'ya think?" she asked Zandaril. "I'd expect to see goods moving."

"Anyone with sense is hunkered down, waiting for things to sort themselves out. Put your goods out on the road, next Rasesni soldier's likely to seize it."

She said, "You're right. Every warehouse and barn is probably full, and the caves in the hills, too, if there are any."

Every so often a track left the road on the left and headed to the rapids. She pointed them out to Zandaril, and he suggested they might be camping places, near the water.

The well-maintained road swung out some distance to the right around the last little fall on the river, and then turned left decisively. Only a small local spur continued upriver the way they had been going.

They paused on the slope to breathe the horses where the first compounds and warehouses sprouted before entering the main body of the north half of the town. From that position, they could see all the way down to the river, to the famous bridge that crossed the Seguchi here, and then up to the much larger south-side town, really a small city.

Zandaril pointed across the river to the wooded summits of the low hills south of town and told Penrys, quietly, "That's where we waited for news from Gonglik, the night we sent Wan Nozu and Tak Tuzap in."

Their taciturn guide circled back to speak with them as they started forward again. "You see, down there in Kunchik, where the buildings widen into a market square, short of the bridge? We've taken back the temple school for the wizards, that one on the left with the colonnade on the second floor. You see it?"

"Clear enough," Zandaril replied.

"It's Venesh's, now. Again. They weren't teaching wizardry here, anymore. We had to bring our own books."

Ichorrog wheeled his horse about, and they followed behind him.

As they entered the market square, with its cobbled paving, Penrys was surprised to find everything looking so… normal. The small permanent shops with their arcades were open, and the temporary farmer stalls were covered with produce. Both uniformed men and apparent townspeople were visible. When she tasted the mood it seemed not exactly relaxed but concerned, as if they were waiting to see what would happen. Even children were out, here and there, despite the threat of rain.

The old stone temple and merchant buildings that surrounded the square, three and four stories high, were weathered, mellowed into place, all except for the broad colonnaded three-story building that made up half of the long east side. The first floor was solid and fortress like, its expanse broken only by a double door, raised several wide steps from the pavement, and a closed-off archway at ground level. It had no windows at all on that floor, not even grilled or barred ones like the other buildings. The long row of thin columns that fronted the second floor for its entire length screened a sheltered walkway, backed by a wall with windows. The solid wall of the third floor was pierced by casements, open to the air, and a flicker of motion within them betrayed curtains.

The visible walls and columns looked freshly cleaned, and the Rasesni characters carved over the doorway had been touched up.

'School of the Secrets of Vanesh,' they said. Pennants hung from the staffs that jutted from the roof corners, bright in scarlet and gold, but she couldn't make out the devices. Nothing like that fluttered from the roofs of the other, dingier buildings.

Without dismounting, Ichorrog pounded on the wooden doors that blocked the tall archway, and they swung inward, allowing them to walk their horses through a long flagged passage and into the interior courtyard of the compound, a place of walkways and exercise spaces interrupted by small gardens whose colors were muted by the not too distant approach of winter. The familiar sounds of smithwork hit Penrys's ears, and her nose told her the location of the stables.

Ichorrog took charge of their belongings and sent the two of them up to Zongchas's office through a simple back entrance with a young woman whom he introduced as Isven. Penrys took her for a student wizard, but her efforts to get her to chat, even in Rasesni, were fruitless. Everywhere she led them, from the stable yard, through the kitchen corridors, and up the back way to the second floor, they passed people who stopped talking when they saw them.

These were clearly not the public parts of the building, but the smells were familiar to Penrys from the Collegium—the ineradicable remnants of hundreds of meals, the cleansers and polishes, the traces of candle soot on the ceilings, the wear in the stone floors of thousands of feet. She wondered how old the students had been who had been schooled here, and for how many generations, some of them Kigaliwen, and some of them, perhaps, not.

As they worked their way forward toward the front of the building following their guide, they passed along one bare corridor unpunctuated by inner openings on the right until a set of carved double doors spread wide allowed them a glimpse of the immense interior room there—bookcases and tables stretched back into dimness.

The shelves were perhaps three-quarters empty, but the familiar smell of moldering covers, dust, and ink stopped Penrys in her tracks. There were lights in this unwindowed space, but no flickering attended them. *Powered devices, they must be.* There were people in the room, too, but she only had eyes for the distant rows of books.

Zandaril halted with her, his eyes widening. "And here I thought I would look for a few books to take back with me. I'd need an entire pack train. Two."

Isven, their guide, circled back skittishly to retrieve them and chivvied them along. They left the library entrance reluctantly and continued down the corridor until it turned the corner of the building. Penrys thought they were now on the side fronting the square.

The first door on the outer wall was ajar, and the girl knocked on it and fled, leaving the two wizards bemused on the wrong side. Penrys pushed it further open, and caught Zongchas in the process of rising from his broad desk to welcome them in.

Behind him, a window let in both air and light, as well as a glimpse of the outer colonnade.

"Surely you didn't find your way by yourselves?" he asked, in Kigali-*yat.*

"Our young guide was in a hurry to leave," Penrys said.

Zongchas raised an eyebrow. "Our students aren't accustomed to meeting foreigners, let alone foreign wizards."

He waved his hand in the direction of the market square. "Neshilik is not foreign to us, not really. We have stories from here, and cousins."

He offered them chairs, in front of his desk, and resumed his seat. Penrys tried without success to make out what the succession of people carved into the smooth walnut sides of the desk were doing.

Zongchas said, "I'm pleased you were willing to come so soon, before we have any… formal agreement."

Penrys waved that aside. "We need to know the story of this 'Voice.'" She leaned forward. "D'ya know where he is now?"

"Still on the Horn," Zongchas said, "Preparing to move. But wait a moment…"

His eyes unfocused a moment. "I've summoned our *Grakeddo*, our Devices Master, and some refreshment."

"Devices Master?" Zandaril said.

"We have all sorts of wizards here—all we could save—and many of them were students. Are students. So we've made of this place a new sort of Mage School, with an unusual number of additional teachers."

He cocked his head. "You must understand, every god in his temple has his adherents and his secret knowledge, and many priests are jealous of what they know. Some of us have started to work on sharing that, but there is resistance. You will find some of our teachers, and their students, are unconvinced this is the right path. Necessity has thrown us all together."

"How many do you have here?" Penrys asked.

"Thirty-seven, counting us all. Twelve are students."

"And in other places?" she asked.

There was a moment of silence, and her heart sank.

"That's all that have survived, that we know about," Zongchas said.

"But we saw, up on the Horn…" Her voice trailed off, but she straightened her shoulders and continued. "Looked to me like maybe thirty, forty people that I took for Rasesni wizards."

"That sounds about right. There were more, but he uses his captives up." She heard the grief in his voice.

Could he be telling the truth about his losses?

"Careless with his tools, eh?" Zandaril muttered, and Zongchas nodded, soberly.

"But I don't understand," Penrys said. "Has your capital… has Dzongphan been destroyed?"

Zongchas grimaced. "No, not yet, but we do fear it, if he turns that way. Many of the wizards have fled."

They didn't stay to defend it? That didn't sound right to her. Or maybe they tried an attack and it failed.

There was a knock on the door, and a tall, thin man stuck his head around the doorway.

"Come in, come in," Zongchas said. "This is Vladzan, our Devices Master."

The thin man came in and pulled over a third chair. He looked them over. "Zan and, what, Ellech, they said? You don't look the part." This last was directed at Penrys.

"Long story, I'll tell you later. But, yes, three years at the Collegium, especially in their library."

Noises outside the door intruded, and then two young men came in with bread, cheese, and fruit. Zongchas cleared space on the end of his desk for the platter, and for the tray with a pitcher of water and glasses.

When they left, they closed the door behind them.

Zongchas pointed them to the food, and leaned back in his chair. "Let me tell you about our great nightmare."

"Two years ago, almost three… No, wait. I need to tell you a bit about our country first."

He waved his hands in the air to illustrate as he spoke. "You've seen maps, yes? We are a spine of great empty mountains with coastal plains on the southwest and northeast, and the inland vale of Nagthari in the east. Most of our people are in the plains, and that's where our cities and ports are. The hill-tribes range widely but they are small, and they share few interests with the settled people of the coasts. Nagthari trades with Kigali, when it is allowed, and holds our holy places.

"It's true that we're not famed for our wizards, unlike *sarq-*Zannib or even the far Collegium, but every place has a few, even up in the mountains, and the advanced ones come to Dzongphan in Nagthari where some of the temples offer them special knowledge and training."

Penrys glanced at Zandaril who looked fascinated. *Not famed? More like well-hidden.*

"So, two years ago it was, and rather more, a… person appeared in Neshred-pur, far up west on the northern coast. He had new teachings, he said, and the local wizards listened to him and were impressed. He struck the ground, and water came out. He offered to teach them how to do that."

Penrys thought of the exhausted wizards pulling the moisture from the air up on the Horn.

"He was not Rasesni, himself. No one knew what he was. He seemed to speak every language, even the hill dialects."

Vladzan added, "He had a chain, snug around his neck. No one thought anything of it, at first, but then it was noticed that he never took it off." His eyes slid to Penrys's throat, and away.

"We think he came alone," Zongchas said, "but others joined him. The local people, those for whom something in their lives was failing, they came first. He had food for them, clothing, money for their debts. A purpose for their lives.

"You understand, we have many temples in Rasesdad, many gods. It seemed harmless enough and, besides, our wizards were keeping an eye on it, and they are educated people and speak to each other."

Zandaril asked, "What was his name?"

Vladzan said, "He called himself the 'Voice of God.' We don't know his real name. We've just been calling him 'Surdo,' as he named himself."

"He traveled from village to village," Zongchas said, "And everywhere he went, a few people left everything behind and came with him. Several wizards reported their misgivings, as well as their news about new teachings. But it takes a while for word to travel, and by the time a couple of the temples in Dzongphan sent investigators, the wizards he met stopped complaining or admiring, and began to disappear.

"He suborned some of the hill-tribes with promises of wealth, to keep order among his followers, and together they began to take what they wanted from each village, and there were reports of murders. The locals named them 'Khrebesni,' thieves.

"Behind him was ruin—crops destroyed, villages laid waste, and every wizard gone. On the first summer, he swept into the foothills of Mratsanag, and then to the upper valleys, and the destruction followed him. He crossed to the high southern valleys for the winter, and then took to the hills again this last summer, and never left them, until he brought his horde to Garshnag, the mountains to the north above Nagthari where many had sought refuge, creating a panic and sending them further, into Neshilik.

"Our loyal hill-tribes fled before him. He is something out of legend to them, something about the end of this cycle of existence, and they will not stand against him. We've sent spies to track him, but none of the wizards who get close enough come back."

"None of them have escaped?" Penrys said.

"You two seem to have been closer than anyone, after the first few villages."

Vladzan said, "We've had some luck with mages riding the minds of birds, but they have to get too close for safety, and when he notices the birds, we sometime lose the bird-rider, too."

"What does he want?" Zandaril said.

Zongchas looked at Vladzan. "We don't know," Zongchas said. "He has sent us no demands. It may be that we can resettle the lands he has passed through, but we can't just bow before him as he passes. Our holy places lie undefended, just waiting for his attention to turn to them. And what is to keep him from returning?

"Our refugees have turned to Neshilik, those that can, while the government and the high priests remain in Dzongphan, as long as possible."

He paused. "Tlobsung is explaining this to your Commander Chang. We can't get close enough to fight. The soldiers in the front lines just… die. We've tried ambushes without men, with devices…"

Zandaril grimaced, but Zongchas didn't seem to notice.

"And those fail, too."

He spread his hands eloquently.

Is this true? My sense of him is that it's true, at least on the surface. Or is it just a way to encourage the Kigaliwen to enter the fight? Spend their blood instead? Or just distract them from the occupation of Neshilik?

Penrys looked at Zandaril, then spoke. "Can we work together, all of us wizards? Put aside the hard feelings between the two quarreling neighbors? Because this is a wizards' problem—if we can't solve it, nothing else will matter."

"We must," Zongchas said, and Vladzan nodded.

"All right, then." Penrys leaned forward and rested her elbows on her knees. *I'll take them at their word - what else can I do?* "How can we help?"

CHAPTER 38

Half an hour into the mage council meeting, Penrys was already sick of it.

The room was handsome, if chilly—a locked interior room, windowless and quiet as a cave when she entered it with Zandaril and Zongchas, their footsteps muffled by the hangings suspended along each wall. She didn't know the events portrayed in their faded colors, but the tall and icy mountains featured prominently left her in no doubt that these were Rasesni-brought, not part of whatever furnishings had already been in place when they arrived.

She wished for that vanished silence now, as the disputes continued around the scarred table. Only four of the five council members were present, but they had no compunction about loud argument. Their minds may have been shielded, but not their voices. She had shielded herself, and covered Zandaril, too.

The pompous Dhumkedbhod leaned back in his chair and crossed his arms, his expression unchanged—nose wrinkled as if combating a foul odor and the rest in an implacable scowl.

He waved one fleshy arm at Zongchas. "You can blather all you want about allies, but you have yet to convince me why we should believe them."

The conversation from the start had remained in Rasesni, and after a couple of protests from Zongchas to switch to Kigali-*yat*, Penrys had just kept a link open to Zandaril and provided a silent running translation. He took advantage of it to provide his own commentary in return.

I don't know what this Dhumkedo god has to say about foreigners, but he certainly says it loudly.

Penrys mentally shushed him. **He can maybe hear you.**

Zandaril snorted out loud. **So you keep saying. Much I care. Strangers get the courtesy they merit.**

Penrys didn't detect any reaction from Dhumkedbhod to Zandaril's scorn, but there was no way to be sure if he couldn't overhear it, or if he was just canny, a survivor of decades of infighting.

Nyagchos, whose religious objections seemed to be more moderate, tilted his gray head and pursed his lips. "If they won't trust us enough to show us proof, why should we trust them?"

There were two sticking points. They flatly disbelieved her account of ignorance, that the last three years were all she could remember, and seemed almost insulted at the story. Among themselves they debated how she could prove it, even if she were willing to let them in and see for themselves. "Nothing easier than to put a barrier in place," Dhumkedbhod had said, "And how would we know the difference?"

The second objection had more possibility of being addressed. After Zandaril had described, in Kigali-*yat*, their encounter with the Voice, Nyagchos had called for seeing exactly what that had been like, in his mind and Penrys's, and Dhumkedbhod pointed out the same difficulty of verification. This time, Vladzan had cut in unexpectedly. "If she shows us people we recognize, it would be easier to believe, yes?"

Penrys was not entirely in favor of this. Aside from the danger of granting access, she'd been successful so far in not describing exactly how they'd escaped. If council got its way, they would have to know about her wings, and she'd wanted to keep that as a surprise, just in case.

She sighed. That just might not be possible.

Holding up her hand, she distracted them from Zongchas's attempts to make progress. "I will show you. I will share it with all of you, Zandaril, too, so that you can feel his testament to the accuracy of it."

Zandaril and Dhumkedbhod broke in at the same time. In *wirqiqa*-Zannib, Zandaril said, "You must not let them in."

Penrys patted the air to urge him to calm, while Dhumkedbhod objected, strongly, "I will not do this, and you would be fools it you did. She's just like him—look at the chain. She'll just show you whatever she wants you to see. Dhumkedo forbids it."

Everyone turned to listen to him as he intoned, "Will you be taken in by another chained monster?"

Zongchas shared a look with Vladzan and Nyagchos, then turned to Penrys. "We will do this."

Penrys straightened in her chair. "This far and no further," she warned. "I will protect myself."

She began with her memory of their capture by the hill tribesmen, the mental voice that had detected and then captured them until they were securely bound. Her audience had to lower their own shields to do this, so she tried to monitor their reactions and their intents while keeping a light touch on Zandaril, too. It was a complicated bit of juggling.

"Show me that again," Zongchas said. "That tribal camp."

She listened to their discussion about the weaponry and clothing of their captors and the camp at the base of the horn.

She wanted to shortcut the tedious climb up the trail at the Horn, but they refused. They paused her again to examine her view of the horde, discussing which tribes seemed to be represented. An undercurrent of dismay began to run through her Rasesni audience. The more they believed the truth of what they saw, the worse it grew.

She muttered, "Captives," out loud, to warn them, and took them through the fettered wizards in rags, pulling water from the air.

"But that's Igzhun," Vladzan said. "I'm sure of it."

"And Drannyal, and maybe Shrigirnang, too." Nyagchos's voice was no longer skeptical, nor his mind, either. "I thought they were dead."

When she finally showed them their enemy, and his chain, she let them feel the throb of her own chain in response. "My chain recognized his," she told them.

Reluctantly, she showed them the end—how they ran off the cliff and fell through the air, with Zandaril's weight dangling from her bound hands, and even the two arrows that hit her, before she cut them off and shoved them out, re-erecting her shields.

She tried to suppress the emotional resonance of the event, to control her breathing and heartbeat, but she knew she had failed when she felt the echo of concerned sympathy from Zandaril.

The council members who had come along with her were blessedly silent for a moment, until Dhumkedbhod's strident voice broke in. "Well? Was it worth it?"

CHAPTER 39

The entire community gathered for their evening meal in the great hall on the first floor. Penrys and Zandaril joined Zongchas and Vladzan at the head table, and Penrys was amused when she noticed the covert glances their presence brought from the rest of the diners.

As in the Collegium, light was provided by devices mounted at head height along the walls, where torches might be expected. Penrys was itching to examine one up close, since they didn't feel as though they operated on the same principles as the kind she was familiar with. When one dimmed, she noticed a young wizard who rose from his seat to tend to it, taking it down from the wall, then rehanging it again once it had brightened. *Charging its power-stone? The task of apprentices, to teach them technique?*

She tried to get a sense for the mood in the room, both apprehensive and hostile. The students all wore armbands in several colors. *Rank, maybe? Student colors were used in the Collegium.*

Many of the people without sashes wore similar clothing, male and female. *Priests. I've seen those garments in illustrations about Rasesdad.* There were three whose clothing reminded her of Pyalshrog, the hill-tribe leader from yesterday's parley, all skins and sashes.

Once again there was no pretense of speaking at the table in Kigali-*yat* for Zandaril's benefit. She translated for him, but she could feel his frustration.

"Tonight," she said to him, as they waited for the meal to end. "You will learn the sharing of language tonight."

"Too bad," he murmured, for her ear alone. "I had other plans."

"I have an idea about that," she answered. "Tonight you will start to learn Rasesni, from me, and I promise you will be happy about it."

He raised an eyebrow, but she refused to elaborate.

Zongchas rose, and everyone in the hall quieted as they saw him.

He glanced throughout the space, catching eyes in every corner, until he had the attention of all.

"Today we have welcomed two wizards from the Kigaliwen, who are not Kigaliwen themselves. They have seen our enemy, recently. He is not far away."

At that there was a rising hubbub throughout the hall, and he waited for it to subside.

"We have a plan to help us, all of us, defeat him. We begin tomorrow."

He raised his hand to request silence after the resulting outburst, and beckoned to his guests.

Penrys rose and walked to stand next to him, where she would be clearly visible, and Zandaril joined her.

She pitched her voice to carry throughout the hall, and spoke in Rasesni, translating for Zandaril via mind-speech. "My name is Penrys, and this is my colleague, Zandaril. As you can see from his face and his robes, he is from *sarq*-Zannib."

She paused. "I am not." She pulled at the collar of her shirt until it was spread wide and the thick chain around her neck was clearly visible.

Not entirely to her surprise, people actually stood up from their seats to get a better look, and conversation broke out everywhere.

Zongchas leaned down and pounded the table with the butt of his knife. "Silence!" It took a few moments before she could speak again and expect to be heard.

"I do *not* know your enemy," she said, "but it may be that I share in some of his abilities. I hope so, for you're going to learn how to fight *me* and we'll see if a motivated and organized group of wizards can defeat him and take their revenge."

She raised her voice as she spoke to penetrate the rising response, until the final words came out in a shout, and it was impossible to say more.

Penrys noticed that several of the older wizards were close-mouthed and unresponsive, and nodded to herself. Skeptics weren't a bad thing—they gave her something to concentrate on. The young ones were easy. If she could convince the others, then maybe they all had a chance.

A sudden assault against her shield got her attention. One of the people in front of her wanted her dead, now. He was young, about

Zandaril's age, and weaker than she was. She fended him off easily, but others joined him.

The crowd was growing aware of the attack. Some watched in silence, monitoring its progress, and many actively cheered it on.

The head table beside her remained neutral. Penrys heard Zongchas mutter, "We should stop this," but someone else, Nyagchos she thought, responded calmly, "Let's see what happens."

With a wry smile, she thought, *I should have expected this. So let's give them a show, since they insist.*

Despite the situation, she enjoyed using her strength without worrying about who saw her.

She pushed back against her attackers, evicted them casually, and waited for the cheers of their partisans to falter before taunting, "Don't you want to learn how to do that right? If you can't beat me, how will you beat the Voice?"

She walked off to the side of the head table so that she could face it, too, and include it in her speech. They were none of them her friends here, except Zandaril, but they all needed to work together, and if she couldn't make them accept her, there was no hope for them.

"Better learn how to work together instead of dying alone."

She could feel their outrage. Some cried out the names of people taken by the Voice, friends or relatives she presumed.

She let them, for a few moments. "Don't you want them back?" She gestured to indicate Zandaril, who remained standing at his place. "We saw many of them alive."

That silenced them all. Penrys looked at the dirty dishes along the table, the servants frozen against the walls.

"Let's do this now, since that's what you want. Who's the strongest among you?"

From different points in the hall three people stood up and glanced challengingly at each other, while anyone else still standing resumed their seat, barring Zandaril. *Clearly there's some disagreement among them about who is best.*

With an inner smile, she waved the implicit dispute aside. "Altogether, then. Try me."

There was little attempt at cooperation and they made no impression upon her shields. She overpowered each of them, and the audience monitoring had no trouble following the details.

She nodded at them, then glanced at the entire room. “Let me know when you want to learn how to do it better.”

Turning, she walked out and felt Zandaril follow her. The noisy buzz rising behind them told her all she needed to know.

CHAPTER 40

"So what's all this about my learning Rasesni?" Zandaril asked.

Penrys waved him aside with a remote look. "Shhh. That's for later."

She cocked her head at the closed outer door to her room on the third floor. The door between them, in adjacent student rooms, stood open, and Zandaril was seated in the one chair in her own room, while she perched cross-legged on the narrow bed. They seemed to be in an unoccupied corner of the half-empty building. "I'm waiting for someone to come. If I did that right, that's what they'll do."

"I don't like you showing them everything like that. They are not your friends."

She sighed. "Of course not. But I have to get their respect, one way or another. If I can't convince them it's better for them to fight with us on their side, they're dead anyway."

"But not us," he said. "Maybe we don't belong here. What are we doing, caught up in their trouble?" The meal had not agreed with him, too different from the Kigali cuisine he had gotten used to. Different seasonings, everything subtly… wrong.

His comment got him her full attention. "Walk away? We could. Why not?"

It still didn't feel right to him, and he spread as his hands as he tried to explain. "Among the Zannib, when there is a *qahulaj*, a bad wizard, one who makes things worse for his people, the word spreads. If other wizards hear of it, they set their tasks aside and come find him. And when there are enough, they remove the problem."

He leaned forward and tried to make her understand. "Because if we don't do it, who else can?"

Penrys said, "But this isn't *sarq*-Zannib. And the wizards here, they're as much our enemy as the Voice. Isn't that what you're saying?"

He nodded.

"Does it ever happen, in *sarq*-Zannib, that one of the wizards who comes when he hears of the problem is another bad one, and they fight on the wrong side together?"

Zandaril muttered, "I don't know." It had to have happened, people being what they were, but what did it mean that he knew no tales of it?

She half-smiled at him. "You understand, whatever I may have implied at dinner, I'm not going to be able to beat a trained attack from this many wizards—I'm sure of it. Once they learn how, it's going to be deadly to us. You might want to get out now, while you can."

He grunted. "If it will be a gamble anyway, we might as well be on the better side making an honest try."

He lifted his head at footsteps outside the door, and Penrys rose and opened it to a knock. The young man in the hall with a masked expression was the first one who had risen to her challenge.

"I am Dzangabtig," he announced with an inclination of his head. "We have decided we would like to study this with you, if you are willing, and I volunteered to come tell you."

Penrys raised an eyebrow. "How many?" She made no gesture to invite him inside.

"All of us," he insisted. "Tomorrow morning, yes? After breakfast?"

"I look forward to it," Penrys said, and shut the door in his face.

"When did you know you would be a wizard?" Penrys asked him.

It was still too early for sleep, but they were disinclined to leave their rooms on this first night, and Penrys was in an odd mood, despite her success at acquiring hostile students. Zandaril had not liked her summation of the danger she would be putting them in by teaching these Rasesni wizards how to fight more effectively, and he wondered if she feared it as well.

"Childhood stories, you want?"

"Why not?" She lay stretched out on the bed, fully clothed. She raised her head and looked at him, seated in his chair. "Unless you would rather not, of course…"

He waved her concern aside. "I was not yet *yathbantudin*, not yet nine years old, and it was the beginning of the spring season, the time of the *taridiqa*, so I was still in the winter camp, with my younger siblings and envious of my brother Butraz, impatient to join him next year.

"I had my chores, like all the children in the camp, and one of them was to bring meals to Umali, when my mother sent me. The women took charge of providing for those who lived alone, and most wizards live alone."

He glanced at her sideways to see how she took that statement, but there was no reaction.

"This was his first year not on the *taridiqa*, for as long as I had been alive. He seemed ancient to me, and all of my friends addressed him as 'grandfather' and stayed out of his path."

They'd made a game of it, in fact. He'd realized years ago that Umali could not have been oblivious to it, but he'd made no sign of noticing at the time. Beneath his dignity, perhaps.

"This time, when I brought him his meal, he was in a bad humor, and he barked at me to get out. I bowed and set down his basket in a hurry, but when I turned to go, he told me to stay. Only this time he said it out loud, and then I understood that the first command had been silent."

"Ah," Penrys commented.

"Yes. So all morning, until my mother came to find out where I had gotten to, we sat together in his *kazr*, on his *jimiz*, what we call a scholar's rug—he unrolled it between us, and my heart sang at the honor—and talked and talked, and never uttered a sound."

A world had opened for him that day, as though he had climbed his first mountain and seen a new landscape on the other side.

"What did your mother think?"

"Wizards run in families, but most of them never marry or have children. It's more like those mules—you have to keep breeding the horses and donkeys to get new ones."

A snort of laughter made him glance at Penrys. **So, something like this?** She pictured a seated elderly man with a turban from which jutted the long and shaggy ears of a mule.

He would have skinned me alive if I'd ever shown him something like that.

"My mother's family had produced no wizard for four generations, but the blood was there. And here I was, proof of it. And young, too, by a few years."

He remembered his mother's face when she found him there, in Umali's *kazr*. "My mother was proud, but sad, too. I didn't understand why, then."

"Hmm?"

"Wizards lead lonely lives. They are respected and cared for, they are important to the clan. But they don't marry or, if they do, it doesn't turn out well."

Penrys turned over on her side to look at him. "Why not?"

Could you marry the mind-deaf?

"It would be hard," she conceded. "Perhaps."

"There aren't many female wizards, *bikrajtayab*, at least among the Zannib—I don't know why. *They* have no problem finding a suitable wizard."

"And what happens with their children?"

"Mixed, some one way, some the other."

Penrys pursed her lips. "There are female wizards here, a few."

"We have songs, we do, about what the ordinary wife of a wizard gets up to, while her husband is away, doing wizard work. They're funny songs, of course, but my mother's face…"

"You must have hated that, thinking that would be your life."

He nodded. "And it made my friendships awkward, most of them. My family, well, they were not afraid of me, a child. But they were sorry for me."

He cleared his throat. "And it worried them, too, as they got older—this reminder that it was in their blood, too."

It was on the tip of his tongue to ask if it had been like that for her, too, when he remembered that she didn't know, and he swallowed the question.

"What was the training like?" she asked.

"We were a big clan, so we had two more wizards who traveled with the *taridiqa*. Very useful for messages, we all were. Umali got me started and passed me along to them when they returned to the winter camp. They taught me on the *tarizd* and in the *zudiqazd*, too, after he died."

He raised his head and looked at her. "I was lucky. Many clans have no wizards, and young ones go unrecognized, sometimes all their lives. I had three of them."

"But…?"

"They all agreed with each other!" It fairly exploded out of him. "There was a single opinion among them on any subject. If I questioned it, if I suggested an alternative, they were united in denial."

Ah, the evening he had raged in Butraz's tent, trying to explain his frustration. His brother had listened sympathetically. "What happens," he'd said, "when the *dirum-malb*, the junior herd-mistress, disagrees with her mentor, over and over?"

"They separate," Zandaril had replied, and his brother nodded.

He framed his response so Penrys could understand. "When a clan has no wizards to provide training, or if an apprentice becomes… restless, they seek out another wizard from some other clan in the tribe or even, if necessary from another tribe.

"So, I bridled my tongue and completed my apprenticeship, and they declared me 'Zan-daril,' a journeyman and presented me with my *jimiz*."

"But that's your name," she said. "You can't have been born to that name."

"I am still a journeyman, until I complete my *nayith*, my masterwork."

If we survive.

"Until then, that name will do. These foreigners,"—his gesture took in Chang's squadron as well as the building around them—"they don't know our customs. It's no matter for them."

"What's your real name? Do you get it back?"

"Not until a *jarghal*, a master wizard, decides I have completed my *nayith*. Until then, only my family…"

He felt her withdrawal and realized she thought he classed her with the other foreigners. It was not his intention to exclude her, and yet it was true.

"I have traveled all over *sarq*-Zannib, and several times to Kigali," he said, "For almost ten years I have bought books and studied with the other wizards I have met. Most were like my teachers, but not all."

The familiar ache set in. "I miss my family. I try to visit their *zudiqazd* each year, and bring them tidings and gifts.

"They wish me well, I know they do." He tapped his forehead meaningfully. "They dust the books I leave behind and introduce me to their children, and tell me about the increase to my herds. But I want to be part of their lives again."

"Why not return for good, then?" she muttered.

"I'm not done. I can't help it—something drives me to find out more, to *do* something with my learning."

He stopped and looked at her. **And then I met you.**

Another mentor? He could feel the constraint in her question.

More than that. Much more.

Zandaril stayed awake, thinking, after Penrys had finally gone to sleep, her back fitted against his chest. He could still feel in his muscles those phantom sensations from her demonstration in the council meeting that afternoon, what it felt like to her to fly, with his own weight dragging her down, the feel of the arrows piercing her.

Her guidance in how he could follow her sensations when they made love was key to showing him how to find her core knowledge, that portion of her mind where fundamentals resided.

The things they had in common, like riding, did not engage his attention, but her knowledge of Ellechen-*guma* became his to employ, and they'd held conversations where he was much more fluent than he'd ever been in the spoken language. As he thought about it, he found he'd even absorbed some of the art of being female, matters of dress and carriage that he had never considered—but this he couldn't mention without embarrassment.

He understood better now how she searched for minds when she scanned her surroundings, and what to look for when seeking animal minds. All of these were new skills for him, and he suspected when she was out of range the knowledge would fade away, but if he worked at them to make them his own, there was no reason the knowledge wouldn't become permanent.

Finally, she'd pointed him at a wizard sleeping in a distant room and told him to talk to her in Rasesni. And he'd been able to do so, drawing upon that man.

In a single night, he'd become a better wizard, a different one. Penrys had asked him to monitor her during the class lessons to come, to learn whatever she was learning, if he could, and now he understood how that might be possible.

He knew there was still one barrier between them. She hadn't pushed him to mind-share in the same way, after he'd explained the Zannib discomfort with it, weeks ago. She'd left him that privacy.

And now he found he neither needed it, nor wanted it.

He leaned down and nuzzled the back of her neck.

"Hmm?" came sleepily up to him.

"I wanted to share with you what you do to me, Pen-sha," he murmured in her ear, "When I do this… and you move, yes, like that…"

CHAPTER 41

Penrys hardly touched her breakfast, anticipating a stormy morning. After the meal, she stood aside with Zandaril and wiped her sweaty palms surreptitiously on her breeches.

"Watch m'back, will you?" she muttered to Zandaril, while they waited for the tables to be cleared away to the walls, and the benches arranged in rough rows.

She walked out and stood in front of three dozen wizards, waiting for them to arrange themselves and quiet down. The teachers, she saw, occupied the back rows. She couldn't spot Dhumkedbhod. *Has he absented himself from this? That's not good.*

Rather than shout, she looked over at Zandaril and mouthed "whistle" at him, and he obligingly set his fingers to his mouth and startled them into silence.

"All right, folks, we don't have a lot of time so let's take this seriously." Penrys made sitting down gestures at the last of them.

"Here are the facts. Yes, I have a chain, and yes, it's like the one your enemy has. My chain reacted to his chain when he saw me." She held up her hand to cut off the buzz.

"Me, I have no memory more than three years old. I don't know him, or any other chained wizard, and I'd like to keep it that way."

One voice cried out, "That's what they told us last night. How do we know that's true?"

She closed her eyes. Clearly last night's demonstration wasn't going to be enough.

"Try and see, if you want," Penrys said, and raised her shield. As she'd expected, he wasn't the only one to make the attempt, but none of the half-dozen made it through her shields. *They don't know how to coordinate an attack like that.*

"Enough," she said, but left her shield up. "Zandaril could teach you something about combining to overpower a stronger wizard. We'll add that to our list. I'm not going to let thirty-odd people in to paw through my mind, but I will, if necessary, show Zongchas whatever he needs to see. Good enough for now?"

The mood in the room was a little more respectful.

"Let me make a few observations first. I've spent the last three years trying to read my way through the Collegium library and experimenting with devices. That's supposed to be the biggest wizardly library in the world, but I've never heard of Rasesni mages, and it took me quite a while to make sense of one of your devices. So, libraries will only take you so far."

There were a few chuckles. They were listening to her now.

"I will tell you what I can do. Everything I can do. Maybe that's similar to what your enemy can do—we're guessing about that, because of the chain, and maybe we're wrong. I'll tell you everything I've learned and, more importantly, how I learn it, because I suspect he can do the same. He probably knows everything you do, from your captured colleagues, but he doesn't know what I do, whatever's unique to the Collegium.

"He's strong, very strong, but he's just one man, and there are limits to what he knows. I'm not at all as strong—I ran as fast as I could—but we can work together and we may know a lot of things he doesn't."

She turned to Zongchas. "Does he have anyone he delegates to, any wizard? Can he make more like himself?"

"Not that we've ever heard. He has fighters in his service, from rebellious hill tribes, from what you showed us in council, but if there are willing wizards, we don't know about them."

Vladzan looked away while Zongchas spoke, as if he disagree.

Penrys smiled broadly. "Good! Then we have a chance."

She looked down a moment, to sort out what she wanted to focus on. There wasn't enough time to take them back to the basics. She would have to use as many shortcuts as she could.

She raised her head and tried to include them all in her speech. "Our individual strength is inborn, more or less, but we can all develop better skills, starting now."

She broadcast to everyone there. **If you can hear me, raise your right hand.**

Everyone, without exception, raised a hand.

"That's a relief. There are places where mind-speech is not universal."

She pursed her lips. "I'll begin by showing you how I mind-shield, and if you do it differently, I'll learn from you. You shield to keep out a serious intrusion, but we'll use simple mind-speech as the test. If I'm shielded, you can't hear my mind-speech, you can't sense my mind at all."

"Zandaril, there, will show you how to gang up and coordinate your ability to penetrate or sustain a shield, using a sort of resonance. We'll take you three at a time, each of us, and I want anyone not participating to try and monitor what we're doing while they wait."

She pointed at the three nearest and beckoned them over to her.

By mid-morning, Penrys felt like she'd made good progress with the basics of self-defense. All but one of the young students had successfully raised a shield and defended it to some degree, and she thought the one failure was just too nervous and would get there on his own if he kept trying.

As they came to her, she checked their own methods but found nothing new for herself. She expected that to change when they switched over to physical magic later, assuming there would be enough time for that.

Keeping a random group of them out of her shielded mind posed no difficulty at all initially, but as the older wizards returned from Zandaril's session, that changed. What they learned from him about a coordinated attack was effective. She could feel the difference in the last group of three.

"Don't go yet. Could you feel that you were more powerful, bonded together?"

Ichorrog was part of the trio, and he nodded, scarred face flushed with exertion. "It was better this time with all of us, instead of the first time when we tried it one by one."

"Up until now," Penrys said, "the defense has been stronger than the offense, in all cases. That's going to change, and when it does, we may do each other damage."

"We have to learn how to spar first, to do it safely," Ichorrog suggested.

"Right, and then how to fight for real," Penrys said.

She swallowed. "If I can hold off three of you, at your current level of practice, how many of you will it take to overwhelm my defense? I'm weaker than your enemy. If you can't beat me, how will you beat him?"

Zandaril's head turned as he listened to her. "This is dangerous."

"Yes, but it has to be done. We need to gauge effectiveness somehow. How many does it usually take to overpower a wizard-tyrant?"

"Five or six is typically enough, rarely more." He paused. "I never heard that the target liked the experience." She could hear the disapproval in his voice.

"Yes, well, want to organize a fighting team from your pupils anyway?" she said.

Zandaril glared at her, but he assembled an uneven team, the three she had just held off, and a trio of youngsters. "They have to learn to work with whomever they find," he explained.

The students looked ill at ease yoked with their elders, but they dutifully went through the linkage exercises Zandaril had shown them. Then Penrys felt Ichorrog lead his team into a bond with the prepared link, and he looked with his eyebrow raised.

She held her shield and nodded.

The attack was much stronger than she expected, but her shield held.

Zandaril pulled another set of three into the group, and then more. Finally, when the last ones joined the attack, her shield buckled and broke.

She found herself on the floor, straddled by Zandaril, with his hand on his belt-knife as if daring anyone to approach. Her head rang like a bell.

"It's all right," she told him, thickly, as she sat up. "It's probably easier for them to just slit my throat, if they mean me harm."

She hauled herself up with the aid of the bench she'd fallen off of, and sat down on it and waited for things to stop spinning.

"See, now we have some useful information," she said. "The Voice kept us both immobilized and broke Zandaril's shield. He was moments from breaking mine. So, either he's as strong as several Rasesni wizards, all by himself, or he was able to draw upon the wizards he held in bondage."

"The next step is to see if I'm stronger than most of you. If I'm not, them maybe he isn't either, and it's all the power of his captives."

Ichorrog said, "I'll volunteer. Only seems fair—we didn't intend to hurt you."

Yet. They didn't intend to hurt me yet, wasn't that what he really meant?

Penrys raised her hand. "Doesn't matter, this is how we learn. I'll try to be, um, gentle."

She looked up at the standing Zandaril uncertainly. "I've never attacked anyone like this either."

Ichorrog braced himself and, when he nodded, she probed his shield and then concentrated on a steady pressure. It blew apart almost immediately, but she thought she was able to hold her punch back from doing damage. Ichorrog paled and staggered, but remained standing.

"You all right?" she asked.

He half-smiled. "You have a lighter touch than I do." He looked over his shoulder to his two teammates. "Let's try it as a group."

Penrys felt them form the link and when Ichorrog gave her the nod, she repeated her simple assault. The combined shield lasted a little longer, then tore apart. *That's disconcerting. How many would it take?*

"Enough for now," Zandaril said, before they could rig a larger combination. "All of you need to practice both attack and defense, or someone's going to get hurt."

Penrys gratefully let him organize groups of three to spar with each other while she waited for her head to stop throbbing.

CHAPTER 42

Well, this is an improvement.

Penrys found the mood at lunch a very different affair from the meal the night before. The excited voices echoed off the walls as the wizards, in groups, argued about what they had been practicing during the morning sessions. She still couldn't spot Dhumkedbhod.

Zongchas himself had participated—all of them had. "How do you think it went?" he asked.

"Fine. It was fine," she said. "Um, where was Dhumkedbhod? Do I need to see him independently?"

"There were important matters he needed to address." The embarrassment she felt belied Zongchas's reply. *So, he won't participate. I hope they try to teach him separately—they're going to need everyone.* Mentally, she shrugged. There was nothing she could do about it.

"I've got one more big lesson for the mental skills this afternoon, and then we need to do some dull work. Calibration."

At Zongchas's puzzled look, she added. "Think of us as weapons. Don't you want to know what we can do, so we can be deployed most effectively? Look, call your weakest student a "unit." That's the least amount a wizard can defend with a shield or attack against a shield. Or compel a shield—that's for the afternoon session, too.

"We can only measure against each other. If a student can barely defend against two of the weakest, but not three, then he's a 'level two.'"

Zongchas was nodding along, and so was Zandaril just beyond him.

Penrys said, "We need to rate everyone, and then measure them in groups, too. First we need to confirm that the levels can be added, in other words, if I take a level two defender and a level four defender, they together can fend off a level five or six attacker. Understand?"

She raised her eyes to see Zandaril looking intrigued. "That's how it works, but we never measured it precisely," he confirmed.

"After that, we need to see what level I am, and make some guesses about your stronger enemy in comparison. Then you'll know if you have enough absolute power, in principle, to stand against him."

She turned to Vladzan, seated next to her, who was following the conversation.

"You, *Grakkedo*, might not think this matters for physical magic," she said, "But why is it the devices aren't working? Is one of the reasons that your wizards can't get close enough to trigger them? What if they could get much closer, in high-level groups? That would make a difference, wouldn't it?"

His expression changed from polite interest to active engagement.

"Right," she said. "I thought so. We'll be exploring your side of things starting tomorrow."

"Try again. This isn't easy."

Zandaril watched Penrys coaching the whole group in a skill that few of them had realized was possible. Three of them stood before her, frustrated with yet another failure.

"Look, you know how to shield and you know how to break a shield. This isn't very different. You're taking your own shield and imposing it on someone else, and leaving yourself defenseless while you do it, so you *must* work at least in pairs, one to attack, and the other to defend you both. And remember, if you're trying to shield yourself and someone else, you're dividing your power with someone else, so you're both weaker. Same for the attack."

She stopped. "Maybe numbers will make this easier. Let's say the target's a level four defender. The first step is to overwhelm his shield, so the attacker must be greater than level four, so let's say he's a six.

Zandaril watched her students struggling to follow her.

"The attacker breaks the target's shield. Easy, right?"

Heads nodded.

"Then he goes to impose a shield and he succeeds. That means he can't shield himself, so his buddy, who's also a level six, defends them both. But *that* means each of them is defended at a level three or so, not at level six. Right?"

Fewer heads nodded.

Penrys continued her scenario. "So, the target has had a shield imposed by the attacker, but if the attacker's concentration slips for just a moment, the target can counterattack, at his own level four. But the attacker is still trying, so he's only defended at a level three. What's going to happen?"

One of the younger boys, who'd been following closely, spoke up eagerly. "The attacker isn't shielded well enough while he's attacking, and the target rips through his buddy's shared field and then his, one at a time, and thumps them both before they can react."

Laughter rose from the group, and Penrys nodded.

"That's right. That's how two level six attackers get thumped by a level four defender. Y'understand?"

Zandaril realized that's what she'd been doing the night she appeared during the attack from the mirror. She'd been dividing her shield among three others, until she reached the limit of what could withstand the attack. *I wonder why she didn't counter-attack instead of just waiting for Chang's bluff and for someone to turn the mirror away. Maybe she couldn't see what to attack, and maybe the attacker couldn't see who was defending.*

"Let's take a break for a few minutes, and start again," she said.

Before Zandaril could ask his question, Zongchas walked over to them. "This is fascinating, a whole area we've never considered. How did you find out about it?"

Penrys's mouth quirked. "Recent knowledge, and it's your doing." At his raised eyebrow, she elaborated. "The attempt to control Chang's command tent? Through the mirror?"

Zandaril watched, fascinated, as an expression of guilty knowledge flashed across Zongchas's face.

"Ah," she said. "Thought you might remember that. That was an imposed shield, so this can't be entirely new to you." She cleared her throat. "I happened to be the one defending."

Zongchas sputtered a bit but didn't elaborate.

Zandaril was struck by one conclusion. *That Veneshjug must have been pretty high-level, at least as high as me. If he's here, he should stand out. But what level was Penrys, that she could defend against him, even divided four ways? Four times stronger?*

Suddenly three dozen wizards didn't seem like very many against the enemy that had so casually imposed a shield upon them both, at a significant distance.

And was Veneshjug here? He hadn't recognized him from the minds around him, but he had little confidence that he remembered his original impression well enough. Surely Penrys would have told him if she'd found him among their students.

It was time.

Penrys had delayed as long as she could, but as the late afternoon light slanted through the windows of the practice hall and lit the dust in the air, stirred up from all the activity, she knew there had to be one more test.

She raised her voice. "All right, everyone."

The wizards wrapped up their current exercises and quieted down.

"All of you have been evaluated by your approximate level of strength. Don't forget you'll improve with practice, to some degree, though most of this is innate."

She hesitated. "Now it's time for the part that matters. Your enemy imposed a shield on both of us." She waved at Zandaril. "He was at least a couple of miles away when he did it, and he had control, too."

It was silent in the hall.

"How strong was he, that he could do that?" She cocked her head at the same young student who had spoken up before.

"Well," he said, "He had to be stronger than the defenses you two could use, right?"

"That's right. Now I want you to sort yourselves into groups by your strength. Weakest on the left, strongest on the right, and leave a little separation between levels."

She waited while they shuffled into ten or twelve groups. There were only two in the weakest group, at level one. Most were clustered in the middle groups around level six or seven. Her first attacker, Dzangabtig was alone at the ninth position, and there were three on the far right, Zongchas among them.

"So, how strong is Zongchas, Zandaril?," she asked.

Zandaril cleared his throat. "That group seems to be something like a level twelve," he said. He himself stood with a trio of level tens.

"That's quite a range."

Dzangabtig called out from his solitary spot. "What level are you?"

"That's what we're going to find out," Penrys said, trying to keep the apprehension out of her voice. "And there's only one way we know how to do that, right?"

Several of the students looked uneasy. No one had liked having a shield imposed upon them, and only the strongest of them had needed to face more than one simultaneous attacker trying to overwhelm them.

"Let's start with the strongest. That'll get us there faster," she said. "A group of you got through my defenses this morning, remember, so you know it can be done. We're testing a different skill, now, one that goes beyond that, and working on getting more precise results."

She pulled a chair over and sat down as a precautionary measure. "Each person step up to the front and add his strength to the others. If it isn't enough, the next one will come and join them. Y'understand?"

She leaned forward in the chair and braced her forearms on her thighs. "Stop when you succeed. Please."

Then she bowed her head, raised her shield, and stared at the floor.

Though not from the strongest group, Zandaril stepped up first, just outside of her range of vision. She felt his attempt as a pressure against the sphere that was her mind's boundary, but it didn't trouble her concentration much. In a few moments, she heard footsteps approaching, and the pressure grew. Then another came, and another.

She lost track of the count. She had the advantage of controlling just one thing, a single shield, while the external pressures wavered and fluctuated, instead of consolidating into a single weapon. Here or there two were joined effectively, but most were not.

Her vision vanished after a bit, and she was conscious only of her internal struggle. She knew they would have to break her shield before they could impose an external one, and she tried not to flinch in anticipation. By concentrating on the roundness of her shield, she helped deflect some of the ill-aimed attacks, but there were too many of them, coming from multiple directions, and, finally, her shield was stripped away, and she felt her mind laid defenseless to the chaotic force pushing against it.

Nothing changed for several moments, and then, like a great muffling cloak, she felt something like the immobility she remembered when they'd hid beneath the hollow of the tree near the Horn. She tried to mind-speak and could not.

A voice that was not Zandaril's cried out, "Enough!" and the pressure vanished in bits and pieces. Penrys blinked repeatedly, but it was a little while before her sight returned and she could feel someone grasping her shoulder and shaking her.

"Are you all right?"

Zandaril's voice. Sounds worried.

"I'm fine," she said, "Or, at least, I will be."

She gathered her feet under her and tried to stand up. Her knees buckled, but Zandaril caught her upper arm and kept her from falling. She made a second attempt and succeeded.

The sweat on her scalp itched, and she turned away from her audience until she was sure she could master her expression.

"How many was it?" she asked Zandaril.

"Turn around and see for yourself."

She turned back, and saw eight wizards standing at the front, including Dzangabtig. Her eyebrows climbed her face.

"What…"

"Adding me, that's about ninety-eight, all our levels together. Took almost eighty to get through, and then another twenty to impose the shield."

"How much do we need," she said, hoarsely, looking up at his face.

"You and I are about a hundred and ten, together. How much stronger do you think he is?"

She sat back down in her chair and tried to calculate it. "Lots," was all she could manage.

"But does that mean sheer power's going to work?" Zongchas sat with a few of the senior wizards around the table in the main hall after the class finished and held an impromptu conference.

Penrys grimaced at Zongchas's question, but she had to answer it.

"A group of your mages defeated me, which is good news for us all," she said. "But, altogether, all of your people only add up to about two hundred and fifty, counting levels, and that's if they coordinate perfectly well together, which we know is unlikely. The fewer individuals trying to bond together, the better, if you want a focused attack. You felt how inefficient it was, yes?"

Zongchas nodded.

"We're guessing I'm about a hundred," she said. He looked at her, clearly missing her point, and she rolled her eyes.

"Look, it took your nine best to do it. What if I were trying to fight back? Who's going to shield them? The other, what, twenty-eight weaker wizards? Remember my example about how a level four can 'thump' two level sixes? You can't attack me and defend the attackers at the same time—you haven't got enough strength to do it.

"Besides, there's only one of me, and that's actually an advantage—I can attack wizards like you one by one from a position of strength, if I'm not overwhelmed or distracted. I mean, I've never tried it, y'understand, but we'll do the experiment and I've no doubt of the outcome."

Zongchas's face changed entirely as he worked through the problem.

Zandaril said, "It's like fighting a bunch of small armies with a big one. You might have more people over all, but if the big one can attack your armies one at a time, it's hopeless."

Ichorrog had been part of the attack group, and he spoke into the silence. "I thought, we thought, you'd be fighting with us." He looked at Zandaril, seated next to her. "Both of you."

"I plan to," she said, "and that'll help, but…" She rubbed her face—it had been a long day. "He's stronger than I am, much stronger. We still don't know if it was him alone who overpowered us, or him somehow drawing on his captives. We're probably better off trying for a physical assault instead."

Vladzan glanced at Zongchas, and Penrys saw the small nod he received. He said, quietly, "I may have a way to help with this."

"I'm listening," she said.

"You and I need to pool our knowledge about devices and what they can do, before we do anything else. I assume you've been skimming my mind for it anyway…"

He waved away her stammered excuse.

"I expected it, but we need to do this formally and see if any good ideas come from it."

"I didn't really get much," Penrys said, stifling her embarrassment. "Just some sense of what's possible, but it's very different from what I've studied at the Collegium."

"How so?" he asked.

"Power-stones, lots of power-stones," she said. "And very clever uses of them."

She cleared her throat. "Have you looked at my own knowledge in this area, yet?"

A slow smile appeared on Vladzan's thin face. "It might be useful to find out how that chain works, yes?"

She swallowed, and waited for the rest of it.

"And the wings," he added, contemplatively. "I wonder how they're powered." Zongchas and the other Rasesni mages stared at him. "Oh, yes," he told them. "They're some sort of device, too, I imagine."

CHAPTER 43

Zandaril had excused himself from dinner early and vanished, as some of the others did, but Penrys lingered over the meal in a desultory discussion of possible plans before breaking away eventually.

She scanned briefly for Zandaril and found him out of the building but not far away and clearly in no distress, so she dismissed the puzzle of what he was doing and paid a visit to the library, something she'd been longing to do since they'd arrived.

As she walked in she inhaled the familiar scents, and smiled. *I would know a library blindfolded.*

An older wizard occupying a table in the front area with a stack of books looked up nervously at her entrance. His face was known to her from the classes, but there were too many names to remember. She nodded at him and picked up one of the darkened hand-lights near the door. In a moment, she'd charged its power-stone and carried it with her into the closely spaced shelving.

When she surfaced again, she was startled to realize almost three hours had passed. What had made her stop was the realization that she was charging the power-stone for the lamp for the third time.

No one was left in the front area. She sat down at the nearest table and stared blankly at its dented and scratched surface, while her body finally recognized that its legs were tired.

So many books. So many that are not in the Collegium's catalogue, I'm sure of it. Not just Rasesni books, none of which are there, but the dozens and dozens from other lands.

She looked at her hands, her fingers flexing, and snorted. *They're not tired—they're itching to steal whatever they can snatch, whatever my conscience says.*

Penrys walked back to her isolated room down empty corridors, her thoughts still on the endless stream of titles. Her mind assembled the bookcases into a single image of all the shelves on one impossibly tall and wide wall. She thought it might equal perhaps a twentieth of the Collegium's collection, and almost all of it new to her.

Such a plethora of gods, and so many of the titles devoted to secret knowledge. Did the devotees of one god read books dedicated to others? Was it allowed? Encouraged?

She'd sometimes thought of the knowledge represented in the Collegium's books as a river with many streams running in to make it broader. Was this more like a forest, each god's tree standing tall, with only superficial vines connecting them together? Surely not—how could they be so advanced in power-stone technology if they didn't share?

When she opened the door to her room, she blinked at the vision of Zandaril stretched out comfortably on her bed. Then her nose caught up with her eyes and she smiled at the reek of alcohol. *So that's what he was doing.*

His eyes popped open at the sound of her entrance and he grinned up at her.

"You're back. I've been waiting for you."

Her lips quivered and she looked down indulgently. "I assume you weren't drinking alone."

She took the chair and stretched out her own legs. "So, tell me about it. I thought they weren't our friends."

"That's why it's good to make *new* friends. One new friend, anyway. Dzantig. That's his short name. You remember Dzantig, yes? The one who thought he could beat you first."

"Yes," she said. "I know Dzangabtig."

"Did you know he helped when they broke your shield? Told them to back off when I thought they might not. Told them if they harmed you they wouldn't be able to learn from you."

"No, I didn't know. That's good."

Zandaril lifted one arm from his prone position to waggle a finger at her. "I am sympathetic foreigner to these wizards. They come talk to me."

His hand waved in the air.

"They think I am brave to travel with you." He nodded his head. "Me, too. They want to know why you haven't eaten me yet."

Penrys told him solemnly, "Not hungry enough." It was hard work keeping a straight face.

He nodded again as if he appreciated her answer. "I am not *very* drunk, you know. I told Dzantig I had to be able to walk back to my room."

With a distinct leer, he added, "*Walking* isn't really what I meant."

A while later, well past the middle of the night, Zandaril rose from their bed and wrapped his discarded robe round him. Enough light from the sky glow of a clear night entered through the window that Penrys could make out his form as he pulled the chair over closer to the bed and sat down.

"I must talk to you seriously," he said, and Penrys judged him nearly sober.

"These wizards, some of them, they tell me things you don't hear. I smile and nod like a stupid foreigner, and they tell me their worries."

Penrys raised herself up to prop her back against her pillow and the headboard.

"What do they talk about?"

"Sacrilege. Some of them are outraged to be exposing the secrets of their gods. Their gods are not all friends, and neither are their priests and followers."

He leaned forward. "Many of the older ones are priests, did you know?

"I thought so, from their dress."

"This did not start with you. It is Zongchas who pushed this policy, who forced them to mingle all the books and writings they brought into exile. And not all of them are unhappy about it. The younger ones are excited to learn forbidden things."

He snorted. "Even wizards behave like children. But this is a big problem for us. For you."

Penrys blinked. "Why us?"

"Because they can't blame Zongchas and do anything about it. But you, you they can blame. You are a great target, just like their enemy, but right in front of them."

"I don't expect them to like me," she protested. "I expect them to understand that they must band together if they want to defeat him."

"That's what their heads tell them, but not their hearts. Not the devotion they give their gods. Some of them think this Surdo arose to punish them for abandoning the old ways."

"I don't have time to sooth a bunch of ruffled feathers that they don't even tell me about."

Zandaril looked at her as if to evaluate her statement, and shook his head. "Pen-sha, heresy is dangerous. Dangerous! It damages our working truce. You are too blind to understand this. You have no gods."

Those words chilled her. She knew this disturbed him about her, but they hadn't discussed it. "I mean no harm to anyone's gods."

He looked at her sadly. "You looked at the library tonight. Those are not books about magic, they're books about the secrets of the gods. You know this—you saw the titles on Veneshjug's books."

"But it's the same thing," she protested.

"Not to a believer."

Silence fell between them. There was nothing she could say to refute him.

He must have seen the worry on her face.

"Well, never mind. Me, I do not believe in their gods, either. And if we ever find a way to loot their library, I expect my share."

CHAPTER 44

The next morning, Penrys and Vladzan huddled at one end of the hall over a long table with loose power-stones and bits of wood. Vladzan kept two of his students running back and forth for example devices.

Zandaril guided ever larger groups of wizards into binding their efforts together smoothly, while keeping an eye on the serious discussion between the two device experts. Penrys and Vladzan looked like any two specialists, meeting by accident and sharing notes. They could have been merchants, or craftsmen—the same intense focus, abbreviated speech, and appreciation for new concepts, spiced with arguments about which methods were better.

Finally, he set his best students to practicing with each other, and sauntered over to see what he could learn.

Penrys looked up as he walked over. "Good timing," she called. "We've just about settled the basic differences between our schools."

"What have you learned?" he asked. "What can we use?"

"Well, it boils down to just a few things. The Collegium seems to have better sensors and better movers for people, but Vladzan's been showing me some great triggers and some clever ways of, I guess you would say, leveraging the applied force. Oh, and they've got some very important insights into what holds substances together. You know, the way I described how their trap works, by breaking the bond that holds a substance together."

She looked over at Vladzan. "That a fair summary?"

He nodded, and Zandaril noted the excitement in his posture. "Seems to me like our native abilities are pretty similar. What she calls 'moving,' 'binding,' and 'destruction'—those are our fundamentals, too. Seems like the Ellech are better with the physical magic, and maybe the Zannib with the mental, while we, and Penrys here, do both. Not all of us can manage the physical stuff, mind you, but most of us."

"They charge power-stones like they do in Ellech," Penrys continued, "But they've got a method of storing the power in a group of stones and using them at once."

Vladzan cleared his throat. "We've sketched out some notions of how we can combine our knowledge." He gestured at several sheets of paper, with hasty notes scrawled on them, and a few sketches. "But we need weapons, and we need them in a hurry. We don't have time for experiments."

That last was accompanied by a pointed look at Penrys.

"Look," she told him, "I've already explained I can charge all the power-stones you can get me. The problem's going to be some sort of tactical plan and, I'll admit, that's not my area of expertise."

Zandaril said, "So what's the next step? What can our enemy do, and how does all this help?"

He didn't like the look of uncertainty that crossed both their faces. Vladzan pulled out one of the pieces of paper, with two short columns on it and put it in front of her.

Penrys hesitated, then explained to Zandaril. "That's a list of what we know, and it's not much. That first column is me. How am I different from, say, Vladzan? First, I'm much stronger with the mental skills. Same skills he has, but much stronger. Second, I can charge power-stones using my chain. Oh, and by the way, he can't see power in it the way we can in the stones. Remember I wondered about that, since I couldn't see the chain m'self?

"Third, the wings. I showed him. We need to do some more tests, but he agrees with me that they're probably something made, like a device, even if they bleed, and neither of us have any idea how that was done or where they go, or much of anything else.

"Finally, there's the healing, the speed of it and the absence of scars. We don't know how that works, either—might be built in, but we don't know how."

She looked down at the paper. "That's it, that's all that's special."

Zandaril shook his head. "Your lack of memory."

"Might just be an accident of whatever happened. It's hardly a skill."

"Maybe, but I think it's a clue of some kind. And don't forget the obvious," he said.

She looked at him, puzzled.

"Who are your people? I didn't get a long look at him, before we… jumped, but I don't think he looked a lot like you. Not your, um, tribe. Where do you belong? And do they all have ears like yours?"

Her hand rose involuntarily to the side of her face, and Vladzan raised an eyebrow. "Oh. I forgot to tell you about that," she told him. She pulled her hair back and gave him a good look, and he sighed and extended the list on the sheet of paper.

Then he proceeded to read from it. "In the other column, for this Surdo, it's a different list. Problem is, we don't know if he has wings or not, if his ears are furry, if he has physical magic—we know very little."

Penrys interrupted. "But we do know he's much stronger than I am. Is that native, or is that assisted, by something like power-stones? Can he draw on his chain directly? Or is he drawing on those wizards? That's my theory."

Vladzan looked at Zandaril. "She wants to test that."

"How?" Zandaril asked her.

Penrys looked down. "It would take two things. I'd need to have a couple of wizards who are high level, that I'd try to draw on and add their strength to my own, without their cooperation. Then I'd need a test like the one yesterday, where we line up enough wizards to overpower me and see if I really am effectively stronger."

She glanced up at Zandaril. "I don't know what that would do to them. And if it hurt them, I don't know if the damage would be permanent or not. And if this is what he's doing, I'd have to look for the weaknesses in it—can he keep it up for a long time, what happens when he sleeps, does he burn out his wizards stealing their power, can they resist…

"These are horrible things, and I don't see how it can be tested without doing harm. Especially since we know his captives haven't been able to bond together to overpower him. Why is that? Don't they know how to? Have they been broken somehow? I don't want to break someone to find out."

Zandaril looked down at her impatiently while she toyed with the list, and thought about how to put it.

"If you bring these wizards," he flung his arm out to include the rest of the people in the hall, "to a fight with the Voice without knowing the answers to some of these questions, you may all die, and hundreds after you. You *have* to make the tests. Even if it hurts people. What choice do we have?"

He turned to Vladzan for support, and the man nodded. "Your friend is right—it has to be done."

Penrys looked haunted at the prospect.

"You'll be careful," Zandaril said. "I know you will, because I'm going to be your first test subject."

They argued about it for most of an hour. Penrys refused to consider it.

She looked at Zandaril's calm face while he tried to persuade her, and pictured him in the group of wizards, drawing water from the air on the Horn—broken, and hopeless.

"No," she said. "You don't learn medicine by starting to experiment on your… brother. Your partner."

That made him pause, and Vladzan, pulled a scrap of paper from his pile of notes.

"I think you may be worrying about nothing," he told Penrys. "I don't think whatever Surdo is doing destroys his wizards, not directly. It doesn't make sense."

He pointed at some figures.

"Let's say he can drain a wizard, like you suspect. Then either the wizard can recover, or he can't. Right?"

She nodded, provisionally.

"If they don't recover, then it's a one-time event," he said. "He uses them up, and that's it."

He steepled his fingers together and looked at her. "There aren't that many wizards. It wouldn't be enough power to be useful for long. If he had captured two hundred of them and drained them all, once, he would have gone through all of that power long since."

Zandaril said, "But we saw his wizards using power to provide water. They were tired, it was hard, but it was also clearly something they did all the time."

He turned to Penrys. "If it broke them, drained them permanently, he wouldn't be so willing to spend it like that, and they wouldn't have constant work to do like that."

He's right. But it's not that simple.

"If I tested a new bow by shooting you with it to see what kind of damage it could do, you might not die, you might recover. But you would still be injured, and I would…" She couldn't finish. *I would still be the person who hurt my (my what?) my partner deliberately, to see if I could.*

Vladzan looked at her. "We will do this thing. It is necessary."

Zandaril cleared his throat. "We need to know if her theory is right, that it can be done at all. Then we need to know how much, for how long, and what the effect is, on both her and me."

Vladzan organized it, and everyone in the hall stopped to gather around and eavesdrop on the process, some on Penrys, and some on Zandaril.

Penrys watched Zandaril take a chair next to her, with an assumed air of nonchalance. "I'm going to start with my shield up," he said, "since surely no wizard would go to this willingly."

She nodded, her mouth dry. The room was silent.

And it began.

She closed her eyes, not wanting to see his face, but changed her mind. *If he has the courage to do this, I'll do him the honor of watching the damage I do him.*

The shield Zandaril raised was stronger than before. *All this practice has helped him. But it's not enough.* Almost effortlessly, she stripped it away and heard his sudden indrawn breath.

She clenched her jaw and suppressed his efforts to raise the shield again. *How would I find his power?* She thought of the power-stones, and how they felt to her mind, then she looked within him for something similar, and found it. As if she were moving something with her mind, she called upon his own power instead of a power-stone, and lifted a mug from the table next to her with it.

Zandaril's shock at feeling the physical magic performed struck her like a blow. It was something he couldn't do by himself, and it seemed particularly nasty to him to be used like a puppet this way.

Penrys choked but held her grip on him. She dropped the mug and lifted his own hand, externally, using physical magic, while he fought unsuccessfully to pull it back down into his lap.

She stopped, then. One more test. She pulled at his power, like sucking on a straw, and swallowed it into herself, somehow. As gently as she could do it, she felt his horror at the sensation, and she stopped before she'd drained him completely, as best she could judge.

His face was white and strained, and she couldn't look at it any more. She cast her eyes down and released him.

Her vision was blurred, but she reached for the mug with her mind one last time and spun it around as though she were using a power-stone. *That part worked, anyway. But at what cost?*

She sneaked a peek at Zandaril.

A ghastly smile flickered on his face. *It hurt him, of course it did.* She leaned in his direction, forgetting their audience, to put a hand on his arm, and he… flinched away. She snapped her hand back and turned her head away. *He sees me as a monster now, and he's right.* She shuddered.

When she lifted her face and looked at the audience of wizards, no one would meet her eye, not even Vladzan.

"I'll be fine," Zandaril said to her. His voice was remote and flat, to her ears.

She stood up abruptly and turned her back to him. She motioned him away with her hands, and walked, almost ran, out of the hall.

CHAPTER 45

Penrys had no idea where she was going when she stumbled out of the hall, but the door to the street wasn't far. Behind her she could hear the rising clamor of voices and she walked faster to put them further behind her, until she reached the door and opened it. Then she stood there at the top of the stairs leading down into the square.

There was a stone bench to the right of the doorway, and she sank onto it and took a few deep breaths to try and calm herself.

So, I can't drink power-stones, any more than any other wizard, but that's all right—I can drink wizards instead.

Her stomach revolted and she concentrated on swallowing.

An image of Chang came to her mind. *A general can't make friends of his soldiers, can he? Or how could he use them in battle?*

The door of the guild hall opened, and Zandaril stepped out. When he spotted her, his face lit up with a tired smile. He sat down deliberately next to her, and she shrank from him.

Zandaril stretched out an arm, laid it around her shoulder, and drew her to his side.

She couldn't meet his eyes. **I am so sorry.**

Look at me. I already have a shield returning.

Penrys reached out tentatively. Zandaril was weak, and bruised, but it was true—he was able to raise a light shield. *If there's this much recovery in a short time…*

It was worth it. We learned important things, and no harm done.

She sighed. *At least he didn't flinch away again.*

"They were worried about you, inside. I told them I'd come get you," Zandaril said. "We have to go back. They need us, and they know it now."

She muttered into her lap. "That a wizard could do what I just did, over and over, and think nothing of it… I don't understand such a man."

"We don't have to understand him," Zandaril told her. "Just stop him."

By common consent, they broke the classes and arranged to resume after the mid-day meal. Penrys was grateful for the chance to settle her thoughts, but she could only pretend to eat.

They established some of the limits to what Penrys could do, before the next session wound down in the late-afternoon.

She could steal the power of another wizard, if she could break his shield. While she couldn't compel his mind, she could control his body from the outside, clumsily.

She wasn't sure where the power went, once she took it, if she didn't use it immediately. Maybe she stored it in her chain.

Vladzan tried to follow her example on one of the student wizards, but Penrys couldn't feel any increase in his strength when she tested his shield afterward. Of course, the power levels were small, from her perspective, so she thought the test was inconclusive.

You can't put more power into a power-stone than it will hold. That's why you sometimes need more stones.

Maybe Vladzan can't get any stronger than he is now, so if he doesn't use the stolen power directly, it's lost to him. That's why no one's exploited this already as a way to get stronger. Easier to just use power-stones.

How much power can I hold?

There was no way to answer that without experiment, and she was unwilling to drain a roomful of wizards to find out. She'd never felt a limit from the chain, but then she hadn't subjected it to a deliberate attempt to exhaust it.

Or had she? *Why could I only shield three men in Chang's tent, when I arrived? By the numbers we've been exploring, it should've been more. Was the chain the source of the power that moved me a quarter of the way around the world? Maybe there wasn't much left afterward.*

"Vladzan," she said. "Where are your power-stones? You must have a lot of them here somewhere, right?"

He eyed her warily.

She waved her hand dismissively. "I don't need to see your armory. I want to try something. How many can you charge, each of you, at a time?"

"Depends on the wizard. Students can do a couple of small ones, every day. I can do several."

"What happens if you do too many?" she asked.

He stared at her.

She shrugged. "It's never happened to me."

Vladzan took on a thoughtful expression. "If you exceed your limit, you can feel diminished for a day or two."

"So, it goes from your own core to the power-stones, yes?"

He raised his eyebrows. "That's how we think of it, yes."

"You see, I don't do it like that, m'self—I never thought to ask. I do it from here." She tapped the chain around her neck. "At least it feels like that to me."

She continued, "So couldn't you use the number of power-stones a wizard could charge as a rough test of his strength?"

He nodded, seeing where she was going. "That would be more precise, and simpler, than testing against each other."

"Right. So, how many can I charge? Just me, with the chain?"

Vladzan beckoned two of the senior wizards over and sent them away.

They returned in a few minutes with two sacks each, larger than the ones Penrys carried in her pack. Word spread through the hall about the test, and Zandaril came over with the others to watch.

Vladzan opened one sack and poured some of the stones out onto a table top where their facets gleamed dully in a variety of colors.

Vladzan scooped up a small handful. "This would be about my daily limit," he said.

Penrys said, "If I'm about ten times stronger, then I should be able to do about ten times as many, right?"

He nodded, and added nine more handfuls to the first one. Altogether, it was about a third of the sack.

Penrys sat down at the table. "So, let's start there," she said. "Feel free to watch with me, everyone."

She felt the mental echo that told her others were watching.

"One stone—that's nothing," she said out loud. She picked up a stone and powered it casually.

"A handful…" She scooped up part of the little pile and powered it. "No different."

"What about the rest of them?" She laid her hand down on top of the heap and powered them all. They glowed vividly to her mind, but she felt no reduction in strength.

She glanced at Vladzan with a question in her eyes, and he gestured at the remainder of the sack.

"All right, let's try the rest of them." She picked up the sack, two thirds full, and powered the contents.

She stood up, and she could hear her footsteps on the stone floor clearly in the silent hall as she walked over to the three unopened sacks. She took a breath, laid her hands on top of them and powered all the stones inside. She felt giddy for a moment, as if she'd taken in too little air, but she didn't think she was actually weakened. The shock of the watchers was perceptible, and she raised her shield and thrust them out.

She smiled uncertainly at Vladzan. "Well, there must be a limit, but maybe there's no point continuing. It's got to be the chain—that's much more than I should be able to do with just my own power, even given the… disparity in our strengths."

"And if I can do it," she said, "so can your enemy. That must be what he does with the captive wizards. He drains them for his own use, and keeps them drained most of the way. The more of them he can keep alive, the stronger he becomes."

Vladzan looked at the sacks of power-stones, one partially emptied out onto the table. "It's a shame we can't boost our own core strength directly from these, but it's a one-way flow."

A commotion at the doorway disturbed the low conversations that had resumed, and a rider, dust-covered and weary, strode in. The servant who escorted him led him straight to Zongchas and he handed over a packet of papers from the satchel slung over his shoulders.

Zongchas scanned through them quickly while all eyes watched. When he lifted his head the conversations stopped. "We're out of time," he said. "They're on the move, east from Nakshadzam. Southeast, into Neshilik."

CHAPTER 46

Penrys didn't like the windowless mage council room any better this time, but at least Zandaril and she were no longer the focus of attention. A private dinner had been provided, but it didn't appeal to her, not after that news.

She noted the reappearance of Dhumkedbhod with an expressionless nod and withheld her reaction to his scowl. The others were the same—Zongchas, Vladzan, and the somewhat enigmatic Nyagchos, the man who had wanted to "see what would happen" when the first attack from the students was launched at her.

Nyagchos questioned Zongchas. "They did *not* descend north of the Craggies to spend the winter in the farmsteads there?"

Where the Kigali forces could be encouraged to confront them, with or without Rasesni assistance. Penrys ticked that prediction off her list.

"No, it's definitely down into Wechinnat, headed for the Linit Kungzet route," Zongchas said.

"They're turning into Nagthari?" An agitated Dhumkedbhod rose from his seat. "To Dzongphan?"

Zongchas patted the table in front of him. "Sit down. We don't know that. It's just the road into Neshilik. If they turn west, well, then… But that hasn't happened yet."

Vladzan pursed his lips. "It's more likely they're planning to shelter here for the winter, in Neshilik itself."

He turned to Zongchas. "Any news about the state of the…force he's bringing?"

"They say the horde looks ill-nourished, but it hasn't dispersed. They hoped it might, after leaving the mountains."

He glanced down at one of the reports. "His guard of Khrebesni has grown. Might be larger than Tlobsung's army now, though I don't imagine it's as effective."

Zandaril muttered, "Tlobsung has no Voice behind him."

"No, but we have her." Zongchas waved a hand at Penrys.

Nyagchos asked, "But what will happen at the Gates if Tlobsung moves west to confront the Khrebesni? Will the Kigali squadron move right in behind him and bottle us up while he's gone?"

He looked directly at Zandaril. "Or will it help us fight?"

Dhumkedbhod commented sourly, "Or will it leave us to do the bloody work while it bypasses the battle, preparing a way through to assault Dzongphan while we're licking our wounds?"

Zandaril just shook his head. "I can't answer for the Kigaliwen. I don't know their plans."

Penrys asked, "One thing I don't understand. Why do those hill-tribes follow him?"

Dhumkedbhod turned to stare at her in disbelief. "What better proof of their god's favor than success at the hands of his servant, Surdo?"

Vladzan added, placidly, "Some of them may hope for reward in this world, too."

"I'm getting tired of this 'throw the foreigners out' policy," Penrys said.

They stood in the hallway outside the mage council room. Inside, the meeting was continuing without them.

"You know this can't be everyone," Zandaril said.

"All the Rasesni wizards, you mean? You're right, of course." She began to stroll back in the direction of the main hall.

"There had to have been wizards involved in getting the information in those reports, spying on the Voice, despite what Zongchas told us," she said. "I wonder how many. Enough to make a difference?"

"And is anyone training them?" Zandaril said.

"You notice Dhumkedbhod reappeared. Where's he been hiding?" She glanced at Zandaril. "I've been reluctant to go probing for him, to maintain the illusion of cooperation. Maybe that should stop."

"Where's Veneshjug?" Zandaril asked. "That's what I want to know. I've been looking for him since we got here, cooperation or not. Haven't found him."

"Maybe he's with the others. It'd be awkward to have him here, after all." She paused. "Unless he doesn't know about the deaths when I triggered his trap."

"Knows, and happy about it, I bet." Zandaril muttered. "I'm going to find Dzantig and make him tell me whatever he can."

Zandaril peeled off in the direction of the main hall. Penrys stopped where she was and considered. The noise and clatter that meant the hall was still full of diners ruled out the more public places. She wanted someplace private to sit, but not her room. Out of doors for preference, while the weather was still mild, for autumn.

What about the walkway, behind the colonnade? There must be some way onto that. Most of those rooms are empty, so it shouldn't bother anyone.

She passed the hall and took the main stairway up to the second floor, then she turned to the north corner of the floor as the logical location for an outer access. She hadn't seen one near Zongchas's office, in the south corner, but there had to be a door somewhere.

It wasn't in the corner, she discovered, but in the middle—an anomalous door in-between the doors of two rooms. She expected it to be locked, but once she had it open and looked more closely, she realized it was locked only from the outside.

Wouldn't do to get trapped out here. She winced at the thought, even if a simple mind-cry would bring rescue.

It was easy enough to wedge a fragment of broken stonework into the mechanism to keep it from re-latching. She gingerly let the door drift shut, and her tinkering held. *I'll bring a bit of paper to use next time, if I come back.*

She stayed along the edge of the wall instead of up front, near the colonnade, to hide herself from the square, but the view was pleasant even so, with the lingering glow of the sunset behind the buildings across the square, and the sun-warmed stonework preserving what was left of the heat of the day. The presence of stone benches every few yards demonstrated that the architects had planned this as a place for people to linger.

Well, things change in a few hundred years, I suppose. No one lingers here now, just as few are found in the corridors. This must have been quite a school when it was new, with several times the number of people that are in it now.

The benches didn't get the benefit of rain, sheltered as they were by the building floor above them. Wind could only do so much to keep them clean. Reluctantly, Penrys brushed a layer of dirt off of the nearest one, then sniffed her soiled hand and wiped it on her breeches as she sat down.

Where *were* the other Rasesni wizards? Where would Dhumkedbhod vanish to? She scanned lightly in the direction of the mage council room and found no one. The meeting must be over.

This time she looked seriously throughout the building trying to match his signature. With fewer than fifty people, it wasn't hard, and she found him. He was shielded, but not successfully against her, now that she was really looking. *He must be relying on his shield, and it's been working for him while I overlooked it. So, where is he?*

The answer startled here—he was quite nearby, on her level and straight south of her. That put him in the corner room of this walkway, and *that* was Zongchas's office. *Who else is there?*

She stood and crept toward the window at the end of the walkway while she looked. *Zongchas, of course, and Vladzan. And one more. Who is that?*

She knew that mind, but this time it wasn't riding away from her in the middle of the night. *Veneshjug. Zandaril was right. It makes sense—they need everyone but they wouldn't have wanted to parade him in front of Zandaril and me. Can I get near enough to listen without giving myself away? After all, their minds may be shielded, but not their voices.*

She suppressed her giggle and slunk along the inner wall as close as she could get to Zongchas's window.

"I tell you if you rely on her for defense you'll regret it."

Penrys didn't recognize the voice, and that made it Veneshjug's, by elimination.

"She's just as dangerous as Surdo, maybe more so, now that you idiots have helped train her and revealed our own weaknesses."

Zongchas's voice agreed, "She's read *your* books, Vejug—she still has them, and *your* power-stones. Tell me again just why you felt you needed to set up that ridiculous mirror business, you and Vladzan."

Veneshjug defended himself. "Not my fault, who could have expected interference by two wizards, from the Kigaliwen? But what she can do with power-stones is unprecedented, Vladzan says, and if she learns how to make more powerful devices… I'm told she's been wandering through the library, unhindered. Why is that, Zongchas?"

Zongchas's voice rose. "We need her to defeat Surdo—what choice do we have?"

The querulous tones of Dhumkedbhod broke in. "Would you trade an old tyrant for a new mistress? What god does she follow? Tell me. Not my god, not yours."

"You're all fools if you let her live a minute longer than necessary." The crisp tone of Veneshjug's voice sent a chill down her spine. "I don't believe this tale about no memory for a moment."

Zongchas protested. "I saw the truth of it in her mind."

"You saw what she wanted you to see," Dhumkedbhod scoffed.

Vladzan apparently agreed. "He may be right. She's so strong, who knows what she could conceal?"

The uncertainty creeping into Zongchas's voice disturbed her. "You think she was toying with us when she revealed her own weaknesses?"

Veneshjug said, "How do we know your tale of her encounter with Surdo is even true? Maybe she's working *with* him, luring us into a trap. She's the same as he is, with that chain, so how likely is it that she's his enemy? That she doesn't even know him?"

"I find it hard to believe that that Zandaril can conceal these lies, too," Zongchas said.

Veneshjug dismissed the problem. "He's either under her control altogether, or working to see how the Zannib can benefit. The more fool he—she'll betray him, wait and see."

That doesn't sound right. Why would he think that? What's he doing, setting something up? Penrys's ears pulled back on her scalp. *This isn't just dislike, this is something else.*

Dhumkedbhod asked, "And what's the Kigali interest in all of this?"

"They're not wizards. They don't understand the danger. Anything that defeats us is good for them."

Penrys marveled at how Veneshjug had an answer for everything.

A commotion at the doorway interrupted them with a summons for Veneshjug. He offered an excuse, "Something I have to go do now," and left. All the others except Zongchas followed him out.

Penrys froze in place until she heard him settle in his chair, then she crept back a few paces. What had she overheard? What were the ramifications? She'd known some of the polite relationship between them had been artificial but this level of active ill-will took her breath away.

She needed to find Zandaril. Could they survive this alliance? Even if they succeeded? She wished she dared to bespeak him, but now she feared they could be overheard.

CHAPTER 47

Penrys scanned for Zandaril within the building but didn't find him. *Must be out with Dzangabtig again. Hope he's successful.*

This time she would be satisfied with her room where at least she couldn't be surprised by anyone.

She peeked into Zandaril's room, just in case he was there after all. It was bare of life, the bed used only to support their packs and to lay out their clothing.

So, they've been through our packs. Well, that's no surprise.

Veneshjug *was* a surprise, though, and a nasty one. He made her flesh creep. He had plans, and she didn't understand what they were. The two of them had walked into his hands in the belief that a common enemy would ensure their safety, at least for a while. They were wrong. Maybe very wrong. And the Rasesni knew a lot more about them now. What did it mean that this temple school was dedicated to Veneshjug's god Venesh?

Where was Zandaril? He had to hear this.

She lay out flat on her bed with her hands behind her head and tried waiting for him, but she couldn't shake her sense of alarm.

Maybe we should leave tonight, when he gets back. Drunk or not.

She pulled herself off the bed and went back to his room. It only took a few minutes to load her pack with everything. When she was done, she tried scanning for Zandaril again, but he still wasn't in the building and she was reluctant to reach further for fear of alerting Veneshjug or anyone else who might be watching her. She didn't want them to find her actions suspicious in any way, not now.

I'll do his pack, too—save time when he gets back.

He was tidy, a lifetime of nomadic habits, and the pack was still half-full. She left his spare robe for last, as padding for the top of the pack. When she lifted it up and started to fold it, she couldn't resist holding it up to her nose and breathing the residual scent in deeply. Suddenly she missed him, terribly, though he'd only been gone a couple of hours. *Where is he?*

A knock at her own door interrupted her thoughts. *Is that him?*

Her mind-scan revealed Isven, her mind nervous. Penrys had thought little of her since their first encounter, and she was one of the weakest of the students. *She's been scared of us the whole time.*

She opened the door, and Isven bobbed her head briefly.

"*Brudigna, brudigdo* Zandaril sent me. He says he's got something he has to show you, out at the stables."

Zandaril! That's a relief. Why wouldn't he just bespeak me? Maybe he's worried about being overheard, too.

Too bad he couldn't find a better messenger. She feels scared half to death.

"Thank you, Isven. Shall I come with you?"

"Oh, no," she babbled, "He doesn't want me back. He said so." She backed out of the doorway into the corridor and hastened away, turning her head back once to stare at Penrys, who was watching her.

Must be important, if he had to reach me so badly he used her. Or maybe he's just a bit the worse for drink.

She suppressed a smile, then stepped out and closed the door behind her. *I better be careful approaching the stables, just in case.*

She retraced her steps from their arrival a couple of days ago. As before, the corridors at the back of the building were empty of students or teachers, and in the noisy kitchens, still cleaning up from dinner, the staff paid no attention to her as she made her way to the rear entrance.

On the threshold, she paused to remind herself just where the stables were situated, out in the inner yard. Then she laid her hand on the door handle and pulled it open.

There was a flash of movement, then nothing.

Voices woke her, voices she knew and now dreaded. She kept her eyes shut and her mind as calm as she could.

Her head throbbed where something had hit her, and there was a foul taste in her mouth. What had they given her while she was unconscious? What did it do?

Veneshjug was arguing with the rest of the mage council, and his voice echoed off the walls. Were they underground somewhere?

"Why would she stay behind once she sent Zandaril back to her master?"

That was Zongchas.

She was lying on something like a bench or a low table, off the ground. She could feel the rough surface against her fingertips, but her fingers wouldn't move.

"Good riddance," Dhumkedbhod's voice announced. "You know what the Zannib are—*zhabbyedum*, way-less heathens! Worse than the Kigaliwen."

"We all agree," Veneshjug's cool voice soothed.

"There's no turning back now," Zongchas complained. "I hope you're right."

"It's the only way we can be sure," Veneshjug said.

He paused, and announced, "And she's awake now."

At that, Penrys threw off her pretense. Before she even opened her eyes she pulled up her shield and probed the people in the room. Or, rather she tried to—no shield, no scan. She couldn't feel them at all. When she broadened her reach, she felt nothing at any distance, no mind-glows.

Despite herself she felt panic accelerate her heartbeat, and over the roaring in her ears Veneshjug's sneering voice penetrated. "Didn't know about the *sedchabke*, the mind-block drugs, did you? Should've spent more time in the library."

The expression on her face, whatever it was, sent Zongchas a few steps back. The rest of them stayed in place, Dhumkedbhod excited and exultant, Nyagchos speculative.

Vladzan was just curious. "I've never seen the *sedchabke* used. Mind and body both, I see. How long does it last?"

"We have all night," Veneshjug said, "and tomorrow, too. There's no hurry."

"When we're done here," Vladzan said, diffidently, "would you mind if I… tried a few things?"

Calm yourself. Ignore the stupidity that delivered you to your enemies. That's in the past, it can't be changed.

She slowed her breathing to try and regain some control. It was only her limbs that seemed to be inert—she could still swallow and open her eyes.

Concentrate on getting through the present. There's no point thinking about what Vladzan just said—after all, you might be dead by then.

Another slow breath. And another.

Moment by moment. Endure it, use it, prepare for the next. That's all that matters. If they kill you, they kill you. Don't give them the satisfaction of fear.

And above all, don't think about what's happened to Zandaril.

She worked on her breathing and glared at Veneshjug, who smiled back at her, pleased.

"Shall we get started, then?" he said.

At Zongchas's nervous nod, Veneshjug turned her resistless head so that he could shove his fingers between the chain and the side of her neck. There was no spare room, and his knuckles poked painfully against her throat when he tightened his grasp. When he pulled at the chain, she choked.

She felt nothing of the chain's power, but neither, apparently did he.

"We need to take it off, first," he said, releasing his grip.

For the next several minutes, Veneshjug with the assistance of Vladzan mauled her neck, pulling at the chain and looking for a catch of some sort. Penrys felt the trickle of warm blood.

"Look how that cut closes up," Vladzan said. "What happens if…"

He picked up her powerless left hand and turned it palm up, then with the knife from his belt, he carved a firm line across the fleshy base of her thumb and watched the blood well up. Her hand didn't so much as twitch under the assault. She could feel the sting of the injury, but not see it, since it was out of her line of sight.

"Observe. Let me wipe the blood away." She felt the passage of a cloth. "Look how the ends knit, almost visibly. In a few hours, I imagine, there would be no trace left."

"Convenient," Veneshjug remarked. "She'll last longer under questioning that way."

What would happen if they manage to get the chain off? What kind of life would that leave me?

Silly question—I won't be around to find out. Especially not if they have to take my head off, first.

What will my makers do with a new owner?

She took another steady breath.

Are they already looking for me? Can they tell someone's trying to get a hold of the chain?

Nyagchos intervened. "We all understand the only way this can end. But not until we get some answers, if you please."

"What message did she give Zandaril for her master?" Zongchas asked.

Dhumkedbhod said, "No, find out where she comes from and who sent her, the way she showed you. See what she's hiding."

Veneshjug glanced at Penrys's face. "Ah, another surprise. You taught some of us how to follow along with someone's recollection, in that first report. Very useful it is, and we give you our thanks. Now it's our turn."

Nyagchos organized them. She had no defenses against them, as though she had no core power at all, and they met with no resistance as they pushed against her past recollections.

She watched herself stand in the catalogue room at the Collegium, and the group voice, led by Veneshjug, told her, **Further**.

A meal in Vylkar's hunting lodge up in the hills, and she was painfully lashed with **Further**.

Her awakening in the snow at night, cold and naked, and the torches and men and horses standing around her.

Dhumkedbhod said out loud, "Now we're getting somewhere."

Further.

She resisted, and they tore through her efforts and thrust her back down again.

And helplessly she fell, dropping into a narrow black hole like a bottomless well, leaving them peering down after her, unable to follow her into blackness.

She flung out her virtual hands to try and slow her passage, but felt nothing.

There's nothing here! It's empty! Can I fall forever?

Is this death?

She felt her chest panting and her heart racing.

I'm still alive. 'What the body knows.' Zandaril—he was right. It can't be empty, m'body knows things, from before. I just can't see them.

This is an illusion. It must be. If I can have the illusion of falling, why not the illusion of flight?

She stretched out virtual wings and caught the illusion of air beneath them, then pulled herself upward against it. Above her was a tiny, shrinking hole, a dim point of light against the utter blackness that expanded in all directions around her. She pumped her wings again, and again, straining her illusory muscles and trying to make the small circle of light larger.

It took forever to pull herself upward, much longer than the endless fall. She barely breathed, saving her concentration for the exhausting effort. *How can an exercise of the mind hurt so much?*

When she finally reached the top of the well, the moment before her memory of snow and torches, she clung there like a bat, and waited.

The wizards were no longer there in her mind, combined in assault, watching. They had withdrawn.

"That's it then." She heard the disappointment in Vladzan's voice. "Two hours, no change in the shallow breathing. Perhaps she isn't coming back."

"It was always a risk," Veneshjug said.

"You promised us answers, Vejug," Zongchas complained. "Now we have nothing."

"We have the chain," Veneshjug said, briskly, "and tomorrow we'll harvest it, after I've prepared a few things. Until then, go get some sleep."

The footsteps of several people receded and a door closed.

Two of them had stayed behind. Veneshjug said, "Vladzan, you've got the watch for the rest of the night."

"Did you see how filling all those power-stones didn't seem to weaken her?" Vladzan mused.

"She came thousands of miles and still had enough power to

hold shields against me, in the mirror. I want that chain, and I want her conscious for it."

"Surdo was not pleased with you, letting the Kigali block him at the Gates." Vladzan's soft tone had a sting in it.

"You're no better off—your note about enslavement didn't quite work, either."

Penrys heard a rasping sound, as if Veneshjug were rubbing his hands together. "I won't care what the Voice thinks, if I can get my hands on that chain."

His footsteps moved towards the door. "Try not to let her condition deteriorate further—I want to find her in the same shape in the morning."

The door opened, and closed again.

"Pity," Vladzan's voice murmured. "Still, there must be something I can learn. The signs should be gone in a few hours."

Pump the heart. Breathe. Circulate the blood. Liquor burns off quickly. It's been hours since they fed me the drugs.

She clung to her hiding place and ignored the outer sensations of the body, the cuts and stings and probes, the touches and grasps, the warm stickiness of drying blood. *It isn't real, it doesn't exist.* Only the heart beating and the breath supporting it mattered.

Push the blood, use up the drug, clean it out.

Pump the heart. Breathe.

CHAPTER 48

Vladzan had apparently tired of his experiments, and Penrys heard the creak of the chair when he sat down. His breathing was regular, but without the deep rhythms of sleep.

Too much to hope for, that he'd just drop off. At least he can't see my toes inside my shoes.

For the last little while, she'd been trying to wiggle her toes, and she welcomed her feeble success. *It's wearing off, finally.*

If her body could move again, eventually her power would return, assuming there was no permanent damage. Vladzan would be shielded, surely, but with her full power that would mean nothing to her.

How long would she have to wait? If she alerted him before she was strong enough, she'd never get another chance, but the others might return before she could be sure.

Pump the heart. Breathe. It's working.

The damage to her body was probably healing, but she didn't dare open her eyes to look.

Vladzan pushed the chair back and she heard the clink of bits of metal. *Chains? If he binds me so he can nap in peace, I'm doomed.*

Now or never.

She pulled up as much of her shield as she could manage, then she broke through his and grabbed at his core power, as if he were a power-stone. She set herself, and drained it all away, into her chain, leaving him nothing, not the barest remnant. With bits of the power that she siphoned off, she reached out and stopped his heart, and held it still as it stuttered, twice, three times, until all the movement ceased. While she worked, she wrapped her own shield around him, to smother any final mind-cry. Without a working heart, he had no time for an audible scream. The only sound was his body hitting the floor with a dull thud.

She listened to his mental confusion and panic, and made no attempt to hide herself while she watched with him as darkness descended and his mind died.

It meant nothing to her, nothing at all.

The next task was to get away, and for that, she would have to move. She opened her eyes. and tried to sit up. The theft of Vladzan's power had no effect on the residue of the drugs, and her body was slow to respond.

She clenched her fists, over and over, and waggled her feet—anything to increase the blood flow. She managed to jerk her body up onto one elbow and held it there while she looked around the room.

There were no windows and just the one door. It was some sort of storeroom, she saw, with sacks of supplies piled up along one wall. *Probably no locks on the inside. Good. If I can walk, I can get out of here.*

She strengthened her shield as best she could, concentrating on being invisible. If one of the others probed the room, it wouldn't matter that they couldn't find her—they wouldn't find Vladzan, either, and that would be enough to raise the alarm.

She swung her legs over the side of the wide bench and winced as her feet hit the floor clumsily.

Pump the heart. Breathe. Keep moving.

It took four attempts before she could stand up, and then all she could do was sway back and forth.

Concentrate. Flex the hands, bend the knees.

Leaning forward, she forced her body to stagger into a step, and then another one. Sensations against her skin distracted her, and she looked down. Her clothes were in rags, cut by Vladzan's busy knives. The pain was distant, and healing, but the sticky blood was a distraction, impeding her motion where it bound the clothing to her.

She did a quick calculation, warmth versus movement, and without hesitation tore some of the rags away where they interfered. Then she returned her focus to the door and let her body take care of itself.

She watched her hand lift the latch while she listened through her shield for anyone else nearby. She still couldn't hear mind-glows at any distance, so she opened the door softly and listened carefully. When she pulled it open all the way, onto an empty corridor, she saw bare and dusty stone stairs ascending into darkness, with recent traces of footsteps disturbing the surface.

The first step up onto a riser almost stopped her. She tilted her body to the left to let her right foot reach the step without bending the knee much. That worked, but making that leg take all the weight again when she tilted back failed for several minutes.

She stood unbalanced there and worked the muscles of her arms and hands, trying to flush more of the drug away. Eventually, the leg bore her weight, and she repeated the process for the next step, and the next, a little more smoothly each time.

The door at the top was invisible in the black, but her groping hand found a latch, and it opened into the cool night air, somewhere in the inner courtyard, lit by starlight.

She swayed on the threshold for a moment, and tried to find mind-glows again, and failed.

Have to get away, not just hide. Can I fly?

She invoked her wings, and nothing happened. Ruthlessly, she suppressed the panic that said "they're gone." *Must need a full recovery to be used, that's all.*

Hide, then. I'll have to hide until everything wears off.

Penrys turned her head at a rustle and the dim shape of a man. *They've found me.* She reached out, and seized his mind, prepared to rip away his puny shield, but it wasn't one of the mage council, and she hesitated.

Dzantig stepped all the way out into the starlight a few feet away, his face distorted and his hands held up in supplication.

"Please, *brudigna*," he whispered. "Please, don't. Don't kill me. I've been waiting for you."

She tilted her head to look at him, and tasted his mind. Fear, but no malice.

Her voice choked her, dry and rusty. "Where's Zandaril?"

"I don't know."

That seemed to be the truth. She released him, and he took a step closer and cautiously reached for her arm.

"You've got to hide. They'll be back."

Yes, hide. Hide first, then talk.

He pulled at her tentatively, and she lurched after him. He guided her about fifty steps to the back of a disused garden fountain and lifted an iron trapdoor there. "Can you, um, climb down?"

She peered down at the iron ladder bolted to the side of the shaft that vanished into darkness, and shivered at the reminder of her fall into the abyss.

"Look, I'll go first," he said. "But you have to close the door behind you. Can you do that?"

She thought about it, and nodded.

When he was a body length down, he reached up to pat her foot, and she backed in carefully, one foot at a time. When her head passed below the surface of the ground, he tapped her leg from below. "The door. Lower the trapdoor. Quietly."

She took one last breath of the autumn garden, sleeping in starlight, and lowered the trapdoor.

They climbed down for several body lengths, until she heard Dzantig step off the ladder onto a stone surface, and she followed. She could hear water dripping into pools in the distance. He pulled a small lantern out of his pocket and tried to power the stone in it, but Penrys could feel him trembling. She reached out casually and powered it, and the darkness was beaten back.

They were standing in a junction of four arched tunnels with the vertical shaft. In all directions the tunnels receded into the black. The air was humid, and little moist noises reverberated in the distance.

Dzantig backed away from her unblinking stare. "It's the water tunnels, and the sewers. Students know about them, a way out of the compound undetected."

He laughed briefly. "The previous students left notes about them. I don't think the mage council knows."

She reminded herself. *This Rasesni is Dzantig. Zandaril's friend, his drinking partner. Not an enemy?*

"Where's Zandaril?" It came out more clearly this time.

"He asked me about Vejug, but I hadn't seen him. He asked me to wait for him in the square. He was going to meet me for… well, it doesn't matter. He didn't come."

She nodded at him to continue. She could see his mind-glow, a little, and it didn't waver.

"I saw this cart come out," he said. "Like they use for vegetables. There was a man driving, and another one riding alongside. A guard for a food cart? At night? It didn't make any sense."

He cleared his throat. "I tried to find a way to look inside but I couldn't see much. I thought I saw a bundle of clothing. It turned north, away from the bridge."

With a catch in his breath, he continued. "And the later Zandaril was, the more I wondered about that guarded cart, and the fabric, thinking about his robe."

She shut her eyes, and heard him gasp as he took another step back.

When she glanced down, she found her fists clenched. When she looked at him again, he said, hastily, "I came to look for you. I went by way of the courtyard, to see if there was anyone to ask about the cart, but it was dark, and no one was there. And then I saw them, carrying you, and they vanished into the stable."

She tasted him again. *Truth, still truth.*

"All of them, all the mage council, even Vejug. Who could I tell?"

He looked into her face as if hoping for agreement. "So I waited and watched, for hours. They all left, not long ago, except for you and Vladzan."

His eyes roamed over her rags in muted curiosity, and she slashed her hand through the air. "*Sennevi.* Vladzan is done." The end of that story.

It was hard to tell in the lantern light, but she thought he blanched. Certainly his mind was scared.

An important question caught her attention. "Why? Why are you helping me?"

He straightened up, in the underground tunnel, and made her a bow. "Dzangab, my god, enjoins me to help the god-touched."

Penrys mused out loud. "But I don't believe in gods."

Dzantig smiled at her, raggedly. "I don't think that matters."

"It's because of Zandaril," he said. "And you. And because we *must* defeat Surdo. And because this is wrong, Dzangab would have me defend the righteous. And I am *not* a traitor—*this* is how we Rasesni will survive Surdo, if we do."

His voice picked up confidence. "I'm not strong enough to change what the mage council wants, but I'm strong enough to conceal you and get you to help, and this I will do. I fear what has befallen Zandaril who came to us as an honorable guest. As you did. If I can't help him, maybe you can."

He spat on the tunnel floor. "And besides, I have always despised Vejug and his greedy god."

CHAPTER 49

Dzantig led Penrys along the tunnels. They walked enwrapped in the limited sphere of light shed by the lantern. Everywhere outside of its reach was blackness.

It seemed to Penrys that she was back in the endless abyss, that she had found its bottom and it extended forever over her head.

She stopped, occasionally, lost in the nightmare, and Dzantig came back and tugged at her gently to get her started again.

He shuttered the lantern when they reached a door, no different in character than any of the others they had passed. He opened it softly and peered outside, and drew her through after him.

They had emerged above ground behind a work shed. She could see the lights of very late travelers crossing the bridge south into the main city.

"We're well south of the market square," Dzantig told her. "You can stay here for a while. No one comes here."

He pushed at her until she sat down on the path behind the shed, and squatted down beside her.

"Is there anywhere you can be safe? I must be back by dawn, but that's still a couple of hours away."

Safe? Who do I know?

"Can you find Kor Pochang? He sits on the town council. Do you know who that is?"

Dzantig nodded. "We've met them all, the councilors."

"Tell him… Tak Tuzap's friend needs help. Careful, there are Rasesni quartered there."

"I can do that," he said. He caught his underlip in his teeth. "I won't be back this way unless I fail—I'll enter the tunnels at a different point. If they catch me and question me…"

He leaned toward her and lowered his voice. "Don't come back. Our strongest wizards are in the mage council. You can't kill them—we're going to need them."

He glanced at her bloody rags. "I'm sorry for what they did to you, whatever it was."

On his knees, he made a formal bow, arms outstretched. "Help us, *brudigna*, please. In spite of this. In spite of Zandaril."

She cleared her throat. "I don't know if I can. I'll… try."

As he stood to leave, she focused on his face and nodded. "Thank you, *tsevog*, for your care. You have been a worthy student."

After his footsteps faded away down the path, a little time passed while she sat unmoving. *Pump the heart. Breathe.*

The fading of the starlight in the pale light of pre-dawn roused her.

Too much light. I'll be found.

She glanced at the deep shrubbery across the path. Dense bushes hid her view of the interior, their leaves still clinging to the branches. Near the ground, the stems rose leafless before they converged, and small animals had made trackways there.

She stretched out on all fours across the path and crawled into the gaps between the bushes until she found a hollow all the way in, still lined with last year's leaves. There she curled up on her side with her head on her arm. She couldn't see the path or the work shed from there.

She wanted to sleep, but she couldn't. Her brain hurt, aching from the inside.

Here and there the first birds woke and began their morning songs. She could feel their mind-glows, dimly. She tightened her shield around herself like a blanket, fearing the searches of the enraged wizards.

Wherever there was a gap in her rags, she felt the cold damp of the leaves against her skin, but it soon warmed up and the sensation faded.

Help him, he said. Help the Rasesni. As if I care about them. The Voice is welcome to them all. Some of them already work for him.

She shuddered involuntarily, and raised her arm to remind herself she was no longer lying paralyzed and powerless on a stone bench underground. She flexed her hand in front of her eyes, marveling at the complex movements it could make, the smoothness of its gestures.

It must have been Veneshjug that had Zandaril taken. Not dead, maybe, not when Dzantig saw him. Wouldn't need a guard if he were dead. But now?

Sent him north. To intersect the Voice? Payment for Zandaril spotting him, weeks ago, as a false herdsman? Or just a random gift—"Here, have another wizard."

If her thoughts were correct, he was hours away. She couldn't reach him in time to stop anything. She tried her wings for a moment, in the enclosed space, but nothing happened.

He can't be dead! She reached out for him, but all she could find were the few mind-glows nearby.

They didn't care about him, except maybe Veneshjug—just wanted him out of the way. I put him in this danger. This is my fault.

A cold thought intruded, that Zandaril was lost to the Voice, or dead, and a chill washed over her. *If he's gone, what stops me from leaving, once the drugs wear off? What do I care about captured wizards or Kigali soldiers?*

Unbidden, her memory presented a glimpse of Zandaril laughing at something she'd said, saying something earnestly with that deep voice, blinking owlishly up at her from the bed and leering suggestively.

Her breath caught in her throat.

And there were others in the path of the Voice. Tak Tuzap, even Dzantig, the enemy who had defended her when she was vulnerable in class, who went drinking with Zandaril, who waited through her ordeal and led her to safety.

I have no duty to these people, no vows. But if I'm not connected to them, what am I connected to? Not the Collegium. Not my unknown or maybe nonexistent family. Not my theoretical maker, the one responsible for that hideous hollow inside me—never that. If I don't make my own connections, fight for something, what am I? A monster, in truth?

Is that's what's wrong with the Voice? He must have some purpose, but what? To what end? Does Veneshjug know? It can't just be survival, can it? And yet, how easy it was to kill Vladzan, to watch with him as he died. And how little I care about it.

The birds in the predawn were all awake, now. Surrounded by music, she gathered her rags around her and shivered.

She was tired, and her head hurt, and her heart ached.

The knock on the window of the room where Tak Tuzap slept woke him. His uncle's house quartered two Rasesni officers, and he had taken a small back room on the ground floor for his own use. Kor Pochang's scullery maid waited nervously for him to throw on his clothes. He armed himself with what was at hand, and then he slipped out the window and crept with the maid through the streets to Kor's house. Once inside the compound, they separated, and Tak made his way to the stable before the stars were even extinguished.

Hearing voices up in the hayloft, he climbed cautiously and froze when he found not just Kor Pochang himself, but a young Rasesni man. When his hand fumbled at his belt knife, Kor hissed at him and whispered harshly, "Never mind that nonsense. Get over here."

"This is Tak Tuzap," he told the stranger, hauling him forward to present him. "'Tak Tuzap's friend,' you said."

Zandaril! It must be about him. After a whole month he remembered me. Tak stood up straight and tried to look competent.

"That's what she told me," the man said, in accented but understandable Kigali-*yat.*

Must be Penrys, then. What would she want me for?

"I'm from the temple school, up in Kunchik. They've been there three days, teaching us ways to defend ourselves against…" He rubbed his forehead. "Against an enemy coming off of Nakshadzam. She was a good teacher. Strong, so strong."

But that meant he was a wizard himself. A whole school of them!

He looked at the man more closely. He looked tired, like he'd been up all night. Scared, too.

"I don't think I should tell you my name. I have to get back before dawn, or they'll question me and we can't keep secrets from the mage council if they choose to look."

He murmured, half to himself, "Though maybe *she* did."

Shaking his head in an effort to stay awake, he said, "I think they seized Zandaril last night, and sent him north, to our enemy."

Tak heard his own indrawn breath in the silence.

"I know they captured Penrys and questioned her. She escaped, somehow, and I got her out of there."

Kor broke in, "Where is she? What do you want from us?"

The Rasesni waved his hand, "I've got her stashed south of the square, and when I asked her, she told me to fetch you for help. That's all I want."

Tak said, "But why are you helping her? You're not her friend."

"It's not that simple, boy. I have to, my god lays this task on me. It's too hard to explain. And besides, Penrys and Zandaril were our *guests.*"

Tak heard outrage in his voice, and reverence for his god.

He addressed himself to Kor Pochang. "Let me go get her, Kor-chi."

"Nonsense, it's too dangerous"

"My uncle would have wanted me to, you know he would," Tak said. "Besides, she knows me."

He turned back to the messenger. "Where is she? What does she need?"

"You know the work shed behind the ropewalk, on the north side, southeast of the market square?"

"I can find that." Tak glanced at Kor and correctly interpreted his resigned expression.

"Bring blankets, clothing, food, water, bandages." A cloud passed over the stranger's face.

"I think, I hope she will look for Zandaril, once she's better. They'll be looking for her at the bridge, so I don't think you should take her south of the river. Don't tell me where!"

He took a step toward the top of the ladder, sticking out into the hayloft. "Be careful of her, boy. Whatever happened to her, she's dangerous now, and strange."

What had the Rasesni wizard meant, when he called Penrys 'dangerous and strange?' That's not how he remembered her. Intense, maybe, but he still smiled thinking about chasing caps in the air with Wan Nozu. Nothing very dangerous about that.

Tak Tuzap clucked to the horse pulling the small buckboard along the outer perimeter of the ropewalk compound. It had long since outgrown its walls, and supplemental storage buildings cluttered the open land next to it. The path curved around to the northeast and there, as the Rasesni wizard had described, was a small work shed inside the path but outside the compound.

The sun was not quite up, and few people were about yet, but Tak had already seen the Rasesni patrols guarding the north end of the bridge, searching the handful of wagons crossing to the south this early. His own buckboard, borrowed from Kor Pochang, had a piece of precautionary canvas stretched across the top, but they had ignored the northbound traffic.

He halted at the shed. Where was Penrys? Mud smeared the surface of the path, and something looked like it had been dragged into the bushes on the far side.

He set the brake, and then hopped down to look. "Penrys-chi?" he whispered. There was no reply.

Following the drag marks, he wriggled under the intertwined branches, and there he found a woman's body in the dim shaded light of the new day.

The sight of so much blood on the clothes stopped his heart, but there was none on the ground, and her chest moved up and down steadily. Her face was hidden, and for a moment he hoped there'd been a mistake. When he shook her shoulder, she mumbled something, but subsided again when he ceased.

This was going to be a problem, he realized. He couldn't carry her, so he would have to get her moving on her own, and quickly, before anyone saw them.

He shook her again more vigorously, but to no effect. After a little thought, he crawled out to the buckboard and fetched a stoneware bottle of water and several bandages. When he sat down beside her again he poured some water onto a bandage and wiped her face with it. That roused her, as he'd hoped, and he put the bottle in her groping hand and helped her drink.

"Come on, Penrys-chi, come follow me. Time to get you out of here."

Her eyes had no focus, but her muttered "Takka?" encouraged him.

"Yeah, it's me, just like you asked for. Let's go, gotta get up."

He pulled up on her shoulder and she half rose to support herself on her elbow. "Where's Dzantig?"

"Is that his name?" Tak asked. "He's gone back, he said."

Her eyes closed again, and her head drooped.

Taking a deep breath, he said, "Sorry, *minochi*, but you gotta wake up," and he leaned over and slapped her cheek.

She snatched his hand, like a snake striking, and her eyes blazed open and held his captive. For a long moment he froze, feeling something in his mind, looming over it. "Dangerous and strange" about described it, after all.

Then she blinked and released him. "Sorry, Takka. I'm… not myself."

She rolled over on her stomach and crawled back out of the bushes and made enough room for him to follow.

He helped her up, relieved to see she could walk, and led her to the buckboard. She leaned on the side of the wagon while he dropped the tailgate, and seemed to be glad of his help to pull herself up onto the wagon bed.

Jumping up beside her, he wrapped her in a blanket, as much to cover the distressing sight of her from his view as to warm her, and laid another blanket over and around her, trying to prop her so she wouldn't roll around too much once they got moving again. After he'd raised the tailgate and covered the whole wagon bed with the canvas cover, he paused on the ground beside the wagon seat with his head down, and shook, thinking about the clutch of her hand and those burning eyes, and the tickling sensation in his mind like threatened lightning, before regaining command of himself and mounting up to drive her away.

CHAPTER 50

Zandaril's eyes bleared open, and he commented thickly, "What are all those birds doing, singing at night?"

And what am I doing sitting by the side of the road? Where am I?

He shook his head to clear it, and discovered he was bound to a young tree, just off a narrow road. He tried to raise his hands to his throbbing head, but they didn't budge.

The sun was rising to his right, and he turned his head aside to keep the piercing light from his eyes.

I was talking to Dzantig about Veneshjug, then I headed to my room for something before joining him in the square, and then… what?

He couldn't make sense of it, but the pounding in his head told its own tale.

The ropes that held him to the tree were coiled around his torso, pinning his arms to his sides. His bound hands protruded in front of him, below where the coils ended. *What is this, the goat in the tiger trap?*

He scanned his surroundings and found the mind-glows of small animals, but only at the edges of his range did he detect other people, and none of them were Penrys.

If someone's taken me, they'll have gone after her, too.

He wore himself out for a couple of minutes struggling with the rope, but it was a professional job, and he achieved nothing other than to wake himself up thoroughly and sharpen the pain in his head.

Something rustled overhead, and he ignored it, taking it for leaves on the tree, but when he glanced up, he saw a piece of paper, tied to the tree above him.

Probably written in Rasesni. Can't read it anyway without one of them around to draw on.

Looking at the low wooded ridges rising in front of him, on the other side of the road, and the trail out of them that joined the road directly across from him, he felt the hair rise on his skin.

I'm facing north, and that's the Craggies, isn't it? And that trail, where does it come down from?

Just to hear the sound of his own voice, he muttered, "The road to Linit Kungzet, I bet that's what this is. And I'm a present, left for the Voice when he comes on by."

He froze, then tried to stand up and move the ropes further up the tree to loosen the coils, but he found his knees had been tied to stakes, out of his reach.

Can't even run away this time.

Zandaril lost track of time for a little while, before he could control his breathing. *Maybe they won't come this way. Maybe they won't find me.*

Despite himself, he chuckled. *Of course, if they don't find me, maybe I'll just starve out here.* He smiled crookedly. *Well, there are worse fates.*

If he does come, I can't let him know about Penrys. Maybe he won't remember me from last time.

He passed the time scanning for people, but it was the animals that told him of the people coming, as they scurried out of the way before them.

The first ones down the trail were scouts from the Khrebesni. They broke into coarse and casual laughter at the sight of him. One adjusted his clothing as if to piss on him, but a command from behind stopped him, and quieted all the activity.

For the second time, he saw Surdo, and this time there was nowhere else to look. The chain recalled Penrys's—*don't think of her!* —but not his face, not at all. Dark unbraided hair framed his clean-shaven face, but his was thin where hers was not, his eyes slightly aslant and the eyebrows sparse instead of shaggy.

His shield was torn away, and Zandaril heard that awful voice again, this time in his head. **Ah, the Zan is back. What are you doing here, eh?**

At his gesture, one of the tribesmen brought him the paper tied over Zandaril's head, and he read it in good humor, and cocked his head at Zandaril. "It seems you are a present, from an admirer. I shall have to remember him."

And then his eyes narrowed.**Where is the woman you were traveling with?**

WHERE?

The probe expanded to fill his mind, until he could hear or think of nothing else. Finally he screamed back, **I don't know!**

The pressure withdrew. Zandaril screwed his eyes shut and hung his head.

Behind the Voice, the captive wizards, and then the horde came pouring out of the trees, spilling over the path on all sides as they came. They were strangely silent, except for the sound of their feet and the breaking of branches. The scouts maintained a clear space around Zandaril and their leader, leaving the road on both sides for the followers.

Zandaril felt the ropes being cut from him, but a loop around his neck kept his hopes from rising. *He would have felt the truth of my answer, and that must have puzzled him.*

He opened his eyes again and found Surdo staring at him. Then the man turned to one of the tribesmen. "I have a use for him with the others, so do nothing that will reduce his utility. But I want to know where his companion is. Find out."

But he knows the truth, he saw it. Why do this?

The first blow to the stomach drove the thought from his mind, and the strikes to the kidneys that followed drove him down in agony. Throughout the beating, a man stood by and shouted at him, "Tell him! Tell him what he wants to know!"

They kept their fists from his head and wouldn't let him escape into unconsciousness, but there was nothing he could tell them. They left him alone eventually with a couple of well-placed kicks.

Surdo returned and looked through his mind casually. **Where is she?**

From the ground, Zandaril muttered, "I don't know."

Someone bent over him and hammered shackles on his feet. The clank of them closing and the clink of the chain smothered his heart.

He felt the draw of power from his core, the way Penrys had done it, but this time it didn't stop. He was left with the barest ability to feel other minds. But then, he didn't want to feel any other minds now, not here.

Hands hauled him up, and he swayed on his feet. The Voice led his people off to the east, and when the other captive wizards reached him, he was shoved into their ranks. He shuffled along with them as best he could, trying to muffle the sound of his chains in the dust, as they did.

CHAPTER 51

Tak Tuzap brazenly drove his buckboard right through the market square, past the temple school with its clean walls. He followed the morning traffic like any delivery vehicle, and no one gave him a second look.

His goal was one of his uncle's warehouses at the edge of town, his warehouse now, which stood full of non-perishable goods in these bad times, awaiting its new master's attention and a more favorable market. He used his uncle's agents to do most of his trades, fearing that his youth would earn him no respect.

This warehouse was staffed only with a watchman who lived in a small cottage on the site with his widowed daughter. It was the safest place Tak could think of, north of the bridge.

When he swung the buckboard under the covered loading shelter, the noise brought his watchman out of his front door, his mouth still working on his breakfast.

"It's me, Watchman-chi," he called. "I've got a special load I'll take care of myself."

"Let me help you, young Tak-chi."

Tak Tuzap held his hand up to stop him. "No, this one's private. Go back home and I'll come in and chat in a while."

He set the brake and hopped down to unlock the heavy iron padlock. He had made his own copies of most of his uncle's keys as exercises in metal casting long ago, but now he had the originals, and it still felt strange to be using the real keys on his own business, instead of sneaking about with the copies.

He pushed the two doors inward and latched them back so they couldn't swing forward and startle the horse, then he led the horse all the way down the main corridor to the back of the building and through the wagon turn-around until it faced forward again.

The watchman had walked over to the entrance and stood there, peering into the darkness. Tak thought he could hear muffled noises out the back of the wagon and he hastily began unharnessing the horse.

Haik Anju started forward, and he waved him back. "I'll bring him to you. Maybe you could put him in a stall for me."

The watchman halted, plainly curious, but obedient. He waited until Tak had finished unbuckling everything and led the horse forward.

"That's not your gear," Haik said, as he took the horse's lead from Tak's hand. "What about the harness?"

"I borrowed the rig. I expect I'll return it tonight or tomorrow, and I'll clean the harness when I bring it back. Don't worry about it."

He have him a little encouraging push and the watchman reluctantly led the horse out the loading entrance. Tak unlatched and closed the doors behind him. He couldn't lock them from this side, but he didn't think Haik would try to sneak in, not with his job at stake.

He walked back to the wagon, spurred by the noises which were becoming more urgent. When he unfastened the cover and threw it back, he found Penrys thrashing in a nightmare, crying out inarticulately.

Should I try to wake her? Does that make it worse?

He reached out his hand to shake her shoulder, and paused.

Remember the last time you startled her awake.

That changed his mind, and he withdrew his hand.

All I can do is wait, as long as she's not still bleeding. But how can I find out without waking her?

She needs to be cleaned up, but I want her awake when that happens.

He snorted softly. *So wake her up gradually. She won't kill you. Probably.*

Originally, he had planned to install her in a locked room at the back of the warehouse, where his uncle kept small, precious goods. But as long as he had the building to himself, there was no reason she couldn't just stay on the wagon, as long as it was comfortable enough.

He thought about their journey over the Red Wall and their mornings in camp.

"Penrys-chi, it's time we were up," he called. "I've got the bacon started, and Zandaril's taking care of the horses."

He gave the wagon bed a jostle to go with the speech.

The murmurs stopped. A hopeful voice muttered, "Zandaril?"

He looked over the wall of the buckboard again. "No, it's Tak Tuzap, Penrys. D'ya remember?"

Some of the confusion left her eyes. "Yes, I remember. Where are we?"

"In my uncle's warehouse on the road north out of town. We're alone."

She pushed herself up and let the blankets around her fall away. Tak tried not to look.

"Look, I need to get you cleaned up, and get you something to eat. You can sleep all day afterward, if you want. I brought clothes, like that Rasesni fellow said, stuff from Kor Pochang that might fit. Men's things, I hope you don't mind."

"There's no time. I need to go after Zandaril," she said.

Tak peered at her face more closely. Her eyes were unfocused, still.

He put command into his voice, something he'd been learning as he took on his uncle's work, and lectured her. "You're hurt, and there's something wrong with you—you almost killed me. You can't be of any use to Zandaril if you're no good yourself."

To his horror, she cringed in shame. "I'm sorry! I… the drug…. It's getting better…"

"Don't make such a fuss," he said, with an assumed sternness. "I'm coming up to help, and you need to let me."

He took her silence for assent and lowered the tailgate to swing himself up. She let him help her soak the cloth loose where was it stuck to her. The cuts were thin and clean, and hardly visible—it seemed impossible that they were the source of the blood everywhere. But there were so many of them. *Not a fight. Something else.*

Her back was undamaged, but blood from an oozing blow on her head had made a mess.

She did as much of the work herself as she could, reaching back for fresh bandages and water, and he let her. There didn't seem to be any wounds that required actual wrapping.

"How do you do that?" he asked. "How do they heal like that?"

"I don't know," she said, curtly. "That's just the way it is. They wanted to know that, too."

Were those cuts experiments?

Tak's mind shied away from following that line of thought.

"Shift over," he said, and she shoved herself to the other side of the wagon. He handed her a shirt to pull over her head. The ends of the sleeves fell well past her fingertips.

He laid out two clean blankets as a foundation, and carefully smoothed out any wrinkles. She had been drinking from the water bottles while they worked, and now he reached into a basket and brought out sweet rolls from Kor's kitchen. When he offered them to her, she blanched and shook her head. "No food."

He put them back. "Maybe later, then."

Then he patted the fresh blankets. "Here. You need more sleep. Get as much as you can. I'll be nearby."

She looked unconvinced, so he put the stern note back into his voice. "The sooner you get better, the sooner you can help Zandaril."

She nodded without looking at him, and stretched out on the blankets. He mopped at some of the stains on one of the blankets she'd been wrapped in and made it clean enough, if a little damp, to serve as a covering.

She was already sleeping again when he gently laid it over her.

He wondered about what had happened and where Zandaril was, but it would have to wait. He put things back into order in the wagon, and by the time he hopped down, she had started muttering, her face twisted.

"Hey, now, go to sleep," he told her. "You're safe."

The sound of his voice must have helped, for she quieted for a bit, and then it happened again.

Patience, his uncle had often told him, it takes patience to wait for the right time. It looked to Tak Tuzap like he'd be waiting all day.

It seemed to Penrys that she wandered for days in nightmare. The image that kept recurring was the fall into the deep wide well, with the tiny lit circle of hostile faces receding rapidly above her. She fell until she was swallowed up in blackness, and never reached the bottom.

Whenever she woke, she heard a young voice reassuring her, and she tried to make her muscles unknot, but nothing stilled the churning of her stomach. She remembered being poised to attack Tak Tuzap, coldly pleased that he was in her grasp, and ready to be killed. She thought she might have done something similar to Dzantig.

What have they made me into? Maybe it's my true self.

She woke more seriously once, and Tak helped her to the privy out back. When she returned, she emptied one of the stoneware water bottles, but refused food. Her whole body felt drained, and her mind even more so.

Tak had described the quantity of blood on her clothes. He thought it was all that blood loss that made her weak, made her drink, and he wanted her to eat something, but she just couldn't face it.

She still felt nothing when she thought of killing Vladzan, and didn't think that would change, didn't even want it to. But that she was prepared to do that to Dzantig, or Takka—that should have given her horrors. And the fact that it didn't bother her enough… her mind shied away from that and found refuge in sleep. It was very strange.

She laid down again and gave herself up to dreams.

It was late afternoon before Penrys finally felt slept out. She was still tired, but there was no more rest to be found in sleep.

She threw the twisted blanket off of her and sat up in the wagon. Tak Tuzap was slumped against the far side, next to the open tailgate, snoring lightly. She tried to ease out without disturbing him, letting herself down over the tailgate until her bare feet touched the ground.

She walked stiffly around the wagon to his side. Up behind the seat she found the clothing he'd brought along. She reached over the buckboard's wall to root through it. The men's breeches were very large on her, but there was a belt. She tied a knot in it for now, over the doubled material—when Tak woke, she'd borrow his knife to cut holes for the buckle. With the crotch pulled up to the right place, the waist came halfway up her ribs, but the tunic she found would cover that well enough. She'd miss having access to the breeches' pockets, though.

A long bandage wrapped around her breasts provided some support, and the shirt was fine after she rolled the sleeves, but the tunic needed its own cord to hold it reasonably close to her body. Tak could probably find her something.

She still had her shoes, and the socks had been rinsed of blood and were almost dry. She leaned against the wagon wall and put them on, before continuing her search.

Ah, two spare packs. Perfect. She added the bottles which were still full to one of the packs, and looked at the food. *I feel like I may never eat again, but that's probably not true. Besides, what if I find Zandaril?*

That decided her, and she added hardbread and cheese, and even Tak's sweet rolls.

All that remained was to roll up a blanket for a bedroll and strap it on.

She looked up and met Tak's watching eyes. *Oh. Two spare packs, not one.*

"Without me? You can't go look for Zandaril without me."

He sat up and rubbed his eyes, his disappointment plain on his face.

She swallowed. "Come," she said. "I want to get a little exercise, and I need to talk to you. You can show me your uncle's warehouse."

She had woken up shielded, something she'd never been able to do before. She took a moment now to cast a scan around her. Her range seemed to be limited to a mile or so, but she was much closer to normal. *The drug must still be wearing off.* No sign of Zandaril, anywhere, as far as she could reach.

"Here's the truth, Takka. One warrior to another."

He drew himself up straight and walked with her while she worked on her limping stiffness as they proceeded down the main aisle in the dim building.

"The Rasesni have an enemy, someone like me—a wizard with a chain. He's got himself a rough army, a bodyguard of mountain tribes, and a bunch of captured wizards which give him lots of extra power. They call him the Voice."

She looked down at him—he was almost her own height. "That's why they invaded Neshilik this time. They were running away."

"Why didn't they fight?"

"They tried, but it didn't work. You told us something about this, remember, when we came up to Gonglik with you and Wan Nozu. Zandaril and I went on afterward, and we found him. He caught us, but we were lucky, we got away."

They reached the double doorway and turned to go back. Her muscles were easing, but she still felt weak. *Blood loss or the drug?*

"Chang made a truce with Tlobsung, the Rasesni commander, and we came in to work with the Rasesni wizards in the temple school, to find out more about the threat and to help them defend against it, if we could."

She could feel Tak listening hard and reserving judgment.

"What happened last night… One of their powerful wizards—the one who owned those books I had, remember? He came out of hiding and sent Zandaril away. Then they grabbed me and…"

Her voice faltered, and she lurched to a stop. "They drugged me and they questioned me but it didn't work for them the way they wanted. They left me alone with one of them and I killed him."

She could hear the toneless quality of her own voice.

"And later I tried to kill Dzantig when he was trying to help me, and then you. I'm not safe anymore, Takka. Not the least little bit."

She started walking again. "Before all that, we heard news yesterday that the Voice is coming down off the Horn and into the corner of Neshilik. He might go west into Nagthari, or come into Neshilik to winter—we don't know. I think this wizard who captured Zandaril, I think he was working for the Voice. I think he sent him there. I hope not, but I have to go look for him."

She leaned against the wagon as they came up to it and looked away from him. "I don't know if he's alive. I can't reach him, but maybe that's the drug. And maybe not. And if I do find him and he's with the Voice, then we're both sunk, because I can't beat a wizard that strong."

She turned finally and looked at Tak Tuzap directly. "And you can't help me. I'm sorry, but it's true. You can't go with me—that's just two of us dead instead of one."

As he opened his mouth to protest, she overrode him and wagged a finger in his face. "What you can do, what you *must* do, is tell all of this to Kor Pochang. Warn him. The Voice will ruin Neshilik, especially if some of the mage council are traitors. You have to retreat in front of him if he comes this way. Ask Kor to get word to Chang. Maybe the main Kigali force can do something when it comes, but that's still weeks away. And they have no wizards."

She challenged him. "Can you be a man and do the right thing, instead of what your heart wants?"

"But what will happen to you?" Tak whispered, "And Zandaril?"

She snorted. "If we're lucky, we won't live to see it. But maybe, just maybe, I can find Zandaril and sneak him out. I won't lie to you—it's a long chance. But maybe."

"How will you get there?" He cleared his throat. "You can have the horse, but I didn't bring a saddle."

"I don't need him." She felt a genuine smile stretch her cheeks. "You know how you wanted to see something wizardly?"

He nodded cautiously.

"Well, what do you think about this?"

She stretched out her arms and invoked her wings to match, and this time they came.

CHAPTER 52

"Psst. Hey, you, Zan."

The man next to Zandaril poked him on the arm, then faded back a pace. Zandaril lifted his face and looked left, to see who was speaking. He'd been walking head down for a long time, concentrating on keeping up and trying not to think about anything else.

A gray-haired woman in dingy clothing took the spot next to him.

"Where'd you come from, huh?" She spoke a rough sort of Kigali-*yat.*

He tried to bespeak her, but nothing happened.

She must have seen his expression. "That won't work, not while he's got us on full drain."

He asked, hoarsely, "Is it always like this?" He stumbled over his chain and she grabbed him by the arm to keep him from falling. He tried not to wince for the bruises already there.

"He's got to keep them under control." She hooked a thumb at the horde of people walking in front of them, silent and dusty. "That's always a big task, especially when they fight."

She scowled. "Sometimes he has jobs for us, and then he let's us keep a little, to get the work done. Then we can talk." She tapped her forehead to show her meaning. "But he can hear what you say that way, if he's listening, so better you talk out loud."

"What's your name?" she asked.

"Zandaril, *bikrajti.*" He tried to sketch a quick bow while walking, but his stiff muscles made a botch of it.

"Well, I'm Rinshradke, from up Shirtan-pur way. I've been with him since near the start."

She glanced around at the other shackled wizards in their ragged clothes.

"I'm a survivor, I am. The others look to me."

She gave him a challenging glance. "So, how'd you get here?"

"It's a long story, *bikrajti.*"

She snorted. "You got anything better to do?"

He pulled his mind away from his injuries. She reminded him of one particularly acerbic *dirum*, herd-mistress, of his youth, and it had never paid to treat *her* with less than full attention.

For the next half-hour as they walked along, he told her about Penrys and the rest of his story.

"Do you mean those honorless scum from the temple school sold you out?"

"Revenge, I think, for finding Veneshjug before he wanted to be found."

"I'm not surprised. Even in Shirtan-pur I heard about Vejug. He'd take it personal."

They trudged along for a few minutes in silence.

"D'ya think you could teach us, like you did those students?"

"What, how to work together?" Zandaril said. "But you haven't got any power."

"Not now, maybe, but who knows what might happen. You live as long as I do, you learn that things change. Even like this, if we touch each other we can follow along with a lesson, an' he can't hear. Might look clumsy, but it works."

Zandaril thought about it. She was asking him if he could *organize* these wizards, help prepare them for some opportunity. Better that than stewing in despair.

"Yes, *bikrajti*. I will, gladly. When can we start?"

"Now," she said, "Just marching along." She reached out to take his hand and stretched her other hand to the man on her left. "It's gotta go a long way, so think slow and loud."

They stopped moving when the sun was high in the sky, and Zandaril turned his eyes back to his surroundings. Once he'd stopped thinking about his feet, his pace had adjusted to the fetters.

Now everyone dropped hands and turned aside to the edge of the road for what little privacy they could manage, to relieve themselves.

Strange how the personalities traveled over the long physical links they formed. He couldn't match persons to faces, but they were nonetheless vivid, some questioning, some despairing, but all bludgeoned into at least a semblance of cooperation by the force of Rinshradke's mind. No courteous persuasion was necessary—Rinshradke just told them "learn this," and the grumbling stopped.

As they returned to their section of the road, some of the wizards nodded to him on their way to resume their places in the rough column. *I wonder which ones those are.*

A whirlwind of noise announced the arrival of a raiding party, whooping up from the south with a mixed herd of cattle, horses, and sheep, every animal that was large enough bearing improvised packs and bundled supplies. They passed by on the way to release their captured provisions to the care of the rear guard.

Rations already cooked the night before were brought down the line from the horde in front, carried by men walking clumsily along the road.

Those Khrebesni can ride when they choose, but they dismount once they don't need the horses any more. Must not have many horses up in the high hills, above the trees.

The tribesmen looked at ease with their heavy packs, the captured animals more food than transportation. This must be the way they travel all the time. Never pack more that you can carry on your own back, in case you need to eat the beasts.

The silent horde carried supplies and water for everyone, while the wizards had no packs at all. I guess we're more valuable. Renewable power, if he can keep us alive.

When he looked down at his feet, he bemoaned the way the shackles were tearing up his boots. *What is it about these foreign lands, that I can't keep a pair of boots intact for more than a couple of weeks?* A glance at some of the others showed him how boot legs became leather-lined shackles, once they separated from the foot portion.

If you can't keep up, what happens? Rinshradke's clothes didn't fit her well, but they weren't as ragged as some, and she'd been there a long time. *Do they loot the ones that fall behind?*

Something in the dust of the road caught his eye. He leaned down and picked up a stone, a little smaller than his palm, flat like a wavy sea with an unsightly hollow in its middle. *Not my usual had-kighat, and yet, there's something about it.*

He pocketed it.

When he reached out to seek Penrys, he found nothing more than a few feet away.

Stay alive. Don't have her come looking for you, and you no longer here.

When the water carrier came by, he drained as many cups as he could before they beat him away.

Penrys waited until evening to leave, alone in the woods behind the warehouse. A disconsolate Tak Tuzap had departed without her, with a promise to warn Kor Pochang and, through him, the rest of Neshilik, on the assumption that the Rasesni occupiers might not. It was the best she could do for them—they were on their own, now.

As soon as the darkness was thick enough to mask her flight, she headed north, scanning cautiously until she landed at the crossroads where Ichorrog had brought Zandaril and her, just a few days ago, on their way from the truce field.

She judged herself to be about five miles north of the temple school, and twenty or more west from Harlin, where Tlobsung's forces were encamped. She couldn't reach the collection of mind-glows that represented Kunchik, much less Harlin, and there were no wizards within her reach. If Zandaril was alive, he wasn't close by.

Where was the Voice? If she could find him, she might find Zandaril. She could still feel the residue of the drug, in the slackness of her muscles and the soreness and limited range of her mind. Veneshjug had said it was long-lasting and in that, at least, he'd spoken the truth.

She should travel some distance to the west while it was dark, high above the road, and then make a camp off of it, somewhere. If the Voice was coming her way, then good, and if not, she could pursue them faster when she was better, when her range was longer.

It felt right, leaving the other people behind, to go on into the west alone. When she woke up in the morning, she'd be able to focus on her task.

CHAPTER 53

When Penrys woke in the dim light before the sun's rising, for a moment she thought she was still hiding in the stand of bushes, abandoned by Dzantig, until the differences in the birdsong registered. *Country birds, not town ones.*

Her shield still held. *Is that a permanent improvement, or can I thank whatever contribution Vladzan made to the chain's power? I wonder how long the stolen power lasts?*

She dressed quickly, settling Tak Tuzap's gifts on her belt. She'd ended up using a cord around the breeches and cutting down the belt for the tunic with his knife, and when she'd made to give it back to him, he'd pressed it on her, with its sheath.

"You'll be needing this more than me, *minochi*. And this, too—I brought it for you."

He'd taken off his own belt, and revealed the weapon that had been dangling from it—a leather-sheathed ax, for throwing or one-handed fighting. Engraved whirlwinds decorated the freshly-sharpened blade, and the bison-horn grips were well-worn.

"That's my da's grandsire's *parkap*, from off my uncle's wall. Hasn't seen war for a while, so I thought now would be a good time."

"You were going to carry that for yourself," she'd accused.

"This is better. You take it."

She hadn't told him she'd bring it back—she didn't want to raise that hope—so she'd just bowed her head to him and slipped it onto her cut-down belt.

Now she adjusted both knife and ax until they hung comfortably with her smallest water bottle and a small pouch for food. She'd practiced drawing the ax until she was satisfied. The grip was a bit large in her hand, but not unusably so.

With her pack ready on the ground beside her, she sat cross-legged to search.

The road had forked the night before, one branch following the river to the southwest through the farms, toward Linit Kungzet at the border, and the other running along the base of the Craggies straight west. She'd gambled that a need for water would make the river route more appealing to the Voice, and if she was wrong about him coming east, it would also be the road he would take west into Nagthari. She'd made her camp accordingly in the woods just south of the river road, a couple of miles past the fork, hoping for more range in the morning to help her make a decision.

Now she reached first southeast toward Kunchik. Today she could faintly feel it, several miles away, the concentrated mind-glows making a dim background for the nearer minds she found as she started to swing more to the east, familiar minds—the Rasesni wizards from the temple school. She touched them only briefly, wary of revealing herself.

They must be on horseback to have traveled so far this early in the morning. Can't be but a mile or so off, on the river road past the fork.

When she turned her attention directly to the east, she found a fainter cluster of mind-glows, with a feel that reminder her of Chang's squadron. *I bet that's Tlobsung's men. Must be on foot, what, an hour away? Less? Not at the fork yet.*

This means they both think the Voice is coming this way and they're going to try and coordinate. Must have been traveling since well before dawn.

She searched to the west for the Voice's people, cautiously. And there they were, close enough that she would have felt them last night, without the drug's inhibition. She would hear them, too, in a little while, close as they were. She peered through the trees that lined the far side of the road and tried without success to penetrate the morning mist from the warm river over the cold ground, hoping for a glimpse of them. They were in the fields a couple of miles away, between the two roads. This quiet spot was shaping up to be a battlefield today.

To her mind, what lay to the west was a complex cluster of people, hundreds of them. A thin layer in front, and then a large group of dulled minds. *I wonder if that's the horde.*

Behind the horde and around the whole body were more like the ones in front, by far the largest of the groups. *That must be the Khrebesni—they have the feel of Pyalshrog to them.*

There was a group on the inside, that seemed like they might be wizards, but the feel of them was weak. *Where's the Voice? In the center with his wizards, where he is best protected?*

No one's mounted, anyway. The horses are all in the rear, with cattle.

If Zandaril was alive he would be there, she hoped, but she didn't dare try to probe more obviously. She was closer to the Voice now than she had been when he first detected her. *Is my shield that much better, or is he just ignoring me for now? If I get too close my chain will feel his—surely it works the other way, too.*

The Rasesni wizards are going to ride right past him on this road, if they don't stop now. Should I tell them?

The subject of long-range searching hadn't come up while she was with them. Was it possible they didn't know?

And why should she tell them?

While she watched and debated with herself, the approaching formation out in the fields shifted. The surrounding tribesmen peeled off at a trot and turned into the woods north of the upper road, heading east, while the rest halted. In a little while, she heard the rustle of their passing across the further road for several minutes, and was grateful her camp was hidden well out of sight on the road they didn't take.

When they reached the portion of the upper road parallel to the lower one where the wizards were riding, she felt the glee on the one side from the running warriors, and the alarm on the other as the wizards heard the noise. They stopped and shielded themselves, but the Khrebesni continued on past them north of both roads, headed for the fork.

What good did the wizards think their shields were going to do anyway, thirty-odd against hundreds of warriors?

The decision about warning them had been taken out of her hands. The one who needed warning now was Tlobsung, and there was no one in his column she could reach, even if she wanted to.

To the west, the horde resumed its march, with the captive wizards behind it, at an angle aimed at intersecting the group from Kunchik on their present course.

And those wizards were still milling about in confusion at the passage of the tribesmen.

I'll give them credit, at least they'll try an attack on the Voice, looks like. It's not going to work, though, not if he sics the horde on them. What a waste.

Well, I can't let him suck up thirty more wizards, now can I?

She abandoned her pack and took to the air, east and low along the road, below the treetops, shielded and trying to keep out of sight of the horde in the fields. Was there anyplace they could take a defensive position, before the horde was upon them? Tlobsung would have his own hands full and they couldn't count on him.

She found them on their horses just a mile or so away, arguing about what to do next. They had two wagons with them, stopped in the middle of the road. When she flared up and landed, it shocked them into stopping their dispute. As soon as they had recovered, shouts of "traitor" and "murderer" rose from some of the riders. A few even tried mind assaults that failed to penetrate her shield.

She caught the eye of Veneshjug and smiled at him, a rigid, fixed smile, as full of promise as she could make it, then turned to the rest of them. "Who wants to attack me first and defend the *honor* of your Mage Council?"

That puzzled them into relative silence, and she raised her voice to carry over them all.

"That sound you heard was hundreds of Khrebesni headed off to set an ambush for Tlobsung, I expect."

They settled down and listened. Only the creak of their leather gear intruded. "Why aren't you with them?" she asked.

Zongchas told her, nervously keeping his horse at some distance. "We got ahead of them."

"Don't you read anything other than mage books?" She shook her head. "Who's going to protect you, now that Tlobsung's about to be tied up?"

An outraged voice cried, "We brought devices."

"Oh, yes? Planning to throw them at the horde out there while they attack? That might buy you thirty seconds. You're idiots—you needed the infantry for support against the enemy. Didn't you know that? Didn't Tlobsung tell you?"

One look at Dhumkedbhod's shocked face gave her pause. *Maybe they've never united like this before, never fought with an army. Did they even coordinate with Tlobsung?*

She stood there on the road and looked up at all of them on their horses, trying to make them understand. "I can't find the Voice. He might be with the tribesmen that passed by or with them out there in the field." She hooked her thumb at the horde coming their way. "They're coming at you, right now. If you're quiet, you'll hear them."

In the silence, they all heard an eerie swishing noise, not the tramp of marching men, but the chaotic push of a hundred or more sweeping through an unharvested field.

"You've got horses, you can probably get away and link up with Tlobsung if you hurry."

She could hear a bitter argument start up among the Mage Council members, and she took a moment to glance around the riders. Too few were bearing weapons—swords, mostly, belted awkwardly over their robes.

The decision was taking too long. She turned to the two wagon drivers. "Get those wagons emptied, right now. We're going to turn them into barricades—upend them on the south side of the road, wheels out, and take refuge in the trees back of them. Tie the horses behind you."

While the Mage Council sputtered objections, Penrys's one-time students stripped the wagons bare and freed the horses. She scanned the sacks as they carried them and detected devices and loose power-stones among them. Others led the horses into the trees and returned.

The noise of the wagons overturning with a crash almost drowned out the horde's measured, inexorable approach. As the mist began to burn off in the warmth of the morning, Penrys could see the first of them in the gaps between the trees across the road. Their faces were blank and tired, not eager like men going willingly to a fight.

Their weapons were primitive, wooden sticks and rocks, but it was more than some of the wizards had. She'd been teaching her students how to attack other wizards, not mundane people, controlled by the Voice.

Can I break that control? How is he doing it?

She called to wizards sheltering behind the wagons. **Shield with me. Don't shield us, you fools—them. Put a shield around them.**

It was a mess of confusion. *Oh, Zandaril, if you were only here to put them into some sort of order.*

Some of them even broke off to prepare small devices that they threw into the horde, cheering when they exploded, like the charms Veneshjug had prepared for Chang's camp. The trees across the road blunted some of the force, and their unskilled aim reduced the effect of the rest. The men coming didn't swerve or hesitate, and the first of them set foot on the road.

CHAPTER 54

Penrys failed to make the wizards into a unified force as the horde arrived. **Listen to me!**

This isn't going to work. Time for a single leader. She reached for Veneshjug's mind. *Him, first.* She ripped through his shield and drained him as she had Vladzan, but left him a portion of his strength, letting her chain absorb the rest.

As quickly as she could she worked her way through the rest of them, a few willing, like Dzantig, but most of them fighting her.

When she had them all under control, she spun a shield around the horde, all of it, and defied the Voice to break it. She felt his resistance initially, but he withdrew. *Where is he?*

The effect on the horde was immediate. The men stopped and swayed on their feet, their faces puzzled. She told them, **Sleep, now, and stay asleep.**

They collapsed to the ground. Behind her, there were cries of horror at having their power ripped away.

She taunted Veneshjug. **Enjoying this?** The wordless hostility that returned pleased her.

Penrys turned her attention back to the field. She could feel resistance coming from the captive wizards—they were trying to raise shields against the Voice, but they were weak. Since there was no longer any point in hiding, she scanned through the group individually, forty or fifty of them, and there! There was Zandaril! She shielded him immediately.

Took a long time. I was getting bored.

She smiled, but he felt terrible to her, his magic feeble, and his body in pain. She stretched her mind out and powered his core, from her chain, as if he were a power-stone, and he blazed vividly to life.

What did you do?!

He stuttered to a stop and pictured the group of captives. **Do them all! I've been organizing them.**

The humor underlying that thought was very welcome. She poured power into each of the captives as she pulled them under her shield.

All this power! It was exhilarating. There was nothing she couldn't do. Her chain seemed limitless.

She tried to be cautious, but she thought she felt a few of them drop out. Was it possible to overfill someone, like a power-stone? She cringed, but she had to be quick. Why hadn't the Voice counter-attacked? Where was he?

All of the captives were sheltered now, under their own second shield. She could feel them coming her way, very slowly, and she remembered the shackles.

What about the Rasesni wizards? Shouldn't they be shielded too? She couldn't release the sleeping horde, or the Voice could seize them back. It was beginning to be a lot to juggle.

Penrys's chain started to throb, and she spun around frantically, looking for the Voice who had to be nearby.

Her control over the wizards around her was stripped away, and she could dimly hear Veneshjug's mental voice, **Allow me to serve you, zendo, great lord.**

The Voice's harsh and well-remembered mind-voice commanded his new captives, **Hold her.**

Some were eager to comply, but were physically restrained by others, and she could feel several of them banding together to try and raise shields to shelter behind, with the remnants of power left to them by the Voice and herself.

In the confusion, before they could reach her, the Voice stepped out from behind the trees where he had hidden while the horde advanced.

Penrys had forgotten how tall he was, tall enough that the two-handed sword slung on his belt seemed to suit him. *How could anyone with that mind-voice look so young, no older than me?*

The Voice's assault was immediate, and frighteningly strong. He'd seized what was left of the wizards' power, and Penrys could feel the difference.

I should have taken it all from them so he couldn't have it. Curse me for a soft fool.

She held her shield over the sleeping horde and augmented the one generated by the captives in the field, but there was nothing left to attack with.

He kept the pressure up, probing methodically for weaknesses, and meanwhile speaking to his new captives in ways she couldn't hear.

He's so much more experienced. Even his chain feels older, stronger. I'm losing this.

Movement caught her eye, and she focused on Veneshjug rushing her with a short sword. He moved awkwardly, as though controlled by the Voice.

Is he a puppet or did he volunteer?

Penrys tripped him and dodged out of his way, but it gave her an idea. *Does the Voice use that sword much? I don't see armor. When's the last time anyone went after him physically?*

She drew Tak Tuzap's ax and ran at the Voice before he could retreat. As she got within striking distance, the burning of her chain around her neck almost stopped her. She could smell sizzling flesh, and the pain distracted her. *Is it happening to him, too? Is he causing it, or do the chains act independently?*

He had time to draw his sword and stand her off with a swing, and Penrys realized how bad her position was—no shield, nothing to parry with. She drew Tak's belt knife as her only option, but her feet felt clumsy, the weapons small and inadequate in her hands.

She managed to slice him with the ax on his left upper arm, but she knew his clothing had blunted the damage. When he advanced on her, she fell back.

Veneshjug tried to join in, but almost tripped him, and the Voice compelled him to the ground, out of the way.

She defended herself against his swings with the ax and knife, but she knew herself untrained and incompetent. Her best success was catching his blade with both of hers, held in an "X," but that was nothing but a defensive maneuver. *I have to attack somehow. Wish m'body knew about this kind of fighting.*

The horridly painful blazing of her chain urged her to back away, but she knew if she couldn't stop him now, her chances would only get worse, so she let the tears run down her cheeks and tried to ignore it.

He swung powerfully from his left, and this time, her attempt to catch his blade failed, and it ran down the back of the little knife in her left hand, right down the hilt, and the knife fell. She felt a chill in her hand, and when she glanced down, she saw fingers in the dust of the road. Her fingers. The bones in her palm seemed to loosen in a horrible way.

The momentum of his swing when it didn't meet the expected resistance spun the Voice around and twisted his body to his right. Penrys sprang from the ground as though she were launching herself into the air, and cleaved the side of his head with the small ax, its blade no larger than her hand. It penetrated so deeply that she lost her grip, and she saw the wound spouting blood around it as they both collapsed to the ground.

She jammed her ruined left hand under her right armpit, to try and slow the blood pumping out. It didn't hurt yet, but the sight of the bare thumb was sickening, and her stomach roiled.

With her mind firmly locked on the Voice's, she felt his own shield drop and then his control of the wizards around her.

She probed him, frantically. **Who are you? Who made you? Did he make me, too? Why?**

There were no answers from the dying mind, just a dimming sense of surprise.

She could feel expertises in areas she didn't recognize, and his native language, one she didn't know.

And then he was gone.

There was silence for a moment. At some point, her chain had ceased to burn, though the pain was still eye-watering.

Veneshjug started to pick himself up and looked for his dropped sword, but Dzantig and others appearing from behind the barricade stopped him from renewing his attack on her, and he turned to the body instead.

Under Penrys's stunned eyes, he reached down, worked the ax loose from the skull, and struck the body at the top of the neck.

She blinked. Rolling over on her left side and keeping her left hand pinned under her right arm, she made her way onto her knees and then staggered up and started to back away, unable to turn her eyes from the sight.

Veneshjug struck again, and again, his blows becoming stronger and more focused until finally he managed to separate the head from the neck.

The head rolled a few feet in the road, heavy as a stone, and Penrys caught a glimpse of ears as it did, ears just like hers, black and furry. One was dusty from the road, and one was covered in blood from the gaping wound. They alternated as they rolled, and she couldn't take her eyes away. The blood leaking from the base left trails in the dust until it stopped flowing.

When Veneshjug stooped to pick up the Voice's chain from the topless neck, and lifted it into the air in both hands in exultation, the hot blood running down his arms steamed in the cold air.

Her chain began to throb again, painfully over the burns, and she shouldered through the wizards standing in shock at the edge of the barricades.

"Get back!" she cried hoarsely. If her chain had a voice, she thought it would be screaming.

When she ducked behind the upended wagon, she glimpsed the carnage behind it. Most of the wizards were collapsed on the ground, and some weren't moving at all.

He sucked them dry. He must have.

Veneshjug on the other side, cried out a dedication to Venesh. Then he invoked the chain, like a power-stone.

A tremendous boom rocked the upended wagons and she heard screams from people on the wrong side of the barricade.

Her own chain was quiet again, resting firmly against burned and scored flesh.

Penrys staggered cautiously around the upended wagon and back into the road. There was nothing left of the Voice, head or body, and not much of Veneshjug, either. Dhumkedbhod and two other men lay dead in the road and there were several injured, groaning.

Dzantig came with her. As she staggered by the wagon, a glint of metal embedded in it caught her eye. "Can you dig that out for me?" she asked him.

He worked around it with his knife and pried it out—a three link fragment of the destroyed chain.

None of the pockets in her improvised clothing were accessible. "Drop it in the sheath, would you?"

She pointed her chin at the empty leather sheath for Tak's knife on her belt. "Stuff it in there."

She leaned against the wagon and locked her knees to keep from falling down. Her gaze was focused on the dusty road at her feet, and she noted distantly that something was still dripping red there, a little at a time. She was cold and very tired, and her fingers were out there, somewhere.

CHAPTER 55

Zandaril shuffled tenaciously through the field, in the trampled path of the horde where he could, desperate to get to the fight before it was too late. Penrys's shield had dropped away before the loud noise, and the shield he'd raised with Rinshradke, pulling in the rest of the surviving captives, was ragged and uneven, despite the power Penrys had charged them with.

He couldn't reach her through the shield, and the screams and cries that succeeded the explosion had him terrified about what he might find.

They had watched the horde ahead of them drop in the field, and it was a surprise to find they'd been sleeping, not dead, and were now waking up, confused and scared. Rinshradke assigned two of the weakest wizards to stay with them and try and keep them together until help could come.

The rest of the captive wizards plowed forward, mowing down the grain as they passed.

Dead and injured bodies from the horde littered the edge of the field, and damage showed in the trees, but finally they managed to make their way through the margin and onto the road.

Zandaril tried to make sense of the chaos before him. Two wagons were upended on the far side, liberally streaked with blood, and there were bodies everywhere.

He dropped his shield. **Where are you, Pen-sha?**

A small body, leaning against the far wagon, raised its head weakly. **Here.**

He dodged the injured awkwardly, impeded by his fetters, and stopped a few feet away.

She was covered in blood, all across her chest and down both arms, all of it dripping into the dust or coagulating, and her left hand was pinned under her right arm. He hoped that was the only source of the blood.

Dzantig was supporting her. "Help me with her," he called.

"What do you need?" Zandaril asked.

"Clamp your hands around her arm above the wrist. She can't lose any more blood. I'll go find something to wrap it in."

Zandaril lunged forward and grabbed her left forearm in a tight grip with both hands. "You can let go now," he told her, nudging her right arm away with his elbow. "I've got it."

She sank to her knees, and he went down with her, saying, "What have you been doing with these ungrateful wizards, eh? Getting yourself into trouble? Let's take a look now."

She let him pull the hand into view and it was all he could do to control his face. The top of the palm had been sliced away diagonally, taking all the fingers with it, and only the thumb remained.

"Ah, we'll get that fixed up in no time, don't you worry."

"He's dead. I killed him," she muttered, into the ground.

"And a good thing," he said. "You'll tell me all about it later."

A foot poked him, and he looked up. Dzantig stood over him with a canteen and a torn shirt.

"Now you just think of something else while we clean this up a little."

She glanced up at the canteen and shuddered in anticipation. "Save some for my neck."

Dzantig met Zandaril's eyes, and then reached down and pushed her hair aside. The chain was blackened and scorched, and raw, blistered flesh wept all around it.

"Hand, first," Dzantig said, and Zandaril nodded. They washed it off as efficiently as possible to see the extent of the damage, and Penrys trembled in pain at the process. Zandaril inspected it, then called Dzantig to take his place holding the forearm clamped.

"I'm going to just tidy things up a little, then we'll wrap it all up and you'll feel much better," he told her. "Don't worry, I do this for horses all the time."

She didn't respond.

With Dzantig's help, he positioned her open hand against the wood of the wagon and used Dzantig's knife to trim the ragged bits of skin and tendon that protruded. Then he wrapped the palm as tightly as he could manage in strips torn from the shirt.

"Loosen your grip slowly," he told Dzantig. "I want to see what happens."

The wrapping reddened wherever it contacted the wound, but the bloodstains didn't spread much after that.

"I think the bleeding has already slowed down," he said. "Now let's take a look at that neck."

He used a strip from the shirt to wrap her hair up, out of the way, and then looked at the chain.

"Not much room, here. Maybe we can put a padded cloth around it, then roll the chain up her neck a little higher to rest above the bandage."

He looked up at Dzantig. "You should hold the chain higher on her neck."

When Dzantig hesitated, Zandaril snorted. "Nothing will happen if you touch it, trust me."

He smiled for a moment, thinking of more pleasant touches, but the trembling body under his hands recalled him. He patted the burns gently with a soaked cloth, then dried it to see how bad the seepage was. *It needs lotions to soothe it, but that will have to wait. Just get it covered for now.*

He wrapped two strips of cloth in a third and laid that as lightly as he could around her neck, tying it firmly at the throat. The released chain lay on the upper edge, but didn't press directly on the damage.

He cupped her cheek in his hand gently. "There, Pen-sha, that should be better. We're all done for now."

She drew her knees up and rested her right arm on them, and her forehead on her arm. Her bandaged hand was drawn against her bloody chest.

Just let me sit here for a little while.

"I'll leave you with her," Dzantig told Zandaril. "And… I'm glad to see you—I was worried."

Zandaril watched Rinshradke and Zongchas together sorting out what could be salvaged. The dead were ignored for now while the walking wounded tended to the others. Some of the captive wizards reunited with friends, and there were little cries of recognition, but most of them seemed to be strangers from other regions within Rasesdad, united now only in their survival.

After a few minutes, Penrys drew a shuddering breath and lifted her head. "That's better. What about you? You're hurt, I can feel it."

"That's nothing worse than a beating. No, it's the boots I mind."

She glanced sideways at his torn boots, the shackles eating into the leather.

"What, again? How do you manage that?"

"It's a mystery to me, it is." He smiled to see her keeping up the banter.

Dzantig passed, and Penrys called out to him. "Dzantig, I want power-stones. I saw at least one sack of them on the wagons from before. Can you fetch it?"

"I know where it is," he said.

In a minute, he returned with it. "What do you have in mind?"

"I'm going to try something. Zandaril, come over here."

Obediently, he stood in front of her, and spread his feet apart at her gesture until the chain between them was taut.

Dzantig put the bag next to her on the ground and opened the top for her. She reached in awkwardly and placed a little heap of stones on top of a link in the middle of the chain.

"Wouldn't it be better at the end where the shackle is?" he asked.

She looked up at him. "Don't know how much control I have. Didn't want it too close to your skin."

Deadpan, she added, "Of course, if you'd rather…"

"No, no, forget I asked. You go right ahead."

She powered the stones, and continued to power them until they overloaded and melted both sides of the link.

Gingerly, Zandaril pulled the chain on either side of the softened link until his chain had separated into two pieces. "I can tie these ends up to the leg shackles and keep them out of the way until we can get them off altogether."

"If you can bring the captives over to me, I'll do them all, as long as I can."

Are you sure?

I'm better, really. This isn't hard to do.

He snorted his skepticism, but nonetheless he walked over to Rinshradke to set it up. Soon a steady stream of tired wizards clanked by, and Dzantig was kept busy finding rags they could use to tie up the broken chains.

The last in line was Rinshradke, and Zongchas came with her, talking earnestly. When Penrys had finished with her chain, she raised her right arm to Zandaril. "Give me a lift," she said.

He pulled her up and looked at her closely. The color in her face was better, and she seemed more energetic, if you could look past the appalling blood on her clothing.

"We need to go help Tlobsung, send everyone who can ride back to him," she told Zongchas. "Can't you hear them?"

Now that the injured were quieter, the distant sound of battle was audible.

Whatever these Rasesni decide, I'm getting Penrys out of here.

"I'll go fetch us some horses," he told her. "Don't move."

She laughed.

"She's lovely, but how will I get on her?"

Penrys looked at the two horses Zandaril brought back and thought about mounting with one hand. She wondered briefly if their owners were living or dead, but it didn't matter right now.

"Leave that to me," he said. He tied both mares to the wagon wheel and unhooked the canteen from the saddle.

"First, you're going to drink this, as much as you can."

"Blood loss," she muttered, and he nodded.

"That's right. Water is good for that."

She took the canteen in her good hand after he opened it, and chugged it down, surprised at how dry her mouth and throat seemed to be.

She stopped when her stomach told her it couldn't take any more, and handed it back. He closed it and hooked it back on his saddle.

"Now, pay attention," he said. "Dzantig and I will get you on your horse, and you don't need to do anything. In fact, you're going to put this on, first."

Another shirt from someone's saddlebag was pressed into service, and Zandaril fashioned a sling for her left arm. The instant he slipped it over her neck and shoulder, it started to soak up blood from her clothing, but it helped keep her hand from knocking against anything.

Zandaril sent Dzantig to the far side of her horse to catch her, then he had her bend her left knee into both his hands.

"Just put your right hand on the saddle for balance, but don't try to haul yourself up."

He fairly threw her into the air and she swung her right leg automatically over the horse's back. Dzantig reached up and kept her torso from swaying too far to the right, and she thumped into the saddle more easily than she would have thought possible, considering how much of a challenge just standing up had been.

As the two men adjusted her stirrups for her, a thought struck her. "Can't be this easy when men do it, surely."

Zandaril chuckled. "Can get a bit painful, it can." Dzantig grinned.

Penrys gestured for the reins, but Zandaril shook his head.

"Can't have you doing that. Leak a little more blood and there won't be much left. You just sit there and try not to fall off."

She was indignant for a moment, but then gave up, relieved.

All around them she saw about twenty of the wizards also on horseback, some of them injured. The remainder would stay behind for the wounded. None of the one-time captive wizards joined them.

Penrys watched Zandaril walk over to the older woman who'd been the last of the captives whose chain she'd separated, the one who'd been talking to Zongchas. He clasped her arm and bowed his head to her, before he returned to mount up.

Dzantig handed the reins of her horse to Zandaril, then mounted his own, and the little troop walked away from disaster and death.

CHAPTER 56

"Stop here," Penrys said, and waited for the throbbing in her wounds from riding a trot to subside.

Everyone had made it to the fork in the road. The sounds of combat were off to the east down the main road.

She scanned the near portion of the battle. It was a swirl of confusion to her mind, the Khrebesni mixed in with the soldiers.

Zandaril looked back at her, her reins clasped in his left hand.

*Got a plan?*

She shrugged. _*I can't just make them all stop. Let me try something.*_

She picked out the nearest knot of fighting and zeroed in on a tribesman in the thick of it. She reached out as she had for Vladzan and stopped his heart, then found another and did the same. That knot broke apart.

*How do you tell the difference?*

With a shock, she realized Zandaril was watching through her, as he was accustomed to do while she was teaching him. Watching her cold-bloodedly killing men. _No help for it now._

*By their native language. It's all the same for the Khrebesni.*

She looked for the next knot of conflict and resumed her work.

Zandaril quietly relayed what was happening to the others.

After half an hour, her interference was clearly having an effect. The groups were separating, and the tribesmen were gathering and retreating back down the road.

Penrys twisted in her saddle and called out, "They're coming this way. Hold your ground."

The noise of a couple hundred men or more jogging down the road was hard to mistake. When the first of them reached the fork and saw the mounted wizards, he hissed and came to a stop.

What must we look like, all bloody?

Like survivors. We look like survivors.

She spoke to him in his own language, in a carrying voice, and made sure her chain was visible. "He's dead. We've reclaimed his captives and the horde."

He lifted a blood-stained spear and stepped forward, and the men behind him followed.

She sighed, and stopped his heart. He wavered in place for a moment before he fell.

The indrawn breaths behind her almost matched the ones in front, and all movement ceased.

Penrys gestured to the western side of the fork and the northern of the two roads. A new leader bulled his way forward and led what was left of his people around the wizards, leaving them alone on the western edge of the interrupted battle.

It's over.

She slumped in her saddle, until Zandaril's voice penetrated.

"Look at them."

She lifted her head and surveyed the wizards. There was apprehension on their faces, and a brief scan showed fear and resignation. They expected her to take over from the Voice, as Veneshjug had tried to do. As she herself had done already, drawing upon them for the power she needed to fight against him. They hadn't come with her to stop the fighting, they'd come because they feared her.

Her thoughts felt slow. Did she want to control them? She looked at their faces, her gaze passing over Zandaril's without pausing. With this much power, she could perhaps hold Tlobsung's force, what was left of it, use it as a better-armed horde. And twice the wizards, if she consolidated the survivors.

I could do it. But why? What for?

She shook her head silently, and restored power to the wizards with her, taking it back from her chain. While the startled wizards before her backed away, she reached to the ones who'd stayed behind with the wagons, and restored them, too, the ones who were alive. It was all she could do.

They still don't like us much.

She smiled sardonically. "Better stay close," she told Zandaril. "They're not our friends."

More noise on the road to the east resolved itself into a marching column. Zongchas trotted over to the officer in charge.

A space grew around Zandaril and her, with Dzantig the only wizard who kept his horse with them.

Zandaril leaned toward her. "Do you want to stay?"

"With them?" She tilted her head toward the wizards sidling away. "There's nothing for us here."

Dzantig said, "My colleagues are fools but…" He spread his hands in a gesture of helplessness.

He bowed to them from his saddle. "Thank you, *brudigna*, *brudigdo*. We would be dead now, or worse. *I* know this, if they don't."

Reaching into a saddlebag, he pulled out the half-full sack of power-stones, what was left after melting through the foot chains. He handed it to Zandaril, then turned and followed the rest of the wizards.

Penrys looked down in bemusement at the wealth in Zandaril's hand. "On the whole, I'd rather have some of their books."

Zandaril snorted, and stashed the sack in his saddlebag.

"Let's go," he said. "Not our fight any more."

They rode at a walk east on the road, keeping to the margin to let clusters of soldiers march past headed west. No one bothered them, after one good look at the blood, and Penrys pulled the remnants of her shirt's collar up and bent her head to let her hair obscure the chain.

After a while, they had passed the worst of the fighting—the dead on the road, and the living tended by their fellows.

When they reached the turnoff to Kunchik, Zandaril stopped, and Penrys brought her head up.

"What…?"

He looked at her patiently. "The nearest help is in Kunchik. You need a doctor, and me, I want to get these shackles off."

She looked down and saw how he'd twisted the tied-up chains around to the outer side of his boots to keep from hitting the horse with them. It looked uncomfortable.

"Do we have to? I want nothing from these Rasesni."

Zandaril stared at her. "What, you want to ride all the way out the Gates to Chang? That must be thirty miles or more."

Penrys glanced at the sun, not yet very high in the sky. "It's only mid-morning, hard as it is to believe. We can do it." She swayed in the saddle, belying her words.

"Kunchik is much closer. What about your packs, the things you brought with you?"

She snorted. "You think they're going to let me take Veneshjug's books and his power-stones back with me?"

She shook her head. "There's nothing there I can't replace. What about you?"

"Everything I care about is back in Hing Ganau's wagon," he said. "Or right here."

He looked at her speculatively for a moment, and she straightened her spine under his gaze.

"Seven hours, it is, at a walk. Less if we trot for some of it. Think you can?"

She forced herself to be honest. "I think so. Maybe. We'll stop if we have to."

She waved her hand in its sling at him. "Won't make any difference to this."

Blinking back the fog that threatened to engulf her, she added, "Oh, Zandaril, I want to. Can we?"

He clucked and turned his horse to the east, leading hers behind him. "We'll do it, Pen-sha. We'll sleep in our own bedrolls tonight."

CHAPTER 57

Down one of the turnoffs that ran to the rapids of Gonglik Jong, where the water rushed over the stepped falls, Zandaril led her to a grassy spot near a backwater and pulled her off her horse, careful of her left arm. He tethered both mares where they could graze the autumn-tinged herbage and walked Penrys over to the bank before letting her rest.

"That hand needs looking at, now that we have lots of water," he said. "And you'll feel better if you can get cleaned up proper."

Penrys let herself be handled. It was pleasant to sit and do nothing, the music of the falls drowning out everything else, and the spray soft against her skin, if a bit chilly.

Zandaril came back with yet another shirt, and someone's tunic, too.

"Well-stuffed saddle bags," she commented.

"I didn't just look at the beasts when I chose these two." He grinned at her.

"Stand up, now, you lazy woman." He grabbed her right hand and hauled her up.

"Another drink before we start."

He shoved an open canteen into her hand and she obediently drank, whereupon her body reminded her of other urgencies.

She looked down and remembered the knotted cord holding up her too-large breeches.

"Um, if you're planning to strip me anyway, I'm going to need your help, as well as your assistance in… other matters."

A look of comprehension crossed his face. "Well, if I keep pouring water into you, what do you think I expected?"

He waved his hand. "Let's get the top off first, so it doesn't stain everything else more than it already has. Then we'll see how far down we have to go."

He flourished a knife. "From the saddle-kit. Good to have a knife again." With it, he cut the shirt and tunic off her left side, and let her pull her right arm through on the other side.

She glanced down and saw that her improvised breastband was soaked with blood. "That, too, I guess."

"Ah, nothing I haven't seen before, Pen-sha. I'll find you something else to use."

The top of the breeches were also sticky with blood, and it was easier to cut the cord than to try and untie it.

"Now that's a puzzle," he said. "Didn't find any spares in the saddle-bags."

"It's only the top part," Penrys said. "If we wash that and keep the rest dry, maybe I can just wear it damp.

"Let me think about it. Meanwhile, off it goes. Everything."

She leaned on him as she hobbled over to a bush, throttling her embarrassment, but what else could she do? He held her right arm solidly and looked away while she did the necessary and escorted her back to the water's edge, naked and cold. She thought for a moment of torches and snow.

"We'll start at the top and see what we find," he said.

He made her lean forward so that he wouldn't soak the bandage around her neck, and he scooped water through her hair. She was shocked to see the red come out—she hadn't realized how much blood there was.

He wrung her hair until it stopped dripping, then took rags from the unstained back of her ruined clothing and wiped blood off of her face until she felt as scrubbed as a kitchen floor.

The bandage around her neck was damp, now, but he left it in place as he started wiping down the rest of her. The worst of the blood was on her clothes, of course, but she was sticky everywhere.

Cold as the water was, the thrill of being clean was better than any fire. He saved her left arm with its bandage for later and worked around it, while she held it up to keep it from getting wet.

When the water finally ran clear, he asked, "Bandages now, or after I get the clothes ready?"

"Do it now, let's get it over with."

"Good girl."

He'd cleared a place for her to sit, on the laid-out bedroll from one of the horses. "You just slip into that and sit up."

He filled both canteens from the freshest part of the water, and brought them back, along with the rags he had prepared for bandages.

"Now you hold that chain of yours, high as you can."

Penrys sat cross-legged in the bedroll and exposed from the waist up. She spread her right hand and used the thumb in front and the fingers in back to try and keep the chain rolled up as high on her neck as it would go.

Zandaril cut the old damp wrapping off and patted at the damage with a fresh rag.

"Not too bad, this is."

He tied a clean multilayer coil of bandage around the burns, and she let the chain roll down to lie against the top of it.

He pointed at her left hand. "Ready?"

She nodded and looked away while he unwrapped the bandage instead of cutting it off. When the bloody mess was gone, he began sponging everything clean under it.

"I can stitch this, like for horses. It would be better, keep it cleaner."

She forced herself to look at what remained of the back of her left hand. From the lower left to the upper right below the knuckles, the Voice's sword had taken everything in one slice. Her thumb was intact, longer now by a good bit than anything else. The back seemed wider, looser, and the feel of it turned her stomach.

It ached and burned freshly now that it was exposed to air and water again without the support of the wrapping.

"No," she said hoarsely. "No sutures. Something will heal, I expect, and that will get in the way."

She looked away again. "Just make sure it's clean and bind it tightly to keep the dirt out."

Pulling up her knees and leaning her head on them, on her right arm, she held her left hand out for him to work on and gritted her teeth.

Eventually it was done.

"Lie down, now, Pen-sha, and I'll get everything ready for you. Won't take but a few minutes."

"We'll keep going today, right? All the way?" she asked.

"All the way. I promise."

She let his words soothe her and she snuggled into the bedroll on her right side to the sound of the bubbling water.

"It's time."

Zandaril shook her shoulder gently and Penrys opened her eyes. When she checked, she found the sun had moved in the sky but it was still shy of mid-day.

"I wanted to let you sleep longer, but I promised to see you back today."

Zandaril gestured at the clothes laid across the foot of the bedroll. "Come see your new robes, *bikrajti.*"

He held up the breeches first. She recognized them, the same ones she'd been wearing, but the bloody top had been cut away and suspenders added, a neatly stitched leather strap permanently attached at the back and divided to cross over the shoulders.

"We'll have to tie it through the holes in front to make it fit, but I think this will work, and you don't need to unfasten anything to take it off."

"How did you manage that?"

He grinned. "Whoever this wizard was, he understood what to carry for a long trip on a horse. Spare stirrup leathers always come in handy, and a repair kit for tack."

"Near as I could tell, you were using a long strip of cloth over your breasts, yes? I hope this will work. Seems to me that's got to go on first, and I've been looking forward to helping with that."

He leered at her as he picked up the cloth he must have sewn together from several shorter ones, and the good-natured badinage lifted her spirits as much as the brief nap.

"Don't get used to it. I'll manage for myself, soon enough," she said.

Still, she laughed as she raised her arms and, with him fumbling and her helping one-handed, they managed to wrap a reasonable support around her and tuck in the ends.

"Shirt next. No matter if it's too big."

That slipped easily over her head and she let him pull her up by her right hand.

"I've been wanting to see how these breeches will work out," he said, as he helped her balance while she put one leg in, and then the other, and shoved her feet into her shoes.

"No socks are better than wet socks, I think, and you're not walking anywhere," he said.

The cut-down waist was in a reasonable position, and she had him tie the braces off in front so that the crotch was comfortable.

She managed to tuck the excess length of shirt in without too much help from him.

"You should turn tailor, I think," she told him.

"Carpet weaving is more respected, in my family," he deadpanned.

The borrowed tunic was snugged in with a new belt. "Let me guess—the other stirrup leather?"

Zandaril nodded.

She looked closely—he had unstitched the buckle from the old bloody belt and attached the new leather to it.

He bored a hole for her once she had it on, and she felt like a new woman, despite her aching hand and throat.

The horses were ready, she saw, and her spirits sank. How would she mount again?

Zandaril followed her gaze. "Ah, nothing to it. Same as before, only you're stronger this time, and I won't let you go over too far."

When he threw her up into the saddle, he was as good as his word, with a grip on her belt that anchored her as she settled.

Then he mounted himself and took her reins again. She protested, but he ignored her.

"If your horse shies at something, you may need a hand to grab with."

She felt a tinge of panic, and she waved her arm in its sling at him. "I can't let this stop me from riding."

"No, no, Pen-sha, it won't. Once it heals, however it heals, you'll be able to use it well enough for lots of things—riding, too. But not right now."

They walked back onto the road and settled in to the rhythm of a long day in the saddle.

CHAPTER 58

"Did I tell you how well they did after the Voice released them?"

Zandaril's voice bubbled over with enthusiasm as he described his success at showing the captive wizards how to organize themselves to raise their own shield.

"They only had half a day's worth of lessons, passed mind to mind while touching. It's remarkable what they were able to do."

She commented, "They were motivated, and they had a good teacher."

He looked back at her, startled.

"Well, you *are* a good teacher. I could always tell the improvement in the students after you sent them back to me. They worked better for you, learned more."

She smiled at the surprise on his face. "In fact, wasn't this what you wanted to do? Organize wizards? I don't see how anyone could have done it any better."

He stopped his horse, and she drifted up alongside him on hers.

"What's the matter?" she asked.

"My *nayith*, my masterwork," he whispered. "Is that what you say, *jarghalti*?"

She nodded. "I think so, anyway. For what that's worth."

He kicked up into a trot and she followed, concentrating on sitting as comfortably as she could without jostling her arm.

Eventually he slowed back into a walk, and they passed an hour or more alternating between the two gaits, trying to make time.

Penrys dozed during one of the longer walking sessions. Images of the head rolling in the dust occupied her mind—the furry ears, like hers, now bloody, now dusty. The feel of his mind as it died, the surprise, the unknown language, the obscure skills.

Zandaril jolting to a stop woke her fully, and he pulled them both to the side of the road as they passed Tlobsung's camp at Harlin to let the traffic pass unimpeded. There were wagons of wounded wheeling into camp, she saw, and other men marching out, to the west.

"Let's get out of here," Zandaril said, and they picked up a trot again, the westering sun behind them lengthening their shadows in front.

It was still daylight, just, when they finally encountered the outermost scouts around Chang's squadron.

Their horses were tired, but the smell of other horses livened them up, and it was with straight spines that the two riders rode, exhausted, into the camp.

Word traveled ahead of them, and both Chang and Tun Jeju stood outside the command tent and watched them stop and dismount, Zandaril, clinking from his tied chains, pulled Penrys off of her horse and supported her until her legs worked well enough.

"I take it there's news," Chang said. "Better come in before you fall down." He waved a trooper over to take their horses.

They helped each other to chairs and collapsed.

Tun looked them over. "Maybe we should reconvene in the healer's tent," he commented to Chang.

Zandaril laughed and held out a booted and shackled leg. "A smith first for me, Notju-chi, and then both of us there, I think. But we can spend a few minutes here, on the way."

Tun waved his hand in encouragement.

"The Voice turned into Neshilik," Zandaril said, "and headed east. Tlobsung took his force out to meet him, north of Gonglik, and the Rasesni wizards from the temple school came to join them. There was a fight, several of them, but…"

He looked to his right, at Penrys asleep in her chair, her damaged arm cradled in her good one.

"Well, it's a long story. We won, the Voice is dead, lots of people died. That part's over."

He stood up. "Come to the healer's tent, in a little while, and I'll give you all the details, but I only know my side, not hers. She's the one who killed him."

The lanterns flickering overhead seemed strange to Penrys. *A tent, a large one.*

She was on a cot, and there were two more nearby, only one of which was occupied, by a sleeping man.

Must be the healer's tent. But I don't remember how I got here…

She overheard Zandaril's voice. "I don't need anything, *Shiksupju-chi*, I'm not pissing blood anymore."

I didn't know he was hurt that bad.

Everything felt clean. She was wearing the shirt Zandaril had given her, and not much else, but the pair of blankets over her kept her warm enough.

She raised her hand to her throat and felt the flat bandage there over a layer of something oily. When she brought her fingertips to her nose, she couldn't identify the soft, pungent scent. The burn was dull, now, not sharp and urgent.

What would have happened if the fight had taken longer? Would it have burned through my throat altogether and killed me?

She wished she could have seen the damage the Voice's chain did to him, if any.

When she lifted her left hand for inspection, she admired the clean and tidy work that had replaced Zandaril's workmanlike wrapping. A padded glove, that's what she needed—something to protect it without exposing it to stares. It didn't hurt so much, just a throb with every heartbeat.

What about the fragment of chain?

Zandaril?

"Here," he called cheerfully, and he walked over to her in ragged boots free of shackles. "How are you doing, Pen-sha?"

He hauled over a camp chair and sat down beside her.

Coughing to clear her throat, she said, "What happened to our old clothes? I need the sheath, the one Tak Tuzap's knife was in. You didn't lose that, did you?"

He raised an eyebrow.

"It's important," she insisted.

"Let me go find it," he said. "Be right back."

She lowered her head again, an apology in her glance in reply to the glare from the healer.

"It really is important," she muttered, defiantly.

When Zandaril returned, Chang and Tun Jeju followed him, with Sau Tsuo and others from Chang's staff, and the area was a flurry of activity as camp chairs were commandeered for all of them.

Zandaril tossed Tak's old knife sheath onto her cot. "This the one?"

"That's it. Look inside. Tell me if anything's there. I had Dzantig shove it in, deep."

He picked it up again and stuck his own knife in to pry around. The point caught on something, and he dragged out the three-link fragment of the Voice's chain, still stained with blood.

"Is that what I think it is?"

At her nod, he held it out to her on the point of the knife, careful to avoid touching it with his bare hand.

She plucked it off and dropped it casually in her lap.

"Help me sit up," she told him, and he arranged a backrest for her while she pushed herself up with her right hand. When he was done, she waved him back to his seat. Then, facing Chang's council, she picked up the bit of chain and slashed the air with it in her hand.

"*Sennevi.* It is done. This is what's left of the Voice. Now, ask your questions."

It took hours, and her voice was hoarse before the end, but finally Chang's council was satisfied.

Penrys had listened with anger as Zandaril described his abduction and captivity. On her side, she'd been circumspect about exactly what had happened that night with the Mage Council, but she could feel Zandaril's fury, unexpressed.

Penrys waited until all the officers had left, then turned to Zandaril. "Are you really all right?"

He waved off her concern. "That was just a beating, nothing broken, no permanent damage."

She looked at him skeptically. *What was it like for you, waking up bound and waiting for the horde to descend? I can't ask you, can I?*

She told him, "You know, Dzantig really did help me, 'cause he was so worried about you. When you went and made a friend to drink with, you probably saved my life, too."

"Good." He gave her a hard look. "And what exactly did their council do to you, and how did you escape?"

"I'll tell you sometime," she said. "The details don't matter."

"I think they do, *bikrajti.* I think I owe Tak Tuzap your life as much as Dzantig, and I want to pay my debts."

"Poor Takka. I took his knife, and that little ax was an heirloom of his house. They're both as gone as the rest of this." She held up the fragment of chain.

Zandaril looked thoughtful. "How big was this ax? Show me."

She sketched it out for him in the air and described the bison-horn grips and whirlwinds on the blade.

He was still angry, she could feel it. "Those Rasesni have a lot to answer for."

She made a crooked smile. "They already did. Only two are left of the original five on their Mage Council, and think how they died."

"That's a start," he muttered.

She adjusted her position in the cot, one handed, to ease her back. "Did you ever find out what Chang did while we were gone?"

"Just what we expected—he bottled up the Gate and let the diplomatic answers wait for his own commanding officers to arrive. I think he was trying to avoid contagion from a wizard war he didn't understand."

He looked down at her. "Tun Jeju told me privately that he thinks the temporary truce will hold for a while. I think everyone assumes Rasesdad will vacate Neshilik again, since they can. Not our problem, anyway."

"Time enough tomorrow for everything else," he said, standing and leaning over her.

He helped her slide down in the cot and she heard him settle back into his chair as she slid into a night of violent dreams and bloody death.

CHAPTER 59

When Penrys awoke for the last time, it was well past dawn. The friendly sound of morning activity around the camp had helped her feel safe at last.

The healers' tent was empty, but she detected the hand of Hing Ganau in the pile of clean clothing laid on the chair Zandaril had been using the night before. On top was a roll of the same wrapping the healer had used on her left hand and a small but sturdy ceramic pot sealed by wax. The fragment of chain lay next to it.

She swung her legs over the side of the cot and, when her head stopped spinning, she picked up the pot and gave it a sniff. *For my neck. Nice of her. Must think I'm going somewhere.*

The sight of new boots made her sigh. *Ah, yes, my old ones are still in Kunchik. I hate breaking in new boots.*

She dressed, tentatively using the thumb on her left hand to help. It was clumsy, and it made her hand ache, but it was much better than no hand at all. No more needing assistance in the bushes like the day before. Her face burned at the recollection. She pocketed the chain fragment, grateful to have pockets again.

All that effort, all those deaths, and that bit of metal is all I have to show for it.

Faced with the boots at last, she contemplated the loops at the top on either side. *That's not standard issue.* She picked one up and examined it more closely. The loops didn't quite match the leather of the boot tops, and the stitching looked new.

Zandaril. So I could use my thumb to help pull them on.

Unexpected tears rose to her eyes and she bowed her head to hide the weakness. *We're done, aren't we. He jollied me along yesterday when I needed it, like the kind man he is, but the things he saw me do…*

She sniffed, and forced herself to stop. *At least he survived, I didn't get him killed. That's something.*

Now what? Where do I go? There's no point staying here.

She took a couple of deep breaths, and pulled on one boot. When her hand stopped throbbing, she tugged on the other one, picked up her pair of shoes, and limped out of the tent.

Penrys found Hing Ganau's wagon where she expected it, the camp not having moved in several days. Neither Hing nor Zandaril was there, and she lowered the tailgate one-handed and climbed in.

The bean sacks were much the same, but all the personal marks of Zandaril's occupation were diminished. She saw one tidy roll bound by leather straps which she suspected was his little rug, the one that had made such a comforting bit of color between them.

The books were gone, and his special stones, no doubt into the open packs she saw lying along the wooden wall. Only his bedroll was still laid out.

Her few possessions, all provided by the squadron, were in a neat pile against the opposite wall, with an old, empty, pack beside them. They included her folded bedding and the half-empty bag of power-stones.

The inference was clear. It was time for her to gather her possessions up and leave.

She set her face and bent to the task. The shoes she was carrying would fit in the bottom of the pack, once she'd cleaned them.

"You're here!"

Zandaril's cheerful voice interrupted her packing.

Penrys made sure her face was under control before turning, and raised her shield.

"I went looking for you in the healers' tent but you were already gone," he said. "Sorry I wasn't there, but I had errands to run."

He dropped a small burlap bag on the floor of the wagon and hauled himself up. He stuck his hand in the bag and pulled out a tidy knife in a belt sheath, and put it aside.

"No, not that one." Rummaging in the bag again, he came out with a different knife and laid it down in front of where she was kneeling.

"Look—for Tak Tuzap. Think he'll like it? I never saw what he gave you, but I had the sheath to give me an idea of the size."

He reached down and handed her the other one while he spoke.

"This one's for you—to replace the one you lost."

She looked down at the sheathed knife in her hand, and couldn't speak.

Into the drawn-out silence, Zandaril said, "What's wrong, Pen-sha?"

She clamped her jaws until she thought she could control her voice.

"When are you leaving?" she asked, her face still concealed by her hanging hair.

"Tomorrow, I think. The smith won't be done with the ax before then."

She heard him reposition himself until he was seated cross-legged in front of her.

"Aren't you coming, Pen-sha?" he asked, gently.

"I… I thought I might find a way back to the Collegium. Maybe I can find some sort of clue now that I have some of the chain, *his* chain, to examine. There must be ships…"

She cleared her throat. "I'll be fine. You don't have to worry."

Her eyes seemed to find the floorboards of the wagon fascinating. Every bit of dust, every scratch—it gave her something to look at.

"And why would you do that?" he asked.

When she didn't reply, he prodded, "You can do better than that…"

It stung her, and she muttered, "Blood. Death. Monsters. Power."

She finally made herself lift her head and look at him. "Next time you'll get killed."

His face wasn't shocked, or even puzzled. It was steady.

"I have better idea," he said. "We go give Tak his *yarab mar uthkahi*, his honor gifts, buy some donkeys from him so I can experiment with mules. You come meet my family. We feed you better, lots of *wishkaz* spices to keep you warm in winter, and we have real winters, not like here."

"You can't! It's much too dangerous. *I'm* too dangerous."

She cleared her throat. "I killed Vladzan—stole all his power, stopped his heart, and watched from the inside when he died."

He nodded, as if it were no surprise to him. "What he deserved. Like the Khrebesni you killed to stop the attack. Killing the enemy is not wrong."

"Not like that. Not reveling in it, not… glorying in the power of it."

"But you gave it back, all the power you stole. You are *not* like the Voice."

"Oh, Zandaril, I *am*. I will be."

"Every warrior learns what it feels like to kill an enemy. Sorrow to kill a man, pleasure to defend family and friends, righteousness to wield justice, pride in success. They learn this, or they are not warriors but murderers. You have learned this now."

"This time around." She trailed off. "The mage council, they wanted to know where I came from, so they robbed me of my strength with a drug and forced me to look."

She unclenched her teeth. "There was nothing there, Zandaril. I don't care what m'body knows, there was nothing there. I'm not getting it back."

Looking at him directly, she said, "I *am* building on sand, and this can't be the first time. M'body got its own memories somewhere. How old am I? Do I just stay this age? How would you tell, if I heal so well? Maybe wrinkles are just something else to heal and I'll never see them. Maybe I did have children… but think what monsters I might breed."

She bit her lip.

Zandaril let a few moments pass, then asked, "Have you looked in the inside pocket of that pack yet?"

Penrys stared at him. She turned and felt around inside until she located a hard lump and fished it out. The small leather pouch was unfamiliar, and when she loosened its thongs with the aid of her teeth she discovered the stone she had picked up on the way from Lupmikya, after stopping at the mill.

"This?"

She held it out on her palm. "I know it's not right. It won't balance on its own, but I… like it."

He reached into his pocket and pulled out a matching leather pouch.

I suppose he must have made both of those pouches. How did he know about my stone?

The stone he uncovered was broad and flat-bottomed, with a deep depression that marred its appearance. He placed it on the wagon boards between them and plucked her stone out of her hand. Its rough base fit the top of his as though they had been made together, and yet they were different minerals—his was a dark gray granite, solid and speckled with black bits, and hers was an orange-gray sandstone with streaky layers.

The combined stone, to her eye, was strong but not simple. The movements were complex, the colors and materials were a contrast, and yet it made a pleasing whole.

She wondered what he saw.

Zandaril told her, "I have never heard of a two-part *had-kighat mar-lud*, and I don't know what it means, but they belong together, you can see that. And they are wrong when they are apart."

He left the conjoined stones between them.

"Listen to me. Just living is dangerous, and yet we embrace it, we must. At least you do not build on sand now."

He gestured at the double stone. "We have real foundations. Maybe you have another family, maybe two, maybe none."

He shrugged. "We will deal with that when we must."

How can hope roil my stomach like this?

"You're not scared of me, like any sensible man?"

He grinned at her. "You? You should meet my *nurti*, my second sister. Much scarier. That's why I bring her donkeys, to distract her from me. She should get along fine with mules."

Sobering, he said, "I need a student, now that I am a *jarghal*, a master, and I need a *taghulajti*, a teacher, too. I teach you, and you teach me. How else do we learn?"

He shoved the two stones over to her, with his own pouch. "Here, you hold them both. Look at them and remember why we do this."

Bowing deeply from his seated position, he took a deep breath. "My name, Zandaril—that isn't really a name, I told you. It's a title. Means one who travels, a journeyman. It's what we call ourselves after we've left our masters, while we search."

He shrugged. "Kigaliwen don't know any better, and they don't approve of Zannib names anyway."

He bowed again to her. "You have recognized my *nayith*, *jarghalti*, my masterwork, and so I take my name back, and you are the first to hear it again. I am Najud, son of Ilsahr of clan Zamjilah, of the Shubzah tribe, and my mother Kazrsulj is the daughter of Khashjibrim of the same clan."

Penrys mouthed his name. "Lucky," it meant, and "Fortunate." Then she tasted *wirqiqa*-Zannib for the intimate forms.

"Naj-sha, would it be?" she murmured, and watched with interest as he blushed.

CHAPTER 60

As they pulled out of the expedition camp the next morning, Penrys followed carefully behind Najud, trying to anticipate his movements. When he stopped at the outer perimeter, she reined back her confiscated Rasesni mare, and checked to make sure the three pack horses abandoned to her by Veneshjug halted with her and waited patiently.

Najud had far better control over his horses. He was riding his favorite black mare, Badaz, and leading a string of all his horses as well as the Rasesni mare he'd stolen. His horses' packs were light, like hers—they'd be getting their supplies in Neshilik.

He held the end of his lead rope in his hand, for better control. Hers was looped over her saddle horn, since her right hand was occupied holding her reins. A neat leather glove covered her left hand, stuffed in the fingers and upper palm with sheep's wool to both pad the injury, and mask the damage.

Najud had switched saddles for her yesterday, giving the squadron's trooper saddle back and getting her a working saddle from the ones supplied for the herdsmen. "The horn will be good for you. Lets you swap hands from one thing to another more easily," he'd said, and today she could see what he meant. She wasn't sure if she could manage both reins and pack string one-handed, but she'd wanted to try, not thinking it fair for Najud to lead all the pack animals while she did nothing.

She couldn't have loaded them, however, not even if she'd still had both hands. Najud had been quick and efficient. He'd made sure yesterday that all the pack frames were padded correctly for each animal's configuration. The farrier had seen to all the shoeing needs and even taken a look at the teeth of the two new mares.

Though the *Maiju* had been unwilling to sell him supplies for more than a day or two, citing the cavalry's need, he hadn't been stingy about equipment parts and repairs. They had more than enough sheepskins and rope to supplement what Najud had brought with him, and the speed with which he assembled the packs and loaded the frames was an education, as were the hitches he used, a complex system that was clearly an expertise in its own right.

Penrys had watched him and tried to take mental notes, but she knew she could only slow him down until her hand healed well enough to allow her to be of some use.

He'd glanced at her once and told her, "Never mind, Pen-sha, we learn how to do this as children. I'll teach you as we go along."

Now, stopped outside the camp, she wondered why Najud had halted.

He dismounted and tied the reins of his horse as well as the lead rope to a tree and walked back her way, past his string.

To her surprise, Tun Jeju walked with him.

What does he want? I thought we were done with farewells.

Najud's reply made her smile crookedly.

What, you weren't satisfied with Chang's dismissal?

Chang, alone in his command tent, had thanked "Zandaril" formally for *sarq*-Zannib's assistance and presented him with a small scroll. Then he'd nodded to Penrys as though unsure whether or not to credit Ellech for her own help, and that was the end.

Well, we're lowly wizards—what did you expect, after all, gratitude?

At least they'd been able to genuinely thank Hing Ganau, themselves, with a gift Najud pressed upon him. *Coins, surely, considering the clink.*

The little girl Tak Tuzap had rescued was talking now and said her name was Tan Omi, though everyone called her Gailen anyway. Najud had left another present for her welfare. "On Tak's behalf," he'd said. "Easy for me, and she'll think well of him when she's older. He'll be pleased, I think."

Najud has interesting notions of obligation. Why haven't I heard him mention Dzantig yet?

"Notju-chi was kind enough to come with me so you wouldn't have to dismount," Najud said, as he came into earshot. "Maybe now he'll tell us what he wants, out here where no one can see him."

Tun gave him a sidelong glance, but proceeded down the trail unperturbed to her horse's shoulder, and bowed to them both.

"Let me begin by thanking you for the *liju*, our Serene Emperor. I am sorry for your losses"—he looked pointedly at Penrys's gloved hand—"and hope you will accept this small compensation for your efforts on behalf of an empire not your own."

He put his hand into his tunic and pulled out two small red silk pouches.

Najud's face froze.

Those are imperial grants. That will be gold inside.

Penrys took her cue from him and bowed from her saddle.

Tun gave one pouch to Najud and reached up to give her the other one. It was small but not at all light in her hand, and she tucked it away carefully in an inner tunic pocket.

After waiting politely for them to finish disposing of his gifts, Tun said, "It may be that someday Kigali might wish to call upon you again. Perhaps word could be sent to find you, through Ussha and the Ghuzl mar-Tawirqaj?"

Penrys reminded Najud. **Better tell him your name.**

"Notju-chi, please use the name Najud, son of Ilsahr of clan Zamjilah, of the Shubzah tribe. I am no longer Zandaril."

Tun nodded. "I had wondered. The archives speak of other 'Zandarils' in the past."

He glanced at her with a raised eyebrow.

"Still 'Penrys,'" she said. "Different customs. That's just my name."

This time, anyway.

Najud bowed to Tun. "*Chan do ne Te ba Gen ka Liju.*"

Penrys bit her lip. *He must have memorized the traditional phrase—A thousand years to the King of Earth and Sea.*

Tun nodded, and walked down past Penrys's string, back toward the camp.

CHAPTER 61

They paused at the top end of the market square in Kunchik, just before entering the square. Penrys shook her head.

It's only been four days since I was last here. Seems impossible.

The market looked unchanged, well populated even as evening approached. If any of the people had fled in anticipation of the Voice, there was no evidence of it now.

Come on up past me. I'm going to attach my string to yours.

She gave him a startled look. **I can't handle that many yet.**

It's not for long.

She led her string alongside his, and then beyond him. He leaned over as the last horse passed and slipped his own lead rope over the end of the pack frame in a double loop, freeing up his riding horse.

"Just hold them here until I get back," he said, as he trotted by her and turned west, off the square to the right.

She watched him disappear left again around the corner, onto a road paralleling the square, then turned her attention to the excellent view of the temple school on her left, illuminated by the setting sun. From the slope of the land and the height of her horse, she could make out the benches against the wall behind the colonnade.

They would be preparing for dinner soon, those who were left. How many had died? She hadn't been able to keep track of who was alive that morning, but their losses were heavy. What had they done with the one-time captives? Were they there, too?

She could have scanned the temple school, she supposed, but she didn't want to expose that much of herself to them.

Najud reappeared around the corner, walking his horse slowly to accommodate the two boys with him.

He left one of them with her. "Give him your rope. He'll take them into the inn."

She lifted the loop off her saddle horn and leaned down to give the boy the lead. "You all right with this?"

"It's our job, *minochi*."

He waited prosaically for Najud to reach the start of his own string and point out the loop to the other boy, who promptly untied it and took charge of the second string.

Then both the boys walked off into the gathering dusk the way they'd come, leading the tired horses behind them.

Najud halted alongside her. "Thought we could stay a night in a merchant inn. Lots of stabling, easy access to market."

"Didn't you want to see Tak Tuzap? Don't they have markets south of the river?"

"Wanted to see Dzantig, too," he said. "Plenty of time for Tak after that."

He looked at her. "I think you'll like this place. Meals, beds, and a real bath, with hot water."

Her stomach growled at the suggestion, and he smiled.

"Good. Thought you'd agree."

An actual dinner, with civilian sophistication. Penrys didn't think she'd eaten so well in a very long time. Somehow it tasted all the better after a long soak in hot water, with Najud in another tub nearby.

She'd held her left hand out of the water but removed the neck bandage, willing to replace it afterward in their room for the pleasure of truly clean hair. When they were done, it was just a simple walk from their room down a flag-stoned passage to the inn's common room and a heavy meal.

Najud thumped his empty mug on the table and raised it for service, while Penrys shook her damp hair and yawned before she could raise her fist to cover her mouth.

"Wake up, now, we're going to have company," Najud told her.

At her puzzled look, he cocked his head at the entrance. She realized he'd been watching it all through the meal.

She peered at the man walking in, and blinked. It was Dzantig, and he carried a canvas-wrapped package under his arm.

"I called him," Najud said, tapping his forehead meaningfully. "Wasn't sure he'd come."

He kicked out an empty chair at the table as Dzantig drew up. "Sit. You've eaten?"

Dzantig looked ill at ease. "I couldn't get away earlier, so I had to wait until after dinner."

Penrys had straightened up in her chair. "You look well, considering."

"And you, *brudigna*." He settled into his chair and a man walking by handed out two mugs, one for him and another for Najud.

"I think I owe you my life," Penrys said, soberly. "Twice. Once in the tunnels, and once bleeding to death at the barricade."

She felt the burden of the debt as an ache in her chest. "I don't know how to repay you."

Najud took a lengthy pull from his mug, and smiled. "Good thing that I do."

Both the others turned to stare at him.

"Here's what we should do," he said. "I want to set up a trade route, over the High Pass, on the border in Song Em. Bring a caravan through regularly, up all the way to Gonglik, right here." He hooked a thumb out in the direction of the market square.

"Trade with the Zannib?" Dzantig said, stunned.

"Why not? Must have plenty to sell."

Dzantig waved that aside. "That's not it. It's never been done."

"So?"

Penrys leaned back and watched Najud in professional action as a trader for the first time.

"What if this truce ends up with us all returning to Nagthari?" Dzantig protested.

"Are there no roads to Linit Kungzet and beyond? Shortcuts, too, maybe."

Dzantig paused with his mouth open, and Najud laughed at him.

"I don't have any authority to do this."

"Who does?"

That stopped Dzantig altogether. "I don't know."

"Would they want this, the Rasesni?"

Dzantig nodded, hesitantly. "Some of them. But what about Kigali? They'll never let it happen, trade with another country that they don't control."

Najud shrugged. "We can adjust as we go along. It's a long border."

Penrys interrupted. "Do *you* want this, Dzantig? Would you like to be part of it?"

He drained the rest of his mug in silence while he thought about it, and they respected his delay.

"Yes," he said, slowly. "Yes, I would. The wizards who want to share knowledge survived better than the jealous ones like Dhumbhod—Vejug the traitor is an embarrassment to them now and they don't want to be linked to him. The new Mage Council would probably agree. That Rinshradke is part of it now, Zandaril, and she thinks well of you. And what the wizards want, they mostly get."

"Priests aren't dumb about what might happen otherwise, eh?" Najud said.

"It's not just that," Dzantig said.

He looked at Penrys. "I told them what happened that night, everything except the names of where you went, and I told them that Dzangab had required it of me. This has created some… divine authority for change. We are at a decision point, some think, about what we should do, and the balance may have shifted.

"What you propose, Zandaril, that might tilt the balance even further."

He swallowed. "Yes, I want to be part of this."

Najud nodded genially. "Good. Here's what you do. I want you to be my factor. Tak Tuzap can probably help you, introduce you to the merchants here in Gonglik. You carry my proposal to the council and tell them—without you, I say there's no deal."

Dzantig's eyes widened and Penrys hid a smile.

"Tell them it will take a year to get the first caravan organized, maybe two. You get paid like any factor, a percentage of the value of the goods. Tak Tuzap can explain how it works."

"But, but…" Dzantig sputtered.

Najud pressed past his objections. "I will check *sarq*-Zannib treaties with Rasesdad and Kigali, and if something needs to change, we will change it. Yes?"

Dzantig finally got his objection out. "You're not in charge in *sarq*-Zannib, you can't just make this happen."

"Well, if we are all at war, you're probably right. If not, what is there to lose by trying?"

Penrys nodded and ticked off a mark on Najud's side. If she'd been keeping score, that would have been a winner.

"Besides,"Najud said, "I *do* know people on the *Ghuzl mar-Tawirqaj* in Ussha, and both of us are currently in favor with the *Liju*, the Emperor, at the moment."

"Long may it last," muttered Penrys, and both heads turned to her.

She thought back to books she had read in the Collegium. "In *sarq*-Zannib, new caravans based in the west would bring in entirely different goods from the established ones in the east, while the outgoing market is barely served. Not so much for the big traders to object to, not much overlap, isn't that right?"

Najud nodded. "It's not impossible."

"And I bet no one knows if Kigali would object, or not," Penrys offered. "Try it and find out."

CHAPTER 62

Najud opened his eyes cautiously in the morning, waiting to find out if he had a headache or not. He moved his head and confirmed the anticipated punishment. *Good thing I don't have to celebrate new deals every night.*

Penrys's side of the bed was empty and no longer warm, and he was alone in the room. He flung the sheets and soft blanket aside and sat up, scratching. When he ran his eyes over his clothing, scattered in the direction of the chair, he missed the flash of color he expected.

Where's my robe?

A mental chuckle returned to him. **I've got it. Get back into bed, I'm bringing a visitor.**

Incoherent outrage seized him, and then he heard footsteps coming and took her advice, pulling the covers back over him.

Penrys knocked once on the door in warning before unlocking it and ushering in her guest. Najud pegged him as a merchant—a tailor, judging by the tools belted around him.

"Najud, this is Chak Zobu. He owns the tailor shop in the square. I wanted to find fabric for another robe—you can't go all the way back to *sarq*-Zannib on a single robe, it's ridiculous. But this is better—he can make you one, he says. He was nice enough to come with me to take measurements so you wouldn't have to spend time there yourself."

Chak looked from the obviously naked man under the bedclothes to the robe in Penrys's hand and clearly decided discretion was his best option.

"*Binochi*, it would be my pleasure to provide fresh clothing for you. The lady tells me you will need everything by tomorrow morning, early. This is so?"

Najud tried to rescue whatever dignity he could from the situation and nodded. "We leave tomorrow, after breakfast, Tailor-chi. Have you made robes to that pattern before?"

He nodded at his one robe still in Penrys's grasp. Since his ceremonial robe was buried in the packs in the stable, he needed to get this one back.

The tailor carefully took it from her and shook it out to lay it smoothly across the bottom of the bed. Najud snaked his feet up to sit cross-legged and give him a flat surface.

Chak ran his hand lovingly over the front of the robe. "The material is very fine, sir. *Himmib*, the fine goat hair, if I'm any judge, yes?"

At Najud's nod, he continued. "Soft and warm, but not very strong, is it? I rarely see such fabric, but perhaps a soft but durable sheep's wool will do for travel? We have some fine dark colors, such as a man like yourself might favor."

Penrys's grin distracted him, but he managed to reply, "Dark colors, blue or brown, would do well for a plain robe. I do not expect you to mimic the ornamentation, Tailor-chi."

His gaze softened when it rested on the garment. His *nurti*, his second sister had embroidered the collar and edges a couple of years ago and given it to him as a *bawi-anit* gift, for his name day. It still fit him, and reminded him of her whenever he saw it. The rougher robe he'd been wearing had been ruined in his captivity.

He glanced up at Penrys, detecting a bit of uncertainty behind her insouciance. It was well-thought of her, to arrange this, he admitted, despite the methods she'd used.

Chak broke into his thoughts. "No, *binochi*, we can't do that in a day, and I suspect it was a hand you know who set this work for you."

Najud gave him a sharp look. "Plain and tough and warm will do well enough for travel. Can you match this one as a pattern?"

"Nothing easier, *binochi*."

He cleared his throat. "The lady suggested that the rest of your apparel might need augmentation. Perhaps you could suggest your needs?"

Penrys said, "I'll just step out for a moment and let you two discuss it. Two robes, mind," she told the tailor. "Your best material for the purpose."

She narrowed her eyes at Najud. "We have plenty of room in the packs. Don't stint on this."

He raised his hands in surrender and shooed her out of the room.

For the next several minutes, he discussed options with the tailor. Small clothes and socks were easily handled, and shirts and breeches to his current pattern as well. When the tailor asked about over-garments for bad travel weather, they settled on cloaks of the type the miller in Lupmikya had given them, long since seized by the Khrebesni, and two sorts of hats, a front-brimmed cap to wear under the hooded cloak for light precipitation, and a full brimmed one for serious rain or snow, to wear on top of the hood. Chak's suggestion for heavy knitted caps for outdoor sleeping was also accepted.

When all the measurements were completed, and Najud had gratefully dressed, Penrys's knock sounded again on the door. *She must have been monitoring to get the timing that precise.*

When he opened to door for her, she looked up at him with a question on her face. **Everything all right?**

"Good idea, Pen-sha," he assured her. "Now it's your turn." He laughed at the dismay on her face.

"What, you thought you'd get away?"

He hauled her into the room by her good arm and presented her to Chak as he closed the door behind her and blocked it. "Good Tailor-chi, you see what she has. Rough-made stuff, fits badly, not comfortable. What can you do, by tomorrow morning?"

Chak looked her over briefly. "Do you want clothing of a similar fashion, *minochi*, but more suitable for rough travel? That would be quite easy to do quickly. Now what are your preferences? Colors?"

As he spoke, he picked up his paper and charcoal to take notes. He ran his measuring tape over her, from bottom to top, but as he started on her shoulders, the chain resting on the top of the bandage around her neck caught his eye, and he dropped his tape with a gasp and backed up, bowing deeply as he went.

"Your pardon, *minochi*—this *posom* should have realized—they said she was traveling with a Zan."

He backed up another step. "They say you killed the demon that was coming."

His face stared at the floor in his deepest bow, and he held that position.

Najud watched the dismay spread on Penrys's face, followed by a deep flush.

Good. Someone here appreciates what she did. She should hear it.

"Never mind all that," she stuttered out, and coughed as if something were choking her.

"Um, look, I would be grateful if you would advise me."

Chak straightened up cautiously.

She removed the glove from her left hand and showed him what was left, wrapped in its bandage. "As you see. Maybe there are fasteners for clothing that would work better for me, encumbered as I am. Toggles instead of buttons?"

He nodded thoughtfully.

"And gloves… see how this one is padded? I need two thin pairs, and two thicker ones, don't you think? And sheep's wool to fill them, yes? More wrapping for the neck, too—it's a long trip."

Chak began to lose his awe as she engaged him in a technical discussion, and Najud approved her tact with him.

"The same kind of outer garments that he asked for should work for me, and the socks, and all. But, um, I will need some sort of breast support I can manage one-handed. Do you think there's something you could recommend?

Ah, now, I'm always happy to help you with that, on or off.

She didn't turn her head to look at him, but Najud watched with interest as a blush warmed her cheeks.

They worked out the rest of the details, and Penrys added two blankets to the list.

When she pressed a gold coin on the tailor, removed ahead of time from the pouch Tun Jeju had presented to her, he backed away and raised his hand to stop her.

"No need, *minochi*. No need."

"Nonsense. You should have money up front, and perhaps extra for the rush and personal attention."

"*Minochi*, this is my honor, that my shop should provide such services for you."

"You will please me by taking the money, and you can say whatever you wish to your other customers about it. I am sure we will be very happy with the results."

Ultimately, Chak pocketed the coin and bowed his way out, clutching his notes.

She closed the door behind her and dropped into the chair with a sigh of relief. "I didn't expect all that. Not used to someone looking at the chain as anything other than an odd necklace."

Najud asked, "If you wanted better clothing before, why didn't you get it, instead of putting up with the army clothes?"

Penrys stared at him. "How? I didn't have any money, and there was no place to get better clothes anyway."

Idiot. Of course she didn't have any money, arriving from Ellech as she did. She took what she was given, like any soldier. I didn't think about that.

His eye fell on Dzantig's package, the one he had brought with him last night.

"I have something for you, too.

He pointed at the package. "Go ahead, take a look."

She bounced up and started to unfold the canvas wrapped around it. She used her bad hand to help where she could, to Najud's approval.

Penrys picked up each book as it appeared and read the title. "Look, two books about wizardry, for Dzangab, his god, and a grammar, and a Rasesni/Kigali dictionary."

She beamed at Najud. "Why did he bring these?"

"I told him it was for me, but I wondered how much Rasesni you might keep after we left."

She nodded as he spoke. "I'd retain a lot of it, since we used it so much, but it would fade. This is perfect, it'll help us preserve it."

"Dzantig warned me the grammar was for the godly language, closer to what the books are written in, not the popular one we've been using."

"It's always that way," she said. "You should see the shelves and shelves of formal languages that aren't used anymore, at the Collegium."

CHAPTER 63

"So this is Tak Tuzap's house?" Najud said.

Dzantig, who had kept up a running commentary ever since they crossed the bridge and entered the densely populated main city with its busy morning traffic, wound down to a stop and gaped.

Penrys replied, "Can't say for sure, but this is where *he* is, anyway." She had followed her link to him, allowing Dzantig to steer her to wider roads whenever the direct route was blocked.

They stood together at the entrance to a *samke* compound that occupied a full block, just around the corner from another one of Gonglik's many broad markets. The gates were open, and a steady stream of people passed in and out, and crossed the inner paths to the various buildings. Only a small portion of it was a family dwelling, the rest appearing to be warehouses, workshops, and even a substantial stable and freight yard.

"No point waiting," Najud said, and he walked up the stone steps to the family door and tapped the *wanbum* with his knuckle. The little gong made a mellow but penetrating sound.

He spoke to the servant who answered, and then beckoned them all to join him.

The small hall was graciously proportioned, its floor tiled with stylized hunting scenes, but Penrys noted empty spaces on the walls giving evidence of missing decorations, and the surfaces of the tables and benches that lined it were curiously bare.

Stolen, or removed for safety?

The servant led them to a back room on the ground floor, tapped on the door and cracked it enough to consult, then opened it wide and ushered them in, Najud in the lead.

Tak Tuzap rose from his chair at a long table, his brush hastily laid down and still rocking on its rest. "I heard about it, everyone knows."

His excited smile took in Najud and Penrys, then lingered on Dzantig. "I found her where you said she was. I'm glad to see you again. Maybe you'll tell me your name, this time."

Dzantig bowed and introduced himself. "No one else knows of your involvement that night, nor Kor Pochang's."

Najud said, "I should tell you both—"Zandaril" was just a name I took for this journey, while I learned my craft. I have presented my masterwork to a master, and now I am free to take back my name. Please call me Najud."

Tak eyed Penrys. "Wizard stuff, I bet."

Penrys noted a tidily-made cot in one corner, and Tak, following her glance, said, "This is my room, for now. The rest is occupied."

At her frown, he continued, "No, it's all right. They've recognized my title to my uncle's business—it's mine now—and they let me run it. We even dine together, very civilized. These aren't the men who killed him that night."

He gave her a brief grin. "I have a lot to learn, but we'll manage."

"I've brought you new business, Trader-chi," Najud said. He explained his caravan plan to Tak Tuzap, and the role he saw for Dzantig in it. "I look to you to help Dzantig learn the trade, as your uncle taught you."

Tak glanced at Dzantig and nodded. "That's easy enough, as long as he can spend some time with me, learning. Nothing too hard about adding more traffic to the perimeter runs in the southern cove, in Song Em, that all the annual traders take. You should just make your base on our side of the pass at Jaunor with an outpost here in Gonglik, or maybe in Kunchik, in case you want to expand west to Linit Kungzet or east out the Gates. Your letters can be carried along the trade network, and accumulate in your posts until someone can carry them to the next stage. And the uncertainty about how much to commit to get started—that's a common problem. We can help with that. We finance many of the small circuit traders, you know."

He ran his hand over his face, making him look instantly a decade older, and Penrys hid a smile.

Must be his uncle's gesture. I wonder if his uncle had a beard?

She'd seen a few beards in Neshilik. They were thicker than the ones in the squadron. Was it Rasesni blood?

"No," he said, "The real problem is politics. I don't know how to help with that. I know my uncle's friends, but they're not my own friends, not yet."

"I have an idea about that," Najud suggested. "What about Kor Pochang? How can we get a message to him requesting a meeting?"

Tak sat down again, laid his pen aside, and took up a brush and a fresh sheet of papyrus to compose a formal message.

He's so young, gangling in his clothing that's he's not yet grown into, but he looks prosperous and here, in his element, he knows what he's doing. What will he be like in a few years?

Tak blotted the ink, picked up a small hand bell and rang it, then rolled the papyrus and dripped turquoise wax on the join, sealing it with a ring that he removed from his thumb.

He caught her eye on him and held it up. "My father's ring. He was my uncle's partner. Too big for me now, but I'll grow."

"I don't thing anything will be too big for you long, Takka," Penrys said, approvingly. "Najud, tell him about Len-len."

Following a knock on the door, a head popped in. "Get me a messenger boy for the central district," Tak told him, and the door closed again.

Najud told Tak Tuzap how the little girl was doing and what he'd done for her. "I gave her guardian information about how to find you. Perhaps you'll meet again sometime. You saved her life, you know—that makes you responsible, though maybe you are too young to just adopt her."

Meanwhile, Penrys pulled Dzantig aside to thank him for the books.

"It was my honor, *brudigna*. I could not just give you books from our library—I hope you understand—but the grammar and dictionary, that's no more than any student would have, and my own god, Dzangab, he would want his word spread, even to unbelievers."

He coughed apologetically at the term, but she waved it away.

With another knock, the door opened and a boy of about Tak's age popped in and bowed to his master. "You needed a messenger, Tak-chi?"

"Take this to Kor Pochang—you know where his compound is? Bring it to the kitchen door and wait for an answer."

The boy tucked the scroll into his tunic, bowed again, and walked out of the room. As soon as the door had been carefully closed, Penrys could hear his running steps receding down the corridor.

Najud took this moment to walk up to the table before Tak could rise again, and he summoned Penrys to join him.

"Tak Tuzap," he said, "we have *yarab mar-uthkahi*, honor gifts, for you, to thank you for your rescue of Penrys and the weapons of your house."

He reached into his robe and brought out the two empty sheathes, with the blood dried upon them. He gave them to Penrys.

But I don't know what words they expect.

She cleared her throat. Awkwardly, she laid the knife sheath onto her deceptively full gloved palm.

"This knife was my only shield in the final combat. It served me well until I was overwhelmed at last."

She took it back into her right hand while she removed the glove to show him the wrapped remnant, then put the glove back on.

He blanched but otherwise heard her in dignified silence.

"After the fight, this sheath carried away all that survived of the Voice." She lay the knife sheath on his table, tucked the ax sheath under her left arm, and reached into her inner tunic pocket to pull out and show him the three-link fragment of chain.

She put it away again and transferred the ax sheath back into her right hand.

"This ax, an heirloom of your house, killed the Voice, saving my life and many others. All honor be to it."

She lay that sheath next to the other one.

"I apologize that neither survived what followed the Voice's death."

Najud reached again into his robe. First he drew out the new knife in its sheath and laid it before Tak Tuzap.

"May this simple tool have as glorious a career as the one it replaces. May it always remind you of your daring journey alone through Seguchi Norwan, the saving of a little child, the warning you carried, and the help you provided us."

It was a fine example of military smith work, Penrys saw, stamped on sheath and blade with the wolf that was Chang's squadron's emblem.

Next, Najud pulled out a small sheathed ax. He held it in balanced on both hands and bowed with it, as if it were a sword in miniature.

"I cannot replace an heirloom of your house. I can only hope this may find your approval as a new heirloom, to remind you of the old."

He unsheathed it and displayed both sides. One was marked with whirlwinds similar to the ones she had described to him. The other bore a single eight-spoked circle engraving in the upper center of the blade.

"The *zamjilah*, the eye of heaven–it's the mark of my clan, to remind you of our debt to you."

Dzantig had stood off to the side respectfully during this ceremony, and Tak was speechless. He fought for control of his features, while Najud and Penrys backed away to give him some privacy to recover.

Finally, he rose and bowed deeply to them both, one at a time. "My house is honored by these gifts, and they will occupy a place where they are always under our sight."

A tap on the door brought welcome relief to the charged atmosphere in the room, and Tak waved in the messenger who bowed and handed him a scroll, then bowed again and left.

Tak cracked the yellow wax seal and read it quickly, surprise on his face.

He looked up at them. "He wants to see us now, we're to use the main entrance. 'Walk right up to the door,' he says."

CHAPTER 64

The Councillor's *samke* was a startling sight to Penrys. The forecourt gravel was raked and clean, and the iron of the gates showed no trace of rust. The main domicile had a charm and balance that was enhanced rather than diminished by the additions that had accreted over time, and the sound of running water from some unknown source overlaid the whole with a sense of peace, despite the noise of activity outside the walls.

Tak Tuzap's clothing identified him as a prosperous, if over-young, citizen of Gonglik, but she felt decidedly dowdy in her own ill-fitting clothes, and Dzantig looked the modest student-priest that he was. At least Najud looked suitably exotic, if travel worn.

Too bad we couldn't do this tomorrow, in our new clothing.

Najud caught her eye and smiled. "You should see Yenit Ping," he murmured. "This place is a backwater, in their eyes."

Tak headed their little party as they walked up the steps, and the door opened before he could tap on the *wanbum*. A grave and dignified elder servant bowed them in and led them through a wide hall into a large and comfortable room, clearly a place for receiving guests. They found two men waiting for them there, one of them in Rasesni military uniform.

One of the officers quartered in Kor Pochang's residence?

Kor was a thin man with an intelligent face. His confidence and self-composure reminded her of Tun Jeju.

Not much escapes him, I bet.

The officer bore a long scar down his face. It originated in the scalp above, and the hair refused to grow along that line.

Honorable wounds. A traditional officer, or a politician?

Kor bowed. "Thank you for coming so promptly. Allow me to introduce one of the officers who does me the honor of residing here. This is Menchos, currently seconded to Commander Tlobsung."

Menchos said, in impeccable Kigali-*yat*, "We have a superfluity of senior officers scattered about Gonglik and the rest of Neshilik.

Alas, I am one of them. We have imposed upon the hospitality of Councillor-chi, here."

I never saw a less superfluous person. I wonder what his role really is.

Tak Tuzap performed the introductions for his guests, and the entry of servants bearing trays with steaming cups of *bunnas* and small pastries reduced the formality of the atmosphere, as Kor directed them to backless, silk-upholstered single benches matched with small side tables, clustered in the center of the room.

Penrys made sure her lips were clear of crumbs, and then addressed the affable Menchos. "Can you tell me, *zendo*, why the regular Rasesni army did not crush The Voice? Surely overwhelming force…"

His eyes strayed briefly to her chain before returning to her face. "His warriors rarely separated from him. When they did, it was always in superior numbers to the opposing force, as you recently saw."

He set his own cup down on the table next to him. "When he was present, our wizards died or were captured, and he slew his way through our men, beginning with the unit commanders directing the actual fighting. Once the fighters were leaderless in the field, he worked his way up and down the ranks, killing more senior officers when he could, or returning to destroy what was left in arms if necessary. He killed thousands. Thousands."

The room was silent, held by the cold intensity of his voice.

"We couldn't get within ten miles of him, not our army, not our spies, and not—as you know—our wizards. To preserve our army, we had to send it elsewhere, to protect our other borders and to put as much of a protective cordon around him as we could afford, knowing we would lose it if he turned in its direction."

And he's talking to me calmly, in this room, though he obviously assumes I could do the same thing to him and this entire city, if I tried. A brave man, if he thinks this. And it's true, isn't it. If not me, then someone else—if there are two of us with chains, there must be more.

He continued as if he had never been concerned. "Both Kor Pochang and I wanted to greet the heroes of the battle at the fork. The wizards have told us how you did to the Khrebesni what Surdo did to us."

Her heart thumped at that comparison and she felt her skin chill.

No, I'm not like that. I gave the power back.

But I could be.

Before she could say anything, Menchos cocked his head. "I don't know exactly what the wizards are dithering about now—not my concern. But I did want to tell you—we in the army remember our friends. As long as they stay our friends."

Penrys felt that narrow edge of balance, that the relationships could change in an instant. Without changing expression, she scanned the room and felt the presence of men positioned unmoving all around the outside. Her imagination conjured up images of hidden holes in the wall, and arrows.

I should have known this could be a trap.

Time for her to make what case she could.

"I admit the comparison, *zendo,* but I did not know your enemy, nor where he came from, nor what he wanted. I didn't even recognize his native language."

Dzantig broke in. "Our own mage council has reason to believe her, *zendo.*"

"Perhaps," Menchos said, as he studied her. "What do *you* want?"

"I plan to travel to *sarq*-Zannib with my friend and colleague. What I want…"

She sighed. "In the long run, I want to learn more about the origins of this." She flicked her chain with a finger. "I spent the last three years *not* destroying Ellech, and I think *sarq*-Zannib, and Kigali, and Rasesdad are reasonably safe from me, too."

She half-laughed. "Hard to prove it, though, isn't it?"

Cocking her head, she challenged him, directly, "Perhaps you should kill me now and be sure."

Her deliberate provocation froze everyone in the room.

Menchos made a tiny shake of his head, and the moment passed.

Kor broke the tension. "Najud, I understand you have plans in *sarq*-Zannib that involve us, is that so?"

Najud laid out his scheme to start a Zannib caravan over the High Pass, with Dzantig as his factor working with Tak Tuzap.

Menchos asked, "You would take it on to Dzongphan, if the Rasesni leave Neshilik?"

"I think it would be a good plan. New market, new goods, excellent trade. What do you think? Will it be allowed? Licensed?"

"It is an interesting thought," Menchos said. "I will consider it."

He slapped his thighs and stood up. "Meanwhile, good host, may I trouble you for writing materials? I will give them both a safe conduct for Neshilik, if they will wait a few minutes."

Tak muttered, "I don't think anyone will stop *her*," and Menchos pretended he didn't hear it.

Kor clapped his hands and summoned a portable desk for Menchos, who took a deliberate position in their midst to do his work.

Doesn't want someone outside the room to shoot anyway? I saw that head shake.

While he pressed his seal to the bottom of the second document, he glanced up at Penrys.

"Where can we find you, *brudigna*?"

"I'll be with Najud for some time," she said. *For how long?*

"Tak Tuzap or Dzangabtig will be able to reach me," Najud added.

He pocketed his safe conduct and turned to Kor, with a smile on his face as though no threats had been implied or acknowledged.

"Now, can anyone tell me where I can buy some donkeys, suitable to breed mules from our sturdy horses?"

Tak lighted up. "That's a specialty of ours, as I told you. I will show you our very best."

CHAPTER 65

Penrys listened to Tun Jeju summarize the crux of the problem in front of the senior officers. The darkness outside the tent's entrance reinforced the sense that they were focused together on a crucial decision.

"It comes down to whether you're willing to cede Neshilik to Rasesdad in exchange for their help against this 'Voice' and his horde."

Chang waved a hand dismissively. "If this Tlobsung had wanted that, he would not have tried to weaken us or to set us up for ambush from their enemy. He would have approached us for help."

"Not the Kigaliwen," Zandaril said, with a sardonic tone. "The Kigaliwen who do not trust wizards won't trust Tlobsung's wizards. The Kigaliwen who've never seen a *qahulaj*, a wizard-tyrant, won't believe us when we tell them what's coming. The Kigaliwen who conquered Neshilik permanently will not give it up again for a buffer state. The Kigaliwen will never ally with us, their traditional enemy."

Chang glared at him, but he went on. "The Kigaliwen who are bringing an army of unknown size for arrival at an unknown time are better diverted north of our seized territory, and maybe our two enemies can weaken each other, or at least give us time to settle in and improve our defenses, for when the survivor comes after us. Maybe they'll give us time to flee into *sarq*-Zannib if we can't stand against them."

"And if they ally with the horde, instead?" Chang said.

Penrys shook her head. "Never voluntarily. No one would. The only willing members are there for plunder."

She leaned forward for emphasis. "I don't know what this 'Voice' wants, but he's bringing tools with him, human weapons, not builders and settlers. And he's collecting and using wizards, which ought to scare you. It scares me." The stableyard of the inn was crowded the next morning. Chak Zobu had come early, to deliver their purchases and to make sure that everything was to their satisfaction. Penrys had been delighted to change to new, well-cut clothing in the dark greens that she loved, and she approved Najud's robes.

Now everything was packed away. The supplies for the journey itself were divided among three of the horses—a luxury, Najud had called it, but he thought there was no reason they couldn't be comfortable and prepared for bad weather and the climb over the pass.

The rest of the horses in their two strings carried trade goods—the silks and linen fabrics that were always popular among the Zannib, buttons and ribbons, fine metal tools, a variety of sturdily packed ceramics, spices, seed for new varieties of crops, especially the oats that did so well in *sarq*-Zannib's colder fields, and many other smaller items. Penrys had monitored Najud's bartering sessions from the inside, fascinated by the complex combination of knowledge, pricing, and negotiation that made up a trader's life.

So much for me to learn, all the skills of packing and travel. Is he wizard or trader?

The donkeys were waiting for them in Tak Tuzap's care, along with the goods Najud had ordered from the markets in the main city yesterday afternoon. They would stop there, assemble packs for the donkeys, and then leave.

Penrys had been surprised at the size of the donkey jacks—they were almost as large as the small horses Najud had brought with him. Tak had been unwilling to sell him jennies, too, but Najud was insistent on building his own donkey herds, not to be dependent on someone else for jacks to cover his mares and produce mules.

"I plan to use mules for this caravan, as soon as they're ready," he'd told Tak, "Mules that are even tougher for the blood of our winter-hardy mares. I'll be buying more donkeys to strengthen the blood of the herd, but these will be a start. No jennies, no deal. I can buy jacks somewhere else."

Tak had looked willing to prolong the argument, but he laughed and gave in. "Only for you," he'd said, "and only as long as you promise to come to me first for new stock."

After they left, Penrys had asked, "What about those two mares you seized from the wizards? Will you be breeding them, too?"

Najud had grinned at her. "That's why I took mares instead of geldings. But we'll see how well they do, crossing the pass. They're larger than our horses, but may not be as suitable for our life. Rasesdad has cold mountains, but it's not horses that they use on them."

Still, the two mares, tethered to posts and waiting for them to mount in the inn's stable yards, looked good to her—sturdy, intelligent, and sound.

A small commotion at the inn yard's gates turned her head, and she saw that Chak was back, and several people came with him. Some were clearly his family—a wife, two adult sons, and a smaller boy and girl, all of them well-dressed, as befit a tailor's family. She couldn't place the others.

Behind them came Dzantig, carrying a small bag. He waved at Najud and her, and then placed himself near the gate and waited.

Chak approached, with his family. He bowed deeply, and they followed his lead. Penrys and Najud returned the greeting, and Penrys said, "As you see, Tailor-chi, we are well-clothed by your efforts. Is this your family?"

Chak bowed again and introduced them. "I wanted them to meet you, *minochi*, hard as they worked. And my wife has a small gift for you."

Penrys tried to keep the surprise off her face as the woman approached.

"My husband told me of his ill manners yesterday, and I wished to apologize on his behalf."

She pulled out a square of fabric in a beautifully-printed soft wool, flowers and plants densely filling a golden ground. Shaking it out and folding it in a diagonal, she reached up and settled it around Penrys's neck, covering both chain and bandage, and tucked the ends inside her shirt collar.

Penrys could hear the intake of breath from her family at the woman's daring, and her own face must have displayed a welter of emotions. From the woman, she felt nothing but sympathy, and a bit of trepidation at her own initiative.

She grasped the woman's hand, and bowed over it, speechless.

The woman gasped and pulled her hand back. She handed Penrys another square. "This is a lighter weight, for indoors. Please take it, *minochi*, with our thanks."

Chak escorted his wife back to her children, and then brought the eldest son forward.

"*Minochi*, my son has prepared a sign that he thinks we should display, but I wanted your approval."

He waved at the other men who had accompanied him. "These men are witnesses, should you agree."

Penrys glanced at Najud, who shrugged.

"Please, show me," she said.

The young man unrolled a scroll, neatly lettered, that declared, in both Kigali-*yat* and Rasesni, "The wizard Penrys, destroyer of demons, is a satisfied patron of this business."

She clenched her jaws to help her ensure a serious expression, and nodded consideringly. "It is no more than the truth, and I wish you well with it."

The son rolled up the scroll, and the whole group of them bowed one more time and left the yard.

Penrys stroked the soft scarf.

Such a thoughtful gift.

It kept her from laughing out loud in front of the grooms and others in the yard and embarrassing those good people.

No scarf will help them if I learn to tap the chain directly for more than restoring the power it steals. Maybe that's the fate of monsters like me, to experiment until we find we like it too much, and only the power matters.

She shook the thought off. It hadn't been many days since the fight, but it was beginning to worry her how long it was taking for the burns from the chain to heal.

Dzantig stepped forward from the shadow of the gate, with the bag in his hand and nodded to them both.

"Before you mount, I would like to give you a blessing, in the name of my god Dzangab. It is permitted?"

Penrys looked uncertainly at Najud, but he bowed deeply. "We would be greatly honored."

Dzantig opened his bag and pulled out a decorated board with short bracketed feet. He placed that on the bare dirt of the stableyard and put a small bell and a tiny brazier on it, blowing on the coals to revive them. He removed a bowl no larger than his palm from the bag and filled it from the water pump. A small bit of dried fish, and a few crumbs of incense for the brazier from which sweet smoke began to rise completed the assemblage.

He bowed to them, turned and faced their riding horses, and then the strings of pack animals, then turned back to his place behind his improvised altar and bowed to it.

He rang the bell and let the echoes die out naturally, and Penrys followed along with him as he intoned, in the old, classical godly language, "Oh, Dzangab, look over these travelers and their beasts and keep them safe from hunger and thirst and the perils of the trail. May their virtuous thoughts rise up to heaven like this smoke, and their enemies be confounded."

He rang the bell one last time and bowed again over the altar as the tones faded away.

Without speaking, he smiled at them, emptied the bowl, covered the brazier, and returned everything to his bag. Quietly, he walked away and out of the gate.

"I was forgetting most of the wizards in Rasesdad are priests," Penrys said.

He nodded. "Got your letter, for Tak Tuzap to send?"

She patted the left side of her tunic and felt the thick crinkle of the packet, addressed to Vylkar. Najud had convinced her it was time to tell the Collegium something of what had happened to her. "Not right they should worry," he'd said.

Her conscience had bothered her a bit on that score, though she didn't think it would have been of any great concern to them.

He followed with a glance down to his replacement boots. "Next time I go traveling I will take extra boots with me, good Zannib boots. Three pair, maybe, or four."

He mounted up, and Penrys listened to his low voice rumbling its mock complaints and hugged the sound of it to her.

I could listen to that all day.

What will sarq-Zannib be like? His family? The other wizards?

Penrys mounted from the wrong side, a concession to her absent hand. A groom gave her a leg up, and she settled into place.

"It'll be cold sleeping out, headed into winter and the pass." Najud waved his hand at the snug buildings surrounding them.

Penrys replied, "Warmer for two than for one," and watched for his smile.

"Straight over the bridge," he said, "Then we stop to pick up the donkeys and get them loaded."

He laughed. "Have I ever explained to you how much fun it's going to be with seven donkeys on a string, following the horses? I think a 'destroyer of demons' will be handy to have along."

Penrys rolled her eyes. She had other things to think about. Like unwrapping the bandage in the bath last night and seeing the new flesh, the little finger buds just starting to show.

How many times has this happened before?

GUIDE TO NAMES & PRONUNCIATIONS

PRINCIPAL CHARACTERS & PLACE NAMES & TERMS

PEOPLE - ELLECH

Aergon (AIR-gohn)
Senior wizard at the Collegium of Wizards.
Penrys (Ryssi) (PEHN-rewss)
The chained adept. Wizard trained at the Collegium of Wizards.
Vekkenfet (VECK-en-fet) - Leadfoot
The jocular nickname of a particularly slow horse.
Vylkar (VIEWL-kar)
Senior wizard at the Collegium of Wizards. Patron of Penrys.

PEOPLE - KIGALI

Gailen (GIE-lehn) - Sunshine
The temporary name given to a toddler found by Tak Tuzap.
Chak Zobu (CHAHK ZOH-boo)
A prosperous tailor with a family shop on the market square in Kunchik.
Chang Zenju (CHAHNG ZEHN-joo)
The *laigomju*, commander, of the cavalry squadron sent from Jonggep to Neshilik.
Haik Anju (HIKE AHN-joo)
An elderly watchman working for the Tak family in Kunchik.
Hing Ganau (HING GAH-now)
A sergeant acting as a teamster while his broken leg heals.
Jip Ngori (JIP n-GOH-ree)
A guard officer who reports to Chang Zenju.
Kep Jungo (KEHP JOON-goh)
A cavalry officer who reports to Chang Zenju.
Kor Pochang (KOR POH-chahng)

A trading partner of Tak Paknau and the head of the *zopgep*, the governing council of Gonglik.

Mu Wenjit (MOO WEHN-jit)

False name used by Rasesni Veneshjug when masquerading as a herdsman.

Nek Kazu (NECK KAH-zoo)

Associate of Zau Tselu, friend of Tak Paknau.

Rai Limfa (RYE LIHM-fah)

A civilian woman providing laundry and tailoring services in the cavalry squadron.

Sau Tsuo (SOW TSOO-oh)

An officer on the command staff under Chang Zenju.

Tak Paknau (TAHK PAHK-now)

The head of the *tengom*, the Trader's Guild in Gonglik, uncle of Tak Tuzap.

Tak Tuzap (TAHK TOO-zahp)

The young nephew and heir to Tak Paknau, an important trader in Gonglik.

Tan Omi (TAHN OH-mee)

The real name of Gailen, the toddler found by Tak Tuzap.

Tun Jeju (TOON JEH-joo)

The *notju*, intelligence master, and imperial representative for Chang Zenju's expedition.

Wan Nozu (WAHN NOH-zu)

Young nephew of Wan Tawa.

Wan Tawa (WAHN TAH-wah)

Headwoman of Lupmikya, aunt of Wan Nozu.

Zau Tselu (ZOW TSEH-loo)

Colleague of Tak Paknau.

PEOPLE - RASESNI

Dhumkedbhod (Dhumbhod) (DOOM-ked-bohd)

Priest and senior member of the Mage Council exiled from Dzongphan. His god is Dhumkedo.

Drannyal (Drana) (DRAHN-yall)

A mage (wizard) captured by Surdo.

Dzangabtig (Dzantig) (DZAN-gab-tig, DZAN-tig)

Priest and member of the Temple School in Kunchik. His god is Dzangab.

Ichorrog (Ichi) (EE-chor-rog)
Member of the temple School in Kunchik.
Igzhun (IG-zhoon)
A mage (wizard) captured by Surdo.
Isven (Svene) (ISS-ven)
Student at the Temple School in Kunchik.
Khrebesni (KHREB-ess-nee) - Thieves
Uncomplimentary term for the hill-tribes that have allied themselves with Surdo for plunder.
Menbyed (Byede) (MEN-byehd) - Nameless
Alias employed by Veneshjug when using the mirror device on the Kigali expedition.
Menchos (Mene) (MEN-chohs)
Senior commander or intelligence master exiled from Dzong-phan.
Nyagchos (Nyacho) (NYAG-chohs)
Priest and member of the Mage Council exiled from Dzong-phan. His god is Nyag.
Pyalshrad (PYAHL-shrahd) - Hand of the Mountains
The collective name for the hill-tribes that work with the priests of Dzongphan to enforce their control over the population of Rasesdad.
Pyalshrog (Pyaro) (PYAHL-shrog)
The leader of the local factions of *Pyalshrad*, the Hand of the Mountains hill-tribes, that have invested southern Neshilik.
Rinshradke (Rini, Risha) (RIN-shrahd-keh)
Senior mage mistress (*Klanna*) from Shirtan-pur.
Shrigirnang (SHREE-geer-nahng)
A mage (wizard) captured by Surdo.
Surdo (SOOR-doh) - The Voice
The chained wizard-tyrant who is wreaking havoc in Rasesdad. The name was given by the Rasesni—his actual name is unknown.
Tlobsung (Sungu) (t-LOHB-soong)
The military commander of the local force holding Neshilik.
The Voice
See "Surdo."
Veneshjug (Vejug) (VEH-nesh-joog, VEH-joog)
Priest and senior member of the Mage Council exiled from Dzongphan. His god is Venesh.

Vladzan (Vlada) (VLAHD-zahn)
Device Master (*Grakkedo*) at the Temple School in Kunchik and member of the Mage Council exiled from Dzongphan.

Zongchas (Chasa) (ZOHNG-chahs)
Mage Master (*Klando*) and overall master of the Temple School in Kunchik. Senior member of the Mage Council exiled from Dzongphan.

PEOPLE - ZANNIB

Butraz (boot-RAHZ)
Najud's older brother.

Ghuruma (goo-ROO-mah)
Najud's oldest sister.

Ilbirs (eel-BEERS)
One of Najud's cousins.

Ilsahr (eel-SAH-her)
Najud's father.

Kazrsulj (kahz-er-SOOLJ)
Najud's mother.

Khashjibrim (khash-jeeb-REEM)
Kazrsulj's father.

Kurighdunaq (koo-REEG-doo-NAHK) - World-bow (Rainbow)
A clan in northwestern central *sarq*-Zannib, part of the Undullah tribe.

Najud (nah-JOOD) - Lucky, Fortunate
A journeyman wizard of the Zamjilah clan, in the Shubzah tribe, traveling in Kigali as an apprentice, or Zandaril.

Nibarzan (nee-bar-ZAHN)
One of Najud's cousins.

Nirkazdhal (neer-kahz-THAHL) - Steppe Thunder
Najud's youngest brother. His name is a joke referring to his very noisy infancy.

Qizrahi (keez-RAH-hee)
Kazrsulj's sister, married into the Kurighdunaq clan, in the Undullah tribe.

Rubti (ROOB-tee)
Najud's second sister.

Shubzah (shoob-ZAH)
A tribe in the northeast central region of *sarq*-Zannib.

Surbushaz (soor-boo-SHAHZ)
One of Najud's cousins.
Umali (oo-MAH-lee)
A wizard of the Zamjilah clan to whom Najud served as apprentice.
Undullah (oon-dool-LAH)
A tribe in the northwest central region of *sarq*-Zannib.
Washi (WAH-shee)
Najud's youngest sister.
Yukjilah (yook-jee-LAH)
Butraz's wife.
Zamjilah (zahm-jee-LAH) - Eye of Heaven
Najud's clan, part of the Shubzah tribe.
Zandaril (ZAHN dah-REEL) - Traveling Zan
The conventional title of a wizard at the journeyman stage, between apprenticeship and mastery, adopted in place of a given name until a masterwork has been produced. Since most wizards only travel to foreign lands (if they ever do) while journeymen, this is the common name that appears in records from other nations about Zannib wizards.
Zaybirs (zye-BEERS)
One of Najud's cousins, son of his aunt Qizrahi, of the Kurighdunaq clan, in the Undullah tribe.

PLACES - ELLECH

Asuthgrata (AH-sooth-grah-tah) - High Region
Upland district of mixed grazing and woodlands, famed for its hunting.
Drosenrolkentham (DROH-sen-rohl-ken-thahm) - Wizard-learning-place
The Collegium of Wizards in Tavnastok.
Dunnarfeol (DOON-nar-fayol) - Winter's House
The highest mountains in the world, forming the north border of Ellech.
Ellech (ELL-ekh)
A northern nation tucked along the southern margin of the Dunnarfeol mountains, with precipitous timber- and grass-covered slopes running down to a deep-water port. Famed for

industry and research, with a well-armed merchant navy to seek out new markets.

Tavnastok (TAV-nah-stok) - City of Wealth
Inland city based on river commerce and industry, in the Asuthgrata region.

PLACES - KIGALI

Fawok Gung (FAH-wock goong)
The largest of the chain of lakes in the Kwatka Kote lowlands.

Fuchoi Jan (FOO-choy jahn) - Old Ferry Pass
The trade route through the Red Wall near Shaneng Ferry.

Galat (GAH-lat)
A disputed region between Kigali and Ndant, with significant mining resources.

Genna (GEHN-nah)
These marshes are the site of a possible canal opening up the Kwatka Kote lowlands to inland water traffic.

Gentu Hanjong (GEHN-too HAHN-jong)
The northeast bay for the harbor city Kwattu.

Gonglik (GOHNG-lick) - The Steps
The largest city in the Neshilik region, named for the extensive stretch of rapids and waterfalls on the upper reach of the Seguchi River which inhibit navigation. It lies south of the river and extends to the north at Kunchik, with the first permanent bridge over the Seguchi River, 1800 miles from its mouth.

Harlin (HAR-lin) - Grassy Field
The floodplain of the Seguchi River just inside Seguchi Norwan, used as a temporary Rasesni military encampment.

Jaunor (JOW-nor) - Cold Wall
The trading village at the base of Tse Jan, the High Pass, at the extreme south of Neshilik.

Jonggep (JONG-ghep) - The Meeting of Waters
The largest inland city, at the junction of the two main branches of the Junkawa River: The Seguchi and the Neshikame.

Junkawa (joon-KAH-wah) - The Mother of Rivers
The longest river in the world, with two main branches: The Seguchi and the Neshikame. It finds its outlet at Pingmen below the walls of Penit Ying.

Jusham Jan (JOO-shahm jahn) - The Low Pass
Caravan route between *sarq*-Zannib and central Kigali, west of Jonggep, the Meeting of Waters.

Kigali (kih-GAH-lee) - Land of the Ki Dynasty
Set in the mid-latitudes of the southern continent, Kigali is a wealthy and hard-working nation with a history of political stability and expansion. The Junkawa River and its hundreds of tributaries provide internal communications, and well-placed ports support its strong mercantile interests.

Koryan (KOHR-yahn)
Fortified high point overlooking the water gap on the north side of Seguchi Norwan, the Gates.

Kunchik (KOON-chick) - North Bridge
The northern extension of Gonglik, across the Seguchi River and connected by a bridge.

Kunlau Himbun (KOON-low HIM-boon) - Kunlau Mountains
The long range that forms the northern border with Fastar and Ndant.

Kwatka Kote (KWAHT-kah KOH-teh)
The eastern rift valley running from northeast Gentu Bay to southeast Pingmen harbor.

Kwatna Jun (KWAHT-nah joon) - Kwatna River
The river linking the chain of lakes with Gentu Bay in the eastern Kwatka Kote lowlands.

Kwattu (KWAHT-too)
The busiest port city, in the northeast on Gentu Bay at the mouth of the Kwatna River in the eastern Kwatka Kote lowlands.

Lang Nor Himbun (LAHNG-nor HIM-boon) - The Red Wall
The eastern border of Neshilik, a low range running north from the *sarq*-Zannib border to the Gates.

Linit Kungzet (LEE-neet KOONG-zet)
The border fort in eastern Neshilik that holds against incursions from Rasesdad on the Seguchi River.

Linyan (LIN-yahn)
An industrial city at a fork of the Junkawa River, above Yenit Ping.

Lomat (LOH-mat)
A disputed region with Rasesdad north of the Craggies, on the upper Neshikame River. Known to Rasesdad as Olmrad.

Lupmikya (loop-MICK-yah) - Millwood
A small village with a grain mill in Neshilik, south of the Steps.

Minchang Himbun (MIN-chahng HIM-boon) – Minchang Mountains
The long, porous range that forms most of the southern border with *sarq*-Zannib.

Neshikame Jun (neh-shee-KAH-mee joon) - Little Sister Water
The northern branch of the Junkawa River. It is navigable well into the Lomat region.

Neshilik (neh-SHEE-lik)
The western district of Kigali, surrounded by mountains and traversed by the Seguchi River. Often disputed with Rasesdad.

Nuntse Tepan (NOON-tseh TEH-pahn) - The Eastern Plateau
The region to the east of the Kwatka Kote lowlands, disputed with Peighar.

Pago Hanjong (PAH-go HAHN-jong) - Pago Bay
The bay into which the Junkawa River flows via Pingmen Harbor. Zannib Ussha shares the southern end of the same bay.

Pingmen Hanjong (PING-men HAHN-jong) - City View
The bay or series of harbors carved out by the Junkawa River.

Seguchi Jun (seh-GOO-chee joon) - Seguchi River
The southern and main branch of the Junkawa. It finds its source in the Mratsanag Mountains in Radesdad above Nagthari, and Gonglik in Neshilik is the site of the last downstream bridge. All crossings are by boat or ferry below that point. It is navigable up to the Steps at Gonglik, and navigable again above the rapids to Dzongphan.

Seguchi Norwan (seh-GOO-chee NOR-wahn) - The Gates
The gorge and water gap of the Seguchi River in northeastern Neshilik, dividing the Craggies from the Red Wall ranges. The river currently hugs the southern side.

Shaneng (SHAH-neng)
An important trade city on the Seguchi River just south of the Gates, with active ferry traffic.

Shirtan (SHEER-tahn)
A disputed region with Rasesdad and Fastar on the far side of the water divide of the Neshikame headwaters. It provides ocean access in the far northwest of the main body of the southern continent.

Shukyun Tep (SHOOK-yoon tep)
A river city on the upper Neshikame.
Song Em (SONG ehm)
The southern cove of Neshilik.
The Craggies
See "Totok."
The Gates
See "Seguchi Norwan."
The Horn
See Rasesni "Nakshadzam."
The Meeting of Waters
See "Jonggep."
The Mother of Rivers
See "Junkawa."
The Red Wall
See "Lang Nor."
The Steps
See "Gonglik."
Totok Himbun (TOH-tock HIM-boon) - The Craggies
The low range that forms the northern border of Neshilik.
Tse Jan (TSEH jahn) - The High Pass
Caravan route between *sarq*-Zannib and Neshilik at Jaunor.
Wechinnat (weh-CHIN-naht)
The northern cove of Neshilik.
Yenit Ping (YEH-nit ping) - Endless City
Capital city, on both sides of the Junkawa River, overlooking Pingmen harbor.

PLACES - RASESNI

Damsnag (DAHMS-nahg) - The Right Horn
The southern encircling range at the eastern end of Mratsanag.
Dzongphan (DZONG-fan) - Temple Quarter
The capital city, which includes the mother temples of all the gods, in Nagthari.
Garshnag (GARSH-nahg) - The Left Horn
The northern encircling range at the eastern end of Mratsanag.
Mratsanag (m-RAHT-suh-nahg) - The Wild Ram's Horns
The second tallest mountain range in the world.

Nagthari (NAHG-ta-ree) - Between the Horns
The region between the eastern mountain pincers, bordering Neshilik.

Nakshadzam (NAHK-shud-zahm) - The Horn's Tip
The intrusive escarpment that marks the extreme end of Garshnag. Known locally as "The Horn."

Neshred-pur (NESH-red-poor)
A coastal town west of Shilit Bay, where the Voice was first discovered.

Olmrad (OLM-rahd) - Wild Sheep Place
Rasesni name for the disputed territory north of the Craggies. Known to Kigali as Lomat.

Rasesdad (RAHS-ess-dahd)
The Rasesni nation includes the Mratsanag Mountains and the well-watered and fertile plains they support on two coasts. It is the western neighbor of Kigali, in the southern hemisphere.

Shirtan-pur (SHEER-tahn-poor)
City at the mouth of the Kabanchir River in northern disputed territory Shirtan.

PLACES - ZANNIB

(Yud) Aziyal (YOOD ah-zee-YAHL)
River flowing into Hilj Wandat at Mard Shimiz.

(Yud) Harin (YOOD ha-REEN)
River flowing into Pago Bay on the east coast at Mard Ussha.

(Jus) Shamr (JOOS SHAHM-er) - The Low Pass
Caravan route between *sarq*-Zannib and central Kigali, west of Jonggep, the Meeting of Waters.

(Mard) Shimiz (mahrd shee-MEEZ)
Important harbor city at the mouth of Yud Aziyal on Hilj Wandat, near the Rasesdad border.

(Jus) Sidr (JOOS SEED-er) - The High Pass
Caravan route between *sarq*-Zannib and Neshilik at Jaunor.

(Mard) Ussha (mahrd OOSH-shah)
Capital city, founded by Kigali, on Pago Bay on the east coast near the Kigali border, at the mouth of the Harin River. Also known as Zudiqazd mar-Sarq, the Winter Camp of the Nation.

(Hilj) Wandat (heelj wahn-DAHT) - Enclosed Sea
Very large almost-landlocked sea in the far west, bordered also by Rasesdad.

(Ardib) Yakush (ar-DEEB yah-KOOSH) - The Fence Mountains
The somewhat porous border range between Kigali and *sarq*-Zannib.

Sarq-Zannib (SAHRK-zahn-NEEB)
The Zannib nation. It occupies the bottom of the southern hemisphere and is neighbored on the north by both Rasesdad and Kigali. The western third concentrates on fishing and small farm agriculture, while the remainder is steppe and grasslands.

Zudiqazd mar-Sarq (zoo-dee-KAHZD mar-SAHRK) - Winter Camp of the nation
See Mard Ussha.

WORDS & PHRASES - ELLECH

Bendu (BEN-doo) - Device
A device for performing *raunarys*, usually made of wood.

Beolrys (BAYOL-rewss) - Mind-skill
The wizardly skill of mental-magic, things of the mind such as mind-speech.

Ellechen guma (ELL-ekh-en GOO-mah) - Ellechen language
The language of Ellech.

Emkenrys (EHM-ken-rewss) - Moving
One of the aspects of *raunarys*.

Felkenrys (FEHL-ken-rewss) - Binding
One of the aspects of *raunarys*.

Hakkengenni (HAHK-kehn-gen-nee) - One who knows
An archaic term for a wizard with unusual strength in mind-skill and thing-skill both. Usually translated as "Adept."

Raunarys (ROW-na-rewss) - Thing-skill
The wizardly skill of physical-magic, things of the real world, such as moving, binding, and destroying.

Rysefeol (REW-seh-fayol) - Device framework
A composite framework, usually made of wood, a level of complexity greater than a *bendu*.

Ryskymmer (rewss-KEW-meer) - Magic detector
A specialized *rysefeol*, for smelling out the use of devices and moving to their location.

Sennevi (SEHN-neh-vee)

"It is done." The customary final phrase that marks the end of a traditional tale, often accompanied by the slash of a hand.

Strekenrys (STRECK-en-rewss) - Destroying
One of the aspects of *raunarys*.

Thennur holi! (THEH-noor HOH-lee) - Wasted sweat!
An exasperated curse.

WORDS & PHRASES - KIGALI

Binochi (bee-NOH-chee) - Sir, Sirs
An honorific.

Chan do ne Te ba Gen ka Liju
A thousand years to the King of Earth and Sea. A customary blessing on the Emperor.

Gepten (GHEP-tehn) - Market Fair
A seasonal market place serviced by traveling traders.

Gwatenno (gwah-TEN-noh) - Traveling traders
Merchants who make their living on the *gepten* circuit.

Juk (JOOK) - Luck charm
Religious or luck charm, small and pocket-sized, usually made of wood or ceramic or metal and brightly painted.

Kigalino (kih-GAH-lee-noh) - A Kigali person
An individual citizen of Kigali.

Kigaliwen (kih-GAH-lee-wehn) - Kigali people
A group of Kigali people, or the collective citizens of Kigali.

Kigali yat (kih-GAH-lee-yaht) - Kigali speech
The language spoken in Kigali.

Kwajigomju (KWAH-jee-GOHM-joo) - Ram unit leader
A military rank roughly equivalent to Sergeant.

Laigom, Laigomju (LYE-gohm (-joo)) - Wolf unit (leader)
A military rank roughly equivalent to Colonel. The unit is the equivalent of a cavalry squadron.

Lakju (LAHK-joo) - Horsemaster
A military title for the man in charge of all the horses for the cavalry unit.

Leipum (LAY-poom) - Silk petal (branch)
An artificial version of the branch-in-leaf that is used to symbolize a truce.

Liju (LEE-joo) - Country Master, Emperor
The title of the Emperor of Kigali.

Maiju (MY-joo) - Tent master
A military title roughly equivalent to Quartermaster.
Minochi (mee-NOH-chee) - Madam, Ladies
An honorific.
Notju (NOTE-joo) - Master of secrets
A military title roughly equivalent to Intelligence Master. Usually this is an imperial representative.
Parkap (PAHR-kahp)
A traditional western Kigali weapon, a small ax suitable for hand use or throwing, similar to Rasesni models.
Posom (POH-som)
A deprecatory reference to self when addressing someone of higher status—"your servant", "your slave."
Puichok (POOIE-chohk)
The standard six-mule military wagon, usually topped with a canvas roof stretched over a bow framework.
Salengno (sah-LENG-noh) - Yak men
A pejorative term for Rasesni men.
Samke (SAHM-keh) - Kin home
A multi-generation compound for a large family. In some regions, it is combined with buildings that are part of the family business.
Shiksupju (shick-SOOP-joo)
A doctor or healer.
Tatgomju (TAHT-gohm-joo) - Bison unit leader
A military rank roughly equivalent to Captain.
Tengom (TEN-gohm) - Trader's Guild
The guild of Traders in Neshilik.
Wanbum (WAHN-boom)
The small gong that hangs on the wall next to a door, intended to be struck with a knuckle.
Yankatmi (yahn-KAHT-mee) - Headwoman
The (female) person who leads a village.
Yekungno (yeh-KOONG-noh)
Civilians (from the military perspective). Non-combatants.
Zopgep (ZOHP-gehp) - Town Council
The governing body of larger towns.

WORDS & PHRASES - RASESNI

Brudigdo (BROO-dig-doh) - Mage
The standard title for a male wizard (mage).

Brudigna (BROO-dig-nah) - Mage
The standard title for a female wizard (mage).

Bzinsabrud (b-ZIN-suh-brood) - Object's magic
The magic related to the use of external objects, especially devices, in contrast to *setsabrud.*

Grakedke (GRAH-kehd-keh) - Stone-carrying thing
A magical device, one using a *granyalig*, a power-stone.

Grakkedo (GRAH-ked-doh) - Device Master
A title reserved for an expert in *bzinsabrud*, physical magic, especially in the use of *grakedke*, magical devices.

Granyalig (GRAHN-yall-ig) - Powerful stone
A power-stone, a special crystal that can store and release magical power.

Klando, Klanna (KLAHN-doh, -nah) - Mage Master/Mistress
A title reserved for an expert in *setsabrud*, mental magic.

Pyalshrad (PYAHL-shrahd) - Mountain Hand
The Hand of the Mountains, the collective term for the hill-tribes used as enforcers by the the ruling priests.

Sedchabke (SEHD-chahb-keh) - Mind stop
A drug that both paralyzes the body and inhibits all use of magic. A tool of discipline for errant mages.

Setsabrud (SET-suh-brood) - Mind's magic
The magic related solely to the use of the mind, in contrast to *bzinsabrud.*

Tsevog (TSEH-vog) - Student
The formal title given to students by their masters.

Zendo (ZEN-doh) - Great Lord
A general title, analogous to "sir" but also used more literally to address men of high status.

Zhabbydedum (ZHAHB-byehd-doom) - Way-less
Those without gods—heathens.

WORDS & PHRASES - ZANNIB

Abin (ah-BEEN)
A stoneware cup, specifically used for the *binwit* or in other ceremonial contexts.

Baijuk (bye-JOOK)
Mead, a drink fermented from honey.

Bawi-anit (BAH-wee ah-NEET) - Name day
The day an infant is named, usually a few days after birth.

Bikraj, Bikrajti (beek-RAHJ(-tee)) - Wizard, Wizardress
The common title for a wizard.

Bikr mar-thulj (BEEK-er mar THOOLJ) - Magic of Things
The Zannib term for physical magic, not practiced by the Zannib.

Binwit (been-WEET) - Mead kit
The collection of materials for drinking mead ceremoniously. It includes the stoneware bottles and cups, often handed down within families, wrapped in an engraved leather rolled pack, usually presented at the transition to adulthood.

Bunnas (boon-NAHSS)
A low wild shrub native to *sarq*-Zannib whose berries are collected and dried as part of the *taridiqa*, the annual migration. The infusion of ground, dried, berries in hot water is high in caffeine. Popular throughout the southern countries and a significant trade item for *sarq*-Zannib.

Dirum (dee-ROOM) - Herd-mistress
The senior woman responsible for all the clan's herds while on *taridiqa.*

Dirum-malb (dee-ROOM-mahlb) - Apprentice to the Herd-mistress
A younger woman learning the position of *dirum.*

Dunaq wandim (doo-NAHK wahn-DEEM) - The World That Surrounds
The Zannib term for the world of reality that exists outside the ordinary world of perception.

Ghuzl mar-Tawirqaj (GOOZ-el mar tah-weer-KAHJ) - Circle of Speakers
The national tribal assembly in Ussha.

Had-kighat (mar-lud) (had kee-GAHT (mar LOOD)) - Stone touched (by a *lud*)
Found stones, usually hand sized or smaller, that have a significance for the finder.

Hadab-makhtab (had mah-KHAHT) - Powerful stones
Power-stones, special dull faceted gems than can hold and focus magic for *bikr mar-thulj.*

Himmib (hee-MEEB)
Cashmere, the very fine and soft wool of a particular species of goat, a valuable trade item.

Irghulaj (eer-goo-LAHJ)
The general title for student.

Jarghal, Jarghalti (jar-GAHL(-tee))
The title for a master wizard (wizardress).

Jimiz (jee-MEEZ)
The scholar's rug, a rug given by a master wizard to a journeyman before he enters his *tulqiqa*. It is used to mark a special space for seating for a wizard and his guest or student.

Jukwit (jook-WEET)
The stoneware bottles used in the *binwit*. They have an indentation around the center to allow them to be hung from a cord.

Kazr, Kazrab (KAH-zer) - Yurt, Yurts
A structure similar to a yurt, made of a wooden framework encased in felt.

Khimar (khee-MAR) - Honey
Honey is a special substance, favored by the *lud* for its unusual locations and properties, and for its use in fermenting mead.

Kuliqa (koo-LEE-kah) - Turn home
The celebration when the *taridiqa* begins the last leg of the annual migration, to the *zudiqazd*.

Lij, Lijti (LEEJ, LEEJ-tee) - Sir, Lady
A term of respect. *Lij-mar-lij*—Master of masters. Derived from Kigali *li*, meaning king or emperor.

Lubr mar-az (LOOB-er mar AHZ) - A string of horses
A pack-train of horses.

Lud (LOOD)
Numinous objects or locations, often referred to as "little gods."

Nal-Jarghal (nahl-jar-GHAHL)
The title for an apprentice wizard.

Nayith (nah-YEETH)
The masterwork of a wizard, the transition between journeyman and master. So judged by another master wizard.

Nibar (nee-BAR)
Hospitality, guest right. Usually offered from senior to junior participant.

Nurti (NOOR-tee)
Younger sister.
Qahulaj (kah-hoo-LAHJ) - Taboo
Wizard-tyrant, one who does taboo things.
Sarq-Zannib (SAHRK-zahn-NEEB)
The Zannib nation.
Shirqaj (sheer-KAHJ)
Warrior.
Sushnib (SOOSH-neeb)
Book.
Sushnibtudin (SOOSH-neeb-too-DEEN)
Trunk to hold a scholar's books when stationary, carried in parts in special packs when on pack animals.
Taghulaj, Taghulajti (tah-goo-LAHJ(-tee)) - Teacher
A wizard or wizardress who teaches others.
Tahaziqa (tah-hah-ZEE-kah)
Traditional verses.
Taridaj (tah-ree-DAHJ)
The people who partake of the annual seasonal migration performed by the traditional Zannib of the central region.
Taridiqa (tah-ree-DEE-kah)
The annual seasonal migration performed by the traditional Zannib of the central region.
Tarizd (tah-REEZD)
The route taken by the annual seasonal migration performed by the traditional Zannib of the central region.
Tayujdaj (tah-yooj-DAHJ) - One who pairs for others
The marriage-broker who introduces potential partners and arranges betrothals.
Tigha (TEE-gah)
Older brother.
Tulqiqa (tool-KEE-kah) - Wander time
The traditional wandering time when journeymen wizards travel to learn and to find opportunities to perform a *nayith.*
Tushkzurdtudin (tooshk-zoor-too-DEEN) - Has sixteen years
An adult, one who is at least sixteen.
Uthah (oo-THAH)
A small fabric square used to mark special spaces by being draped over a cushion or other object.
Wirqiqa-Zannib (weer-KEE-kah-zahn-NEEB)

The Zannib language.

Wishkaz (wish-KAHZ)

Hot spice.

Yarab mar-uthkahi (yah-RAHB mar-ooth-KAH-hee) - Honor gifts

Gifts made in payment of an honor debt.

Yathbantudin (yahth-bahn-too-DEEN) - Has nine years

A child between nine and sixteen. Old enough to join the *taridiqa*.

Yawd-Rub (yowd ROOB)

An aromatic sap burned for scent.

Yawd-Suragh (yowd soo-RAHG)

An aromatic ground bark burned for scent.

Zamjilah (zahm-jee-LAH) – Eye of heaven

The central crown at the top of the *kazr* that holds the rafters together and lets the smoke escape.

Zan (ZAHN)

An individual member of the Zannib nation.

Zannib-hubr (zahn-NEEB HOOB-er) - Free or Swift Zannib

The Zannib who continue a nomadic tradition of annual migration.

Zannib-taghr (zahn-NEEB TAHG-er) - Slow Zannib

The Zannib who live a settled life.

Zarawinnaj (zah-rah-wee-NAHJ) - One who rides in front

The leader of the *taridiqa*.

Zudiqazd (zoo-dee-KAHZD)

The winter camp, from which the *taridiqa* begins and ends. It houses those who do not go on the migration.

IF YOU LIKE THIS BOOK…

MORE GOODIES

You can find **more information** and **maps** at: KarenMyersAuthor.com/link-the-chained-adept/.

Continue reading for an **excerpt** of the first chapter of **Mistress of Animals**, the next book in **The Chained Adept** series, and find out more about it here: KarenMyersAuthor.com/link-mistress-of-animals/.

Sign up for the **newsletter** to stay informed of new and upcoming releases and to get occasional bonuses, like free short stories: KarenMyersAuthor.com/signup.

Let other readers know what you think by leaving them a review where you bought the book.

CONTACTING THE AUTHOR

You can contact Karen Myers at KarenMyersAuthor.com or by email at KarenMyers@KarenMyersAuthor.com. You can also follow her on Facebook: Facebook.com/KarenMyersAuthor.

ALSO BY KAREN MYERS

The Hounds of Annwn

To Carry the Horn
The Ways of Winter
King of the May
Bound into the Blood

Story Collections
Tales of Annwn

Short Stories
The Call
Under the Bough
Night Hunt
Cariad
The Empty Hills

The Chained Adept

The Chained Adept
Mistress of Animals
Broken Devices
On a Crooked Track

Science Fiction Short Stories

Second Sight
Monsters, And More
The Visitor, And More

See KarenMyersAuthor.com for the latest information.

EXCERPT FROM MISTRESS OF ANIMALS

The Chained Adept: 2

Available from Karen Myers and Perkunas Press

"Demon, I swear I'm going to eat your ears for breakfast."

Penrys halted her horse, dismounted, and stomped back past her three pack horses to the beginning of the string of seven donkeys, the first of which had dug in his feet on the trail of the High Pass and was bawling like three demons instead of one.

The other donkeys fidgeted nervously and seemed inclined to join him, so Penrys probed to see if there was anything more than a fit of donkey sulks responsible.

Demon's dominant mode was generally offended pride, but this time his mind showed her something different.

Najud, something's wrong. I think he's afraid of something.

Her companion's mental voice chuckled. **Sure it's not you he's afraid of, Destroyer of Demons?**

After three weeks, the joke had worn thin to her. Perhaps the wizard they had destroyed had deserved the name, and maybe this donkey did, too, but she found the full title, applied to her, both ridiculous and embarrassing.

Guess Najud's not going to bother to dismount and leave his own string to take a look.

She ran her hands over Demon and scratched under his chin in the spot he liked, and gradually he calmed down, placated by the attention. The others took their cue from him and settled.

She looked down their back trail. The view of the southern part of Neshilik, laid out below them, had been lost two days ago. Now only the steep scrambling slopes on either side were visible, along with the winding trail itself.

Footsteps behind her made her turn. Najud had come back to check on the donkeys, after all.

"Is he all right?"

"See for yourself."

Najud had been making progress on his mind-probes of animals. He was cautious about relying on it—as he said, "I can *see* the start of a pack sore before the beast begins to feel it."

"He's calmer now, but you're right, I think. Something alarmed him," he said. "You can see why many clans put donkeys with the sheep herds, to act as guards against wolves."

"Do they fight the wolves, or is it just the braying that makes them run away?"

Najud snorted.

Penrys scanned the area. "There're no other large animals around, except our own."

"The wind has shifted. Maybe he smelled something, and now he doesn't."

Despite the rock walls, the pass was high and fairly exposed, significantly colder and windier than the sheltered, settled land behind them. And it would only get colder, the further south they went, with the autumn solstice two months past. Penrys had never experienced winter in the south of the world and was still adjusting to the concept that "south" implied "cold."

"Let's get going," Najud said. "We'll see the other *lud*, late today, if we don't keep stopping."

"How do you know that? I thought you'd never taken this route before, over the border between Kigali and your *sarq*-Zannib?"

Najud grinned at her. Since the weather was dry, if cold, he still wore his small turban, the blue one today. Penrys was grateful for the wide-brimmed hat pressed upon her by the tailor back at Gonglik—it kept her shoulder-length hair from blowing in her face.

"It's described in one of the travel stories," he said. "Each landmark is a part of the tale."

He waved his hands in the air. "We tell our children these stories so that we can know a place before we see it. The *lud* are some of the characters."

The little gods, the Zannib called them—the special places or objects, a crooked tree, a rock formation.

It sometimes seemed from conversation with Najud that the lud were everywhere. She wasn't sure how seriously he thought of them.

"Remember the one we passed two days ago, the last spot for a view?" he said.

There *had* been something unusual about that lone, massive rock that seemed to keep watch over the trail.

"She's a character in the story. When you come from the south, she opens the door so the traveler can finally see the green of Neshilik spread out in front of him. Coming this way, she waves farewell. See?

"The travel story of this trail starts in the south, in *sarq*-Zannib, and it helps you find the exact spot where the trail to the High Pass begins. Going the other way is simple—just start at Jaunor, and that's easy enough to find—so that's where the way-back story starts, in the inn-yard."

Jaunor was part of the circuit of market inns that surrounded the southern cove of Neshilik, named "Cold Wall" for the border range at its back and the chilly winds that plagued it when the weather was bad.

"They told us there'd been no travelers through here for a couple of years."

Najud shrugged. "They don't come every year. The Kurighdunaq clan holds their *tarizd* below, the route of the migration, unless something has changed." He hooked his thumb south, at the trail ahead of them. "It's their young men who would get together and make an unplanned visit, during the *taridiqa*, to pick up courting gifts and special supplies for the *zudiqazd*, the winter camp. Not a formal trading caravan."

"Like the kind you're thinking of setting up," Penrys said.

"That's right." He smiled at her. "Besides, it's too late in the year to meet anyone up here. The Kurighdunaq would have started their *kuliqa*, their turn-home, two months ago. We'll have to make very good time to join a *zudiqazd* once we get down, the nearest we can find, and not be too picky about whose clan it belongs to."

"There it is."

At Najud's call, Penrys lifted her head from her horse's footing. His string of four horses some distance in front of her had stopped, but the leader was out of sight around yet another bend in the enclosed trail.

There was still light in the sky, but no shadows were cast in the narrow passage, the sun having been invisible for a while. She hoped for a wider spot for their camp. Bad enough that they had to pack fodder for the animals all the way from Jaunor to make up for the bare, rocky, trail—the limited water they could carry was running low. Najud had told her of an unfailing spring just the other side of this next *lud*, this landmark, and she hoped they could make camp there.

Najud's horses didn't move, so Penrys dismounted to walk up and join him. He hadn't seen the view before, either, and she could share that with him.

After she passed the horses, she found him, bent over a pile of something on the east side of the trail. When she raised her eyes, she saw that the trail curved to the left, and the western rock face fell away from a wide and level extension of the trail, leaving the lowering sun free to illuminate the corner of the eastern wall where the trail passed it, where Najud stood. The texture of the stone changed in that spot, and small embedded crystals sparkled in a patch twice the height of a man.

This must be the lud.

As she reached him, her eyes were carried involuntarily to the promised view. The trail curved down to the left and turned again, out of sight, but nothing blocked her sight to the south and west. The sun blanketed a soft and rolling land with broad strokes and long shadows. On either side, low spurs of the range extended.

She couldn't see directly below her, where the pass began, but Najud had told her there was a sheltered cove there, and those spurs must be the arms around it.

"You're right," she said aloud. "It's a wonderful view. Looks like there's even a good spot for a camp."

Najud's silence drew her from the view and she turned back to him. He hadn't moved from his spot and was still staring at the base of the *lud*.

Am I disturbing something… religious for him?

She was reluctant to intrude, but his posture conveyed worry or even alarm to her. She walked over to see what he was looking at.

There were half a dozen packs on the ground, ordinary trail packs, like a man might carry, not the large packs used for animals.

"Are they gifts for the *lud*, those packs?" she asked quietly.

He shook his head. "The *lud* don't need gifts, just respect. Sometimes a flower, or a pebble, maybe a bit of honey—simple recognition."

He straightened and looked down the short fragment of trail that was visible before the next bend.

"This is wrong."

His taut posture declared his uneasiness. "I'm going to look down the trail before we stop for the night. You stay here, with the animals."

Penrys raised her eyebrows but took the order in silence, and Najud walked down and out of sight.

She checked for mind-glows around them, but there was nothing except themselves for a mile or two, other than the small creatures that managed to live in this barren place, and the larger ones that lived on them.

The packs on the ground were not all the same, she realized. One was quite small, the size a child might carry. But Najud said it was just the young men who used this trail, not families.

They looked relatively fresh—she couldn't imagine they had already experienced a winter here. But in Jaunor they said no one had come over the trail for two years. Where did these people go? Didn't they need what was in those packs?

Najud reappeared, ascending the trail. His face was troubled.

It's bad, but whatever happened, it was at least a couple of months ago. Nothing we can do about it tonight.

"Demon had cause, this morning," he said, as he joined her. "Dead horse. The wind must have brought him the scent, before shifting."

Find out more about this book here:

KarenMyersAuthor.com/link-mistress-of-animals/

ABOUT THE AUTHOR

Karen Myers is a fantasy and science fiction author, best known for her heroic fantasy novels.

After a degree in Comparative Mythology from Yale University and a career as an industry pioneer building software companies, she has devoted herself to writing speculative fiction. Her stories feature heroes in real and imagined worlds filled with magic, space travel, and adventure.

When she's not writing, she enjoys hunting, fishing, photography, and playing her fiddle.

Karen lives with her husband, dogs and cats in an old log cabin in the mountains of central Pennsylvania, surrounded by wildlife. Bears, coyotes, deer, and possums visit often, and when she fiddles on her porch, the wild turkeys talk back.

She can be reached at KarenMyers@KarenMyersAuthor.com.

Made in the USA
Lexington, KY
13 December 2017